The Tru

"A big, juicy family sa... humor and tragic twists, *Truth* is lively and engaging. . . . The story gets more and more absorbing as it moves briskly along."
—*St. Louis Post-Dispatch*

"Barrows . . . hits the mark again with this delightful yet at times heart-wrenching story of life in a Depression-ridden small town. Fans of [*The Guernsey Literary and Potato Peel Pie Society*] will find parallels in this novel's blend of narrative and epistolary chapters. . . . A warmhearted Southern charmer that is sure to captivate readers."
—*Library Journal* (starred review)

"[A] heartwarming coming-of-age novel . . . sparkles with folksy depictions of a tight-knit family and life in a small town . . . In a novel full of richly drawn, memorable characters, bright, feisty Willa is the standout. . . . Add *The Truth According to Us* to the stack of repeat-worthy literary pleasures."
—*The Seattle Times*

"Barrows brings a deft, light, yet crisp probing touch to this confluence of tender people confronting tough circumstances."
—*Booklist*

"Fans of Annie Barrows' bestseller [*Guernsey*] . . . will recognize the author's affinity for breathing life into her characters. . . . Barrows has crafted a luminous coming-of-age tale that is sure to captivate her grown-up audience. Against a lively historical setting, the joys and hardships of the rollicking Romeyn family will keep readers eagerly turning pages."
—*BookPage*

Praise for
The Truth According to Us

"Barrows has written an intricate and moving family novel that explores the possibilities of forgiveness—and that will render readers nostalgic for the curiosity of childhood and the magic of summer."
—*Knoxville News-Sentinel*

"The characters are engaging, the historical details appear thorough and accurate, and there are sufficient conflicts and plot twists to render a compelling story. . . . A pleasant summer read."
—*The Roanoke Times*

"Barrows follows up *The Guernsey Literary and Potato Peel Pie Society* with a small-town story filled with big characters. . . . [*The Truth According to Us* is] a warm family novel of love, history, truth, and hope."
—*Library Journal* (Hot Summertime Reads)

"Barrows, who co-wrote the surprise bestseller *The Guernsey Literary and Potato Peel Pie Society*, takes a similarly panoramic approach to the insular hamlet of Macedonia, West Virginia, using multiple points of view with epistolary interludes. . . . This unique corner of Americana—a mélange of Yankee and Southern cultures—is re-created as vividly as the very different Anglo-European milieu of Guernsey. . . . Undeniably entertaining."
—*Kirkus Reviews*

"In *The Truth According to Us*, Annie Barrows leaves no doubt that she is a storyteller of rare caliber, with wisdom and insight to spare. As she subtly unpacks the emotional intricacies of the Romeyn family and their small West Virginia town in the wake of the Great Depression, we're struck by the slipperiness of history—how the stories we tell each other and ourselves often demand to be interrogated; how the things we're driven to know about our families, our towns, our closest intimates, will always change us, sometimes over and over. Barrows is at her best here. Every page rings like a bell."
—PAULA McLAIN,
New York Times bestselling author of *The Paris Wife*

"*The Truth According to Us* is an irresistible novel, a sly charmer of a story about a small town in Depression-era West Virginia whose history is rewritten by a debutante on the run. Family histories, too, are unraveled, but mended by the fierce, strong women who dominate this delightful page turner, a tribute to the power of love and forgiveness to heal even the most heartbreaking betrayals."
—MELANIE BENJAMIN,
New York Times bestselling author of *The Aviator's Wife*

By Annie Barrows and Mary Ann Shaffer

The Guernsey Literary and Potato Peel Pie Society

By Annie Barrows

The Ivy and Bean Series
Ivy and Bean
Ivy and Bean and the Ghost That Had to Go
Ivy and Bean Break the Fossil Record
Ivy and Bean Take Care of the Babysitter
Ivy and Bean: Bound to Be Bad
Ivy and Bean: Doomed to Dance
Ivy and Bean: What's the Big Idea?
Ivy and Bean: No News Is Good News
Ivy and Bean Make the Rules
Ivy and Bean Take the Case

The Magic Half
Magic in the Mix

The Truth
According to Us

A Novel

Annie Barrows

THE DIAL PRESS • NEW YORK

The Truth According to Us is a work of historical fiction, using well-known historical and public figures. All incidents and dialogue are products of the author's imagination and are not to be construed as real. Where real-life historical or public figures appear, the situations, incidents, and dialogues concerning those persons are entirely fictional and are not intended to change the entirely fictional nature of the work. In all other respects, any resemblance to persons living or dead is entirely coincidental.

A Dial Press International Edition

Copyright © 2015 by Annie Barrows

All rights reserved.

Published by The Dial Press, an imprint of Random House, a division of Penguin Random House LLC, New York.

THE DIAL PRESS and the HOUSE colophon are registered trademarks of Penguin Random House LLC.

A hardcover edition has been published in the United States by The Dial Press, an imprint of Random House, a division of Penguin Random House LLC.

ISBN 978-0-399-58844-0
ebook 978-0-8129-9784-2

Cover design: Laura Klynstra
Cover images: Laura Klynstra (girls), Shutterstock (postcard)

Printed in the United States of America on acid-free paper

randomhousebooks.com

9 8 7 6 5 4 3 2 1

For Jeffrey

Romeyn Family Tree

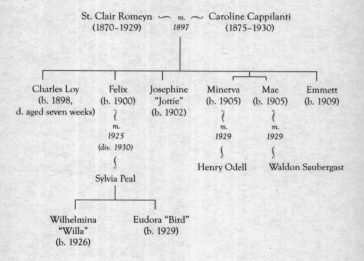

St. Clair Romeyn ∽ m. ∽ Caroline Cappilanti
(1870–1929)   *1897*   (1875–1930)

Charles Loy   Felix   Josephine   Minerva   Mae   Emmett
(b. 1898,   (b. 1900)   "Jottie"   (b. 1905)   (b. 1905)   (b. 1909)
d. aged seven weeks)   (b. 1902)

m.   m.   m.
1925   *1929*   *1929*
(div. 1930)

Sylvia Peal   Henry Odell   Waldon Saubergast

Wilhelmina   Eudora "Bird"
"Willa"   (b. 1929)
(b. 1926)

The Truth According to Us

I

In 1938, the year I was twelve, my hometown of Macedonia, West Virginia, celebrated its sesquicentennial, a word I thought had to do with fruit for the longest time. In school, we commemorated the occasion as we commemorated most occasions, with tableaux, one for each of the major events in Macedonia's history. There weren't many, hardly enough to stretch out across eight grades, but the teachers eked them out the best they could. If it hadn't been for the War Between the States, I don't know what they would have done. When Virginia seceded from the Union, western Virginia got mad and seceded right back into it, all except four little counties, one of them ours, that stuck out their tongues at West Virginia and declared themselves part of the Confederacy, a piece of sass with long consequences in the way of road-paving and school desks.

Tucked up in a crook between the Potomac and the Shenandoah, Macedonia was a junction for generals and railroads alike, and by the time Lee hung up his sword at Appomattox, the town had changed hands forty-seven times, six of them in one day. Our teachers dearly loved to get up a scene of the townspeople stuffing their Confederate flags up the chimney as the Union troops marched in and yanking them back down again as the troops departed. The fourth-, fifth-, and sixth-graders got the war scenes, and the seventh- and eighth-graders got the short end of the stick, because not a thing happened in Macedonia after 1865, except the roundhouse blowing up and the American Everlasting Hosiery Company opening its doors. Half the town worked in that mill and the other half wished it did, but there was not much about the American Everlasting Hosiery Company that looked good in a tableau. Sometimes the teachers gave up and killed two birds with one stone by making the seventh-graders march across the stage, waving socks, while the eighth-graders sang "The Star-Spangled Banner" behind them. In 1938, though, the eighth grade hit pay dirt, because Mrs. Roosevelt drove through town. She stopped at the square, took a drink from our sulfur-spring water fountain, made a face, and drove away. That was plenty for a tableau, except that instead of making a face, the eighth-grade Mrs. Roosevelt said, "The people of Macedonia are lucky to receive the benefits of healthful mineral water." My sister Bird and I laughed so hard we got sent into the hall.

Once the curtain had clunked down on our tableaux and we'd been herded back into our classrooms, I supposed that Macedonia's sesquicentennial festivities were concluded. Hadn't we just covered one hundred and fifty years of history in twenty-three minutes flat? We had. But not a week later came the Decoration Day parade, and that, I realized later, was the real beginning of the sesquicentennial. Later still, I realized that everything began that day. Everything that was to heave itself free of its foundations over the course of the summer began to rattle lightly on the morning of the parade. That was when I first heard of Layla Beck, when I began to wonder about my father, and when I noticed I was being lied to and decided to leave my childhood behind. I have since wondered, of course, how my life—and my father's and my aunt Jottie's, too—would have been different if I'd decided to stay at home that morning. This is what's called the enigma of history, and it can drive you out of your mind if you let it.

Jottie and I were packed tight on the sidewalk, together with everyone else in town, to watch the parade. Usually it wasn't much, the Decoration Day parade, just a matter of assorted veterans looking grim and the high school marching band. But this year, in honor of the sesquicentennial, we'd been promised an extra-fancy show, a real spectacle. And that was what we got: The United Daughters of the Confederacy flounced out first, with the Ladies of the Grand Army of the Republic hot on their heels. Then the Rotary band struck up with patriotic tunes, which was a lot to manage on four trumpets and had a terrible effect on the pony brigade. The veterans marched along, and a pair of girls in skimpy outfits flung batons in the air, just exactly like a movie parade, except that only one of them could catch. We even had a float, The Apple Princess and Her Blossoms, smiling away on the back of a truck. Out came the mayor, waving from his big green car, and behind him was Mr. Parker Davies, who had got himself up in a sword and knee pants to look like General Magnus Hamilton, the founder of Macedonia, which put me in mind of a question I had always wanted to ask. I nudged my aunt Jottie. "How come he called it Macedonia?"

She tilted her dark eyes down to mine. "The General was a great admirer of the Macedonian virtues."

"Huh." That was news to me. "What are they, the Macedonian virtues?"

"Don't say huh. Ferocity and devotion." The Apple Princess joggled by. It was Elsie Averill in a white dress. A lady standing just behind me leaned forward for a better look, and a big whiff of Jungle Gardenia went up my nose.

I squeezed closer to Jottie. "Did he have them?" I asked.

Jottie's eyes followed Elsie for a bit. "Did he have what?" she murmured.

"Jottie!" I recalled her. "Did General Hamilton have the Macedonian virtues?"

"The General?" She lifted one eyebrow. "The General once chopped off a soldier's toes to keep the poor man from deserting. You tell me, Willa: Is that ferocity, devotion, or just plain crazy?"

I eyed Mr. Parker Davies, imagining his bloodied sword raised high, a little toe speared on the point. That was ferocity, I was pretty sure. "Do I have them?" I asked hopefully.

Jottie smiled. "Ferocity and devotion? You want those?"

"They're virtues, aren't they?" I asked.

"They surely are. Ferocity, devotion, and a nickel will get you a cup of coffee at the Pickus Café." I made a face at her, and she laughed. The parade passed by, turned around on itself, and straggled back up Prince Street.

I thought maybe I had a chance at devotion.

Now the Macedonia Chamber of Commerce made the turn and marched by, eight men in identical tan hats and overcoats. They looked like a set of matching boy dolls, only embarrassed. Jottie chuckled and flapped her little flag. "Hooray!" she cheered. "Hooray for our brave boys in the Chamber of Commerce!"

They pretended they didn't hear, all except one. "Jottie?" he said, swiveling around. Jottie drew in a sharp breath, and I saw two spots of pink appear on her cheeks. She started to put up her hand, let it drop, and then changed her mind and lifted it in a little wave. That set him up; now he started smiling like crazy, and even though the parade was moving again, he called out to her, "I was hoping I might see you today, Jottie, I was thinking I might—"

A man behind bumped into him then, and he had to walk on, but he kept turning around to wave at her as he went.

"Who was that?" I asked. Nothing happened, so I gave her a poke. "Who was that, Jottie?"

"Sol," she said. "Sol McKubin." She opened her purse and rummaged inside. "I had a handkerchief in here this morning."

And that would have been that, if I hadn't heard a low laugh behind me. It was Mrs. Jungle Gardenia. "*Shoo-oo,* good thing old Felix ain't here," she hooted softly to herself.

What? I whirled around, wondering who she was and how she knew my father.

She didn't look like someone he would know. She was wearing a young lady's dress, even though she wasn't a young lady, and her face was white with powder. She caught my stare and wiggled her drawn-on eyebrows at me. I turned back to Jottie quick.

"Jottie," I said, giving her another poke. "Who's Sol McKubin?"

"Is that Miss Kissining there across the street?" Jottie squinted at the sidewalk opposite. "In that polka-dot dress?"

I looked. It wasn't any more Miss Kissining than it was the Lindbergh baby. "You must be going blind, Jottie," I began scornfully, but I was drowned out by the Rotary band giving their final honk on "The Battle Hymn of the Republic." The parade was over.

That was all right with me. My favorite part came after, anyway. I took hold of Jottie's hand, and we sailed out into the wake of the marchers.

It was like a second parade, with all of Macedonia milling along Prince Street, busying themselves with the real entertainment of the day: calling out, stopping to chat, and gathering into little knots to deliver up their opinions about the ponies, the batons, the float, and the mayor's car. I dearly loved to walk down a street with my aunt Jottie. When I went alone, I was a child, and grown-ups ignored me accordingly. Sometimes, of course, they'd stop me to offer improving advice like Tie your shoelaces before you trip and knock out those teeth of yours, but for the most part, I was a worm in mud. Beneath notice, as they say in books. When I walked with Jottie, it was a different matter. Grown-ups greeted me politely, and that was nice. That was real pleasant. But the best thing, the very best thing about walking through town with my arm through Jottie's was listening to her recount the secret history of every man, woman, dog, and flower bed we passed, sideways out of the corner of her mouth so that only I could hear. Those were moments of purest satisfaction to me. Why? Because when she told me those secrets, Jottie made me something better than just a temporary grown-up. She made me her confidante.

We were strolling up the street when we came upon Mr. Tare Russell in his bath chair. He wasn't real old, Mr. Russell, but there was something the matter with him, and he had to be rolled around town with a blanket over his knees. When he saw us, he yelped, "Jottie Romeyn, you just come over here and let me feast my eyes on you!" Then he waggled his fingers so that his Negro servant would push the bath chair faster. It didn't seem right; that poor man looked a lot older and feebler than Mr. Russell.

"Tare!" said Jottie. "What brings you here? I've never known you to come to the parade before!"

"Civic duty," said Mr. Russell. "What kind of a person would miss Macedonia's sesquicentennial parade?"

Jottie grinned. "I've been asking myself that very question, Tare, all morning long. How'd you like The Apple Princess and Her Blossoms?"

He didn't answer. In fact, he almost interrupted her, he spoke so quick. "I thought Felix would be marching with the veterans. But he wasn't. I didn't see him."

"Felix is away on business," said Jottie.

"He's been gone all week," I added helpfully.

"Business," repeated Mr. Russell, bunching up his mouth. "Well. Felix works like an old mule, doesn't he?" Suddenly, he swung around and glared at me. "Tell him, when he comes back, not to forget old friends. You just tell your daddy that, would you?" he snapped.

I took a step backward. "Yessir."

Jottie's little hand closed around mine. "Of course we will!" she said cheerily. "We'll tell Felix first thing!"

Mr. Russell waggled his fingers again. "Take me on home," he barked to his old Negro servant. "You trying to fry me like an egg?"

We watched him go, and Jottie's hand squeezed mine. "Let's go window-shopping," she suggested. "Let's pretend we've each got ten dollars, and we have to spend it this afternoon or we'll lose it all."

So we did, and we were wrangling away about whether I could borrow two of her imaginary dollars for a pink silk dress, when we ran up against Marjorie Lanz. She lived down the street from us, and she talked all the time. She started up before we could even see her. "How-you, Jottie?" she shouted from inside Vogel's Shoes. "Look here at these sandals." She came out, holding a big yellow shoe. "How'd you like the parade, I thought Elsie looked real pretty, the Rotary could use some new blood, don't you think? Where's Mae and Minerva? Oh hi, honey," she said, catching sight of me. "Aren't you just cute as a button?"

I was too old to be cute as a button, but I nodded, being polite.

Now she was swinging the shoe back and forth. Mr. Vogel was standing nervously in his doorway, waiting to grab her if she walked away with his sandal. Marjorie gabbled on, "I heard you're getting yourself a new boarder, Jottie, that's nice, with all those extra rooms you got." I shot a look at Jottie. First I'd heard of any new boarder. "Who-all you going to get, Jottie? Hope it's someone with more starch in him than Tremendous Wilson, I don't know how you stood that man, is it someone nice?" She paused and looked at Jottie expectantly. So did Mr. Vogel. So did I.

Jottie gazed at Marjorie Lanz for a moment, and then she leaned close. "My new boarder is a representative of the United States government," she murmured. She looked suspiciously at Mr. Vogel. "That's all I can say."

"Ooooh." Marjorie clutched the sandal tight. "It's a *secret*?"

Jottie nodded regretfully, like she wished she could tell more, and turned toward Mr. Vogel. "That's a nice sandal you have there, Mr. Vogel. Does it come in blue?" He shook his head no. "That's too bad. Well, Marjorie, Willa and I had better be getting along. We have to clean out that new boarder's room. The United States government doesn't like a lot of clutter." She looked at me. "They like it neat as a pin. Don't they, Willa?"

Out of pure loyalty, I nodded, and then I waited until we were three storefronts away from Vogel's Shoes before I asked, "Are we really getting a new boarder?"

"Yes, ma'am," said Jottie.

"Is he really part of the government?"

She smiled. "No. 'Cause it's not a he."

"A lady?"

"Yes. A lady."

"A lady in the government?"

Jottie raised an eyebrow. "Sounds like you don't believe a word I said."

"I do," I said slowly. "But how come I didn't know about it?"

She reached out to brush my hair away from my face. "I thought you did know. Didn't you see me move all those things out of the closet? You were sitting right there on the bed."

I tried to remember but I couldn't. I'd probably been reading.

I was usually reading.

It occurred to me that I missed an awful lot of what went on. Silly Marjorie Lanz knew more about my life than I did. Even smelly, powdery ladies on the street seemed to know things about my own father that I didn't. That was downright humiliating, now that I thought about it. Was I a mere baby, doomed to live in benighted ignorance? No! I was a person, a whole person, and I had a right to know things!

"You should have told me," I fussed at Jottie.

She patted my cheek. "You want to know things, sweetheart, you've got to start paying more attention. You've got to keep your ear to the ground."

I opened my mouth to say But I'm your confidante! Then I shut it up again. Maybe I wasn't Jottie's confidante, after all. Maybe I only imagined I was. I pondered. There was the man in the parade, Mr. McKubin, the one who made Jottie blush— she hadn't confided a thing about him. She hadn't even answered my question about him, because she'd gotten distracted by Miss Kissining. Except—I looked at Jottie in surprise— maybe it wasn't a mistake; maybe she'd done it on purpose to distract *me*!

Well!

The morning had been rife with unanswered questions. Mysteries, even. "Good thing old Felix ain't here." What did that mean? And Mr. Russell—why had he gotten so angry when we said Father was away? And just who was this new boarder who worked for the government? Mysteries abounded, and the biggest one was why hadn't Jottie told me about any of them.

I'd been duped.

I'd thought I was Jottie's trusted adviser, the repository of her innermost thoughts. But I wasn't. I'd been fooled. Kept in the dark. Lulled and diverted. But no longer! I resolved to change. Then and there, I made a vow to pay attention, to find out, to learn those truths that the grown-ups tried to hide. I will know things, I promised myself. I will get to the bottom of everything. Starting now.

I was just clenching my jaw with resolve when I felt a tug on my sleeve. There was Bird, her curls stuck to her head with sweat. "That Trudy Kane is going to dance again. I want to see and Mae says she's going to have a stroke if she has to watch Trudy Kane one more time, so you got to come with me." Bird was trying to learn how to tap dance by watching Miss Trudy

Kane. She could already shuffle off to Buffalo on a washtub. She yanked my arm. "Come on."

I looked do-I-have-to at Jottie. She nodded.

"I don't see how I'm supposed to keep my ear to the ground when I have to spend every blessed moment of my life following Bird around," I said bitterly.

Jottie was peering into the windows of Krohn's Department Store, but she turned to grin at me. "What you need is some of that Macedonian virtue," she said. "You just summon up a little ferocity and devotion, and you'll find out more than you ever wanted to know." She turned back to the windows.

Bird yanked on me again, but I stood stock-still. Jottie was right. Macedonian virtue was exactly what I needed.

2

May 17, 1938

Rosy,

Please forgive—can't come to luncheon. Father on warpath: Nelson, sloth, poorhouse, et cetera. Speaks ominously of work. Must stay home and knit socks to make good impression.

Layla

Ben,

Layla needs a job. Can I send her to you?

Affect^{ly},
Gray

May 19, 1938

Senator Grayson Beck
Senate Office Bldg.
Washington, D.C.

Dear Gray,

No.

Sincerely,
Ben

May 20, 1938

Mr. Benjamin Beck
WPA/Federal Writers' Project
1734 New York Ave. NW
Washington, D.C.
Dear Ben,

I am disappointed by your answer. It reveals a lack of brotherly feeling, and a poor memory to boot. Think back, Ben. Think back to 1924. I did not think that it would be necessary to remind you of the time, the money, and the reputation I expended for your sake *and without question* during that summer, but evidently I was mistaken. Perhaps the jail cell has become hallowed in your memory, or perhaps you believe that the judge was inspired to lenience by your worthy ideals. Don't fool yourself. You owe me.

What time shall I send her up? Tuesday at 2:00?

Gray

❖

May 21, 1938

Senator Grayson Beck
S.O.B.
Washington, D.C.
Dear Gray,

Tuesday at 2 is fine. What job do you want me to give her?

Ben

❖

5/23/38

Ben,

I don't give a good goddamn what job you give her. I want her out of the house and off my dime.

Affect^ly,
Gray

[Telegram]

May 23, 1938

Charles: Please meet 11:32 tonight. Must talk.
Situation dire. One solution possible. Love.
Layla

May 25, 1938

Layla—

I'm sorry you were crying when I saw you off. It disfigures you to give way to tears. Not your face—I consider your beauty your least significant attribute—but your mind and your soul. You dread work; you fear it, but this terror is the delusion of your class. Work is noble. It dignifies; it elevates the spirit. I can imagine no better fate for you than to learn firsthand the transcendent effects of labor; you, who sucked the platitudes and superficialities of your class with your mother's milk, can only exterminate the false consciousness that permeates your existence by making common cause with the laboring men and women of this country. Throw yourself on the mercies of work, Layla. A period of shock is to be expected, but in due time, you'll find true companionship in the hearty clasp of callused hands; in labor, you'll find nourishment for your underused mind and deserving objects for your uncontrolled emotions. As you rise from the ashes of your degenerate life, you'll see your banal nuptial dreams for what they truly are: a bourgeois charade, a tinsel ritual that has no place in the Workers' Future.

On the chance that you, with your talent for willful misinterpretation, find me unclear: I mean no. And good-bye.

Charles

May 27, 1938

Mr. Benjamin Beck
WPA/Federal Writers' Project
1734 New York Ave. NW
Washington, D.C.

Dear Ben,

Let's pause for a moment and discuss this calmly, just the two of us, without Father's lash of fire cracking over our heads. Now, Ben, I don't know what Father's got on you, but it must be something pretty awful to bring you to the point of hiring me—and for the WPA, too. Have you killed someone? Even if you have, there must be a better way to expiate your crimes than putting me on the Writers' Project, which is nearly a crime in itself. I certainly understand that if Father's twisting your arm, you have to give me some kind of job. I understand and I sympathize. But consider: Father will be perfectly satisfied if you put me in a dainty little secretarial position, and so will I. Simply by offering me a temporary place in your office, you'll meet Father's requirements, and your arm will be your own again. There's no need to go to extremes. I refer to West Virginia. Sending me to West Virginia is extreme.

Not to mention ostentatious.

Toadying.

And mean.

Yesterday afternoon, after I had got over my first shock at your letter, I betook myself to the library to read up on the Writers' Project (You see? I do know where the library is) and discovered that your arguments in favor of West Virginia (state flower: the rhododendron) are completely erroneous. Yes, I was born in Washington, D.C., but it's ridiculous to say that I'm obliged to work in the state closest to my birthplace. You made that up, you know you did.

Do you know the motto of West Virginia? It's *Montani semper liberi:* Mountaineers are always free. Need I say more? Do you and Father think that by packing me off to the Mountain State, you will turn me into a fresh-faced, wholesome girl in ankle socks, bounding over the rocky heights? You're mad. You'll drive me to drink, and in West Virginia the drink is probably moonshine, which will rot my entrails and make me blind.

Not only will I be miserable, I'll be terrible. I'll be the worst researcher in the history of the Writers' Project, and that includes the seventy-year-old Stalinist morphine addict you told me about. Can you picture me interviewing the farmers' wives and coal miners? Asking tactful questions about baths and head lice? Counting pigs and dogs and babies? Honestly, Ben, they'll shoot me, and I won't blame them if they do.

Please reconsider. You're my uncle. You're supposed to dote on me, and I'm supposed to be the sunshine of your lonely bachelorhood. Perhaps I haven't lived up to my end recently, but give me a chance. Indulge me just this one last time: Take me off the West Virginia project and give me a job in your office, and I swear to you that I'll be the best secretary you ever saw. I'll arrive at your office by 8 (in the morning!). I'll type my fingers to the bone. I'll be lovely on the telephone. I'll contemplate serious topics. I'll be a credit to you.

Just don't send me to West Virginia.

Please.

> Your loving and usually obedient niece,
> Layla

May 28

Layla,

Do you realize that nearly one-quarter of the employable citizens of this country are out of work? Do you realize that I receive dozens of letters each week from diligent, well-educated men and women imploring me for a job, any job, on the project? These people are desperate, Layla. They've been unemployed for so long they've forgotten what it's like to work, they've sold everything they had for pennies, they go to bed hungry—inside if they're lucky, outside if they're not—and they wake up hungry. They've been wearing the same suit of clothes for years, sponged off each night because if they scrub it on a washboard, the cloth will shred to rags. Their children are sick because they don't get enough to eat, and they're dirty because there's no place to wash. These are people who never thought they'd have to beg, and yet here they are, begging me for a job that won't pay them enough to keep food in their stomachs.

There's an opening on the West Virginia Writers' Project. I have, against my better judgment, given you that position. Be grateful or be damned.

Ben

May 30, 1938

Miss Layla Beck
c/o Mr. Lance Beck
Department of Chemistry
Princeton University
Princeton, New Jersey
Dearest Layla,

I must say, it's very inconsiderate of you to run off to cry on Lance's shoulder and leave me here to cope with Papa in the state he's in, and I certainly hope you're not having a rendezvous with that awful Charles Antonin, because Papa will find out, and he'll be even more furious than he is right now. Nothing I say moves him even the tiniest bit, and I can't help it but you simply have to take Ben's tatty old job. I know what you think—and imagine *my* feelings at the thought of you among grubby coal miners—but I'm afraid Papa won't budge, darling. He says if you won't marry Nelson—I'm not lecturing, I'm only repeating what Papa says—then you have to face stark reality. I wept and said I was sure you'd get ringworm, but that just made Papa fuss the more. He said it was time you understood what you were throwing away and if it took worms to make you understand it, that was fine by him (I didn't tell

Papa, but I don't believe there are real worms in
ringworm).

I never thought my own daughter would be on relief. I
could just *strangle* Ben.

Your loving,
Mother

P.S. Lucille saw Nelson at Bick's Saturday. She says he
looks *terrible,* absolutely heartbroken and thin as a rail. You
can't call a man insincere when he's lost weight like that.
You just think about that, young lady.

June 6, 1938

Miss Rose Bremen
"The Waves"
Gurney Street
Cape May, New Jersey
Dearest Rose,

Your letter came like the King's Pardon, just after the
severed head thumped into the straw. Thanks for the kind
offer, but the die is cast, and I'm to arrive in Macedonia,
West Virginia, next Tuesday to begin work for the Federal
Writers' Project. I took the Pauper's Oath yesterday, and I
am officially on relief.

I can't tell you how it happened because I don't
understand it myself, really I don't. I've been a frivolous
person for years now, and Father's never been bothered by
it in the least. If anything, he seemed pleased by my
success: Once, I overheard him bragging that I had been
invited to every house party from the Adirondacks to the
Appalachians. Everything was *fine* until Nelson appeared
on the scene, and then the worm turned with a vengeance.
They wanted me to marry him in the worst way, both
Mother and Father did. I thought they were joking. He was
so obviously, completely awful—and they knew it. They
knew it and they didn't care. Nelson! He's the Citronella
Scion and hugely rich, but he's also vain and tedious and

shallow as a dewdrop. That whinny laugh, that tiny
mustache—I'd rather kiss an eel. His most cherished
ambition is to be mistaken for Errol Flynn. Within ten
minutes of meeting Nelson, I despised him, and if Nelson
ever had a thought about anyone but himself, the feeling
would have been mutual. I thought Mother and Father
knew what a disaster he was, and when he proposed, I
thought we'd all laugh about it. How wrong I was. They
wanted me to be a good girl and say yes. Father was
blinded by the glint of Citronella (he's running again next
year), and Mother was blinded by Father, and Lance
refused to concern himself with such trivialities. I didn't
know what to do, and when Father demanded an
explanation, I panicked and made a fatal error: I said I
could never respect a man who didn't work. The moment I
said it I wished I could take it back. Father's face turned
perfectly purple—I thought he was going into apoplexy—
and they probably heard him on Capitol Hill. On and on he
went about people in glass houses and the walking
definition of sloth and wastrels who bring nothing but
anguish and shame to their parents. And that was just
warming up. Once he hit his stride, he included bootstraps
and paperboys in the snow and Abraham Lincoln and
Brother, Can You Spare a Dime? and Oklahoma and
migrant workers in Model T's, until I lost my head and
shrieked that I was going to take a job and become an
independent woman and make Father eat his hat.

Oh, it gets worse. After Father stormed out of the house,
I decided that if I laid low, he would forget about it, just as
he always had before. So, like an idiot, I went to New York,
and when I sashayed back into the house two days later,
expecting an affectionate paternal greeting, Father
growled, "You have an interview with Ben at two." You
remember Ben, don't you? Father's possibly Socialist
younger brother who is some kind of muckety-muck at the
Federal Writers' Project. Evidently, what I had viewed as a
cease-fire, Father had viewed as an opportunity to oil his
musket, and before I knew it, I was down at Ben's office,
demonstrating my literacy by reading the newspaper aloud

to a bored assistant. I realize now that I should have muffed it, but I didn't, and, as you know, I am a *fiend* on the typewriter. By the end of the afternoon, I was feeling pretty smug. Fine, I thought. I'll show them. I'll be Ben's secretary. I could just see it—I'd be one of those ornamental secretaries, you know the ones, clad in an elegant black dress with crisp white organdy cuffs falling around my perfectly manicured fingers as I riffled through the mail, a picture of competence. "I don't know what I did without her," Ben would say fondly to Father, who would likewise say fondly, "How could I have ever thought she should marry that despicable cur Nelson? She was right and I was wrong."

You know the rest. I had no choice, Rose. I had to accept the job. Father really has cut me off, and there really is a Depression going on. Work is scarce and I have exactly $26 to my name. What was I to do? Mother says he'll relent by Christmas, but that's months away. I don't know how I'll bear it—trudging around Macedonia, West Virginia, in the blazing heat, taking down the reminiscences of a town full of toothless old hicks. I can hear it now: "Along about '95 or '96, the cows died o' the worm and we din't have a lick o' meat for ten year and all the chirren got rickets . . ." I don't know why the federal government wants a record of those people, I really don't.

And the worst of it is, Father is still so furious that I have to *live* on my salary, which means that I have to board in a poky little room in a house belonging to "a respectable family of Macedonia." The house and the respectable family are probably encrusted in coal dust, and I will probably die of starvation or lice within weeks. You may read this letter at my funeral—from beyond the grave, I'll watch as Father writhes, which means, I suppose, that I'll be in hell. I'll feel right at home there after Macedonia.

There's one last thing I haven't told you: Everything with Charles is finished. Please don't send me a sympathetic letter. I can't bear it.

Love,
Layla

P.S. In the heat of that first argument, Father called me a "canker on the social body." Have you ever heard of anything so unjust? All this spring, I have been hemming washrags for the deserving poor and reading uplifting literature to Relicts of the Confederacy on the last Thursday of the month. How can I be a canker?

❦

June 13, 1938

Dear Charles,

  Now that I'm one of the proletariat, don't you think you could

June 13, 1938

Charles dear,

  Last week I took the Pauper's Oath—without lying, too. Briefly, Father cut me off in a rage, I haven't a penny to my name, and tomorrow I begin working for the WPA Writers' Project. I'm to interview villagers in West Virginia. Now that I'm a member of your beloved proletariat (at least I think I am), perhaps you'll reconsider the terms of my banishment the quarantine perhaps you'll be willing to see me perhaps you'll reconsider perhaps we could

June 13, 1938

Dear Nelson,

  I just have to tell you about a funny little incident: You know our maid, Mattie? This morning she was dusting your portrait—I keep it on my bureau—and she said, "I don't know what he sees in that scrawny Olivia de Havilland." I was utterly baffled—until I realized she had mistaken you for Errol Flynn! Isn't that darling?

  It's been *ages* since Mother and Father have been missing You haven't come to see poor little me in

❦

June 14, 1938

Dear Brother,

It's 3:14 and I can't persuade myself to go to bed. Once I'm there, nothing will stand between me and my fate. My dreadful suitcase is packed, along with my dreadful hatbox and dreadful trunk. Mattie pressed my white suit for the train, and it's hanging over my chair, gleaming like the full moon, impossible to ignore. It's been a horrid evening. Mother insisted that we dine at home, just the three of us, but Father is still not speaking to me, and I was too oppressed to swallow, so Mother chattered on and on about something—azaleas? dressing gowns?—for a solid hour. The moment he had stowed the last bite of ham in his mouth, Father lurched to his feet to make his getaway—but he patted my head as he went by. I wanted to wail like a baby.

Oh, Lance, I'm going to be all alone, and I've never been that before. Even when I was sent off to Miss Telt's Seminary, they all knew who I was—Senator Beck's daughter. I don't suppose that will cut much ice in the hog wallows of Macedonia, West Virginia. How will I know what to do?

Layla

P.S. Won't you please try one more time to find it in your heart to take me in? Please, Lance? I've been thinking about what you said, and I know you were right about lots of it, but I'm sure I would improve with your brotherly guidance. You could be my model. Please?

3

In later years, Bird said she knew from the very beginning that Layla Beck was trouble. "From the moment I saw her," Bird would say, sticking one finger straight up in the air, "I knew she was a harbinger of doom." There are times when my sister talks like an old man.

I can't say, myself. I wasn't with Bird when she saw Layla Beck for the first time. I was lying face down in the gutter with tire tracks on the backs of my knees, which Bird says is proof of Layla Beck's being a harbinger and I say is proof of Bird's being a skunk.

We had been sent to the train station to greet Miss Beck and show her to our home. If she had arrived on the 10:43 or the 12:10 or the 5:25, Bird and I would not have been nearly important enough to be her welcoming committee. All three of our aunts—Jottie, Minerva, and Mae—would have gone in their Sunday hats and gloves. But Miss Layla Beck came in on the 2:05, and that was plunk in the middle of my aunts' sacred resting time. So they consulted among themselves and announced that meeting Miss Beck was valuable social grooming for Bird and me.

Jottie, who cared how we looked, made us wash our knees, and after that, she brushed Bird's curls. She started to braid my hair, but that turned out to be beyond the powers of mortal man, just like it usually was. It was slippery, my hair. Anyway, we looked nice, or at least clean, when we set out to meet Miss Layla Beck on the 2:05 from Washington, D.C. Our aunts waved us good-bye and went off to do their resting, Jottie in her chair in the front room, and Minerva and Mae upstairs in the room they shared when they stayed with us, flung down on the beds, breathing in and out at the same time, the way twins do.

It was up to Bird and me to make a nice impression, Jottie said. I said I would do my best but not to get her hopes up, and she laughed.

Outside, it was dead quiet and hot. The birds had given up for the day, and heat steamed from our neighbors' lawns in shining columns. Nothing stirred. The ladies and the little babies were taking their naps, and the Lloyd boys, who would be quiet on the day they died and not before, had gone off somewhere. The men were at work, except for Grandpa Pucks, who never spoke except to tell us to get lost, and Mr. Harvill, who was a high school teacher and on summer vacation just like us.

Bird and I trudged along Academy Street in silence. I suppose if you'd never seen them before, the houses on our street all looked the same, big and white-brick. If you gazed through the polished lens of experience, though, each one was different. You could tell where the Lloyd boys lived, just from the frayed stump of rope that dangled from their maple tree. The swing had crashed to the ground when all three of them plus Dicky Ritts rode on it at once. Grandpa Pucks's porch was bare because he believed that burglars would steal his rocker if he left it out. Every evening, he toted it out to the porch to sit in the cool, but he wouldn't tote Grandma Pucks's. She had to sit inside. At the corner was the Caseys' house, empty and sad. Mr. Casey got sick and died, and Mrs. Casey and the children had to go live with her brother. Sometimes on Sundays, Mrs. Casey came back to water her peonies. It didn't help much; they were dying.

I looked sideways. Bird was concentrating on her feet. The road had melted soft and we had to pick our way along, like cats. We could have walked the fences, but that would have grubbed up our fronts, and we were supposed to look nice for Miss Beck.

"Willa!"

It was Mrs. Spencer Bensee, behind her grape arbor. The grapes tasted awful, but the arbor was pretty and she spent loads of time in it, thinking about the roses of yesteryear, according to Jottie.

"Afternoon, Mrs. Bensee. It's hot, isn't it?"

"You-all should be napping. Does Jottie know you're running around in this heat?" she said sharply.

"Yes'm," I answered. The things children have to put up with.

"Humph," said Mrs. Bensee doubtfully. Then she relented. "You're looking pretty as a picture today, Bird," she called.

Bird didn't say anything, not even when I nudged her. That was always the way. No matter how nice and polite I was, Bird was the one people fussed over. It was because she had those fluffy golden curls, just like the good girls in books. Not that Bird was especially good; when she put her mind to it, she was downright awful, but she looked good, like a Christmas card girl.

"Bye, Mrs. Bensee! We've got to get to the station!" I hollered, so that she wouldn't notice that Bird had been rude. "Why can't you be nice?" I hissed when we were out of earshot.

Bird shrugged. "I'm nice."

"Not to her, you're not."

Bird shrugged again. "She sits in that arbor waiting to kill people."

We got to Race Street, and from there we had to cross over to the United Garage and go around the corner. Radio music was floating out of the United Garage, and I could hear them banging on something in there, metal on metal. Which is why I didn't hear Teddy Bowers on his shiny new bike as I stepped out to cross the road. I didn't see him, either, because I turned my head to look both ways, just like they were forever telling us to do. Before I knew it, I was flat out on the macadam, with Teddy Bowers moaning and screaming about his bike being ruined. I never liked him after that. The bike had come to a stop on top of me, and as I lay there, kicking my legs out like a sick horse, I felt a little tap on my shoulder. It was Bird.

"Don't you worry," she said. For a moment I thought she was trying to comfort me, and I was surprised, because she didn't usually comfort anyone. I should have known better. "I can meet the train all by myself." Very carefully, Bird looked both ways to see that no cars were coming. "Bye," she called over her shoulder as she walked away.

She disappeared around the corner, and Teddy finally summoned the wit to yank his bike off my legs, scraping off plenty of skin as he went. I called him a few things I wasn't supposed to know about, before I saw the blood running down my legs; then I began to cry, and one of the United Garage men heard me and came out.

He paid no mind to Teddy howling in the street—What did Teddy have to howl about? No one had run him down—and he was real nice about me bleeding all over the front seat of his truck. I told him where I lived, and he said he knew already. "The president's house," he said. He sounded solemn, like the president of the United States lived there, but he was really talking about my grandfather, St. Clair Romeyn. He'd been the president of American Everlasting, back when he was alive. "I know your aunts, too," added the United Garage man.

"All of them?" I asked, to take his mind off the blood that was dribbling onto the floor of his truck. He kept looking at it, kind of nervous.

"I went to school with Miss Minerva and Miss Mae."

"Oh." I searched my mind for something to say about that. "I've got three of them. Aunts."

"They sure were pretty," he said, like he was remembering.

I thought they wouldn't like to hear him talk as if they weren't pretty now, but I didn't say that, because his old truck was stopping in front of our house. A moment later, Jottie burst out of the front porch, letting the screen door bang behind her. I opened my mouth to explain, but she was already flying down the front stairs, and then her fingers were curling tight around my shoulders. She held me close for a second. "You're all right," she said. "You're all right," she repeated, like she was telling herself.

"Yeah, Jottie, I'm—" I began, but now she whirled around to glare at the United Garage man.

"What happened, Neely?"

Poor United Garage man. He swallowed weakly and said, "Hey there, Jottie, I just picked her up off the street—over there in front of the garage, you know where—and," he stammered, "and—I didn't do nothing!"

"Yes, ma'am, he picked me up from being run over," I said fast. "Teddy Bowers ran me over on his new bike and stupid Bird left me lying in the street and went on to the station, at least I think that's where she is, so he"—I nodded to the United Garage man—"he brought me home in his truck, and the blood is mostly in my shoes."

"Why, Neely!" Now Mae came down the steps, just as light as a feather. She glanced around at the three of us. "What happened?" she asked, but the way she said it was a lot friendlier than the way Jottie had.

His eyes got big and scared-looking. He didn't say anything, just jerked his thumb at me. Mae looked like she might laugh, but I felt sorry for him, so I spoke up and said again about Teddy and how Mr. Neely had brought me home.

Mae smiled at him. "Aren't you nice."

He nodded, but he still didn't say anything, so I kind of yelled, "Look, Mae, look at my legs! That rotten Teddy ran into me, and then he scraped all the skin off my legs. And then he had the nerve to cry about his bike. Can you believe that?"

"Bowerses are crybabies, every last one of them," she said soothingly, just as Minerva came out to see what all the fuss was about.

"Why, Willa! You're blood-drenched!" she said.

"I know it," I said, but she had already turned to Mr. United Garage.

"And Neely's here, too! What happened?"

We all swung around to see if he would answer this time, but that seemed to shake him worse. "Ha-ha," he mumbled.

"I've got blood all in my shoe!" I said.

Minerva nodded. "You look something terrible."

"I was just trying to help Bird across the street," I said, real noble and self-sacrificing. The grown-ups who circled around me made sympathetic noises. My leg had almost stopped hurting, and I began to enjoy myself some. "I scraped up my hands, too," I said, stretching out my bloody palms to show them. Obediently, they leaned in to look.

All at once, Jottie clutched her throat. "It's a sign!"

Minerva giggled. "Why, so it is."

"The stigmata!" Jottie gasped. "She's got the stigmata!" She did some staggering.

Mae began to laugh. "Call Reverend Dews!" she cried. "It's a miracle!"

And at that moment, Bird's voice wafted over the heads of the grown-ups. "May I present Miss Layla Beck."

Suddenly all the faces that had been looking at me turned away, and I was left staring at a circle of backs. I pushed through them and saw a young lady with shining dark curls. She was wearing the whitest suit I ever saw and white high-heeled shoes to match. She could have been getting married in that suit, except she was wearing a red bow around her neck. She had big brown eyes and a mouth the exact shade of her neck bow, but one lip was tucked into her teeth. "Miss Romeyn?" she said, looking, for some reason, at me.

"No," I answered. But then I reconsidered. "Well, yes, but"—I pointed to Jottie—"she's really Miss Romeyn. I mean, she's the Miss Romeyn you're talking about." I shifted on my feet, and blood came up out of my shoe.

Jottie was trying to straighten her face out. "Please excuse us—"

"She doesn't really have the stigmata," said Mae weakly.

"Not yet, anyway," whispered Minerva.

There was a strangling sound as all three of my aunts tried to swallow their laughs.

And after that there was a long, empty space where Miss Layla Beck should have said something about being pleased to meet us but didn't. She stared at my legs, and then her eyes moved over Mae, Minerva, the United Garage man, and, finally, Jottie. She looked at us like we had escaped from the asylum.

The tap of shoes against brick broke the spell. We all swiveled round to see my father striding up the front path.

"Father!" I cried.

He stopped and smiled. "Miss Beck," he said, taking off his hat. "Welcome to Macedonia." He held out his hand.

※

"Welcome to Macedonia," said Felix, stepping forward into the circle.

In the time it took him to do it, Jottie's eyes swept around the ring of faces, examining the citizens of this tiny world. Neely, she saw, was scared. Poor Neely. He was scared of them, and he was scared they were going to invite him into the house. He was scared that if he went inside, he'd break something or track dirt on the rug. Don't worry, she wanted to whisper to him. It's not like it used to be. It's not so fancy anymore.

Neely swallowed nervously.

Beside him stood Minerva, reviewing Miss Beck with narrowed eyes. Mae was doing the same. Jottie watched as their opinion made its identical appearance on their faces: They were offended. They were offended primarily by the stranger's suit—a white suit, the nerve!—but they were also taking offense at her gleaming curls, her wide eyes, her red lips, and her slender waist. She was a boarder, a border. She was supposed to be meager and pale, clad in a one-dollar dress and last year's hat, eager to please and easy to ignore. She was not supposed to make them the second-prettiest women in the house.

Now Bird strained forward around Miss Beck, trying to catch her father's eye, so he might witness her in her moment of glory. Under Jottie's gaze, she assumed the noble visage of a child who had fulfilled her duty when others fell by the wayside, a child who struggled on alone to guide a stranger to safety.

But Felix wasn't noticing Bird's glory; he was extending his hand to the newcomer. "Felix Romeyn," he said, tapping his hat against his chest, his eyes warm and welcoming. Oh, Felix, don't smile at her, Jottie thought. The poor girl.

He smiled.

The stranger smiled back, her hand rising to meet his and grasp it, clearly relieved to encounter this envoy from the realm of the normal. "I'm Layla Beck," she said, the furrows smoothing from her brow. "Delighted to meet you." They shook hands, and she turned, newly fortified, to Minerva. "Miss Romeyn?"

Felix placed two fingers against her shoulder and gently spun her toward Jottie.

Her turn. Jottie stepped forward. "I am Miss Romeyn," she said, a bit breathlessly. Stigmata. Honestly. She didn't know what got into her sometimes. She smiled. "You must think us utterly—" The girl gazed at her coolly; she thought nothing at all. Abashed, Jottie veered to: "So pleased to meet you."

As she beheld the two tiny, inconsequential versions of herself reflected in Miss Layla Beck's eyes, Jottie permitted herself a fraction of a second to mourn for Tremendous Wilson, the perfect boarder, meek as living man could be, who each night retreated upstairs to his own dim circle of lamplight, casting no shadow on the Romeyns below. Tremendous Wilson had lived in Macedonia all his life. He knew what they'd been and what they'd become and how it had happened. But Tremendous was gone, not to be retrieved, and now there was this girl, glinting and fresh and ignorant as an egg. A girl so smooth and empty that her thoughts could be read like telegrams. There it was, appearing on her face as Jottie watched, the certainty that Macedonia and the Romeyns were minor elements in the plot of her life, ants who happened to be plodding through her picnic, rather than the other way around. It was written in the careless determination with which she was shaking hands now with Mae and Minerva, in the way she was pretending not to see the blood browning on Willa's sock, in her unnecessary, brilliant smile for Neely. She had no need to know them. She would soon move on.

I will never move on, thought Jottie, and a stab of envy nearly broke her in two.

Quickly as she foundered, she retrieved herself. Greet the stranger. Now smile. Shake her hand. As her arm obeyed instructions, Jottie took refuge in her ballast, counting her treasures, her darlings: Willa, Bird, her sisters, even Felix—all of them loved her, needed her, held her dear. She didn't want to move on anyway.

The ship righted itself, and Jottie drew a breath. "Please do come in out of the heat of the day, Miss Beck. Thought you weren't coming home until Thursday, Felix. Mae, will you take Willa upstairs and put something on that leg of hers—and take that sock off, too, honey. Thank you kindly, Neely, for bringing her home. And there's no call for you to look so puffed up, Miss Bird. You shouldn't leave your sister lying in the street."

For a moment, the circle held, unmoving, and then, as though touched by fire, it broke apart, whirling away on the updraft of Jottie's words.

Walking toward the house, Jottie heard a familiar one-note whistle and dropped behind the others. Felix slipped his arm companionably through hers. "The girls behave themselves?" he asked, as he always did.

"Tolerable," she answered, as she always did. "Where were you this time?" she asked.

"Obion, Tennessee."

"Nice?" she asked.

"Sure," he said wryly. "I'll tell you all the high points later. Won't take long. Put this inside." He pressed some money into her hand. "I got to go downtown for a bit."

She glanced at the bills. "Come home for supper."

He nodded solemnly, patted his hat back in place, and walked away.

June 14, 1938

Dearest Lance,

I am here, and you were right about the coal mines. There aren't any. According to local informants, I am in apple, cow, and sock country, never ever to be mistaken for coal country. My ignorance is already a scandal, and I only got here three hours ago.

I was greeted by a reception committee composed of one sweaty little girl. I don't know what I expected—an official from the project? A respectable club woman in a flowery hat? A brass band? Whatever I was secretly hoping for, it was not what I got. After the train hurtled away, I stood on the platform, trying to look as if I didn't care that no one was there. Then I persuaded myself that the furtive man by the bench had come to meet me but had been paralyzed with shyness. Unfortunately, the furtive man noticed my encouraging glances and began to whistle "I like the girls and the girls like me," which forced a decision. I took one step toward the station and nearly jumped out of my skin as I felt a tap on my back.

"I am Miss Bird Romeyn. Are you Miss Layla Beck? I presume." She did look like a bird, too, a scrawny little thing with big blue eyes and curls popping out around her head. I said yes, I was Layla Beck, sounding stiff even to myself.

"*Miss* Layla Beck," she corrected me. "I am delighted to make your acquaintance."

We were obviously working our way through a page in an etiquette book, so I tried to respond in kind, and she inclined her head graciously. "I shall accompany you to our abode, if you please." She held out an arm for me to take, which I did, though I had to stoop to hold it. "We will inform the man where your trunks must be sent," she said grandly.

I mumbled something about it being only a few suitcases. "Miss Layla Beck," she said, "do not concern yourself."

I was trying desperately to keep up my end and *not laugh* when suddenly the page was finished. "Hold on," she said. "I'll go tell Mr. Herbaugh. You stay here." And she bounced off into the station.

We walked home (strange to use that word) through a maze of charmless streets. I do believe you were the one who told me I would be entranced by the natural beauty of the Shenandoah Valley. You may be right, but in downtown Macedonia, natural beauty has been crushed by red-brick buildings and splintery storefronts, punctuated every now and then by a limestone monstrosity with Latin on its cornice. The Depression here seems more than ever a depression, a sag. The center of town is tired and ugly and dismal, with crumbling, dusty sidewalks and knots of men in worn overalls. My little scout pointed out a fountain in the barren town square as a great attraction, but I have no idea why. We wound along empty streets half-melted in the heat, and I noticed that every business—even the closed ones—was shaded by an identical green awning, each bent in the identical spot. Did the awning salesman gleefully break them, one by one, as he left town with his pockets bulging?

After six or seven blocks of this, I succumbed to despairing visions of my destination—it was going to be a tawdry boardinghouse with broken stairs, dirty windows, and a single threadbare sofa in the front room. Dead flies in the corners. An oleograph of George Washington crossing the Delaware hung crookedly in the hall. Oh, dear, it depresses me to think of it—and, as it turns out, I needn't think of it, because the Romeyn house is nothing at all like that. At some invisible border, the red brick stopped, and the streets got wider and more shady. The houses began to retreat from the sidewalk until they got to quite a respectable distance, and I could practically feel ladies taking their afternoon naps inside the houses.

We rounded a corner, and Bird announced, "That there's our dogwood." I would have said a silent hallelujah at the sight of the house—white-brick and gracious—except that I was temporarily distracted by the crowd of people milling about on the front walk. I don't know how to describe the Romeyns—in fact, I'm not entirely sure which milling people were Romeyns and which were bystanders. They were gathered around a girl—Willa, I believe her name is—who was bleeding profusely into her socks and hopping up and down, while a woman shrieked that the poor child had the stigmata. At the sight of me, she went silent, but do you suppose that I've fallen in among a family of revivalists? What will I do if there are prayer meetings after supper? Or, worse, *before* supper? And what—I know it's not possible, but still—what if the child actually does have the stigmata? What's the etiquette for boarding with one who bears the wounds of Christ? Surely I'll be in the way if pilgrims arrive.

As I stepped up the walk, every single one of them turned to glare at me. Perhaps they were looking into my sinful heart. I got an awful shrinking feeling and couldn't summon up a word, and I suppose we would have stood there until doomsday if Mr. Romeyn hadn't come along and welcomed me like a gentleman. He shook my hand

and introduced himself while the rest of them gaped at me. Can they all live here? The one certainty is Miss Romeyn, because I have a letter telling me she's the owner of the house. But who is Mr. Romeyn? A brother? I suppose there is a resemblance between them—they're both dark— but she's rather cold, while he has charming, civilized manners. Besides him, there were two other women— identical twins, can't tell them apart, can't remember their names, am terrified they board here, too—and the children, as well as a mute (perhaps he'd come to be healed). Where do the children come in? Could Miss Romeyn have a lurid past? Doubtful. She seems too austere for such shenanigans.

My room is better than I dared hope, though there isn't much in it. Just a big creaking bed, a towering dresser with drawers that stick, and a table. No, there's an armchair, too, by the window. And now that I'm looking, I see there's a spindly little side chair shoved in a corner. My God, there's one of those hair pictures on the wall. What shall I do?

Love,
Layla

P.S. It's after dinner now, and I've retired to my room to pace like a caged tiger. It's dreadfully hot, and I can hardly breathe up here, but I can't go for a walk because I'm certain to get lost if I do, and, besides, I can't bear to face the Romeyns again. They're kind, but I'm horribly out of place here. I wore a silk dress to dinner and looked like a fool, but how was I to know what to do? Lance, I'm sure I'd be entranced by the natural beauty of the Shenandoah Valley if you showed it to me. Couldn't you pay me a visit? I expect there's a hotel somewhere in this town. Shall I find out? I'm sorry to be such a weakling, but I can't help feeling as though I meant nothing at all to anyone. I'm terribly lonely. How will I bear this for three more months? Today alone has lasted years.

4

Ladies don't smoke in public, Jottie said. In public included a lot of places, even our front room because of all the windows, so Jottie smoked like a stack in the kitchen. Bird and I liked to watch her stirring at pots, frowning through a curtain of blue smoke swirls. Her hands were busy with spoons and chopping and saucepans, so it was rare that she touched her cigarette. Mostly, she tucked it into a corner of her mouth and left it alone. We'd watch without even breathing hard as the ash grew long: Would it fall? Would she catch it? She never seemed to pay it any mind, but just as the dead gray cylinder began to crumple, her hand would flash up and tap it, one-*two,* into a coffee cup. She never had an ashtray. What was the use of an ashtray, Jottie said, when she didn't smoke?

In all the years I watched Jottie charge around that kitchen with her head tilted back to cast up the smoke, I only once saw the ash fall wrong, and that was when Minerva came in to tell her that Mr. Hannaway's bed had fallen right through his bedroom floor into his front parlor. "Huh," Jottie grunted around her cigarette. "Can't blame the bed for trying." Minerva gave a whoop, and then Jottie started laughing, and after that they were both bent over double and slapping their hands on the table, and when they came up for air, the cigarette was missing. We found it in the corn bread, and Jottie scooped it out, leaving just a little hole in the middle of the yellow.

The day Miss Beck arrived, Jottie seemed distracted in her cooking. For instance, she lit a second cigarette while the first one was still in her mouth. I'd seen her smoke two at once before, but only for a joke on my uncle Emmett, who said smoking was bad for you. "Silly," muttered Jottie. "I'm a silly old lady, Willa." She stubbed out the second cigarette gently, so she could light it again from the end of the first one.

"You're not an old lady," I said.

"Yes, I am. I'm thirty-five years old. Double thirty-five, what do you have?"

I pretended I didn't hear her. I hated doing math in my head.

"What's double thirty-five, Willa?" she insisted.

"Seventy," I mumbled.

"And that's hardly likely, is it?" Jottie asked. "With Mother dead at fifty-five and Father at fifty-nine. No, I'll be lucky to make sixty-two, which means I'm more than halfway done with life. That's old."

I should've said No, no, you're young, but I didn't. I was worried she was going to ask me what fraction of her life was over. Fractions were worse than anything. Even Bird was better at fractions than I was.

Thank the Lord, Bird clomped into the kitchen just then. "What're we having?"

"Ham, fried apples, string beans," said Jottie. Her knife slit into an apple.

"Couldn't you make something fancy?" Bird asked. I wouldn't have dared.

"No, I could not. It's a good country ham, anyway."

"We having rolls or just store bread?" Bird went on.

Jottie closed one eye and glared at Bird with the other. "I'm going to poison you all." She always said that when we complained about her food. "I bet if I cry, the sheriff'll believe I did it by mistake." She heaved a sigh. "It won't be easy, though. I'll have to think of a dead puppy."

I giggled, but Bird was stubborn as a mule. "Miss Layla Beck looks like she lives pretty fancy."

"Yes, she does, but she's on relief, just like half the people in this town," said Jottie.

"I've never seen a suit like that in the poor barrel." It was Mae, leaning against the doorjamb. She looked put out.

Jottie sighed again, for real this time. "*I* don't know. Mrs. Cooper asked me did I have room for a new boarder and

I said yes, who, and she said a new girl on the WPA. Fine, I said, seven dollars and fifty cents a week, and that's all I know."

"How'd Mrs. Cooper get her?" Mae pressed.

"She's got some cousin down in Charleston, works on the Writers' Project."

"Humph." Mae settled herself into a chair. "I guess the WPA pays better than I thought. How much you think a suit like that costs?"

"Maybe she sews," said Jottie. None of us sewed. A few times a year, when it looked nice with her dress, Mae brought out a pillowcase she'd been embroidering for as long as I could remember. She'd take a few stitches in it and then lay it down in her lap. "We could learn how to sew," Jottie added.

"Even if we did, we couldn't make that suit," said Mae. "There's sleeves."

"You want me to ask her where she got it?" asked Bird. "I know her the best."

Jottie wheeled around so quick that smoke rose up from the back of her head. "Don't go asking her personal questions, Bird. You know better than that. You just behave nice and polite, and we'll all mind our own business." She looked hard at Bird and then turned away to put some bacon grease into the skillet.

"I never know what's a personal question," grumbled Bird. "They're all personal."

"You just ask yourself how you'd like it if someone asked you that question," said Mae. "That's how you know."

"I don't mind any questions," said Bird.

"That's because you don't answer any," I said.

Mae reached over to slide a cigarette out of Jottie's pack.

"They're bad for you, you know," said Jottie.

"Stella said she saw Emmett eating a club sandwich at Petersen's last Saturday," said Mae. "I wonder why he didn't come by."

Jottie glanced up from her apple stack. "He wasn't with a girl or someone?"

"No. Stella didn't say. She *would* have said if he'd been with a girl."

Jottie scraped the slices into the skillet. "How about you string those beans, Mae?"

"Where's Minerva?" Mae asked, her lips streaming smoke.

"I don't know. How about you do it? And get the tea from the icebox, would you? Here, Bird, you stir this."

I slipped off my chair. I knew what was next. As I slid into the front room, I heard Jottie say, "Where did that child get to?"

Miss Layla Beck was standing in the front room, just standing. Now she was wearing a silk dress, of all things. It had brown roses on it. There are no such things as brown roses, but she looked like a princess. And maybe she is, I thought suddenly. Maybe she is a crowned head of Europe forced to flee for her life. It was possible. They were having a lot of trouble back in Europe; I had read about it. This was exactly the kind of thing that wouldn't have occurred to me before the parade, and I congratulated myself on my keen observing. If you're going to unearth hidden truths, keen observing is your shovel. I had to admit that it hadn't helped me unearth much of anything yet, since, for all my efforts, I had been unable to discover any answers to the questions that had antagonized me so at the parade. Mr. McKubin was just a man who worked at American Everlasting, and Jottie said she didn't know any ladies who wore Jungle Gardenia perfume. But now here was Miss Beck in her silk dress, radiating mystery. She was a mysterious stranger. What a stroke of luck! A mysterious stranger was liable to change everything, and that was a thrilling thought. Of course, I wasn't silly; I knew it wasn't likely that she was a princess. But she was exotic and beautiful and wonderful, and I could hardly wait to gain her trust and then find out every last thing about her.

I smiled winningly. "Hello," I said.

She jumped. "Oh!" and then, "Hello. It's—it's Willa, isn't it?" She spoke in an elegant way, each word clear and nice, like tapping on a glass.

"Yes'm."

She smiled on–off. "Miss Romeyn told me dinner was at six?"

If she wore silk dresses, she was probably used to butlers and silver trenchers. I glanced through the archway to our table. We had silver knives and forks with my grandmother's initials on them, but our plates were chipped. "Well." I was reluctant to expose our shoddy ways. "Jottie doesn't really mean six when she says six. She means *close* to six." Our dining room wasn't very nice, now that I looked at it. "I can ring a bell to call you, if you want." I thought that might make her feel at home.

She didn't seem to care about the bell. "Jottie?" she asked. She didn't know who I was talking about.

"Jottie—that's Miss Romeyn."

"And she's . . . ?" It was a refined way to ask questions, with just your voice. "She's your . . . ?"

"Jottie's my aunt. So're Minerva and Mae, too."

"Minerva and Mae?" She did it again!

"Oh. Minerva—you met her; she's Mrs. Odell. And Mae is Mrs. Saubergast. They live here. During the week, anyway."

"Oh." She looked confused. "My." Then she said, "And Mr. Romeyn?"

"That's my father." She peered into my face then, finding the ways I looked like him. I stood up straight, proud that I looked like Father, and like Jottie, too. "He's Jottie's brother," I added helpfully.

Suddenly Father was there, stepping in from the hallway. "Someone talking about me?" he asked. He always did that way, appearing out of the blue. He moved fast, and by the time you heard him, he was already there. He was famous for it. My great-aunt Frances Tell had once fainted dead away when he popped up at her elbow, holding a plate of yams.

I reached out to touch his sleeve. I was glad he was back, but I knew better than to make a big fuss over him. He didn't like it when people fussed.

"Good evening, Miss Beck," he said, putting his hand to his head like there was a hat to lift. "Oh," he said, and then turned, smiling, to me. "How's the knee, sweetheart?"

"It stopped bleeding. It was the back." I turned to show him.

"Mm," he grunted, looking. "That is a mighty big scrape."

He brushed his hand over my hair. He knew I loved that. "All settled in, Miss Beck?"

"Yes, thank you. My suitcases arrived from the station very quickly."

"Does the room suit?"

"Oh. Yes. It's very nice. I like the—the wallpaper." She blushed pink. She looked even prettier when she blushed.

Bird came out of the kitchen, her face screwed up with trying not to drop the ice-teas she was carrying. Three of them. She always tried to carry three at once.

Father made a special soft whistle—he said it was his Bird-call—and Bird looked up, smiling. "Daddy!" she cried. "You're home!" All three of us—Father, Miss Beck, and I—jumped to save the tea. We each grabbed one, and Father laughed even though Bird had almost shattered glass all over the room. Bird scowled. "I was doing fine," she said. "I wasn't dropping them."

"Not yet you weren't," he said. Carefully, he set the glass he had rescued on the table and turned back to Miss Beck. "As soon as she can balance them on her head, we're packing her off to the circus," he said.

Miss Beck looked confused again.

"I'm joking," he said. Then she knew to smile, but she still looked confused.

The ice-tea sweated cold in my hand as I watched Miss Beck. I didn't suppose a princess would lift a finger to save a glass of ice-tea, but I wasn't ready to rule it out altogether. One thing I knew for sure, though. She'd never been in a house like ours before.

Mae swung through the door, holding a bowl of string beans. When she saw Miss Beck in her brown roses, she stopped and carefully moved her cigarette to the side of her mouth. "Dinner is served," she said.

✳

The lamplight grew yellower as the dusk drew in, making them look hotter, even, than they were. Layla Beck, lustrous in her silk dress as dinner began, was now gleaming with perspiration and surreptitiously dabbing her napkin to her neck and temples under the guise of patting her mouth. Minerva and Mae exchanged smug glances, the girl's discomfort adding some minor honey to the uniform sourness of their grapes.

Jottie's eyes flicked around the table automatically, check-ing plates. Miss Layla Beck did not care for her apples; that was clear. Jottie watched her pushing them around her plate and told herself that it made no never mind to her whether Miss Beck swallowed a single mouthful. It was just that Bird was watching her like a hawk, and now, Jottie knew, she'd have to hear about how fried apples were so revolting that no one could eat them, no one, when last week the child had downed half a pan. Jottie suppressed a sigh; next time she would tell Mrs. Cooper that she only took boarders who ate every last bite. And didn't wear silk dresses. Or white suits, either. Jottie wiped the sweat from her palms with her napkin and switched from plates to manners. Willa's arms were be-neath the table—good—but she'd gone dreamy and silent—bad, because her head would sink lower and lower over her plate until she looked like an ape-girl. Mae, who never cared about food, was idly tucking her beans under her ham, while she listened to Miss Beck and Felix chatter about—what? Oh. The führer.

"To me, the change in Berlin seemed quite striking," Miss Beck was saying.

"So you'd been before?" asked Felix, and Jottie busied her-self by imagining the saga of Miss Beck's sorry fall from riches to relief against the backdrop of her perennial—though defunct—picture of Berlin: the kaiser's pointed helmet glint-ing among dark columns.

"Oh, yes, years ago; was it 1930?" Layla paused. "Yes, 1930. Of course, I was only a *child*"—Mae shot a lightning look at Minerva—"but I remember how terribly gloomy it was. The streets were lined with beggars and people selling things, old family heirlooms and so on, for *nothing.* Mother—" She paused again. "Well, it was terribly gloomy. But last year—obviously, we went there in the spring, so there was *that,* but the people seemed to be much more cheerful. And the buildings were so clean." She glanced at Felix and put down her fork. "Not that I approve of Hitler, you know."

"Of course not," murmured Jottie, adding to her picture a frivolous yellow-haired mother who frittered away the family fortune on German heirlooms. No, better, ran off with a strapping Nazi, leaving Miss Beck to earn her passage home by— what? Dusting? Seemed unlikely. English lessons? Yes, much better. Jottie was just manufacturing an ill-fated romance between Miss Beck and a piano-playing consumptive when Willa came to.

"We've got dessert after this," she assured Layla earnestly. "We've got a dessert course."

Jottie smiled at her niece. Dreamy Willa—who knew how her thoughts landed where they did? "As long as we're on the subject"—Jottie stood—"do you care for sugar or cream in your coffee, Miss Beck?"

"Sugar and cream, I'm afraid," said Layla. "Thank you."

Felix chuckled. "Uh-oh."

"Is that not done?" she asked gaily.

Felix lifted his dark eyes to his sister's. "What about it, Jottie? You going to toss Miss Beck out on her ear?"

She raised an eyebrow at him. Traitor. "Miss Beck can have whatever she likes in her coffee." She turned to enter the kitchen. "Mae, will you help clear? And you, too, Willa, since you saw fit to disappear before dinner."

"I'd be glad to help," called Layla, looking after her.

"No, no, you just sit right there," said Jottie. "Willa."

Willa scraped back her chair. She loaded her own plate on her arm and set her glass on top of it. Then she put her fork in her glass. She sighed heavily and stumped toward the kitchen.

"It's a shame how that child suffers," said Minerva, assembling plates as she rose. Laden, she backed expertly against the swinging door and entered the kitchen, joining her sisters at the sink. In silence, Jottie scraped Mae's plate.

"Go on, Willa," said Mae, pointing her chin at the door. "Go get some more dishes."

Willa plodded away.

Silently, Minerva and Mae watched as Jottie placed the knives and forks in the sink.

Mae cleared her throat. "Used to being waited on, isn't she?"

"She didn't even stand up," said Minerva.

Jottie set a platter carefully on the counter. "Of course, she's only a *child*. And clearing the table is so terribly gloomy," she said.

Mae's face brightened. "Not in the spring. Obviously."

"Oh, *obviously*," said Jottie. "I just love the spring."

"That's funny," said Minerva. "So do *I*!"

The three sisters snickered and returned, rejuvenated, to the dining room.

"Close tonight," Jottie sighed, waving her napkin to and fro.

"I heard you make yourself hotter doing that," said Willa. "The waving makes you hot."

"Let's us go sit in the cool," said Mae. "We can do the dishes later."

Jottie rose. "Care to join us on the porch, Miss Beck?" she asked, pitying the girl in spite of her silk dress and uneaten apples.

Layla's eyes veered to Felix, but there was no help there. He was watching Bird as she took a guilty finger-scoop of Spanish cream from Mae's half-filled bowl and crammed it into her mouth. He tossed her his napkin, and she caught it with a practiced gesture.

"I think—I'm rather tired—and tomorrow—" stammered Layla. "Well, I think I'll say good night. Thank you for the delicious dinner, Miss Romeyn." She stood, clutching her napkin against her dress, her face glistening in the dull yellow light.

"We have breakfast at seven," Jottie said. "I hope that's convenient for you?"

"Oh! Yes. Seven," repeated Layla. "Yes, of course."

"Now I'm done," said Bird, licking her fingers.

"I should think so. Good night, Miss Beck. Come along, girls." Jottie nodded with what she hoped looked like friendly detachment and led the procession to the porch.

"Good night, Miss Layla Beck," simpered Bird as she went.

"Good night," Layla said flatly.

Felix stayed behind, his arms crossed over the back of his chair, his eyes on the table. "Good night, Miss Beck," he said after a moment. He turned his head to look at her and added gently, "You'll get used to it."

Layla nodded, hard, and walked stiffly toward the stairs.

5

The screen door slammed behind them as they came out onto the porch, exhaling the final labored breath of day, taking in the first calming draft of night. Up and down Academy Street, supper was drawing to a close, the last brittle ping of spoons sounding on coffee cups, the collective woody rumble of chairs moving away from tables. The houses that lined the street looked alike in the thickening light, their massive horizontal bulk broken by golden rectangles of windows and doors. And now, as one, they began to disgorge their inhabitants, pouring them out into screened porches to lower themselves into wicker divans and decrepit rockers. Voices, high and low, wheeled like bats over the wide lawns.

Same as ever, same as ever, Jottie thought, sinking into her shredding seat. She watched her nieces commence their nightly rite of selecting chairs. They were young and they didn't understand. They believed that one chair was better than another. They believed that it was important to make distinctions, to choose, to discern particulars. Like crows, they picked out bits from each evening and lugged them around, thinking that they were hoarding treasure. They remembered the jokes, or the games, or the stories, not knowing that it was all one, that each tiny vibration of difference would be sanded, over the course of years, into sameness. It doesn't matter, Jottie assured herself. They'll get to it. Later, they'll know that the sameness is the important part.

After deliberation, Willa picked a desk chair that had migrated on an unknown current from the parlor, and Bird arranged herself across a rocker, lolling her head over the arm to better accommodate her full stomach.

"I'm stuffed," she announced. No one said anything. "I ate too much," she explained. "My stomach is distended."

"Oh, hush," said Mae.

The night was no different from any other. Soft-edged in the gathering shadows, the adults talked and drank coffee. The children waited for something interesting to happen. Idly, Bird rubbed her stomach and half-listened as her aunts talked about the price of something or other. Her eyes moved to her father, his dark head bent over a cigarette. "Daddy?" she inquired, for the pleasure of seeing him look up.

"Hm?"

A second ticked by while she searched for something impressive to ask. "Was Jottie ever bad when she was little?"

"Never," Jottie said at once. "I was good as gold. A model child, virtuous and pious and kind to the little animals. And clean! So clean!"

"Jottie." Felix shook his head reprovingly. "You'll fry for such lies." He smiled at Bird. "Jottie did so many terrible things that it's hard to pick just one."

"Felix! You were far worse than she was," cried Minerva. "Than anyone was."

"Slander. Base slander and calumny," Felix said, dismissing her words with a flip of his fingers. "Did you know Jottie almost drowned a man once?" he asked his daughters. "On purpose, too."

"You helped!" Jottie protested.

"Tell!" Willa looked between her father and her aunt, her face shining with happiness. "Tell!"

Felix lifted his chin at Jottie, delegating the task.

"It was nothing," Jottie began. "Nothing terrible. The Reverend Holy James Shee came to town once a year to save everyone's soul. Every year, he'd go to the quarry and walk on water, and folks would scream and cry and get baptized and give Holy James Shee all their money."

Felix chuckled. "Jottie couldn't stand that part."

"Well, I knew he was walking on something," Jottie went on. "So Felix and I drove out to the quarry and went swimming around, and sure enough, we found a big board stuck right under the water for Holy James Shee to walk on, the old sinner." She paused. "So we took it."

"And then what?" urged Willa breathlessly. "Did he fall in?"

"He did," Jottie said. "He didn't notice that the board was gone until he stepped out of his little holy boat and sank like a stone."

"Jottie stood there and laughed," Felix said.

"I did not! Not the whole time, anyway. Once his white robes got wrapped around his neck and he started shrieking for help, I didn't laugh."

"You ran," said Felix. He grinned at Willa. "Jottie turned tail and ran, and that was how everyone knew it was us who'd done it."

"I was only a child! I was scared!"

"She was guilty," said Felix. "And do you know who our daddy whipped? Me. He whipped me until his switch broke, and he had to go out and cut himself another one to finish up."

"Poor Father," mourned Willa, reaching to touch his sleeve.

"I'm sorry, honey," said Jottie sympathetically.

"Don't be," said Felix. "Daddy got a lot of pleasure out of it."

"Felix! Daddy whipped you because you were so bad the rest of the time, he figured it was your idea!" said Minerva. "You were the worst boy in town!"

"Wasn't," said Felix.

"Oh! You!" Her wicker chair crackled with her indignation. "Who practically chopped Jottie's hand off with a sword? That you stole! Who put that ladder on the roof of the Statesman Saloon?" Her voice rose. "Who took Daddy's barn apart piece by piece until it fell over? Sold his own baby brother to the Gypsies? Stole Gaylord Spurling's coatrack every single week like *clockwork* and put it in Miss Shanholtzer's parlor?" she demanded. "Who?"

"I give up," said Felix blandly. "Who?"

"Yoo-hoo! Jottie! You-all up there?" Harriet and Richie bobbed out of the darkness, the first of the evening visitors.

"Wait!" Willa held out a hand to stay the moment. "Tell about the coatrack. Why did you put it in—" But it was too late. Felix was rising to his feet. Willa slumped back in her chair.

"Harriet!" cried Jottie. "How-you, honey? Hey, Richie. Come on and sit down!"

"Why, Felix! I haven't seen you in a hundred years!" Harriet cried. She flapped her hand at him. "Lord, honey, sit down! It's too hot to stand up." She squinted across the gloom. "I don't know why you don't get any older, Felix. The rest of us look like something the cat dragged in, and you're just the same as twenty years ago."

He grinned at her. "I got gray hair."

"I don't see any gray hair," said Harriet. She moved toward him across the dark. "Show me a gray hair."

He bent his head, and she stretched out her hand—

There was a loud crack as Richie shifted in his chair, and Harriet snatched her hand away. "Dark as a pocket tonight, isn't it?" she said to no one in particular, plopping down beside Bird. "I'll bet we're going to get a storm before the night's out, don't you?"

Underneath the talk of heat, the low voices of the men began. "How's the chemical business these days?" Richie asked.

"Can't complain." Felix drew on his cigarette.

"That right?" said Richie. "Then you're the only one who can't."

"I heard everything down at Everlasting was fine."

Richie made a disgusted noise in his throat. "Shank fired forty-four men this afternoon."

Like a ripple, like a stone dropped in water, Jottie, Harriet, Mae, and Minerva shifted in their chairs. In the darkness, Willa lifted her head.

Felix whistled softly. "Hard times."

"Yeah, and he don't make them any easier. Forty-four guys, all off the line. Management stays put." Richie's low voice was rising.

"Look at that Packard out there," Harriet said nervously. "I've never seen that car before."

"You're all right, then," Felix said.

"That's not the point. Your father wouldn't have done it," Richie replied.

"Mm."

"Shank don't give a"—Richie glanced at the children—"a hoot about what's right. Sol"—someone drew in a breath, and Willa's eyes circled, trying to discern who—"he does what he can, but Shank don't care. Sol says he'll get on a loom himself if he has to."

Felix said nothing.

"He'll do it, too," Richie said with satisfaction. "He would. Sol's a right guy—" There was an audible intake of air as Harriet kicked him. "Well," he said, after a second. "It's hard times for everybody, just about. It sure is."

"You girls, look at all those lightning bugs out there in the yard," said Jottie calmly. Willa watched Minerva and Mae collapse slightly against their chairs. "I wouldn't let such a chance go by, if I were you."

"I'll get you-all a jar," said Felix, rising. He slid inside the house.

"Hey-you!" called a voice from the sidewalk. "You girls sitting out?"

"We're just sitting here waiting for you, Belle!" called Jottie. "Come on up."

Through the flurry of greeting, of coffee-cup getting, Willa waited. Then through the talk of rain, the mayor, Mrs. Roosevelt, cows . . .

Felix did not return.

Willa leaned forward to put her hand on Jottie's arm. "Where did Father go?" she whispered.

"Oh, I guess he needed some cigarettes," said Jottie carelessly.

Willa's eyes narrowed and she sat back in her chair.

Well, I'm damned, thought Jottie in alarm. She knows I'm lying.

The rain came, finally, in the early hours of the morning. Jottie awoke in a brilliance of white as lightning made a ghost of her room. She counted, and the thunder rocked her on two. She yawned, rose, and went down the hall to the children's room. They always slept through it, and she always checked. Yes, fast asleep, both of them, Bird splayed flat in her bed as if she'd been dropped from the ceiling, Willa curled up tight as a snail. Jottie moved to the window and slid the sash down quietly against the rain. She touched Willa's smooth cheek as she passed back toward her own room and was reassured. Still a baby, really. The old mattress sank beneath her as she lay down. She thought of the porch chairs, rockers thrashing drunkenly to and fro in the wind, fallen ash growing sodden on the floor. A wave of deep, cool air blew in her window, and she shivered ungratefully. Pulling her sheet close around her, she wondered whether Miss Beck had been awakened by the storm. No matter. The girl would get used to it.

6

May 28, 1938

Mrs. Judson Chambers
Deputy Director, Federal Writers' Project
Works Progress Administration
The Smallridge Building
1013 Quarrier Street
Charleston, West Virginia

Dear Mrs. Chambers,

I am in receipt of your letter of May 14, regarding the *History of Macedonia* to be sponsored by that city's town council. Your objections to the project have been noted, but as stated in the General Memorandum on Supplementary Instructions #15, the Central Office is exceedingly interested in these local and other-than-State Guide publications and wishes to encourage them as far as possible. In order to relieve the personnel deficiencies you mentioned and thereby allow your office to undertake this important local publication, I have assigned a new field worker to the West Virginia project. As she will be conducting her field work exclusively in Macedonia, rather than in the Charleston office, and as the town council is eager to have the publication as soon as possible, in order that it will coincide with their sesquicentennial celebrations, I did not feel it necessary to send her down to your office but rather directed her to Macedonia, where she will begin work on the history of the town within the month. She will, however, be an employee of the West Virginia Project and her Field Editorial Copy will be filed to your office. I trust that you will convey the information of this new staff member to Mr. Oliffe, as he, the State Field Assistant, will necessarily have the most involvement in this publication.

Yours very truly,
Benjamin Beck
Field Supervisor

May 30, 1938

Mr. Benjamin Beck
Field Supervisor, Federal Writers' Project
Works Progress Administration
1734 New York Ave. NW
Washington, D.C.
Dear Mr. Beck,

I am in receipt of your letter of May 28. Given that the research assistants who are available to gather agricultural and industrial information for the State Guide are entirely inadequate to the task of writing about it, I am most strongly of the opinion that any new personnel should be hired by me in order to complete that task. I cannot but regard the hiring of this field worker for the purpose of a publication other than the State Guide as a usurpation of my authority as Chief Research Editor for the West Virginia Writers' Project, and I protest most vigorously. I will inform Mr. Alsberg of this breach of administrative protocols at once.

Yours sincerely,
Ursula Chambers

[Telegram from Benjamin Beck to Mrs. Judson Chambers]
June 1, 1938
HOLD FIRE. ALL WILL BE EXPLAINED. BEN

June 1, 1938

Private and Confidential

Dear Ursula,

My hair is singed and my fingertips charred by your last. Hush your screams of rage for a moment, and I'll explain what happened. Rely upon it, you'll be grateful to your old friend Ben instead of demanding my head from Alsberg. My previous letter was composed with the official file in mind; this one is for your personal perusal. If you show it to anyone, I'll deny that I wrote it and accuse you of forgery.

The new field worker is none other than my niece Layla, daughter of the Senior Senator from Delaware. Surely you remember his faithful support of Federal One last year? He believes—and given affairs in North Carolina, how can I deny it?—that he is entitled to some patronage in return, and he therefore demanded that I find a job on the project for his daughter. In view of his position on the Appropriations Committee, I thought it unwise to disappoint him, and hired the girl at once. She is, to put it bluntly, spoiled, frivolous, and ignorant, and she's exactly as fit to work on the project as a chicken is to drive a Buick. She was a hair-raising child, and I was quite fond of her, but my brother likes his women purely ornamental, so she was packed off to a finishing school at the age of fourteen, and it was the ruin of her. They taught her to dance, play tennis, drink cocktails, and act as though she hadn't a brain to call her own. However, Layla has brains enough to know which side her bread is buttered on, so she learned her lesson well, and she's spent the past six years wrapping my brother around her little finger. Imagine his shock last month when she (to her credit) unexpectedly dug in her heels and refused to marry a bankroll. The reprisals were swift and severe—King Lear has nothing on Grayson Beck—and within days, Layla had been banished from the lap of luxury and told to support herself. The

Senator from Delaware does not tolerate domestic dissent, you'll be pleased to know.

In any case, she was deposited on my head, together with some burning coals, and we were both left to make the best of it. The prospect was not heartening for either of us. When she came down for her interview, I was pleasantly surprised to discover that she had heard there was a Depression. And somewhere she has learned to type. Aside from this, she knows nothing. She's never worked a day in her life. I've spent the last week cudgeling my brains for a place to put her. Upon whom could I foist such an albatross? Anything west of the Mississippi is too far from home, wails her mother. No daughter of mine will interview Negroes, declares my brother. In New York, the Stalinists and the Trotskyites would lay down their arms to wage war against her. Vargas says she's no use to him if she doesn't know Spanish, and Wayland would kill her within a week.

Then my thoughts turned to you, Ursula, and West Virginia and *The History of Macedonia.* It is the perfect solution, not only for me but for all of us. It's true that Layla will be no help at all with your present problems (incidentally, I must have the agricultural chapter by June 15), but think of the praise and honor you'll receive for taking on the Macedonia project simultaneously with the State Guide. You'll be held up as a model of industry and devotion to the aims of the Washington office, and Alsberg will send out a memo disparaging the work ethic of all the other state directors. They'll gnash their teeth while you bask in glory.

In the meantime, Macedonia will keep Layla out of the way and out of trouble. It's east of the Mississippi, and the town council prefers to pretend that it has no Negro population, so Layla won't be required to record their history. She'll work alone, so she won't irritate other field workers. And it's possible that the chivalrous councilmen of Macedonia will be so stirred by the spectacle of a Gentlewoman in Distress that they won't notice the quality of Layla's prose. It's ideal.

She need not derange the progress of the State Guide in any way. You simply inform the State Field Assistant for the district of her existence and ask him to supervise her work. I suppose he can provide her with a description of the project's requirements.

I hope you take my view of the matter, Ursula, because the thing has been done and would be difficult to undo. Reflect and you'll see that the advantages outweigh the drawbacks. You get the acclaim, Macedonia gets a book, and the project gets its appropriation renewed for a year.

Yours ever,
Ben

❖

June 15, 1938

Dear Ben,

Observe postmark. I am residing in Macedonia, West Virginia. Thy will be done.

Layla

❖

June 17

Dear Layla,

Blame your father. Blame yourself. Don't blame me.

Ben

7

The morning after Miss Beck's arrival, I awoke earlier than usual. I spent a few moments fingering my new scab, and then I remembered the night before. Had Father come back? Sometimes he went away and didn't come home for days. I quick bounced out of bed and into the hallway to take a look through his keyhole. Father's door was kept closed, so you had to peek through the keyhole if you wanted to know whether he was there. I couldn't see him, but I could see that the curtains were drawn, which meant that he was inside, asleep. So that was all right.

I sat down on the stairs to wait for Miss Beck. I had it all planned out. When she opened her door, I would pop up and pretend to be on my way downstairs for breakfast, just like her. Over breakfast, I would peruse the newspaper and converse on world events.

That would be the beginning. After that, I would insinuate myself into Miss Beck's favor by becoming her faithful assistant. Authors always needed assistants, to help them sharpen their pencils and copy their notes. Maybe she'd even send me to the library to look things up for her. Soon we would work side by side, exchanging a few cryptic words that no one else would even be able to understand. When her book was printed, it might say in the front, Special thanks to my assistant, Wilhelmina Romeyn, without whom I could never have completed this work.

But that would be gravy.

My hours of toil would naturally win Miss Beck's heart, and before long she'd reveal the secrets of her (possibly royal) past.

To me alone she'd confide the truth of her palatial home and pampered youth and how her father had come to lose his fortune in the Crash. Or maybe Miss Beck had run away from home. Anything was possible! I'd lend her my hankie if she started to cry and give her my youthful counsel and we'd be friends, at least as much as a lady like her could be friends with me. And, best of all, I for once would know something that no one else knew. I'd never tell, though. I'd be a vault.

Miss Beck didn't come out of her room, and my bottom went to sleep. I decided I would go downstairs and eat some breakfast while I waited for her.

The back door was open to the morning cool, and I gobbled up my breakfast while Jottie drank coffee and read the newspaper backward, the way she did. The last of my milk gulped, I wiped my mouth with my napkin. "Think Miss Beck'll wear that white suit again today?" I asked Jottie's newspaper.

A newsprint corner flapped down, and Jottie's eye blinked at me. "No. Yellow dress with a square neck. Looked real nice."

She had already been and gone. Jottie didn't know where. Or when she'd be back. I'd been thwarted. I moped around thwartedly for a little while, until Jottie said something about idle hands being the devil's playthings, and I made tracks out the front door before she could give me some awful chore to do. I sulked a little more out on the sidewalk, because no one was up yet. Then I took myself off to Capon Street, to the headquarters of Geraldine Lee's army.

For how many years had I longed to be in Geraldine's army? It must have been three or four. It seemed like hundreds. It seemed like I'd stood on the banks of Academy Creek for my entire life, watching the battalions of plum-throwing children as they advanced, retreated, and bayed like wolves, wishing with all my heart that I could join them. If I had been offered a choice between salvation and induction, I know which I would have chosen. But I couldn't pass muster. The rules were straightforward. There was only one: To get into Geraldine Lee's army, you had to fight Geraldine. Fighting Geraldine was mostly symbolic; you didn't have to beat her up—no one could do that—you only had to wrestle her to the ground. But wrestling Geraldine to the ground was no cakewalk. She was a year younger than me, but she was great big and fat, and she had six little brothers and sisters who skittered up while you were grappling and kicked you in the shins. All six of them were mean and skinny; Bird said Geraldine ate their food and it had turned them.

I had always been puny, and I was puny still. From first grade on, children had demonstrated their muscles by picking me up and lugging me around the playground, and it did me no good to holler about it. They thought it was funny. I was taller now—I had grown four inches since January—but I hadn't gained any weight to go along with it, and I was altogether a pitiful specimen of a twelve-year-old, according to Miss Nellie Kissining, the basketball coach at the Race Street School. She had washed her hands of me. Mae said I looked like I'd been put on the rack. Jottie said I'd fill out before I knew it, which was an unnerving idea. I was weak as a kitten from all that growing and, I suppose, from so many years of sitting on the sofa with a book in my hand. There were some days I couldn't even hold the book up and I had to set it on the floor and drape my head over the side of the cushions to read.

All of which explains why I had been standing for long years in the dirt while the scourge of war laid waste to Macedonia. Specifically, Geraldine's army was scourging Sonny Deal's army, except when they stopped fighting each other to band together against the Spurling children. I had tried to worm my way into Geraldine's ranks by helpfully calling out the location of Sonny Deal's troops from the branches of the red oak in our backyard, but her soldiers would have none of it. They told me to shut up. It only increased my longing to be one of them.

I had to bag Geraldine first. Geraldine was real nice about it—she was always willing to let me try. She'd stand there, big as a shed, and I'd leap at her, thinking that if I could just get going, I could push her over. A couple of times, she tottered a little, but I think she was only doing that to make me feel better. Mostly, she shrugged me off like a horsefly.

In former days, I had despaired. But since the parade—since the birth of my ferocity and devotion—I'd devised a cunning stratagem. The cunning part was the element of surprise. Frank and Joe Hardy and Mr. Sherlock Holmes were all of them big believers in the element of surprise, and I guessed what was good enough for them should be good enough for me. My plan was to sneak up behind Geraldine and knock her flat.

On Capon Street, I approached Geraldine's house with caution, but I needn't have. Mr. and Mrs. Lee were too worn out from all those children to trim their hedges. I crouched low inside a rhododendron and waited. Sure enough, Geraldine came out, smacking her lips and burping, and then began to stroll about. The other children must have been eating her scraps, because she was alone. All at once, she did the strangest thing: She began to dance. Not a real dance like the foxtrot, nor even a tap dance, which you couldn't do on dirt, anyway, but a swaying, whirling dance. I guessed it was a ballet dance, and for a moment or two I was just thunderstruck, but then I realized that this was a fine time to employ the element of surprise. I got myself ready, and the next time Geraldine spun by with her back turned, I burst whooping out of the rhododendron and pounced on her. She fell pretty heavy, but I had my legs around her middle and my arms around her neck, so it didn't hurt much.

"Gotcha!" I hollered, and that Geraldine was such a nice girl, she didn't take a swipe at me. She agreed that I had knocked her down fair and square and welcomed me into her army. She'd been pulling for me all along, she said, and she was glad I'd finally made it, because she needed a spy and she knew I'd be fine at that. How do you know, I asked. She said the way I'd snuck up on her showed natural talent. I had to agree that it did.

We did a lot of talking, there in the rhododendron. It turned out that the war with Sonny Deal's army was just to keep in practice for the real war, which Geraldine said Mr. Lee said was against the Reds. According to Geraldine, the Reds were running Washington, and that was only four hours away on State 9, which meant we needed to get ready. I thought that if the Reds were in Washington, I would have heard about it, and when Geraldine told me that American Everlasting was full of Reds, I said I didn't think so, because I knew folks who worked there and they weren't Reds. How do you know they aren't,

Geraldine asked, and it occurred to me that this could be yet another matter the grown-ups had not seen fit to reveal to me. I fell silent, and Geraldine said it didn't matter if I didn't believe her about American Everlasting, as long as I took a vow to fight the Reds. So I did, and then we got down to the business of training, which was mostly creeping around in the bushes to spy on Mrs. Lee. She didn't do anything except hang sheets on the line, but Geraldine thought highly of my creeping and promoted me to officer on the spot. She said I was a born sneak.

When I heard the noon whistle down at the mill, I zipped home for lunch. I wouldn't have if I'd known it was hash. We all despised hash, every last one of us, but Jottie felt obliged to make it because it stretched leftover roast to two meals.

"Is this enough, Jottie?" said Bird. She had eaten two bites.

"No. Two more." Jottie clamped her mouth shut to get her hash down. "It's good for you."

"You should be grateful," said Mae. "Some poor little children, all they have to eat is okra and lard sandwiches."

"You!" yelped Bird, pointing her chin at Mae's plate. "You ain't even had *one* bite. At least—"

"Bird," said Jottie. "What have you been doing this morning?"

Bird scowled. She knew she was being diverted. "Secret," she said grumpily.

"Fine. You can have your secret," said Mae. Bird scowled worse than ever. She had thought they'd try to wheedle it out of her. Mae turned to me. "What about you, Willa?"

"Geraldine and I are getting ready to fight the Reds," I said.

"Oh. You got in," observed Bird. She swallowed another lump of hash and shivered all over.

"What Reds?" Jottie asked. She fixed me with her eyes. "Got in where?"

"Geraldine's army. Geraldine says that American Everlasting is full of Reds." I paused to see what effect this announcement would have.

"She did, did she?" Jottie didn't seem too worried about the Reds.

"Yes, and she says the Reds are running Washington and

we've got to be prepared to fight. Even kids have got to get out and fight the Reds. Says Geraldine."

"I swear, I don't know what possessed Irma to marry that man," said Mae.

"It was that suit of his. Remember?" said Minerva. "She even said so at the time."

"Now listen here, Willa," said Jottie, frowning at Minerva and Mae. "There are no Reds at American Everlasting, and the Reds aren't running Washington, either."

"Mr. Roosevelt is running Washington," said Mae. "You know that."

"And just you remember to keep your politics to yourself, young lady," Jottie said. "You'll bring the wrath of Cain down on our heads if you go around telling people that American Everlasting is Communist." She put another forkful of hash in her mouth, and her eyes watered. She swallowed and then smiled. "Though I'd like to see Ralph's face when he heard it."

Minerva and Mae snickered. In earlier days, I might not have noticed, but now I did. "Who's Ralph?" I asked, as innocent as a baby.

Jottie lifted one eyebrow. "Mr. Shank, and as for the Communists," she went on, "maybe they have their reasons. That czar was no great shakes. Drinking champagne when his people had nothing to eat but rotten potatoes. And letting that Rasputin come into the palace with his big burning eyes and dirty hair."

"Who's Rasputin?" I asked.

"Lionel Barrymore," said Minerva.

"Rasputin was a monk who turned his burning eyes on the czarina until the poor woman was hypnotized and handed over the crown jewels. Emeralds and rubies trickled through his fingers like water," said Jottie, wafting her hands through the air to show trickling. Father said that if Jottie sat on her hands, she wouldn't be able to talk atall. "The czarina ground up pearls to put in her bathwater, and the poor people trudged through the snow in little felt shoes. I don't blame them for turning Communist. I don't blame them a bit."

"Yes'm, but . . ."

"But what?"

"You sound like you think they're all right. The Reds."

"I just say they might have their reasons," Jottie said. "People usually do."

"Everybody else hates them."

Her eyes glinted. "Whatever gave you the idea we were like everybody else?"

She was practically admitting she didn't hate the Reds. Geraldine would blow a gasket if she found out. I sighed. "I wish we were like everybody else. I get real tired of lying."

Jottie's coffee cup froze midway to her mouth.

I'd hurt her feelings. "That wasn't what I meant," I said quick. "That came out wrong." I took a big bite of hash to show I was sorry.

✳

Layla peered uncertainly down a dark corridor. "Pardon me?" she called. Nothing happened. She walked along the scarred linoleum until she reached an open door. "Excuse me?" she said. "Is this the library?"

A man with a white face looked up from his desk. He was rabbity and soft. "No, ma'am," he began.

"A dame!"

Layla looked up, startled, and noticed a jail cell tucked away in the corner of the room. From within, a florid prisoner eyed her avidly. "Dale! Help the lady!"

The rabbity man turned around and glared at his captive. Then he swiveled back. "The library's upstairs, ma'am. Third floor."

Layla smiled. "That's an unusual combination—jail and library."

"They didn't mean for it," the prisoner said eagerly. "It was courthouse and jail once, but they built a new one for the courthouse."

"Hushup, Winslow," said Dale. "Third floor, ma'am."

"The judges didn't like to see what they done," Winslow went on. "It ate at them. Now they can lock a man away and never look on him."

"Thank you," said Layla to Dale. She turned to go and nearly collided with a policeman packed firmly into his dark uniform. He had an old-fashioned walrus mustache.

"Look, Hank! A lady!" bellowed Winslow.

Layla laughed as she looked up at the newcomer. "I guess you don't get many lady prisoners," she said.

The policeman bowed slightly. "No, ma'am. Not what you'd call ladies."

Winslow was delighted. "Aw, you got such nice manners, Hank! Looka-you, bowing! See that, Dale? That's what you shoulda done." His yells followed Layla down the dark corridor. "You come back and visit, lady! Bring me a book from the library! I can read!"

The library was dim and quiet and, except for some children deep in the thrall of their books, empty. Layla took an appreciative sniff as she stepped through the door: dust and paper and glue. She walked on her toes to the desk.

"You can put your feet down," said the librarian, glancing at her over gold-rimmed glasses.

"I was trying to be quiet," murmured Layla.

"I wouldn't worry about that," said the librarian crisply. "Winslow keeps us from being too persnickety about quiet."

"Is he—intoxicated?" asked Layla.

The librarian smiled. "No. If he were intoxicated, you'd know it. You're the one from the WPA, aren't you?"

Layla laughed self-consciously. "How'd you guess?"

"I've never seen you before."

Layla laughed again. "I forget, I'm in a small town."

"It's not so small, but I've lived here thirty-nine years and I know everyone in it." There was a pause. "I'm Caroline Betts."

"Layla Beck." They shook hands over the desk. Caroline Betts's handshake was, like her composure, firm and cool, and Layla was beset by the sudden certainty that the woman before her would have been the best possible author of *The History of Macedonia*. It was obvious; her competence was so solid and complete it could have taken a chair. "Mrs. Betts—" began Layla.

"Miss Betts."

"Miss Betts, I wonder if you can help me find a general history of Macedonia, so I can get some background—"

"Aren't you writing it? A history of Macedonia?"

"Well, yes, but just for background," floundered Layla. "I'd like to read what's been written on the subject—"

Miss Betts's amused laughter was not especially soothing, Layla thought. "Nothing's been written, Miss Beck! You are our first historian!"

"But—" Layla's forehead folded into anxious furrows. "I don't know anything about the history of Macedonia. The town council has given me a list of topics that must be included in my book, but how am I to research them? How am I to write about them?" Notwithstanding Layla's efforts, the last sentence ended considerably higher than it began.

There was a slight pause. "You ask," said Miss Betts.

"Pardon?"

"You're not supposed to know. You're supposed to ask."

It was as though she had risen to the surface of dark water. She took a breath.

Miss Betts smiled. "Feel better?"

"Yes, thanks," said Layla, grateful that a heart beat under Miss Betts's pristine blouse. "Who should I ask?"

"Whom," said Miss Betts. "Me."

Layla's eyes circled the dusty library. "But . . . I don't want to be a bother—"

Miss Betts lifted her eyebrows. "You say the town council has given you a list?"

"Yes, a letter," said Layla, flustered. "From a Mr. Davies. But I didn't bring it with me." She glanced at her white purse, wishing that it conveyed a sense of purpose or resolve or anything besides a frivolous concern with prettiness. "I can get it, though."

Miss Betts's eyes followed hers to the purse. "Tomorrow," she said. "Bring Mr. Davies's letter here tomorrow morning, and we will begin our work on the history of Macedonia." She nodded kindly at Layla. "I shall quite look forward to it."

8

After lunch it was my turn to do the dishes, and I'd promised Geraldine I'd come back to her house after that. I was going to show her where there were some buckeyes already. A storm of buckeyes could bring Sonny Deal's army to its knees. I hurried through the dishes, but not as much as Bird hurried through the drying.

"You can just dry those coffee cups," I began to scold, when there was a knocking, hard and fast, on the back screen. A voice called, "Jottie? You there?" It was Mrs. Fox from down the street.

We heard the worry in her voice. "She's here, Mrs. Fox," I said. "Come in, and I'll get her for you."

She stepped into the kitchen. "Run and get her, honey. Vause Hamilton is at it again."

Before I could turn and run, another, softer voice came at the door. "Miss Josephine? It's Sallie here, from Mrs. Lacey." Sallie was Mrs. Lacey's Negro maid.

"Oh, Sallie, I'm just getting her," said Mrs. Fox.

I ran, calling, "Jottie! Come quick!"

She was settling down into her chair for her rest, but she jumped right up and bustled after me into the kitchen. She didn't need but one look at who was there to ask, "Vause Hamilton?"

"Yes, ma'am," said Sallie. "Mrs. Lacey says if you please, can you come?"

"Of course," Jottie said. She was already halfway to the door. We followed as she sped along the path and then the sidewalk. Around the corner, on Kanawha Street, the sidewalk petered out right at Mr. Vause Hamilton's house. Mr. Hamilton was old, and he'd been rich a long time ago, but he wasn't now. Now he was sort of crazy. Jottie said he'd lost his mind from grief when his son died. His son was named Vause, too, and he'd died young, and ever since then, when Mr. Hamilton remembered him, he got upset and burned a rubber boot in his front yard. Once or twice a year he did it, and it smelled just terrible. Jottie said he wanted to make his neighbors feel as miserable as he did, and I guess he succeeded. They came running to get Jottie because she was the only one who could stop him.

I could see black smoke billowing over Mr. Hamilton's spirea bushes as we hurried along, and I sure hoped Sallie had given Mrs. Lacey a handkerchief to put over her nose, because Mrs. Lacey lived just behind him and she was real old and that smoke might kill her. I pinched my nose shut and watched from the edge of the yard with Mrs. Fox and Sallie and Bird, but Jottie went on ahead, out to the lawn, where old Mr. Hamilton stood, looking at the fire. Back when I was a little girl, he'd been a tall man, but now he was bent. His white shirt stretched tight over his shoulders as he hunched over the flames, and tears ran down his cheeks. He reached out to grab Jottie's hand. "My boy is dead," he croaked. "Vause, his name was."

"Yes," Jottie said. "Vause is dead."

He lifted his head. "He was born on this day. June the fifteenth. In the new century."

I saw Jottie flinch, but she said calmly, "That's right. Today is Vause's birthday."

He lifted his head and recognized her. "You. You knew my Vause."

"Yes. I did."

He peered at her. "He liked you. Better than all the other girls."

Jottie didn't say anything.

"But he died," the old man moaned. "He died in a terrible battle."

"Mr. Hamilton, you've got to stop burning this boot," Jottie said firmly. "You let me put this fire out, all right? Fouling the air and making people sick—that's no way to remember Vause."

"He's *dead,*" repeated Mr. Hamilton, as though she hadn't heard.

"I know it. I know he's dead. But let me put this fire out. It smells bad." Jottie bent at the knees and picked up a handful of dirt, which she tossed on the fire. It didn't make much of a dent in the smoke, but Mr. Hamilton didn't object. He just watched her.

Sallie sidled forward with a little spade. Jottie nodded at her and took Mr. Hamilton's hand.

"Now, let's us sit down and you tell me what's bothering you," she said, leading him away toward his porch. Slowly, they climbed the stairs and she helped him into his chair. Then she sat down next to him and bent her head toward his.

"She's a saint," sighed Mrs. Fox. She looked down at me, kind of sharp. "Your aunt is a saint."

"Yes'm," I said. "I think I'll go help Sallie."

When Minerva and Mae woke from their naps, they were sorry they'd missed it.

"Mrs. Fox says Jottie is a saint," I reported.

"All she did was tell him to stop burning that boot," said Bird. "Doesn't take a saint to do that."

"You hushup," said Mae. She snapped on the radio, just, I thought, to snap something.

Minerva sighed. "Poor Jottie," she said under her breath.

I pounced on it. "Why? Why poor Jottie?"

Minerva and Mae looked at each other and shook their heads identically. "Poor Jottie has to smell Mr. Hamilton's nasty old boot," said Mae.

"Who killed him?" asked Bird.

"What?" Minerva said, kind of startled.

"The boy Vause. Mr. Hamilton said he'd died in a terrible battle," Bird said. "Did someone beat him up?"

"No, of course not." Mae frowned. "And he wasn't a little boy, either. He was—how old, Minnie?"

"Twenty or twenty-one," said Minerva. She looked sad.

"Oh. He was a grown-up," said Bird, disgusted. "Why does

everyone call him a boy when he wasn't one?" She lost interest and wandered away into the kitchen.

I stayed put. I'd been hearing Vause Hamilton's name for years, but I hadn't paid attention until now. He was just Mr. Hamilton's dead son. "Where was the battle?" I asked.

Minerva and Mae exchanged glances. "He didn't die in a battle," Mae said.

I waited, but she didn't say anything more. "How did he die, then?"

Mae looked at Minerva again and lifted her eyebrows into a question. Minerva lifted her eyebrows back and shrugged. "He died in a fire."

Mae twitched at the words. Her eyes were on the dogwood tree in our front yard, but she twitched just as plain.

"What?" I asked.

"What what?" Minerva asked back.

I didn't know, but there was something they weren't telling me. "Why was it so terrible?"

Mae turned on me. "Don't you think it's terrible when a young man dies?"

The Andrews Sisters came on, singing one of their stupid songs. I persevered. "Yes, but—lots of people—well—I don't know."

Minerva took pity on me. "He was a friend of your father's," she said. "And of Jottie's, too."

"Oh," I said. I couldn't think what to ask. "Did you like him?"

"Like him?" Minerva repeated. She glanced at Mae. "Well. He was kind to us when we were children."

Mae smiled suddenly. "Remember when he came back from the war? How he took off his hat and bowed?"

Minerva laughed. "Because he didn't recognize us."

"Because we were all grown up. He asked Felix to introduce him. There on the porch." Mae's face shone, thinking of it. "In his uniform."

"He was the nicest thing," said Minerva dreamily. "Just the nicest thing in the world."

They stared off into nothing.

"We thought," said Mae. She gave the radio a disgusted

look. I couldn't tell if it was the Andrews Sisters or something else.

I tried to look like part of the wall so they would keep talking, but they only nodded at each other and mused in silence. After practically forever, I cleared my throat a little bit. "So he wasn't nice after all?" I asked in the most soothing way I could.

Their faces were empty. "No," said Minerva finally. "Turns out he wasn't."

"What did he do?"

Minerva sighed. "Oh, honey." She looked at Mae again, and Mae inclined her head just a little. "Turn that off, will you?" Mae twitched the radio off, and Minerva turned to face me. "Vause Hamilton died in a fire at American Everlasting in 1920." The words shot from her mouth like she wanted to get them gone. "He broke into Daddy's office and stole money from the safe and then tried to burn down the factory to hide what he'd done."

"And then he couldn't get out," Mae added. "He got trapped and he smothered on the smoke. They found him there in the ashes, the day after, with two thousand dollars in a sack."

I looked from one aunt to the other, flummoxed. Vause Hamilton had robbed my grandfather and set his factory on fire? He sounded bad. He sounded terrible. But my aunts looked sad, not mad. "Why—"

They looked up together, eyes wary.

"Why'd he do it?"

"Money," Minerva said. "He was running away, to California, and I guess he needed money. Though why he couldn't work for it like everyone else, I don't know."

"Did he steal from anyone else or just us?" I asked.

"Just us," said Mae. "Just Daddy."

I pressed ahead. It was like trying to slide around a door as it was closing. "Why does Jottie help Mr. Hamilton, when his boy was so bad?"

"Because she's a saint," said Mae.

"Because Vause was a friend of hers," said Minerva at the same second.

I remembered something. "Mr. Hamilton said Vause liked Jottie. Better than the other girls, he said."

Mae sucked air quick through her teeth. "The old hound!" she snarled. "It's a wonder God didn't strike him dead where he stood!"

Well! "Why? What'd he do?" I asked alertly.

"He made Jottie and Vause miserable, is what he did! The nerve of that man!" Mae fumed, but Minerva caught her eye, and she stopped and took a breath. "Listen, Willa, it's all over and done now, and don't you go bringing it up with Jottie."

"Or your father," added Minerva.

"But why?" I begged, hearing a whine in my voice. I couldn't help it—grown-ups were downright infuriating. The least they could do was say *why* they wouldn't tell me what I wanted to know. "They already know about it, don't they? How bad he was?"

"Well. They don't want to talk about it," Minerva said. "You'll understand when you're older."

"Least said, soonest mended," said Mae, real prim.

That wasn't fair atall, and I got mad. "You don't think that!" I exclaimed. "Nobody thinks that!"

Their faces closed up like fists. Silently, Mae reached out and turned the radio on again. I wasn't going to get anything now, I realized.

Maybe later.

✳

Jottie slipped wearily into her room and lowered herself onto the bed. Her eyes stung from the smoke. They were red, too, she knew. Just a little rest, she thought. She opened one eye to look at the clock. Three. She had time for a little rest.

"Hey, Josie."

Her heart thudded once and she stilled it. If she didn't move, if she kept quiet, she could have him back for a minute, maybe two. She let her breath out, slow and even.

"Vause?" She scanned the rain-heavy garden.

"Here." He stepped out from the shadow of the barn into the watery sun.

The apparition made her breathless. *"What're you doing out here so early?"* she managed to say.

He grinned crookedly. *"Early for some. Late for others."*

"You've been up all night?" she asked, instantly jealous of whatever, whomever he'd been with. *"What were you doing?"*

"Felix and I took an unexpected trip," he said, and winked at her. That meant they'd hopped the train. "And were unavoidably delayed on our return." That meant they'd had to walk part of the way back. He shook the rain from his shining hair and added, "You're looking pretty this morning, Josie."

She blushed, more breathless than ever, and he stepped closer, his eyes curious. For a moment, it was as if they were all alone in the garden for the first time, watching each other like animals.

"Josie?" he murmured at last.

She nodded dumbly.

"Today's my birthday."

"I know," she said, and then wished she'd pretended surprise. "Happy birthday."

"Thanks," he said. "I'm eighteen."

"Of age," she said, feeling like a child.

"Of age," he agreed. He snickered suddenly. "I could get married."

"Don't," she blurted, and her cheeks flamed once more.

He laughed, delighted. "Don't, huh? You don't want me to get married?" He bent down so he could see her face. With her eyes on the ground, she shook her head. "All right," he teased. "I'll tell Thelma." Thelma was his girlfriend. "Good old Thelma," he added absently. There was a pause. "Say, Josie, I've got a present for you."

"But it's your birthday," she protested, relieved to wash up on the shore of a new topic. "I should give you a present."

"Shh. Close your eyes," he said, stepping near. His warmth furled around her, cloaking her against the cool of the morning. "Give me your hand. Like this." He placed her hand in his. "Now. Close your eyes."

She obeyed, feeling the landscape of his palm—calluses and softness—under her fingertips. There was a tiny, cool touch on her hand. Then another and another.

"There," he said. "You can look."

She looked. Her finger glittered with raindrops.

"See?" He smiled. "Diamonds."

A brisk tattoo of footsteps arose from the front walk.

"Why, Mr. Romeyn, you're home early," cried Layla's voice. *"Josie?"*

Jottie rolled onto her stomach and thrust a pillow over her head. There, that was quiet. *"Vause?"* But he was gone. Miss Beck had driven him away. No, she knew that wasn't fair. Vause was always an elusive visitor.

"I could say the same to you," Felix's voice replied. "Aren't you supposed to be chasing down the history of Macedonia?"

Layla laughed. "I was! I went to the library and the jail, by mistake. I came back here to ask Miss Romeyn if I could borrow a map, but Bird tells me she's resting."

"Is she?" said Felix. "Well, I bet I can find you a map. You wait right here."

"I don't mean to keep you from your business, Mr. Romeyn."

"No trouble at all. Don't want you to get lost in the great metropolis." Felix's voice faded as he entered the house.

Now Jottie was curious, and curiosity was guaranteed to send Vause packing. He slipped in only when she hung between sleep and wakefulness, only when she was weak enough to long for him. She could fend him off when she was upright. You just get out, Vause Hamilton, she commanded, punishing herself for her weakness. You're a liar and a thief. And I don't care if it's your birthday. She threw the pillow back to the top of the bed for emphasis.

Layla's voice again: "Oh, thank you, Mr. Romeyn. That'll be a big help."

Paper crinkled. "See, here's where we are. Academy Street."

"I've got to go see Mr. and Mrs. Davies tomorrow," said Layla. "Do you know where Locust Street is?"

"You ride high, Miss Beck." Felix laughed. "Locust is over here. So Parker's going to give you his version of things?"

"Yes. He said he had a lot of material about General Hamilton. You know, the founder of Macedonia."

"Sure, sure, our noble founder. You want to know a secret?" Felix's voice lowered. "General Hamilton wasn't really a general. But don't tell Parker. It'll break his heart."

Layla giggled. "He sent me a long list of people to interview.

He says the book is supposed to include accounts of Macedonia's first families."

"Huh. Some history," said Felix. "Aren't you supposed to write about what happened around here, the War Between the States and all?"

"Well, that, too," said Layla. "And a little bit about civic and natural sites of moment."

Felix burst out laughing. "What civic and natural sites of moment?"

"Um. Flick Park?"

"Flick Park?" Felix snorted. "A natural site of moment? It's a park."

"The Caudy House? Macedonia's oldest structure?"

"Macedonia's oldest chicken coop, more like."

"Dolly's Ford?"

"Well, okay, that's historical. How are you going to get out there, though?"

"I don't know, exactly." Jottie could hear the tiny lift in her voice. "Where is it?"

"Look." He was sitting next to her now, Jottie knew. She'd be watching his face, a little dazed, hoping he'd smile again. Jottie had seen it a hundred times. More. "It's all the way out here," Felix explained. "You can't walk that far. Especially in those shoes."

"I have other shoes."

"Uh-huh, but it's still too far to walk." There was a pause. "How about I take you?"

"Oh, Mr. Romeyn, that would be wonderful! But—you're busy and all . . ."

"I'm not so busy. Listen, will you stop calling me Mr. Romeyn? It makes me feel like a grandpa. My name is Felix."

"All right." Layla sounded shy. "And mine is Layla."

"I know. I can remember all the way back to yesterday. Okay, Layla. We'll go to Dolly's Ford on—well, let's see—better make it Saturday. Will that suit you?"

"Oh, yes!"

Flutter, flutter, thought Jottie sourly. Felix making plans! Felix never made plans. Or maybe he just didn't tell her about them, she reflected. Maybe this was the way he did with all those girls she never met. Jottie frowned at her ceiling. Didn't seem like a fair fight, Felix going after a girl who had to board in his house. My house, she corrected herself. Pooh. She was being foolish. A girl as pretty as that surely had a man somewhere. Maybe she wasn't watching Felix atall. Maybe she was impervious to his charms. And that, thought Jottie, cheered, is a show I'd like to see.

"You got any more natural sites of moment on that list of yours?" inquired Felix.

"Yes, a few. It's in a letter that Mr. Davies sent me. Upstairs."

"Well, you show it to me before we go. Maybe we can kill a couple of momentous sites with one stone."

Layla laughed. "Thank you so much for helping me, Mr.—Felix."

"Close."

"Um, Felix."

"Very good, Layla." He broke her name into two slow sounds.

"Father! You're home!" Willa let the screen door slam behind her.

"Hey, sweetheart," he said easily.

"Guess what."

"Hm?"

Willa paused for effect, and Jottie braced herself. She knew what was coming. "Mr. Hamilton burnt a boot today."

"He did, did he?" Could anyone else hear the ice in his voice? Jottie wondered.

"Yes, but Jottie got him to stop."

The porch creaked as he got to his feet. "Is that right?"

"She's a saint." Jottie smiled at the echo of Belle Fox.

"She sure is." His voice faded as he went indoors.

And he's gone, thought Jottie. Poor Willa.

On the porch, there was a silence with little crackles in it as Layla Beck folded up the map. "What have you been doing today, Willa?" she asked.

"Watching Mr. Hamilton burn his boot," said Willa patiently.

"Who's Mr. Hamilton?" asked Layla.

"He lives around the corner."

"Why did he burn his boots?"

"Just one. He just burnt the one. Because he's sad about his son dying."

"Really?" said Layla, surprised. "That's an odd thing to do."

"Oh, he's always doing it," said Willa breezily.

"My! When did his son die?"

"A long time ago. He smothered to death. In a fire." Upstairs, Jottie took a sharp breath. Who told her? How long had she known?

"Oh, how awful!" exclaimed Layla.

"He was stealing money from my grandfather, and he smothered to death while he was doing it," said Willa with grisly satisfaction.

Stop it, thought Jottie.

"That's just awful!" Layla said again.

"Well. I guess. But don't you think it served him right? For stealing?"

Stop it. Stop it right now. You didn't know him; you can't talk about him. Blindly, Jottie reached for her pillow and pulled it over her head, but the muffled nothing didn't help her. Vause was gone and gone and gone.

✳

It was late in the afternoon, and flies were thick in front of Macedonia's oldest structure, their idiot careening providing the only movement in the landscape. From behind the snaggled remains of a picket fence, Layla batted away flies and tried to find a way to be interested in the stricken building before her. The Caudy House, built in 1824. Could it have been a gathering place? Could it have held dances or meetings or tragic deaths? She eyed the flimsy, bowed walls and the narrow windows and couldn't care. It must have been a terrible place, even in its prime. Its existence was a fact without meaning. And yet she was supposed to find a meaning in it. She sighed, stepped into the yard, and approached the splintering front wall. On an impulse, she slapped it and felt the whole edifice sway from the blow. Hastily, she backed away and stood gazing, in the airless heat, at history.

On Layla's return, Prince Street was crowded with men in work clothes. She paused and moved close to the building beside her. They were all moving in the same direction. Must be closing time at that American Everlasting factory, she thought, and, pleased with her acumen, she smiled genially at a cluster of four or five men arrayed around a lamppost. Their narrow faces stiffened in response; hands went automatically to caps, and one young man—lounging at a dramatic angle against the post—straightened up in a caricature of attention. Embarrassed, Layla turned away, affecting interest in the window behind her, which was usefully full. Teenagers sharing sodas over tables, a child dribbling ice cream, his mother fruitlessly dabbing at his shorts, two older ladies in dark suits—how could they, in this heat—and a man turning away from the counter with a carton: It was Felix! Layla smiled and waved, and he looked at her curiously. His smile grew as hers faltered—it wasn't Felix at all. This man was taller and bigger, and he didn't move with Felix's swift, peculiar grace. But his eyes were almost black, and his hair, too, was thick and dark. Through the glass, the man who wasn't Felix pointed to himself and then to her and lifted his eyebrows in a question. Layla suddenly realized how long she'd been staring at him and began to blush furiously. He lifted a finger, detaining her, and moved toward the door. Layla glanced at the men around the lamppost, raised her chin haughtily, and plunged into the stream of passersby.

The tall man looked after her from the doorway. "You know her?" he called to the group at the lamppost.

"Hey, Emmett," one of them said.

"Hey. You know her?" Emmett repeated.

"Nope. Wish I did," the man replied.

"You can just get off right here," said the one who had been lounging on the post. "I saw her first."

Emmett snorted. "I'll tell Louise you said so."

"You hear about Shank?" the first man asked.

Emmett's eyes scanned the distant sidewalk for one more moment. Then he turned. "No. What?"

They told him—forty-four men fired, just like that, yesterday, that bastard Shank, he didn't care, Tom Lehew, what's he going to do, sixty-three and his land all run out—and Emmett listened. Then he told them what he thought, and at first they laughed. Union? You're crazy. He talked some more, and they glanced at one another, jutting their chins out, which was how it looked when they began to agree. Emmett shrugged. Don't listen to me, he said. Talk to someone who knows. Talk to someone who's done it. Huh, said one of them. Maybe you're right. Could be, said another. Maybe. Maybe. Well, Emmett said, I'd better get on home. See you, Emmett. See you. See you. See you later.

But not once did he stop thinking about the girl outside the window, how she'd smiled at him. He didn't forget about her for an instant.

9

"Oh, for God's sake," muttered Jottie.

"I hates to be beholden to you."
   *"Hell, Ma'am, they ain't too many of us shiftin' for a
livin' out here. I'd be a pore man—"*

Jottie slammed *The Yearling* shut and burrowed into a corner
of the sofa.

"I don't know why you keep reading it if you hate it so
much," said Mae, pausing at the foot of the stairs.

"I want to get to the part where the deer dies," Jottie replied
with her eyes closed. "Hush, now. I'm thinking."

"Looks an awful lot like sleeping to me," said Mae. "Good
night, honey."

"Night," yawned Jottie. She was thinking. There was never
enough time to think, during the day. Especially this day, she
reflected, which had begun so long ago with Willa asking after
Miss Beck—who knew why—and then Geraldine Lee and her
army and her Reds. Cautiously, Jottie approached the painful
spot: "I wish we were like everybody else. I get real tired of
lying." It hurt. She examined the wound: Willa lies about us.
Why? The enemy voice that lived inside her head supplied the
answer readily enough: She's ashamed. Jottie's eyes snapped
open. Had Irma Lee said something? Had she hinted something about Felix or mocked Willa about her mother? Had she
been the one who'd told Willa about Vause? Had she dared?

I'll kill her, Jottie promised, breathing shallowly with rage. I'll kill anyone who makes Willa worried or ashamed.

It's not just Irma, her enemy voice continued implacably. You can't kill everyone in Macedonia, and you can't keep Willa shut up in a box. She's going to hear it all, sooner or later. She'll hear about Felix, she'll hear about you and Vause, she'll hear about the fire, and she'll hear about Sol—she's already beginning to wonder about that; you saw it last night—and she'll be worried and ashamed, and there is not one thing you can do to stop it.

"I wish we were like everybody else. I get real tired of lying." It was a special distillation of shame, to have to lie about your family, and a special distillation of agony to learn of it. Jottie's mind flicked over her own heedless childhood, recalling the protection and authority she hadn't even known she enjoyed. How light and lordly she'd been, how free, how certain that her happiness was the product of her own virtues and powers. How wrong she'd been. How foolish. And how very, very lucky.

If only Willa could have what I had, Jottie mourned. If only she could be so certain and proud. It was an illusion every child should have. And Willa was losing it, right before her eyes.

If only we were still respectable, thought Jottie disconsolately.

Her own thoughts shocked her. No! We're still respectable! We certainly are! Lots of people like us. And believe in us. And we have the house, too, the Romeyn house. We're *respectable*.

But safe? asked the enemy slyly. What about safe?

Her heart sagged. Yes. That was what she wanted for Willa. Safety. She wanted them to be safe for Willa. Unremarkable, irreproachable, and safe.

She imagined how it might sound, being unremarkable: Oh, the Romeyns, yes, of course. Nice people. Real pleasant.

The comparison came along, an uninvited guest: Why, sure, the Romeyns. They used to be a big family in town. Poor old Mr. Romeyn would just about die if he could see what that Felix is up to now. He always was a shady one; remember the way he used to sneak into every place in town? Jottie? Well, she always pranced around like the Queen of the May, but she got her comeuppance when Vause Hamilton threw her over. Didn't surprise me any, but she took it real hard. Nobody even saw her for almost a year after the fire, and I'll tell you, plenty of people think Sol McKubin was right about that fire. Now? I guess she's raising those girls, Felix and Sylvia's girls, and oh Lord, what a fiasco that was, after he practically got himself killed marrying her. After all that, they fought like cats and dogs. I heard stories about the two of them that would curdle up all the blood in your body. It wasn't long before he brought the children back here and Sylvia stayed up in Grand Mile, and you won't believe it, but she and Parnell Rudy are living, well, like man and wife—

Jottie groaned softly to herself and spread her fingers over her face, listening to the clock soldier forward. The darkness inside her hands was calm and soothing. She reached up and turned off the lamp, and her agony ebbed a little.

There's got to be some way I can change it.

For Willa and Bird, I'll do anything.

But what can I do?

I can—she leapt into the abyss—join a ladies' club. There! That's respectable! That's something I can do! I can be lady-like. Why, I can be more ladylike than anyone, as long as I can keep myself from saying the first thing that pops into my mind.

I'll fix it, she thought with returning energy. I'll fix everything. I'll make Willa safe. I'll make all of us safe. I'll start with the ladies' club. And after that, I can learn about flower-arranging, maybe. And, why, there's knitting. Anyone can knit. What about canasta? I'll take up canasta. I can have one of those card parties. And maybe Felix would help, if I asked him. He could do a little gardening. Clip the hedge, maybe, or rake leaves. People like a man who works in the garden. I'm sure he'd help, if I asked him right. And then we'll be safe, safe . . .

When Jottie opened her eyes again, Felix was there. He was sitting on the coffee table, smoking, silent.

"Felix?" she whispered. "I've been thinking—"

"Listen," he broke in, "you don't owe him a damn thing."

"Who?"

"Hamilton. Mr. Hamilton." He ran a hand through his hair, standing it on end. "I don't know why you do it. Let him burn his house down. What do you care?" His eyes were bright and hot. "And if you've got some crazy idea you're doing it for Vause, forget it. You sure as hell don't owe Vause anything, either. I don't know why you can't remember that." He ground his cigarette viciously into the ashtray.

Jottie tilted her hand to shade her face, wishing she were still asleep. "It was his birthday today. Vause's."

"I know," he said. "Thirty-eight." Of course he knew. She realized that he knew it with the same involuntary timekeeping that told him his own birthday. He would never not know it. "Doesn't mean you have to celebrate the occasion with his father."

"Mr. Hamilton is an old man," she said slowly. "He's old and confused. He thought Vause died in France. That's what he thought today. He was fussing about his medals."

"Medals? Jesus." Felix shook his head. "Vause didn't get any medals. He got the Argonne clasp, but we all got that."

She watched her brother's face soften. Tell me, she begged silently. Tell me how it was, with Vause in the Argonne Forest. Tell me everything. But she couldn't say it out loud. If she said it out loud, Felix's face would tighten again. Remember how he double-crossed us, he would say. Remember how he lied. And then she would have to pretend to despise Vause. She should despise Vause. She did despise Vause. She loathed him.

"Well," she said. "I told him that they buried him with his medals. He calmed down."

One eyebrow up and scornful. "He's off his rocker."

She nodded. Change the subject. "You never told me about your trip."

He smiled. "My trip? To Obion, Tennessee? Home of the white squirrel?"

That was better. She curled toward him cozily. "What's a white squirrel?"

Felix's eyes glinted. "It's a squirrel. It's white. Town's full of them and they're real puffed up about it. They got a big statue of one in front of the jail. Six feet tall. Scared me half to death."

She laughed—and then stopped. "What were you doing in front of the jail?"

"Pure happenstance," he said with dignity.

"You weren't in it?" she pressed, thinking of Willa.

"Honestly, Jottie! You got a suspicious mind, you know that? I wasn't doing anything *to* be in it!" He grinned at her. "A man can't even sell a few chemicals without you getting—"

"Felix?" Impulsively, she reached for him. "Sweetheart, don't you want to try to get a job right here in town?" Stay home, she thought. Stay home and do something irreproachable, and I'll arrange flowers. We'll look like everyone else, and the girls will be happy and safe.

He frowned at her. "What are you talking about? There's no jobs here. Maybe you heard? There's a Depression on."

"What about Equality?" she asked, trying to sound offhand, an effect she immediately ruined by adding, "You could ask, couldn't you?"

"Equality Mill?" he said, his frown growing. "Don't know what rock you've been under; they're barely making payroll. And anyway—no thanks. I worked in a mill, once." He waved the idea away.

She nodded, remembering. Felix, shoes glittering, shirt blinding white and crisp, hand raised—So long!—setting off for American Everlasting at their father's side. That was the first day. It was different later.

He eyed her ruminatively, his thumb scraping the rim of his jaw. "You want me home, is that it?" he asked. "I was thinking the same thing. I was thinking I'd stick around for a while."

That startled her. "Really?" And then, dubious, "Why?"

"Whatsamatter? I thought you wanted me here!"

"It's not that girl, is it?"

He smiled. "Maybe."

"You just met her yesterday!" Jottie protested.

"I know. I like her. I think she's cute." He was still smiling, but his words were very distinct.

"She's only a *child,*" said Jottie recklessly. "She said so herself."

"Meow."

"No, Felix, listen—she's—well, she probably has a man somewhere, don't you think? Girl like that?" She nodded hopefully at him.

He shrugged. "Not my lookout. You shouldn't leave a girl that pretty on her own."

Jottie rolled onto her back and looked at the ceiling. "Think," she said. "For once in your life, think about what could happen."

"I'm already thinking about one thing that could happen," he said, and laughed when she turned to glare at him.

"There's probably some law against that—besmirching the morals of the WPA or something," she said. "You'll probably end up in jail."

"Won't be the first time," he said cheerfully.

"No! Felix, listen, we've got to be more careful!" Her hand darted out to catch at his. "You've got to think of Willa—Bird, too, but Willa's growing up! You can't carry on right in front of her! She'll know what it means and she'll be . . . embarrassed."

She had gone too far, she saw; she had accused him. Felix pulled his hand free and drew his cigarette case from his pocket. "Embarrassed," he said coolly.

"Well," Jottie mumbled, retreating. "You know."

"I *don't* know." He tipped his cigarette to a match, and she heard the faint crackle of tobacco consumed by flame. "Suppose you tell me. Suppose you tell me why you got nothing better to do than nag at me like a little old lady. What the hell's going on, Jottie?" He scowled at her through a curl of smoke. "You want me to get a job at Equality and you want me to stay away from girls, and you're trying to tell me it's all for Willa?" The eyebrow rose again. "I think it's for you, honey. I think you're jealous—"

"I am not," she began, but he talked over her.

"You're jealous," he repeated. "You're jealous because you never go anywhere. Why don't you go out on a date, Jottie? Don't let me hold you back." His smile was bright with malice. "You think I can't see what you want? I can. You want me to act like Daddy. That's it, isn't it?" he sneered. "Showing off in a suit, tipping my hat right and left, smiling like a sucker—so you can make believe you're an eminent gentlewoman of Macedonia." He hissed with disgust. "It's not going to happen,

Jottie. If you think I'm going to join the Elks and go to church, you can think again." He leaned forward, his hands closing into fists. "Never."

"That's not what I—"

He didn't hear her. "You want to pretend Daddy's still the president of American Everlasting, don't you? You want it all back again. Forget it. It's over, and none of it was ever worth a damn, anyway. None of it was worth a nickel."

Oh, Felix, she thought, why do you take it so hard, what Daddy was? In spite of everything, old pity released its warmth into her veins, and she reached out to pat his fingers. "It wasn't worth a nickel," she agreed soothingly.

"I should have left," he said bitterly. "After the fire and Vause, I should have gotten the hell out of here."

"But I needed you, and you stayed," she said. "I couldn't have borne it without you." It was the truth.

"I'd rather have gone," he snapped. "I'd've lit out faster than you can spit if you hadn't needed me. If you're saying now you don't want me here, I'd be happy to leave. I'll do it tomorrow."

"No, Felix, I don't want that—"

"I'd be glad to see the back of this town," he spat. "I'd be glad if the whole damn place and everyone in it were blown to kingdom come."

He was so angry. She was the only one who could help him stop; it had always been that way. She owed it to him, and she would owe it to him forever. "Shh," she murmured. "You don't want to get like that. Everything's fine." Gently, she patted his fingers again. "Why, the church would fall right on your head if you went, anyway." He glanced at her, grateful as always for the reprieve. "And the Elks? You'd bring the whole order to its knees, you know you would," she said. "You'd teach them all dirty songs and curse words, and the boy Elks would raid the lady Elks and"—she shook her head—"nine months later there'd be a whole slew of bastard Elks. It doesn't bear thinking about."

"That's right." He exhaled slowly, returning to himself. "It's no good trying to reform me."

He'd be all right now. She smiled at him. "You'd better start saving if you're going to buy your way into heaven. It's going to cost you plenty."

He dropped his face into his hands. "I wouldn't know anyone anyway," he mumbled through his fingers. Then, with a sigh, he rose.

When he was gone, Jottie lay back against the pillows, exhausted, but her mind skittered like a mouse: He'll never change, he'll never change.

I'll have to do it all by myself.

10

June 11, 1938

Miss Layla Beck
47 Academy Street
Macedonia, West Virginia
Dear Miss Beck,

As Head Councilman of the Town Council of
Macedonia, I hope you will allow me to welcome you to
our town and express my hope that your stay here will be
as pleasant for you as it doubtless will be for us.

The town of Macedonia this year celebrates its 150th
Anniversary, and in order to suitably commemorate the
occasion, we seek a dignified yet lively recounting of its
history. In turning to the Federal Writers' Project for the
creation of a short book or "booklet" on this topic, we hark
to the call of national duty, but as a proper and elevated
treatment of the subject must be of the first importance to
all truehearted Macedonians, who are after all the sponsors
of this project, we wish you to be guided in all particulars
by those who have been selected for the task, namely
Mayor Silver, myself, and my wife, Belinda.

With this requirement in mind, I herewith present to you
the material necessary of inclusion in *The History of
Macedonia*. To wit:

Macedonia's history begins in 1758, with General
Magnus Hamilton, whose valor and derring-do cleared this
area of Indians in six short years. As I and my wife,
Belinda, are both descendants of the General, you may

look to us for historical papers and artifacts which are in our home. Several of my fellow council members are likewise possessed of valuable documents and relics of Macedonia's "Golden Age," and I have been authorized to inform you that they will make themselves and these important historical possessions available to you, when you are writing.

The history of General Hamilton will represent the Colonial era. Other historical events to be included are the Revolutionary War, the incorporation of Macedonia in 1788, not excluding General Washington's famous compliment to the town ("I know of no other town so well situated as Macedonia"), the religious renaissance of the 1820s and '30s, with particular attention to the Presbyterian, Methodist, Episcopal, and Baptist churches, the contributions made by Macedonians in the building of the B&O Railroad in the 1830s and its effect on local industry, the valiant struggles of the town during the War Between the States (no favor to be implied to either side, if you please), and the founding of the West Virginia Academy for the Blind by Doctor T. Wiffen White in 1889. The opening of the American Everlasting Hosiery Company in 1900 may also be discussed.

In a separate chapter, we wish to have detailed descriptions of Macedonia's finest edifices and public buildings, some of which are held to be the best in eastern West Virginia, including the recently completed Fire Station No. 3, the Union Hotel, the Race Street School, the Second Presbyterian Church, and the Equality Mill. Indian Creek Cemetery, as the final resting place of the late Governor Alexander Spurling, should not be overlooked, nor should the statue of "Charity," by renowned sculptor Isaiah Michael Biggs, in Flick Park. The Academy Building is worthy of notice, as is the Town Hall, recently built at great expense. The American Everlasting Hosiery Factory is considered to be a superior example of an efficient modern factory; it should be described. There will be no need to include downtown shops, as they are of generally low quality. Other areas that are not of interest are the neighborhoods on the southeast edge of the town beginning at Zackquill Avenue, sometimes called Cake Creek, and the area bordered by Unity Street and Prince Street, known as Leadbend.

In addition to historical epochs and public buildings, the Town Council has agreed that the book or "booklet" should include accounts of Macedonia's First Families and their homes, which in many cases are genuine monuments of architecture. In view of the great deeds and storied pasts of these Macedonians, we believe a brief chronicle of each of these families will add a pleasing informality and "human interest" to the book. The notables of Macedonia have graciously agreed to open their homes to you in order to discuss their ancestors and allow you to see family heirlooms of historic value.

In order to assist you in this endeavor, we have drawn up a list of Macedonia's most illustrious families:

Mayor Eugene Silver and Mrs. Eugene Silver
Mr. and Mrs. James Beville
Rev. Dr. Leviticus Dews and Mrs. Leviticus Dews
Mr. and Mrs. Holmes Cladine
Mrs. Alexander Washington
Dr. and Mrs. George Averill
Mrs. Hartford Lacey
Mr. and Mrs. Walter McKubin
Mr. and Mrs. Arwell Tapscott
Mr. and Mrs. Sloan Inskeep (not the Arnold Inskeeps)
Dr. and Mrs. Casper Tare
Mr. and Mrs. Tyler Bowers
Mr. and Mrs. Wyncoop Rudy
Mr. and Mrs. Ralph Shank
Mr. Tare Russell
Mr. and Mrs. Baker Spurling
Mr. and Mrs. John Sue
Mr. and Mrs. John Lansbrough
Mr. and Mrs. Parker Davies

Some mention should also be made of civic and natural sites of moment, such as Flick Park, Morgan Creek, Spurling Square (often called Town Square) as well as the sulfur-spring water fountain there, the Caudy House (Macedonia's oldest structure), Pella Plantation (once the estate of the Hamilton family), Mount Level, False River, Dolly's Ford, Sandy Mountain, and the site of the former roundhouse. You may enumerate schools, roads, and other local sites of interest as space permits.

I propose that you begin your work by meeting with me and my wife, Belinda, at the soonest possible date. You would be wise to obtain a good map of Macedonia. It is possible that Miss Romeyn can oblige you in this matter.

I look forward to the early commencement of *The History of Macedonia*.

> Yours truly,
> Parker Davies,
> Esq.

"Well"—Miss Betts exhaled, handing the letter back to Layla—"Mr. Davies leaves nothing to chance, does he?"

"Not much," said Layla.

Miss Betts gave the letter a disdainful look and lifted her shining glasses to Layla. "I am a believer in artistic liberty, myself. How shall we begin, Miss Beck?"

Not wanting to disappoint her crusader, Layla said cautiously, "Well, I'm engaged to have tea with Mr. and Mrs. Davies later this afternoon, and—uh—I was hoping that you could give me some background on the early history of Macedonia."

"Certainly! We will prepare you to face the Davieses head-on," Miss Betts said, energetically resetting a hair comb. "Now, as Mr. Davies rightly notes, the recorded history of Macedonia starts with General Magnus Hamilton. He settled slightly to the north of the—good afternoon, Willa," Miss Betts called with resounding clarity. "Back again already?"

Layla turned with a friendly smile. "Why, Willa! Fancy meeting you here!"

Willa paused uncertainly at the door. After a moment, she swallowed and stepped toward Miss Betts's desk, determination written on her face. "Yes'm, good afternoon," she said to Miss Betts before turning brightly to Layla. "Hi, Miss Beck. I'm just here to do some research." She nodded. "I do that a lot. Researching. Today it's Albania. That's what I'm looking up. Albania." A toothy smile stretched to include Miss Betts. "I saw where that King Zog—of Albania—he just got married." She looked probingly at Layla. "King Zog of Albania," she enunciated. "So that's what I'm going to look up. In the encyclopedia. The royal kingdom of Albania."

Layla nodded, baffled.

"You'll find the encyclopedia on the reference shelf," said Miss Betts, suppressing a smile.

"That girl he married, she's twenty years younger than him," Willa continued conversationally. "They call her the White Rose of Hungary, can you imagine?" Again, she looked probingly at Layla. "Can you?"

Layla frowned in perplexity. "Can I what?"

"Imagine being called the White Rose of Hungary," pressed Willa.

"No," said Layla. "No, I don't think I can." Her smile grew fixed as Willa continued to watch her closely. Whatever was the child thinking?

Suddenly Willa's face flamed. She took a half step back. "'Scuse me," she mumbled. "I'll—I'll—just go." She lurched toward the stacks, her shoulders hunched, radiant with embarrassment.

Layla turned to Miss Betts in amazement. "What happened?" she whispered.

Miss Betts's penetrating blue eyes softened as they followed Willa's coltish figure. She shook her head ruefully. "The awkward age," she murmured. "Poor child."

"Do you know what she was talking about?" asked Layla, curious now.

Miss Betts shrugged. "No idea." She lowered her voice and leaned across her desk. "A very bright child. Voracious reader. She's close to having read through our entire collection, not that that takes a lot of doing." Miss Betts's gaze circled her small domain before returning to Layla. "Anyway, she's quite imaginative—"

"I guess so. Albania," interrupted Layla, casting her eyes upward.

Miss Betts smiled. "Yes, but I expect there was method to her madness."

Layla hesitated. "The family seems—well, they've been very kind."

Miss Betts's smile broadened. "Seems a bit unusual, you were going to say. Yes, I suppose. To the outsider. And the insider, as well, in a way. To be clever in a town like Macedonia is something of a social hazard—"

"Mr. Romeyn, you mean?" interrupted Layla eagerly. "He *does* seem quite sophisticated for a town this size, and well traveled, too. I understand he's been to France and—"

"I was referring to Jottie," said Miss Betts.

"Jottie? Miss Romeyn?" Layla said. "Really? I would have thought—well, she seems quite pleasant. And she's certainly a good cook."

Miss Betts sighed. "The epitaph of the spinster."

"She was never married?" Layla asked, wondering how long she would be obliged to dwell on Jottie before she could reintroduce Felix.

"Never married." Miss Betts looked at Layla severely. "And therefore without interest?"

"I didn't say that!" Layla replied, irked. "Really, Miss Betts, you're putting words in my mouth."

"I apologize." Miss Betts blinked remorsefully. "As a spinster myself, I am perhaps sensitive to the imputation of dullness."

Layla smiled. "I don't find you dull."

"Thank you." Miss Betts gazed at her blotter for a moment and added, "The Romeyns were—and still are, to some degree—a very prominent family in Macedonia. Figuring in some of our most historic and . . . well, I suppose you could call them dramatic episodes."

"Dramatic episodes?" asked Layla, raising her eyebrows. "Do tell."

Miss Betts was not to be seduced. "There is a fine line between history and gossip, Miss Beck," she said. "I believe I'll confine myself to history."

Layla nodded, abashed. "Yes, of course." There was a moment's pause, and then she ventured, "They aren't on Mr. Davies's list—what he called Macedonia's first families. I know it's silly, but if they're prominent, why—" Miss Betts lifted her eyes to the shelves among which Willa was presumably standing, and Layla, following her, blushed. "Never mind," she said hastily.

"I believe you mentioned yesterday that you intended to learn how to do research," murmured Miss Betts. Then, louder, "Let us take up the cudgels of history."

As the two women bent their heads together to speak of George Washington, his survey, and Lord Fairfax, Willa, well-hidden inside a capacious dictionary stand, sat as still as the dictionary above her, scarcely breathing, her eyes fixed blindly on the small forest of chair legs that obstructed her view. An hour ticked by as she waited, futilely, to hear more of dramatic events and first families, gossip and history.

Only after Layla took her leave did Willa extract herself, rise, and begin to move, crabwise, around the perimeter of the library. Fondly believing herself inconspicuous, she looked up in astonishment when Miss Betts called out a ringing "Did you find Albania?"

"Albania?" she stammered, and then, "Oh. Yes'm. Albania." She paused. "It's small. I got to go, Miss Betts." She lifted her hand in a clumsy wave.

Miss Betts returned the wave and watched the slender figure disappear. "Good-bye, child," she murmured.

Out on Prince Street, Willa stood for a long moment, gazing in abstraction at a passing car. Then, galvanized by some invisible force, she made a sudden lunge to her right, walking by the weary storefronts without seeing them. Mechanically, she brushed her hand over the smooth face of the wooden Indian standing outside Shenandoah Tobacco and Cigar, circled a knot of gaunt men waiting for nothing around a stairwell, and moved with an automaton's gait to the end of the block. There, wiping the sweat from her upper lip, she stepped off the curb, stepped back on, looked both ways, crossed Prince Street, and turned the corner.

11

At the corner, I wiped some sweat off my face and stepped off the curb. Then I remembered Teddy Bowers and stepped back on it. I looked both ways about a hundred times, and then I crossed the street.

It was heating up. Along Prince Street, I could mostly keep to awnings, but once I turned onto Opequon Street, the buildings didn't have them, nor much else, either. Opequon was just chipped brick, dirty windows, and faded signs. One sign said Cooey's Red Apple, and I wondered what it could be.

I stopped suddenly without knowing why. It took me a minute or two to realize that I'd seen my father's car, parked at the curb. He wasn't in it. I looked up and down the street. There wasn't anything on it that seemed like somewhere he would go—there wasn't hardly anything atall, for that matter. Then I thought, Maybe he's inside Cooey's Red Apple. The hot from the sidewalk sizzled through the soles of my shoes as I peered into Cooey's window. The glass was so dark and gritty, I mostly saw my own reflection, but there were people inside. I could see bodies, moving slow, like bees in a hive. I contemplated marching in the front door, but then I thought better of it. Actually, I was scared to. I decided to sit in Father's car and wait for him. I'd surprise him.

"First families." I whispered the words to myself, wondering what, exactly, they meant: a family that had been here for the whole hundred and fifty years? Or did they mean first the way George Washington was first in the hearts of his countrymen? The upholstery was hot against my legs. I sat and sweated, fingering my scab. Dramatic events—now that sounded wonderful. I poked through my father's hot, tidy car. I opened the little pocket that was supposed to hold maps and papers. It was empty. I turned and pushed my face over the front seat. The backseat held nothing, but on the floor was my father's case, the one he carried his chemicals in. It was a big black leather case, sturdy and solid. Near to the handle were his initials in gold. I ran my finger over them: F. H. R. For an experiment, I tried to pick it up. It didn't budge. I couldn't even move it an inch, it was that heavy. Well, but I'm weak, I told myself. I hung over the seat, breathing hard, and yanked. Nothing. I pressed down the button that popped the clasp, but it didn't open. It was locked up tight. Whatever was in there, I wasn't going to see it.

Thwarted again. I slumped back into the front seat. Chemicals cost a lot of money, maybe. He'd locked them up tight because they were valuable. I could ask him. I could say, Father, will you show me what's in your case here? And he would.

I heard a hubbub behind the car, a *creak-slam,* and a low "heh-heh-heh." Something made me cautious, and I slid down till my head was beneath the edge of the window. Then, feeling just exactly like a Hardy Boy, I rolled over onto my stomach so I could peek out the back window. Four men in hats were standing in front of Cooey's Red Apple. One of them was short and wide. He had a white hat on, a white hat with a black band. I'd never seen such a thing in my life. Then there were two men who must have been brothers, they looked so much alike, lank and stove-in. The fourth was my father. The white-hat man and one of the brothers were laughing, haw-haw-haw. My father wasn't laughing. He was looking at those men quietly, and I felt a little thump of pride at how he was handsomer than the rest of them and more refined, too, because he didn't guffaw like they did. I guessed he was selling them chemicals, though his case was in the car.

Their voices rumbled on. I couldn't hear exactly what they were saying, until suddenly the white-hat man clapped my father on the shoulder and said, real loud, "That's the ticket, Romeyn!" My father smiled, and I saw it the way you see things by lightning, suddenly pulled free from their tracks. This was his other world, and it didn't touch the one he had at home with Bird and Jottie and me. In this place, with these men, Father didn't talk about me or even think about me at all. He was another person altogether. It made me feel lonesome when I thought about it.

After a moment or two, they all walked away, down the street, and climbed into a car. The man in the white hat was driving. I slouched down farther and heard them pass by, heard the engine mutter down to the corner and fade.

I waited a few minutes before I sat up. I could have gotten out of the car, but I didn't. I sat, hot as I was, and thought. I'd been silly about Miss Beck, I could see that, silly and childish, and now she thought I was odd. I cringed a little inside myself, recalling it. She wouldn't ever ask me to copy her notes for her, or say in her book, Special thanks to my assistant, Wilhelmina Romeyn. But it didn't matter. It didn't matter what she thought of me, because I had other things to do. I didn't have time to be her assistant. Keeping my ear to the ground had been just as fruitful as Jottie had said. I was learning all sorts of things, like Father locked his case, and we were at the center of dramatic events, and Vause Hamilton had set my grandfather's mill on fire. And now I had glimpsed Father's other world. I was starting to know things, and I wanted more. I wanted to know about Father and his other world at Cooey's Red Apple. It was research, just the same as I had imagined doing with Miss Beck, but it was my own. I had my own research to do.

I didn't recognize my uncle Emmett's truck until it passed me a second time, backward. He bent forward and squinted into my window. "Willa? Is that you?"

"Yeah. It's me. Hey, Emmett."

"Hey." He craned his neck, looking up and down the street. "Where's Felix?"

"I don't know," I said truthfully.

He nodded and pulled his truck over to the curb. I watched him as he came across the street and leaned in at my window. He was real tall, so he had to lean a good ways. "Any particular reason why you're sitting here in his car?" he asked.

Jottie always said that Emmett was a mystery. I guess she meant because he didn't talk as much as everyone else in our family and he generally looked as sober as a judge. But Bird and I knew better. He had a way of asking us questions, real perplexed and formal, that sent us into stitches. He only did it when we were alone, just the three of us. Sometimes we'd get to howling, out on the porch, and Jottie would come and stand at the door. "What's happening out here?" she'd ask, sort of hopeful and eager.

"I think these children are defective," he'd say gloomily. "I can't understand a word they say." He'd wave his hand at us. "And they're dirty, too."

I giggled again now, just thinking about it. "Father went somewhere with some men," I explained.

"And he left you here?" Emmett asked, kind of surprised.

"No. No, he doesn't know I'm here," I said, and explained how I'd come to be in his car. "He left his case behind." I rolled over and pointed at the floor of the backseat. "It's locked."

Emmett glanced over my shoulder at the black leather case. "Ah." He returned to looking at me. His eyes were the same as Father's and Jottie's, dark, dark brown. "I don't suppose you know that because you tried to open it."

"Well. Yes." I was surprised to hear myself admit it.

"Why?"

"What do you think's in there?" I asked. "Chemicals?"

He nodded slowly. "Yes. Chemicals. Now." He opened the car door and gestured for me to come out. I did. "I am going to give you a piece of good advice, Willa. People pay money for this kind of service, but as your uncle, I'm going to give it to you for free."

"Are you about to tell me to mind my own business?" I asked.

"No I am not," he answered. "My advice is this: Don't ask questions if you're not going to like the answers."

I folded my arms. "Well, honestly! How can I know I'm not going to like the answers until I ask the questions?"

His smile flashed bright. "Easy. You ask yourself if there's any answer that would endanger something that's precious to you, and if there is, don't ask the question."

Endanger? Nothing was endangered. "That's silly. No one would ever find out anything that way!"

"Finding out isn't all it's cracked up to be, Sherlock," he

said. The Presbyterians' bell went four, and he glanced up, toward Prince Street. "Hey, honey, I got to get. You go on home, okay? Don't sit here anymore."

"Okay," I said.

He raised an eyebrow. "I wasn't born yesterday. I want to see you leave."

I smiled. "Okay." I took a step and stopped. "Say, Emmett?"

He had turned to cross the street, but he turned back. "What?"

"What's Cooey's Red Apple?" I pointed to the sign.

"Bootlegger's," he said.

I looked toward the gritty little storefront, surprised.

"See what I mean?" said Emmett. He waited for a moment. "Go on. March."

I started home.

✳

In the theoretical cool of the porch, the twins were draped like wet flowers across divans. Upright and scowling at *The Yearling,* Jottie jumped at the *wheeze-slap* of the screen door. "There you are!" She patted the decayed wicker chair at her side.

"Hey," said Willa, thumping into it. "Hey," she said to Bird.

Stolidly chewing day-old gum, Bird grunted.

"Help yourself," said Jottie, nodding at the pitcher of ice-tea.

"No thanks. What's a first family?" inquired Willa.

Jottie lifted an eyebrow. "A what?"

"A first family. Mr. Davies gave Miss Beck a list of Macedonia's first families, and we're not on it."

Minerva lifted her head, her eyes finding Jottie's.

"Oh, isn't that Parker all over," said Jottie carelessly. "He don't think you're important if you're not related to him."

"Huh." Willa contemplated this. "We're not, are we?"

"No, we are not, and I go down on my knees every day to thank the Lord for it," Jottie said gaily. First families indeed, she fumed. Damn your eyes, Parker Davies, if you make my Willa ashamed.

"So do I," said Minerva. "Sometimes, on special occasions, I thank him twice."

We were a first family when your mama was catching frogs for her dinner, Jottie seethed. You scratch a Davies, and you'll find yourself in a mess of crackers—

"There's Miss Beck," said Bird around her gum. "Out on the sidewalk."

Jottie glanced up, and her rage was quickly adulterated by solicitude. Poor thing looked like to die of the heat. "You want some ice-tea?" she called.

Layla's head jerked up. "Oh, yes, please!" She was almost panting. She entered the shadowed porch, nodding shyly to Minerva and Mae, Willa and Bird.

"Welcome to Droopsville," Mae sighed.

Jottie poured, and Layla watched greedily as the tea popped and cracked on the ice. "Oh, thank you," she breathed, taking it.

Jottie eyed her flushed face. "You have a long walk?"

"Yes. Well, maybe it just seemed long. I was on Locust Street, visiting Mr. and Mrs. Davies." Layla took a greedy gulp of tea.

Jottie's eyes flicked to Willa, who was looking intently at the hem of her skirt. "Didn't Parker give you anything to drink?"

"Hot tea," answered Layla. "In a silver teapot."

"My," snorted Jottie. "Bet you were real impressed."

Layla caught her eye and smiled. "I didn't hardly know how to behave."

Well now, thought Jottie, pleased, maybe this girl isn't so bad. "Have a cookie." She gestured affably to the plate. "Keep up your strength."

With two fingers, Bird removed the wad of gum from her mouth and said, "Dex Lloyd can bite his own toenails."

"Famed across five continents for her sparkling repartee," said Mae, dabbing at her forehead with a handkerchief.

"Was Parker a help with your book?" Jottie asked.

"Oh." Layla hastily swallowed a large bite of cookie. "Why. Yes." She smiled uncertainly. Was she supposed to be polite about him? She tried to evince some enthusiasm. "Mr. Davies and his wife have several items belonging to General Hamilton in their home."

"His sword, his gun, his powder sack, and his sainted knee pants," said Minerva in a bored voice.

"Minerva used to go with Parker Davies," said Jottie.

"I was only a girl." Minerva glowered. "I didn't know any better."

"And neither did he!" crowed Mae.

Layla laughed with relief, and, emboldened, she asked, "I wondered—is General Hamilton related to the Mr. Hamilton who burned the boot yesterday?"

There was a split-second pause. "Yes," answered Mae.

"Well!" Layla smiled happily around the circle. "It *is* a small town, isn't it? I wonder why he's not on my list. To interview, you know. As he's a direct descendant." She looked, questioning, to Jottie.

Across the porch, Willa did the same.

Minerva intervened quickly. "Mr. Hamilton's unhinged. He's not in a state to be interviewed."

"Oh dear," said Layla, rattled anew by all she didn't know.

"These old families," Jottie said thoughtfully, gazing at the street. "Sometimes their blue blood doesn't do them a bit of good."

"What's that mean?" Willa said at once.

"Well, you look at the Hamiltons." Jottie waved her hand vaguely, indicating a world of Hamiltons. "Here's poor old Mr. Hamilton, unhinged, like Minerva says. But it's not his fault. All Hamiltons are unhinged. It runs in the family."

Layla suppressed a smile. "What a shame for Mr. and Mrs. Davies," she said gravely. "I understand they're both of Hamilton descent. They were quite particular on that point."

"They've got a while yet. It usually doesn't come out until they're old," Jottie reassured her. "Take General Hamilton, for instance. He was born mean. And stingy. But he didn't go crazy till later."

"General Hamilton was crazy?" Willa asked. "That isn't what they say in school."

Jottie gave a shrug. "I just don't know what else to call it when a man drives a sword right through his own son's foot."

"He never did!" gasped Mae.

Willa frowned. "I thought you said it was a soldier."

"I couldn't bear to tell you the ugly truth," Jottie replied. "I wanted to shield you. But"—she shook her head sadly—"it was his own boy. Stabbed him right in the foot. Mrs. Lacey told me all about it."

"This is a little different from Mr. Davies's version," Layla said. She set her ice-tea down and reached into her purse, withdrawing a notebook. "But a good history book includes different perspectives."

Minerva grinned. "Hear that, Jottie? Give her some different perspectives."

Jottie allowed a moment for drama to accrue. "Well," she began in her smoky voice, "you know that the General came to these parts in about 1758, dragging his poor measly little wife and baby girl along behind him. There are plenty of people who say he was the first white man west of the False River, but that's not true." She looked at Layla. "He was just the meanest. The Indians were already here, of course, living in peace, but the General didn't consider them when he picked a spot to settle. He took land up near Everett's Pass, right in among them. Now, I'm sure Parker told you how partial the General was to God. He was one of those Calvinists. Harsh?" she asked. "They invented it, and the General was the harshest of them all. Some folks thought that bringing the Gospel to the Indians would be the Christian thing to do, but the General pooh-poohed that idea." Jottie batted the air with the General's disgust. "According to his way of thinking, they were all of them damned, and that suited him fine because he figured there was no such thing as a sin against the damned. He'd make a pact with one band of Indians and then turn around and sell them out to their enemies, till they were all murdering one another. He paid rum in exchange for scalps—that powder sack of Parker Davies's is made out of someone's skin, you know—"

"It isn't!" Minerva cried.

"It is," Jottie said, implacable. "The General had a horse blanket made from the hair of scalped Indians, but there's nothing left of it these days. Pretty soon all the Indians were dead or dead drunk, and the General was snatching up their land right and left. Upshot was, seven years after he arrived, he was the fourth-largest landowner in western Virginia and a big hero to the new settlers. That's when the 'General' business started. It was what you call a courtesy title, for killing all those Indians. But lo"—her voice sank ominously—"he came to believe in it and took to sashaying around with a sword at his hip."

"I want to get to the foot," said Bird.

"You are awful bloodthirsty for a nine-year-old child," said Jottie. "Now. The General had a passel of girls. That poor wife of his had a baby a year for fourteen years. Some of them died, of course, but nine of them lived. Eight girls, and then, finally, a boy. The General named him Philip, after some Macedonian king . . ." The story of Philip unfurled, how his sisters took any husband they could get and left their little brother behind, to be worked half to death by the General. How, after years of misery, he wandered, lost, on a snow-lashed mountain, and met a girl—

"She wasn't an Indian, was she?" asked Minerva.

"'Course she was," said Jottie. "Who else would be up there? But Mrs. Lacey said she was real civilized and all."

"How old *is* Mrs. Lacey?" asked Layla in alarm.

Jottie smiled. "In her eighties. She was just telling me what she'd been told." On she went to recount the secret meetings between the boy and girl, how they'd managed for a time to be happy, until one day the General undertook to pace off his land—just in case he was being overtaxed—and discovered Philip in the woods, trysting with his Indian girl. "Out came that fancy sword, and the General made for the girl's throat." In the nick of time, Philip jumped between them, and as the sword hovered in the air, he declared that he was leaving Macedonia, he and the girl together. "Which was a pretty brave thing to say." Jottie looked around for their agreement. "The General said, 'Nonsense, you're the heir to the kingdom of Macedonia, and you're staying right here.' 'No,' Philip said. 'No, I'm free and independent and I can go where I like.' And then"—Jottie's eyes widened—"the General lifts his sword up high and slams it right straight down through the boy's boot.

Right through his foot, pinning him where he stood. 'You'll stay,' he says."

"Eew," squeaked Bird, wincing.

"I know." Jottie nodded.

"And then what?" asked Willa, leaning forward.

Jottie gazed into space. "Nothing hurts so much in the first minute as it's going to. In the first minute, you can bear all sorts of things. But when Philip saw the blood oozing up around the slit in his boot, he knew that something bad had happened inside. So he took the boot off and shook out three little toes. People say that's the moment when Philip began to go crazy himself." She sat back in her chair. "The end."

There was a pause.

"Wait," said Willa.

"Wait," said Layla at the same moment. Their eyes came together and apart. "What happened then? Did he die?"

"Who?" said Jottie.

"Philip."

"Oh. No. It was just toes, that's all. You can get along fine without toes."

"But you said he went crazy," Willa pressed.

"Oh. That didn't show for a while. He went off, fought in the Revolution. Came back, got married, had plenty of children. Everything was fine—and then one day he burned his own house down."

"Why?" asked Willa.

"Crazy," Jottie said. "Just like his daddy. It runs in the family. Like a curse." *Taste good?* she inquired of Parker Davies in her imagination. *It's your very own medicine.*

"Parker always did seem a little crazy to me," mused Minerva.

"You drove him crazy," Mae said.

"That was an awful story," broke in Bird bitterly. "He didn't marry the Indian girl?"

"No. Left her behind," said Jottie.

"That's awful," said Bird again. "I wanted a happy ending."

"It's history," Jottie reminded her. "You don't get what you want."

"Reality is always so bleak." Mae sighed.

"The truth will out," Jottie said crisply. "No matter how hard Parker Davies tries to whitewash it."

Layla lifted her notebook. "As the official historian of Macedonia, I have a duty to the citizens to make the true history of Macedonia known."

"My, my," Jottie marveled. "A duty." She gave Layla a sidelong glance of approval. Maybe more than just a pretty face. Maybe a little backbone, too.

12

June 18, 1938

Dearest Lance,

Thanks for your not particularly comforting letter. I know you are terribly busy and important, but you might have given a bit more thought to the matter before you advised me to chuck the project and beg for Father's forgiveness. I expect I sounded slightly watery in my last letter, but anyone would be shaky on her first day in a new land. I only wanted sympathy, not instruction, and I couldn't think of leaving Macedonia now, as you so cavalierly suggest. It would seriously inconvenience the town council, as they depend upon having their book in time for their sesquicentennial in September, and it would embarrass Ben and make him despise me more than he does already. I can't go crawling to Father, either. Don't you see that it would be the height of hypocrisy to demand the advantages of being his child while refusing to do his bidding like a child? I won't marry Nelson, I simply won't—oh, no, I mustn't start thinking of Nelson! When I think of Nelson, I begin to brood morbidly on his apple cheeks and his starched hankies, until great shudders ripple down my spine.

In addition to my recently acquired (yet uncompromising) sense of duty, I intend to remain at my post because I am becoming a little interested in the history of Macedonia. Not much, I admit, in *The History of Macedonia* that the town council wishes me to write, but in the actual history. Character fascinates me—the power of it, I mean. One hero—or madman—may beget an entire history. For example, the little town of Macedonia exists solely because there was a lunatic named Hamilton who took it into his head to settle here and destroyed everything and everyone that opposed him. I suppose circumstance plays its part, too, but I think character, even a nasty one, holds a stronger hand, and I intend to give characters their proper due in *The History of Macedonia,* even if I am run out of town on a pike for my trouble. The town council, which is sponsoring the book, has firm ideas about its content: The centerpiece will be detailed descriptions of Macedonia's "First Families." Mr. Parker Davies, the head councilman (or Head Councilman, as he prefers), outlined my obligations in a long letter, and it appears that I am not to dally upon little details like local industry and the Civil War. Mr. Davies very generously offered me the honor of visiting him and his wife, Belinda (!), in order that I might see the relics of his ancestor, General Hamilton, who founded the town. From the tone of his letter, I was convinced he had the General's head in a box.

Nevertheless, I replied like a young lady of breeding and found myself ushered over the Davies doorstep Thursday afternoon by a butler in a waistcoat. He led me to the Davies library, where Mr. and Mrs. Davies awaited me, sitting silently on a silken sofa. They shook hands gravely; their somber expressions were, I think, intended to indicate their general disapproval of relief, the people on it, the New Deal, and President Roosevelt, rather than particular disapproval of me—but I felt vaguely criminal, anyway. It's very demoralizing to be regarded as a problem rather than an individual.

Of course, they were perfectly polite—in the most condescending way. The waistcoat butler brought in tea without a scrap to eat alongside, on the theory, I suppose, that food would encourage me in my headstrong determination to be hungry. They did give me a silver spoon to stir my sugar, but I could tell it pained them. I should have pinched it—I learned how at boarding school, and it would have served them right. Of course, I could have smote them a deadly blow simply by mentioning "my father, Senator Beck," but I didn't do it. I haven't told a soul. I feel that if Father has spurned me, I must spurn him back, if only to prove that I really can be on relief like hundreds of other girls. I *can* get up and go to work and take my lunch in a cheap café and wash my hose in the sink and spend my last dime on a fan to cool my garret— and then find myself despised because of my poverty. One begins to understand the appeal of the guillotine.

Oh dear. I seem to have lost my story in a sea of righteousness. Where was I? In the parlor with the Parker Davieses, yes. After a few moments of dismal small talk— too much rain, apple crop ruined—Mr. Davies signaled with a dry cough that it was time to get down to the business at hand. I took out my stenographer's pad and pencil and sat, fingers poised, ready to record all the glorious details of General Hamilton's long life. There were quite a lot of details. Even as a lad, the General was marked out for greatness by throwing a rock an immense distance. And as a young man, the General was noted by George Washington for his exemplary morals and invited to dine at Ferry Farm, where Washington's descriptions of the land beyond the Blue Ridge Mountains filled young Hamilton with a longing to see this earthly paradise. I was solemnly shown the knee pants that the General wore to dinner, spotted with Washington's own gravy, and then we pressed on through the rest of the General's remarkable career. Oh, Lance, I'm making it sound funny—and it was—but Mr. and Mrs. Davies were horrid. Mr. Davies spoke slowly, with round O's and long throat-clearings and ponderous silences. Sometimes I couldn't tell if he'd finished his sentence or forgotten it, and I'd start to nod encouragingly, and then the old goat would hold up one finger to stop me, as though I were interrupting him. "Hold your horses, hold your horses," he said to me. "Now. The General. Had nine healthy children. Read out their names, Belinda." Then Mrs. Davies shuffled through her papers until she found the list and read it while I furiously scribbled away. Why didn't they just give me the silly paper? Hours passed and my stomach roared and groaned, but they just kept plodding on through year after year of the General's life, until I was on the verge of desperation. Finally, the General passed on to his eternal reward, which I hope was roasting, in consideration of a little skeleton in his closet that I know of (and am planning to include in the history). Mr. and Mrs. Davies heaved themselves out of their easy chairs, and I put out my hand—but no! They weren't going to let me off so easily. I had to tour their house. "I know you'll be interested in the General's chiffarobe," said Mrs. Davies, wringing her hands with excitement.

"Actually, you are completely wrong," I replied. "The General's chiffarobe is of less interest to me than you can possibly imagine. In fact, I think the only thing that can approach the depth and quality of my lack of interest in the General's chiffarobe is my desire to see you and your husband go to hell."

What I really said was, "Of course. How delightful."

The chiffarobe, I quickly learned, was a pretext. They led me up one hall and down another, through miles of parlors and dining rooms, bedrooms and dressing rooms, all the while pointing out their antiques and heirlooms and then *pausing* ever so casually beside them. After a few of these interludes, it dawned on me that they wanted me to include descriptions of their furniture in *The History of Macedonia*. They were pausing to allow me to take notes on the wonders I beheld. Oh dear. I quickly got out my pad and made some scribbles that looked like shorthand to satisfy them. I would have done anything at that point. My spirit was broken. I was so terribly hungry. When we finally got to the chiffarobe (dark and creaky), I admired it dutifully and then mumbled something about not wanting to be late to the Romeyns' dinner—

Mrs. Davies's face soured up like lemons. "You're boarding with the Romeyns?"

"Yes. On Academy Street," I replied.

"Such an unusual family," she said, still sucking lemons.

"Oh, yes?"

"What a shame Jottie has to take in boarders." She tried to look mournful, but her tongue was running over her teeth all the while. "Poor Mrs. Romeyn must be whirling in her grave."

How I wanted to draw myself up and say, Do you imply that my presence dishonors her home, madam? But I wanted to find out what she meant even more. So I said, "Really?"

"Mmm. They were quite well off at one time, you know. Old Mr. Romeyn ran the mill—American Everlasting?"

"Yes, of course," I murmured. "The mill."

"And I'm sure the poor man *hoped* that Felix would take over the business, but, *well,* that was impossible after—"

Just at that fascinating moment, Mr. Davies broke in like an elephant lumbering through the jungle. "Please give the Romeyns our regards. Tell Jottie that the town council appreciates her contribution to the sesquicentennial festivities." His wife opened her mouth—to tell me more of Mr. Romeyn's lost hopes? To spread scandal about the family?—but he shut her up with one of those restraining hands on the arm, the kind that says, Not One More Word. "Thank you for coming to visit us this afternoon, Miss Beck. If you find you have further questions, you may consult with Mrs. Davies or myself at any time, mumble, mumble, ponder . . ."

I took my leave, more interested in the last two minutes of conversation than anything that had happened in the previous three hours. What a dreary afternoon—how on earth am I to turn it into something at least a bit, a tiny bit, interesting? For as dreary as the Davieses are and all the other First Families may be, I have decided to try to make *The History of Macedonia* something good, something worth reading and keeping. I've been thinking about history a good deal in the past few weeks, and I believe it fails when it offers only a tepid recitation of events and dates. A successful history is one that captures the living heat of opinion and imagination and ancient grudge. You are not the only Beck with ambition, and mine is to make my little book the best history of Macedonia that has ever existed (not that there's much competition).

Poor Lance. Have I annoyed you with my girlish prattle? Actually, dear, in point of fact, the foregoing isn't girlish prattle but a chronicle of my professional doings (I'm saving the girlish prattle for Rose). I do hope you aren't one of those tiresome men whose eyes glaze over when women talk about their work. Even the docile Alene may someday grow discontented with the contemplation of your virtues and seek a career, and you must be sure not to be dismissive about it. For you are a little dismissive sometimes. I notice it particularly when you smoke your pipe—you stretch your neck against your collar like a turtle, you clamp your jaw like a colonel, and you deliver your opinions like a bishop. I believe you should give up smoking.

Nine pages! This is the longest letter I've ever written, and that is no paltry distinction, as you know. I do hope this letter isn't overweight, because I really did spend my last cent on that fan for my room, and I can't afford an extra stamp. It was necessary, though. It seems hotter here than in Washington.

Love always,
Layla

. . . *The annals of American history are replete with bold men and true but none more obdurate than Magnus Hamilton, who came to western Virginia when he was little more than a youth and vanquished his enemies with steely resolve and clever stratagems. Early imbued with the harsh rectitude of his Calvinist faith, Hamilton's strict morals won him the admiration of George Washington, who, during a dinner at Ferry Farm, regaled the young man with tales of his surveying expedition in the Shenandoah Valley. These were undoubtedly the inspiration for Hamilton's decision to go west in the summer of 1758, accompanied by his docile wife, Rebecca, and the first of their fourteen children, Mary.*

Their early years on Mount Everett could not be said to be tran-

quil. The General's lust for land overtook his morals, and he is known to have instigated more than one bloody massacre among the Indian tribes that lived peacefully in the area before his advent. Indeed, within six years of the General's arrival in the region, the local Indians were almost completely annihilated, by drink if not by the sword. A gruesome trophy of this desperate era remains in the possession of Hamilton's descendants: a gunpowder pouch fabricated from human remains.

By 1765, having fully subjugated the Indians of the region and earned the epithet "General" from the grateful settlers who followed him to the new lands, Hamilton might have enjoyed a pastoral and peaceful existence, laboring in the fields he had won so dearly, but it was not to be. The General's intractable nature ensured domestic strife, and these years were marked by an ever-increasing irrationality, even insanity, which led his children to flee the family home and culminated in an episode of violence that left his only son maimed for life.

Hamilton's belligerence was turned to good purpose during the Revolutionary War, when a militia under his command met with Brigadier General "Mad Anthony" Wayne's regiment in the Virginia Campaign of 1781. Though Hamilton was well beyond the age of soldiering, confusion caused by his honorary title precipitated an unexpected role in the Battle of Green Spring. Upon being informed of his mistake, Brigadier General Wayne is reported to have said laughingly, "I don't fear for him. It must be a true marksman who can hit a target so small as Hamilton's heart."

Upon the conclusion of his brief military adventure, the General returned to Macedonia and took up the duties of farming the plantation that was by that time known as Pella. Having abandoned an early, ill-conceived sheep-farming venture, he now planted his acres with apple trees and tended his ever-proliferating stock of cows, rich in both money and acclaim, until September 24, 1788, when the town of Macedonia was officially incorporated and he was invested as mayor. Later that year, he had the honor of greeting Bushrod Washington, the favorite nephew of George Washington, at Pella, where Bushrod repeated for the first time Washington's famous compliment to the newly established town, "I know of no other town so well situated as Macedonia." Surely, the two illustrious men raised their glasses to honor the Father of Our Country and the fledgling city of Macedonia alike.

Though the heroic age of Macedonia is long past, and the General's striding step can no longer be heard in the forests atop Mount Everett, memories of General Magnus Hamilton may be summoned when one visits the gracious Locust Street home of his descendants, Mr. and Mrs. Parker Davies. A smiling Mrs. Davies points out the portrait of the General presiding over the mantelpiece in her magnificent parlor. "It was painted by Werner Bliss in 1811," she confides, looking with fond familial eyes upon the grim visage of the General. "Grandpapa—I call him Grandpapa—died the next year, in 1812, at the age of seventy-four." Next the visitor is led through oak-lined halls to see the General's chiffarobe, the last survivor of the original Hamilton cabin on Mount Everett. Dark and creaking, it stands in the sunny hallway it stands as testament to the reverence each successive generation it holds many a rattling skeleton

13

Geraldine was right: I was a natural-born sneak. The day after Cooey's Red Apple, I caught sight of Sonny Deal, walking along with his head lowered furtively. I followed him, just as furtively, keeping to the other side of the street. He didn't notice a thing but ducked under the Race Street Bridge and came out whistling. I let him wander off, then I quick squeezed under there myself. And what did I find but two pails of green plums! Ammunition! I toted the pails right back to Capon Street, and Geraldine decorated me with a safety pin.

We caught Sonny that afternoon in the creek and subjected him to a blistering fusillade of his own plums. As usual, I couldn't hit anything, but Geraldine got him good, right in the neck.

"Willa Romeyn! What in Sam Hill is going on down there?" It was Mrs. Fox, crackling through her boxwood hedge to look down the banks of the creek.

Geraldine, big as she was, knew how to fade into the underbrush. Sonny Deal let out a squawk and bounded like a dog through the water. I was left high and dry.

Mrs. Fox peered after Sonny. "Did that boy hurt you?"

I sniveled. What other choice did I have? "He probably didn't mean to hit me in the eye," I said, gulping bravely.

"Why! That bully! I've got half a mind to call the police!"

I shook my head quick. "No, ma'am. He won't do it again, I expect."

"Humph. Well." She looked at me doubtfully. "You want some lemonade?"

This is what they call serendipity. Maybe it was wrong to get lemonade for lying, but there was nothing I could do about it. We settled down nice and comfortable in Mrs. Fox's lawn chairs, sipping our lemonade and talking about the weather and such. Then I got an idea.

I held my lemonade in my mouth for a moment, thinking, and then I swallowed. "Mrs. Fox," I began. "The other day, when Mr. Hamilton burnt that boot, you said Jottie was a saint." She nodded. I tried to look innocent but not idiotic, which is uphill work. "Did you call her that because Mr. Hamilton's boy burnt American Everlasting?"

She pursed up her lips. "Your aunt has got a heart of pure gold—"

"Why'd he do it?" I asked quick, before she could go on to tell me how good Jottie was. I already knew that part. "Was he crazy?"

"Vause?" she asked.

I nodded.

She shook her head. "No, not crazy, exactly. He was—well, everyone treated Vause Hamilton like he was the Second Coming when he was in high school, and I guess he got to believing it." She frowned. "I'll admit, he had me fooled, too. He always seemed nice as could be, but I reckon he was hiding his other side."

"Like Dr. Jekyll?" I suggested.

She smiled. "Well. Maybe. More likely he got spoiled. Everyone thought he was the most wonderful thing in the world and they told him so, every time he turned around. Vause this, Vause that. It ruined him. Why, look—when he came back from the war, he didn't bother to get a job; he just loafed around for almost a year. Then, when he decided he needed some money—what did he do? He robbed your granddaddy, the most generous man on God's green earth, the father of his own best friend!" She shook her head indignantly. "And he *burnt* the factory. He didn't have to do that! He had the combination to the safe, after all! He took six thousand dollars out of there, and you'd think that would have been enough for him. But, no, he had to burn the place down and put everyone out of work for months!" Mrs. Fox leaned forward, her face pink. She was mad. "Your granddaddy was just heartbroken! And poor Jottie! She was well rid of him, that's what I say!" She sat back in her chair with a thump.

Jottie? Rid of him? What? I shaped the words carefully with my mouth. "Jottie? Was she . . . um"—I didn't know what to say—"did she like him especially?"

The pink faded from Mrs. Fox's face. She took a sip of lemonade. "Oh, I don't know about that!" She gave a little laugh that didn't sound real.

"Is that why Jottie's a saint?" I pressed. "Because she liked him especially and then he stole from the mill and all? And she's still nice to Mr. Hamilton? Is that it?"

Mrs. Fox looked out over her lawn. "Yes," she said. "That's it."

I came slowly across our back porch. I could see Jottie through the kitchen window, head bent over the table. She had liked Vause Hamilton especially, was the most I could get out of Mrs. Fox. Had he broken her heart? Jottie's heart? For the first time in my life, I wondered why Jottie wasn't married. Why she took care of us instead of having her own husband and children. Her own children? Would she rather have her own children than us?

I bolted into the kitchen and put my arms around her.

"Why, honey!" She sounded glad. "You want to hear a disgusting recipe? Jell-O with canned peas! Makes me sick to—" She broke off when I squeezed her tighter. "What?"

"I love you," I said.

"Good thing, because I love you, too," she said, squeezing me back.

"More than anything?" I asked. I wanted to hear her say it.

"Same as Bird and more than anything else," she answered, like she always did.

I felt better, but I couldn't help myself. "How come you never got married, Jottie?"

I don't know what I saw, exactly, but it made me afraid. I'd seen Jottie cry, plenty of times, from laughing. Only once, though, from sadness. I never did know what she was crying about, that long-ago time, but I remembered the awful, sick feeling of it. I remembered standing in the doorway, just stiff with fright, watching her shoulders shake and telling myself, no, Jottie wasn't really crying, she was hiccuping probably, or maybe shaking with laughter. Because if Jottie could be hurt, nothing in the world was safe.

I gripped on to her, dreading to see her cry, dreading to know that I had made her cry, and, more than anything, dreading to hear her say she wished her life were different.

And then it was over. She smiled and her hand curved around my cheek. "You trying to get rid of me?"

I almost cried myself, from relief. "No! No, I just—just—wondered if you'd ever met anyone nice enough to marry."

"No," she said. "No, I didn't."

I tried to think of a nice man who wasn't married. "What about Mr. Russell?"

She hooted. "Tare Russell wouldn't marry me if you paid him!"

"He might," I said.

"No, he wouldn't. And I wouldn't marry him, either," she said firmly.

"Who would you marry?" I asked.

"No one," she said.

"If you *had* to."

"No one. Even if they dangled me over a pit of alligators."

"Clark Gable?" Most ladies thought he was handsome.

"No thank you. I'd have to spend the rest of my days making antimacassars."

"Don't you think he's handsome?"

"He is. But he's not my type."

"What is your type?"

"Tall and golden," she said at once. I didn't know what she meant by golden, but I didn't ask, because she looked flustered that she'd said it so quick. "Clear," she added.

"Clear? What kind of clear?" I prodded her. This was about the most interesting conversation I'd ever had. "You mean clear-pure? Or clear-understandable? Or clear-tidy?"

"I mean clear so that the way he seems is the way he truly is," she said. "I mean clear-truthful. And clear-understandable, like you said." She gazed at me without really seeing me, and then she came back into focus and smiled. "What about you?" she said. "What's your type?"

I giggled. "I'm only twelve!"

"Not a moment to spare," she said. "That's marrying age, down in Georgia."

Was it true? If it was, it was terrible. "I'm not marrying anyone," I said.

"Clark Gable?" she teased.

"Oh, he's too old!" I said, wrinkling my nose. "He's way too old. He has to be younger than that!"

"That's all?" She shook her head disapprovingly. "Youth is your only requirement?"

"No! Young, but also funny." I tried to explain. "Fun. You know, like Father is. Someone who makes me laugh, but not with jokes, just with the way he says things. Someone who makes everything funny and interesting, even doing nothing."

"Just by standing there." Jottie nodded. "Some people can just stand in an empty room and make it seem like the center of the world."

She was talking about Vause Hamilton. That's how she had felt about him. And then he turned out to be bad. He turned out to be a liar. That's why Jottie wanted to marry someone clear and honest—because he had been the opposite. Suddenly I wished Vause Hamilton were still alive, so that I could kill him for breaking Jottie's heart.

✳

Pausing in the hallway, Jottie reached into the pocket of her apron and felt for her box of cigarettes. There they were. She jiggled the box for the reassuring thump of many cigarettes.

You can have one just as soon as you telephone Inez Tapscott and ask about that club.

I don't want to be in their club. They'll sneer at me.

No, they won't.

Some of them will. Louise Silver will. So will Auralee Bowers. And Belinda Davies. Mrs. John, too.

Never mind them. Inez will take care of you. Inez has a heart of gold.

A heart of gold.

Think of Willa. She'll probably get invited to tea parties if you join.

And I'll probably have to eat Jell-O with peas in it. I'll probably have to make it and eat it both. It'll be just like the Rose League.

Mama was president of the Rose League.

Even in the kitchen, Jottie could hear her mother speaking. ". . . he just takes to the work. I believe it must run in his veins, the way he grasps the business—"

Myrtle Loring's rasping voice broke in, "Caroline, this olive whip is heavenly. You didn't make it yourself, did you?"

The faintest of pauses expressed Mrs. Romeyn's genteel rebuke at the interruption. This was followed by a silvery laugh. "Well, no. I told Nettie how to make it, and she followed right along. She follows along real well." Louder, but still silvery: "Jottie, bring out some more of those olive sandwiches for the ladies."

In the olive-less kitchen, Nettie's face fell, and Jottie could feel hers doing the same. "Could we chop up some pimientos?" she whispered hopefully.

"Pimientos is red, and them ladies ain't blind," growled Nettie. "They should be on to the cake by now." She gripped her hair with both hands and pulled.

"It's all right. I'll fix it." Jottie touched Nettie's shoulder. "I'll fix it."

She swished toward the parlor, fluttering her pink dress. The only good thing about Rose League days was that she got to wear her prettiest dress. She entered the parlor, pretending to be modestly unaware as every eye turned to her, and sidled to her mother's chair. "Mama?" she said in a stage whisper.

"What is it, honey?" said her mother benevolently.

Jottie twisted her hands together in what she hoped looked like maidenly confusion. "Felix and Vause came in and stole the rest of the olive whip," she whispered. "They tried to steal the cake, too, but Nettie wouldn't let them."

Again, the faintest of pauses occurred while Mrs. Romeyn decided how to present herself in the face of this infraction. Then she chuckled.

Other chuckles echoed hers as the ladies nodded and gurgled, understanding food larceny to be part of the male prerogative. Jottie, smiling with relief, glanced through the window and beheld Felix and Vause coming up the front stairs.

Everyone else beheld them, too.

"Felix!" called Mrs. Romeyn in a carrying soprano. "You just come right in here and apologize to these ladies!"

Felix appeared at the parlor doorway, lean and careless, his uncanny good looks on full display. Behind him came Vause, shining and smiling. The ladies sighed with appreciation.

"What did you say, Mama?" asked Felix politely.

"What do you mean, you wicked boys, by stealing our olive whip?" cried Mrs. Romeyn. "Good thing Nettie saved the cake. You-all apologize this minute!"

Almost imperceptibly, Felix flicked a glance at Jottie. She widened her eyes: Help!

As the Rose League watched, Felix's gaze circled the room and came to rest on a plump, rosy lady whose hat boasted an artificial peach. He beamed at her as if he had woken that morning from a dream of her, and she smiled back, growing rosier still. "I cannot tell a lie," he began. The ladies giggled. He pointed to Vause. "He did it." Without hesitation, Vause nodded. "You know, I try to keep him on the straight and narrow, but," Felix appealed to the ladies' compassion, "he's weak. He couldn't help himself. He struggled with the demon olive. And he lost. Didn't you?" he demanded, turning to Vause.

Vause nodded. "It was real good olive whip," he said, his blue eyes ashamed. "I'm awful sorry, Mrs. Romeyn. We don't have olive whip at my house."

Mrs. Romeyn inclined her head, acknowledging this compliment to her provisions. "Well," she said, "I guess I'll accept your apology this time." She smiled beautifully at Vause and her son, and swiveled with regal aplomb to collect any expressions of esteem—or, better yet, envy—that might appear among the Rose League at the contemplation of the tender ties between mother and son. "Run along with you, now."

Jottie's eyes followed Felix and Vause, watching hungrily as they turned away, released from captivity, free to do whatever they pleased, free not to please, free not to serve, free not to lie about olive whip.

In a state of high gratification, Mrs. Romeyn commanded her daughter, "We'll have the cake now, Jottie. Tell Nettie to bring out the coffee, and just be careful with those plates!" She leaned toward a nearby lady. "They're Wedgwood, and I just hold my breath with all these children around." The lady tittered. "Hurry up, Jottie," Mrs. Romeyn urged. "Don't be poky."

"Yes, Mama," said Jottie.

Vause, departing, dropped her a wink.

Jottie sighed and picked up the receiver.

". . . Why, Jottie Romeyn, we'd be pleased as punch if you'd come! We never thought you'd want to! Oh, I'm just so *glad*!"

14

On Saturday morning, Bird and I listened for the sound of Jottie slapping her gloves together. It came—a soft *whap*—and then Jottie called, "Come along, girls! Time to go!"

We raced down the stairs, each trying to beat the other. Bird won; she always did, because she pushed. Mae was waiting for us at the bottom with her little suitcase. She was going to see my uncle Waldon, like she did every weekend. His farm was right between two of ours, the north farm and the big farm. My grandfather had owned three farms, and when he died, he left them to Father and Emmett and Jottie. I once asked Jottie why he hadn't included Mae and Minerva, and she said that he'd figured they had enough to do, taking care of husbands; they didn't need farms, too. Grandfather had been right about that, because those farms were a lot of trouble. As far back as I could remember, they'd been failing. All you had to do was mention them, and the grown-ups would start moping about sick cows, broken machinery, sour milk, drunk farmhands, on and on, until you were sorry you'd brought it up. Every Saturday morning, Jottie had to drive out to check on north farm and big farm, and every Saturday, there was some new and awful problem that she had to try to fix. Pretty near every week, she'd come home declaring that we were all going to die in the poorhouse. There was another farm, too, but it was way over by Mount Edwards, and only Emmett ever went there. It was called the mountain farm, though it wasn't on the mountain.

Jottie was poking at her hat in the hall mirror. "Into the car with you," she said.

Bird and I bounced out to Jottie's car. We settled ourselves in the backseat and rolled the windows all the way down, even though it wasn't real hot yet. Jottie glanced back at us over her shoulder. "Just roll them up when we get to Sam's."

"Oh Lord," groaned Mae. "Can't you drop me off first?"

"No, ma'am, I cannot," said Jottie firmly. "It'll only take a minute."

Mae moaned again. Sam Spurling lived on our north farm. His brother Wren ran north farm and big farm, too. There were hundreds of Spurlings around Macedonia, so you always had to make clear which one you were talking about by saying the Up-the-River Spurlings or the Sideling-Hill Spurlings or the Winchester-Avenue Spurlings (those were the fancy ones). There were a whole set of them called the B&O Spurlings (we tormented the life out of those children). But everyone knew Sam Spurling without any other words attached. He lived in a little falling-down house—more like a shack—with a million cats. Jottie said they were all descended from two cats he got to clear rats out of my grandfather's barn in 1918.

The cats had been multiplying ever since. Once, when she was in a snit about my education, Jottie set me the problem of figuring out how many cats Sam had. Four kittens to each cat, with each cat having one set a year. I got up to 1923 and a thousand and something, and then I went and hid under the house. Later on, while I sat on the sofa not having cake in punishment, Bird said, "Oh, that's easy. Let me just think for a minute . . ." She rolled her eyes up in her head and twirled her spoon and said, ". . . carry the two makes seven, he's got seven thousand six hundred and forty-eight cats." All the grown-ups gave puffs of admiration. It was years before Bird admitted she made that number up.

We rolled the windows up as soon as we turned off the main road, but it didn't do any good. The smell came through the bottom of the car. Jottie set the brake, took a deep breath, and climbed out with a box in her hand. Bird scooped up the bag Jottie'd given us, and then we filled our cheeks with air and ran to the apple tree that crouched over on one side of the yard. A flood of cats came yowling and creeping and scraping after us. They were almost all of them scrawny and mangy and mean from hunger, but they pretended they liked us, until we set down their scraps. Then they stopped winding between our ankles and lunged for it. I always tried to hold some aside for the littlest, weakest ones, the kittens just tottering along.

The cats turned Jottie's stomach. She said they smelled. But what really smelled was Sam's house. I don't know how Jottie managed to stand on the front porch and knock on the door. You can plug your nose from the inside, but not while you're talking.

"Sam! It's Jottie. I got some applesauce and some meat loaf out here for you, but you got to come out and get it or the cats'll be in it."

I couldn't hear what he said.

"Sure you can, Sam. Come on. I don't care. I won't even look. I just don't want the cats eating my good meat loaf."

He said something else.

"I'm not even looking. I'm standing here with my eyes closed. Come on, now, Sam."

The door opened a crack, but it was dark in there. He wasn't on the electricity.

"There you go, now," said Jottie, handing him a bundle. "Anything else you need? Want me to bring some milk down from the big farm? Or eggs?"

Mumble.

"You sure?"

Mumble.

"You're welcome."

Jottie picked her way through cats and muck back to the car, where Mae was scrunched down with a handkerchief over her nose. Jottie looked at us, thronged with cats, and shuddered. "Come on back, girls, before the fleas eat you alive."

We piled into the car. I turned to look at Sam's falling-down house as we drove away. There was a cat walking along the swayed back of the roof. I leaned over the front seat. "Why does he live like that?"

"Sam?" Mae removed the handkerchief from her nose. "I guess he likes it that way."

It was a silly answer, the kind you'd give a child, and I was beyond it. "Why?" I asked. "Why would he like all those cats around?" I turned to Jottie. She could be relied upon.

She smiled at me, quick and understanding. "He never cared much for people," she explained. "He couldn't talk—remember, Mae, how he stuttered so bad it sounded like he was choking?"

"I guess that's right," Mae said.

"He could talk fine if there was no one around," Jottie added.

"How do you know?" I asked.

"I heard him once," she said. "When he didn't know I was there."

"What does he look like?" I'd never seen all of him, only his hands and his leg once, when he'd stuck it out the door so Jottie could pour some peroxide on it.

"He looks like a cat," Mae said, giggling.

Jottie laughed. "You know, he does! He doesn't shave, so his hair's grown over most of his face. Might have a tail, for all I know."

"That's a sight I can live without, Sam Spurling's tail," Mae mumbled.

Bird meowed, and we all laughed, but I wondered. I wondered if something had happened to Sam to make him the way he was or if he had grown that way without noticing. If a person could grow to be like Sam without noticing, there was a chance that I was just as strange and hadn't noticed it. What was I like? I wondered. Did most girls my age feel the way I did, as if the people I thought I knew had turned out to have a thousand little tunnels leading away from the face they showed the world? Was this something everyone else had already grasped? The buried parts, now, they were fascinating but ominous, too. And I thought, Maybe that's why Sam Spurling decided to live with a million cats. Maybe a million cats were easier to understand than one or two people.

The next stop was Waldon's farm. It was a nice place, his farm, but Mae didn't reckon herself for a farmer's wife, and after she married Waldon, she kept trying to name it something pretty, something that didn't sound like a farm. She

called it Liondel for a while, and then she changed it to Wil-
lowdeen Hall. She put that one on a sign, but Waldon took it
down. The summer of Layla Beck, she was calling it Hampshire Downs, but no one else called it that.

My uncle Waldon was on the porch when we came up the
drive. Bird and I loved Waldon. He was the kindest man who
ever drew breath, the only grown-up who never, even under the
most dire provocation, lost his temper with me and Bird. He
was long and narrow, and his face was long and narrow, with a
white band at the top where his hat kept the sun out. When he
wasn't smiling, he looked real serious, but just let him catch
one glimpse of Mae and he'd start smiling.

"I have to make myself comfortable," I yelled over the seat.
That's what Jottie liked us to say when we had to go to the
bathroom.

"Me too; I'm about to burst," Bird said at once.

We saw Jottie's eyes narrow in the mirror.

"I *do*," Bird said. We all knew she was lying. She just wanted
to talk to Waldon. She talked his ear off every chance she got.
When she was a little girl, she'd stowed away in his laundry
hamper because she loved him so much, but then she'd wrecked
it by calling his name. She'd wanted him to find her.

"You can just wait until big farm, missy," Mae said to her.

"I'm going to wet my pants," Bird said.

"Not if you know what's good for you, you're not," Jottie
warned. She pulled up in front of Waldon's steps, and Mae and
I hopped out.

"How-you, Waldon?" Jottie called from the front seat.

"Just fine, Jottie," said Waldon. "Right as rain. How-you?"
He caught hold of Mae's arm and held it tight.

"Oh, fine. Did you go up to Martinsburg this week?"

"A-yup, on Wednesday. Saw Wren."

"Willa's got to go inside for a second," Mae broke in. "I'll
just go with her."

She picked up her little suitcase and we went inside Waldon's house. It was cool in there, and Mae had put a dish of
tiny soaps in the bathroom to make it smell nice. After I did my
business, I picked up each soap and gave it a sniff. There was

a rose one and a violet one and one that smelled like grapes. I used regular soap to wash my hands.

When I came out, the house was quiet. "Well, bye," I called, but no one answered. I walked down the hall to the kitchen. "Bye."

There they were, Waldon and Mae, and I saw why they hadn't answered me. They were busy kissing, hard. They didn't even know I was there. Waldon picked up Mae and set her on the counter, and she wrapped her legs tight around him, all while they were still kissing. I had never seen anything like it before. I watched and then I couldn't stop watching, even though I wanted to run away, too. Then Waldon made a sound, and I got scared they'd notice me and I tiptoed backward into the hall and went around through the parlor.

I flopped into the backseat of the car, and Bird said, "What happened to you?"

"Nothing," I mumbled.

"Why're you all red?"

I looked up and saw Jottie's eyes in the mirror again, looking at me kind of curious. I wondered if she knew what was going on in the kitchen. Before, when I'd heard about the things that grown-ups did, I'd thought it sounded terrible and embarrassing. But Mae hadn't minded. She'd been part of it. She'd *wanted* to. Maybe it wasn't like what I thought. Still, I felt funny. I turned to Bird. "I'm hot," I said. "Ain't you ever been hot?"

Up at the big farm, Jottie shooed us away. "I got to talk business with Wren," she said. "Don't chase the chickens." Bird and I rolled our eyes at each other. We didn't chase chickens anymore, ever since we found out that it killed them.

"Let's go jump in some hay," Bird said.

I thought about hay and sweat stuck together. "No," I said.

"You want to scratch the pigs?"

"No. They smell," I said.

"Well, ain't you just a lady," said Bird. "You smell, too, you know. Probably to a pig, you smell like you-know-what."

I stuck my tongue out at her and then, to show that I was above it all, I went to sit on the fence. I thought about Mae and

Waldon kissing until I was so nervous I almost fell off the fence, and then I watched Jottie talking to Wren. Her hands were cutting the air, one, two, three. Had Jottie ever kissed anyone? Had she kissed Vause Hamilton, so long ago? She must have kissed somebody, sometime. Or maybe not. How common was it? Wren listened to Jottie and nodded and turned his hat in his hands. After a while, Bird forgave me and climbed up beside me. We called the cows, and they galumphed over, drooling, and stared at us.

"That was boring," said Bird, when we were back in the car. "This whole morning has been boring."

Jottie laughed and jiggled the steering wheel, and the car careened to the other side of the highway while Bird and I screamed.

15

Emmett was sitting on the front porch when we opened the screen door. "Why, Emmett! Honey!" Jottie cried. "You never said you were coming!"

He smiled at her. "I didn't know I was until about an hour ago."

"Stand up and let me look at you."

Emmett stood. He was so tall that Jottie had to reach up to pat his shirt. It was a funny thing Jottie did when she saw him, patting his shirt. I think she wanted to hug him, but she was afraid he wouldn't like it. Now she frowned at him. "You're looking mighty thin, honey."

"So're you."

"Puh. You eating enough?"

"I eat plenty." He winked at me over Jottie's shoulder, and I relaxed all over. I'd been pretty sure Emmett wouldn't squeal about my father's car or Cooey's Red Apple, but now I knew it. "I'm fine, Jottie," he said.

"Did you see Felix?"

His eyebrow shot up. "Felix is here?" He looked at the front door. "No. I went inside and didn't see a soul, so I came out here. Thought I'd wait for you to turn up."

"I was up at big farm," Jottie said.

"And we took Mae to Hampshire Downs," I said.

He laughed. I always liked to make Emmett laugh. When he laughed, his whole face lit up, and you could see that he was younger than the others. A lot of the time, you couldn't tell.

"Hampshire Downs?" he said. "And let me guess: Mae is the Duchess of Bedford County."

"Waldon doesn't mind," said Jottie.

Emmett laughed again. "I know he doesn't."

Suddenly I understood what they meant. As long as Waldon got Mae, he didn't care what she called his farm. "Oh!" I cried out. The two of them turned to look at me, kind of questioning. "Nothing," I muttered, but inside I felt proud. I knew more than they thought.

"How's big farm?" asked Emmett.

"Same as always," Jottie said. "Butter's up a little, Wren said."

"Good thing. Might as well feed it to the pigs at ten cents a pound."

Jottie plunked herself down in her chair. "So. Why'd you come to town?"

Emmett sat down, too. "I got to talk to Sol."

Jottie's eyes slid to the front door, and she almost whispered when she said, "Sol? Why?"

She looked worried, and I remembered the parade, how she'd turned pink when she'd waved to Mr. McKubin by mistake. And then Richie, too, getting kicked by Harriet when he talked about Sol. There was something the matter with Mr. McKubin, but whatever it was, Emmett wasn't fussed about it.

"I heard a couple of things about American Everlasting, and I—"

Father's voice came floating out of the front hall. "Gloves? Well, that's real nice. All those fishes up at Dolly's Ford are sure going to appreciate that."

Miss Beck's voice laughed back. "The WPA strives to maintain the highest standards of gentility."

"I can see that." Father held open the screen door and they came out together, Miss Beck glossy and happy and beautiful as the day. Emmett stood up, and Father broke into a smile. "Well, what do you know? This is my brother, Emmett Romeyn," he said. "Emmett, this is Miss Beck."

Emmett's mouth opened, but Miss Beck spoke before he did. "Ohh," she said. "I understand now." She smiled up at

Emmett like she'd known him for years and held out her hand. They shook hands, and she said to Father, "I thought he was you. The other day, I was walking down Prince Street and I waved to"—she gestured at Emmett—"Mr. Romeyn through a shop window. Did you think I was a lunatic?" she asked, turning to Emmett.

"No," he said quietly. "No, I didn't."

"I don't see how you could mistake us," Father said, grinning. "I'm the handsome one."

Emmett spoke like he hadn't heard. "You're writing the history of Macedonia?"

"That's right," she said.

"I'll be real interested to read it when you're done."

"So will I," Miss Beck said, kind of rueful.

Father put his hand on her arm. "We'd better go get us some sites of historical moment, then, hadn't we?"

She laughed. "I'm still reeling from Flick Park."

"I know it," he said. "It's like London and Paris put together, isn't it? Come on."

Together, they stepped across the front porch and out into the sunshine. "Bye, honey," he called over his shoulder. I guess he was talking to me.

I watched them drive away, down Academy Street. They didn't wave.

Emmett sat down hard.

Jottie looked at me. "Go get some lunch, Willa. Make a sandwich for Bird, too, while you're at it."

I gave her the fish-eye. I knew when I was being got rid of.

"Go on. Don't cut your fingers off."

I went in the door and slid myself between the coatrack and the wall next to the front door, where I could hear everything. I was a natural.

For a stretch of time, they didn't say anything. Then Emmett said, "That is a real pretty girl."

"I guess," Jottie replied.

Then he asked, low, "Do I look so much like him?"

"Only to someone who doesn't know you," Jottie answered. It was true, too. They were both thin and dark, and they had those eyebrows, same as Jottie, but I'd never before thought that they looked alike. If I were blindfolded and I heard one of them walk in the front door, I'd know which one it was, just by the sound of his shoe against the floor.

"Mm."

"And you're taller."

He laughed a little. "Are you trying to comfort me?"

"Well, you are. You're real good-looking."

He groaned. "Stop that. Honest to God, Jottie, you sound so sorry for me."

I pondered that. She did sound sorry for him, and I couldn't figure out why. I didn't understand what Emmett said next, either. "How is it that Felix gets everything he wants?" he muttered. "How is it that he never pays for a damn thing?"

"Oh, honey, don't be like that. She's not worth all this fuss."

"I wasn't talking about anyone in particular," Emmett said.

"Good. Girls like her are a dime a dozen."

"Oh, yeah? Where?"

Jottie cleared her throat. "What's all this about Sol?"

"So you can say his name out loud now?" Emmett said, kind of snide.

"That's enough of your lip, there, mister. I'm your older sister, remember?"

Emmett made a sound that Jottie would have killed me if I'd made. When he did it, she laughed.

"I heard that Shank fired some fellows, that's all," Emmett said. "Charlie Timbrook and George were telling me about it the other day, and it sure as hell sounds like a rotten business, because afterward Shank gave them the big old talk about how they have to pull together like a family, meaning that the rest of them have to make their orders just the same and he's not paying any extra."

"Sounds like Ralph," said Jottie.

"Yeah, well, it's not right, and he wouldn't dare try it on if there was a union. I got kind of riled up about it and told them they should strike—"

"Oh God, Emmett! They'll lose their jobs, every one of them."

She sounded panicked, and I understood why. Losing your job was just about the worst thing that could happen. I thought of all those poor people with hungry eyes and dirty children, how they held up signs that said Will Work for Food.

But Emmett didn't sound scared. "No, they won't. Not if they do it right. And if they get a union out of it, it'd be worth it. Once they've got themselves a union, their jobs are safe."

"Not *once* they've got a union! If! *If* they get a union! Which will be when hell freezes over, if Ralph has anything to do with it. And until then, he can replace each of them five times over without even thinking about it. Everyone in town is out of work except for the folks at the mill."

"But look at General Motors!" He was excited now. "If they did a sit-down, they might have a chance; that's what I was telling them. They're skilled workers, a lot of them! Shank's not going to be able to—"

"Are you trying to start a war? Emmett, what were you thinking? I hope they didn't listen to you."

"I think they did, a little." He sounded uncomfortable. "It's because of Daddy. They still think he walked on water down there, and they take my word on anything because I'm a Romeyn. That's why I need to tell Sol."

"You're going to tell Sol that you encouraged his men to strike?"

"Well. Yeah. Feels like going behind his back, otherwise."

"Emmett, honey, you don't even work there. It's not your problem and it's not your strike if they're fools enough to try it."

"I know. I know that. But Charlie and the others—well, I felt like I should tell Sol what I did. Sol's always been real good to me." I could hear the floorboards creak as Emmett stood. "I guess I'd better get on with it."

"Give Sol my best," Jottie said.

Emmett made that sound again, but this time Jottie didn't laugh.

All of a sudden the back door slammed. "Don't anyone care about lunch around here?" Bird yelled from the kitchen, so I quick slid out of my hiding spot before she caught sight of me and told.

I went into the kitchen with my elbows out. " 'Bout time you came in," I said, real huffy. "Jottie told me to make you a sandwich."

Bird didn't scare easy. "I don't want a sandwich you make. You cut it wrong."

✳

Cicadas seethed in the motionless landscape of Dolly's Ford. A trickle of sweat dodged down Layla's back, and she resisted the urge to swat at it through her dress. "Wait," she said, taking a gulp of nearly liquid air. "He was in prison for three years?"

"Yup. By the time he got back to the ford, he weighed about eighty pounds. They didn't feed them much in Confederate prisons. Rats, mainly." Felix bent to pick up a stick and tossed it carelessly into the massed green beside the path.

She smiled sideways. "They did not."

"They surely did." Felix stopped walking to face her. "Rats were a treat in Danville, a real delicacy. Better rats than the other prisoners. You can make a nice soup from rats." He smacked his lips.

"You're making that up."

"I'm not making it up! They made soup from rats when they could or mixed up wormy cornmeal and river water when they couldn't, and that was dinner." His eyes searched her face for signs of belief. "Dolly said it was like a nuthouse there in Danville—the prisoners were so hungry they couldn't think straight; they made big plans to escape, forgetting that they couldn't walk more than a few feet. The lucky thing was, the guards didn't have much ammunition left. They just let them lay where they fell, and most of them lived."

The frenzy of the cicadas broke, and in the silence Layla turned to look back at the small, muddy landing that was Dolly's Ford, imagining an eighty-pound man lying on its banks. The way Felix talked, you'd think he'd had the story from Dolly himself. "Did you know him?"

"Joe Dolly? Sure. He was still around when I was a kid. Still weighed about eighty pounds, too. But he carried a big paddle, and if you got fractious on the ferry, he'd knock you off." Felix's eyes crinkled with laughter. "Right into the water. My mother was like to die." He began to walk again.

"I bet you were an awful little boy," murmured Layla, stealing another sideways glance to see his smile.

"I don't know what you're talking about," he said, his eyes catching hers. "I was an angel-child. Every mother in town used to pray her children would turn out like me. Ask Jottie."

"I will."

Their feet kept pace as they walked.

"Why do you think they want a history book?" Layla asked suddenly.

"Who?"

"The town council, Mr. Davies, whoever it was that decided on it."

"I guess they want to make Macedonia look respectable. Enduring and steady and all."

"You know what I think?" Layla said. "I think they want history to show that what they are now was inevitable."

Felix swung around and looked at her intently. "Smart girl."

Layla blushed. "They don't want to think it was luck or someone else's bad luck or just chance."

"Luck is too damn democratic, isn't it? Lots of riffraff get lucky."

"They want to be foreordained, especially Mr. Davies," Layla said. She looked up at Felix. "But that's crazy, isn't it? If history is, well—destiny, then we're all completely trapped forever. And that's ridiculous. That's not the way it is, is it?"

"Whew," he said, breaking into a smile. "You're pretty young to be so smart."

"Pooh. And, anyway, you don't know how old I am."

"You're twenty-four," he said.

"How'd you find that out?" she asked, surprised.

His eyes were amused. "I got my ways."

"No, really."

He shook his head. "Trade secret."

She smiled. "Fine. How old are you?"

"A lot older than you."

She burst out laughing. "Very cagey. Well, I like old men," she said. "I like them old and wise."

"That's good news." He nodded soberly. "That takes a load

off my mind." For a moment they stared at each other, and then he brushed the back of her hand with his fingers. "You hot?"

His fingers were warm and dry, she noticed with embarrassment, while hers were damp with sweat. "Yes," she said a little more emphatically than necessary. "I'm broiling."

"I know someplace cold."

She looked at him, dubious.

"God Almighty, the girl doesn't believe a word I say!" he cried. "Come on, you. Let's get in the car. I'll take you there."

⁂

Sol opened the door to his study. "I'll walk you out," he said to Emmett.

"Honey, maybe Emmett would like some ice-tea," said his sister, Violet, as they appeared in the front room. She smiled encouragingly at Emmett.

"No thanks, Violet," said Emmett. "Thanks anyway, but I got to keep hungry or Jottie will be after me about not eating enough."

Violet nodded brightly, looking between her brother and Emmett. "Well."

"Back in a minute," said Sol, leading the way to the porch. He stopped by the screen door and pulled a cigarette case from his pocket. "Thanks for telling me," he said, eyeing the neat row of cigarettes. "You goddamn rabble-rouser."

Emmett, who had been watching his face anxiously, laughed with relief. "Thought you might take it that way, you capitalist."

"Red," said Sol, patting himself in search of a lighter. "Smoke?"

Emmett shook his head. "No thanks."

"Oh, that's right. Pure as the driven snow."

"Ah, dry up."

Sol sighed. "Emmett, you know I agree with you. But they signed that pledge when they got hired, and Shank'll fire anyone—man, woman, or child—who says union at American Everlasting. I figure the best I can do for them is try to keep them employed."

"But they've got no guarantee of that. He can fire them for nothing."

Sol nodded. "He doesn't, though, not unless he loses a big account. That's why he did it last week; we lost—well, never mind. Anyway. That was tough." He grimaced, remembering, and rubbed his face. "I'm the one that has to do it, too. God help me, I fired Jerry Gale. You know how many kids he has?"

Emmett shifted on his feet. "Well. I guess Jerry knows it wasn't your idea."

"Maybe. He's pretty dumb. He'll probably come and shoot me when he runs out of money." Sol sighed again. "Eh. They should unionize. They have to unionize. But don't say you heard it here."

Emmett nodded. "Heard what?"

Sol smiled. "And if they strike, I won't tell Ralph that a Romeyn was at the bottom of it."

"Funny you should mention getting shot," Emmett said. He hesitated. "Listen, Sol, I know you're in bad if they strike, and I—well, thanks for not being sore."

Sol nodded and looked out at Emmett's truck, parked before his house. "How the hell old is that jalopy, anyway?"

Emmett followed his eyes. "Eleven years, almost twelve. My father got it for the farm."

"Ah."

"Go ahead and say it. Everyone else does."

Sol smiled. "Nice truck."

Emmett put his hand on the screen door. "Well, thanks again, Sol. I appreciate—"

"How's Jottie?" Sol asked quickly.

"Why, she's fine." Emmett looked at the floor. "She sends you her best."

Sol's hovering smile disappeared. "Did she? Well, give her the same from me."

"She's real busy with the girls," Emmett said hastily. "And she got a new boarder, too. A girl on the WPA. She's writing up a town history. You know, for the sesquicentennial."

Sol nodded gloomily. "I heard she was a looker, that WPA girl."

"Yeah," Emmett said. "But Felix already got her, seems like."

Sol looked gloomier than ever. "What else is new?"

"You *sure* you don't want some ice-tea, Emmett?" sang Violet, her bright teeth flashing through the front-door screen. "I just hate to see you standing there like an old horse. Whyn't you sit down? I baked some real nice cookies. . . ."

"Thanks, Violet, but I'd better be on my way," Emmett said, smiling gratefully at Sol.

Sol and Violet watched as the old Model T fired to life and coughed away down the street. Sol bent to smash his cigarette into an ashtray. "You and I should stay away from Romeyns, Vi."

Violet stiffened. "I don't know what you're implying, Solomon McKubin. Emmett is just a *boy,* and I certainly don't think of him in—in—any way at all." She picked up the ashtray between two fingers. "I was just trying to be *hospitable.*"

16

***

I felt his hand on my head before I knew he was there.

"Father."

He leaned on the back of the sofa and read over my shoulder, "'Uttering a shrill cry, the youth flung himself forthwith upon the slavering catamount.'" He twisted the book around so he could see the front cover. "*Cato: Boy of the Lake,* huh?"

I rolled over so I could look at him. "It's not very good." I checked the edges of the room. "Where's Miss Beck?"

"Who wants to know?" He smiled. "Listen, sweetheart—"

"Did you have a good time?"

"Where?"

"Wherever you were, you and Miss Beck."

He pulled my ear gently. "Had a swell time. Listen, Jottie's run downtown. When she gets back, will you tell her I got a telephone call and I have to meet a man tonight?"

I tried to summon myself up to say, real casual, Oh, you going to Cooey's Red Apple again? But I couldn't. "Business?"

"Mm-hm."

I hesitated. "Who—when you sell those chemicals and things, who do you sell them to?"

He watched me without saying anything for a second. "Different people."

"Tonight."

He smiled. "A fat man. A big fat man named Clayton V. Hart."

He'd answered me. I couldn't believe it. Just like I was a

grown-up, only he didn't tell grown-ups much, either. He was telling me a secret. He was trusting me. I flushed with pride.

He reached down and pulled my other ear. "I don't know why you like that."

"It makes room in your head," I said. I was so happy. I put my hand up and pulled his ear. "See?"

He gave his head a little shake. "Now my brain's all loose. Tell Jottie, huh?"

I nodded, trying to look businesslike and responsible. "You going to be gone for a long time?"

"Nope. This'll be short."

"How short?"

He smiled at me. "I'll be back yesterday."

"Father."

"It used to work. When you didn't know the difference between yesterday and tomorrow."

"I know. I'd go ask Jottie which one it was, and then I'd start crying." By that time, he'd be gone.

He drummed his fingers on the back of the sofa. "It was a lousy trick to play on a little kid."

I shrugged. "It's okay. Can't you stay to supper? Emmett's coming."

He lifted an eyebrow. "That right? He still here?"

"No. He went out, but he said he'd be back."

"Huh. Well, I can't, honey, much as I'd like to. I've got to get gone."

I pinched the cloth of his cuff between my fingers. "You want me to tell Miss Beck?"

"Tell her what?"

"That you're gone."

"Think she won't notice if you don't tell her?" He grinned at me. "You trying to hurt my feelings?"

I shook my head. "I meant like a message from you."

"I see. No need. But thanks, anyway." He looked down at his sleeve. "Unhand me, would you, sweetheart? I got to go."

I didn't want to, but I unhooked my fingers and watched him slide away. Sometimes he moved so fast he seemed imaginary. I opened *Cato: Boy of the Lake* again, to the page he'd touched, and pressed my face against it. Nothing was left of him there, either. I dropped the book on the floor and stood. I could go in his room. No one had ever said I couldn't, and, anyway, no one would know. I was pretty sure I could open the door without making any noise.

But his door was *open*. I stopped at the head of the stairs. It was never open. I walked softly down the hall, cat-foot, and looked in to see Miss Beck, standing there as if it were her own room, as if she had some right. I was appalled. I was so appalled I almost gasped, but then she would have turned around and seen me, so I swallowed my gasp and watched her. She didn't touch anything, not really. She dropped a paper on his desk and then she stepped back to the middle of the room and just stood there, breathing in and breathing in. I thought maybe something was wrong with her, until I realized she was sniffing—she was smelling Father's room, just like I had smelled the page he touched.

I wanted to slap her.

Layla—

I never saw a girl eat so much ice. I sincerely hope you haven't got a frostbitten mouth, as that would cast a pall on the sesquicentennial celebrations, especially mine. If you thaw out by next week, I'll take you down to the United States Fish Hatchery, which is a site of moment if ever I saw one and offers better eating besides.

Did I wear you out, marching over hill and dale this afternoon? I'm meeting a fellow on business tonight, so I won't see you at dinner. Be a good girl and leave me a note, so I know you're alive.

F

Felix,

As far as I can tell, my mouth and I remain in status quo. I wish I had some ice, though.

Layla

P.S. Thank you for taking me to Ice Mountain. I loved it.

In the shadow of Sandy Mountain lies Dolly's Ford, which traverses the False River between the settlement known as Licksburg to the south and, to the north, the terminus of the old False River Turnpike. A natural gorge formed by sheer two-hundred-foot walls of granite borders the landing, where a ferry has tirelessly plied the waters for over a hundred years. During the War Between the States, Joseph Dolly, the proprietor and ferryman, made a reputation for himself as a vehement Unionist. So ardent a patriot was he that, upon the requisition of his ferry for Confederate supplies, he poled to the middle of the False River and there sank the goods, together with his own vessel, for the sake of his country. He was held in one of the infamous Confederate prisons in Danville for the next three years, but upon his homecoming, he declared, "I'd do it again, twice."

Twelve miles to the south of Licksburg on Cold Stream Road is Ice Mountain, a formation of stone chimneys where ice may be found on even the hottest summer days. Ice Mountain was used as a local refrigerator by early settlers, and even today it remains a favorite spot for Fourth of July picnickers, who come with their freezers and take advantage of nature's bounty to make ice cream in honor of the day. Nearby, the euphoniously named Raven Rocks were Confederate strongholds during the difficult winter of

Layla Beck seemed to glow in the dim dining room, radiant against the dull luster of wood and tarnished silver. There was a kind of electricity coming from her, Jottie thought. You could almost see it, a thin rim of gold hovering over her brown curls and the soft curve of her cheeks. Emmett had clammed up even more than usual in the presence of such splendor, and without Minerva or Mae to help bear the load, Jottie plodded through inquiries about Dolly's Ford, the weather, and the ride. The dullness of the material freed her thoughts to glide and hover in their own private jungle. Emmett hadn't said a word about Sol; had he been angry? Sol, angry? It wasn't a thing she'd ever seen much. And Emmett, why was he so grim? Felix, of course, taking poor pretty Miss Beck; it wasn't right, it wasn't fair, but Felix didn't care about fair, not when it came to women; he never had, he never would. Oh dear, she fretted, look at Emmett, so solemn, Miss Beck would never look at him twice with Felix in the room; he acts like someone died. My Lord, she is just beautiful and real smart, too, about Parker the old stuffed shirt, him and his first families! Maybe she'll be smart enough to have Felix's number, maybe she will. She's sophisticated, been around, New York, probably—what was it, the Rainbow Room? I bet she's been there, dancing or something. Champagne cocktail? Why, thank you, I do love a champagne cocktail. I'll tell her about Felix, I'll warn her—but she won't listen. I warned Raylene and Letty, and they didn't listen. I even warned Sylvia, for all the good it did, but this girl, maybe she's not what I think. Oh God, look at her, look at the way she's shining; she's already crazy about him and he's going to break her heart—maybe she won't let him, maybe she's one of those pure girls, maybe she's a big Christian, though so was Mrs. Selman and it didn't stop anything atall. I guess I'll find out tomorrow if she goes to church. I guess I'll wear my pink, it's ironed. Emmett, honey, why don't you *talk,* you used to talk, to me at least. If she gets pregnant, I'll kill Felix with my bare hands. And Willa! She'll know, she'll know what it means—wonder what she saw at Mae's. At least they're married. She'll have to learn about Felix and women sometime, but not yet, not yet. She's too young now, she'll—what?—she'll hate it, she'll think it's her fault—oh Lord, they're waiting on me again. Talk, Emmett, show her that you can talk! Oh! "Now, Miss Beck, did you know Emmett here teaches history over in Morgan County?" she asked brightly.

Layla lifted her face to Emmett, smiling. "I had no idea. Nobody tells me a thing."

Unexpectedly, Willa spoke up. "Nobody tells *any*body anything. You've got to find it all out for yourself."

Emmett gave Willa a dark look before he turned to Layla, saying, a bit stiffly, "Yes, I teach at the high school. Not much local history, though. United States history."

"Don't they have to learn the history of West Virginia anymore?" asked Jottie. "We had to hear about Governor Spotswood and the salt trust and the Cumberland Road until we were blue in the face. I remember it still."

"Governor Spotswood," giggled Bird.

"I've just begun researching the religious institutions of Macedonia," said Layla, looking alertly at Emmett. "It seems as though there was an enormous increase in the number of churches in the 1820s and '30s."

"Oh. Well, I don't know much about that," he said, dropping his eyes to his plate.

"I do," said Jottie, exasperated. "You just ask me, Miss Beck, and I'll tell you all about it. Quite a story."

Emmett snickered, looking more like himself. "I give you Miss Josephine Romeyn, noted scholar of the religious history of Macedonia."

"Pooh," said Jottie, cheering up. "You teachers don't know much if you don't know about Reverend Goodacre and his sister."

"Who?" asked Layla.

"Reverend Goodacre—oh, he was a rascally thing," she began. Emmett lifted his dark eyes and rested them thoughtfully on her. "I'll tell you all about him tomorrow, Miss Beck, though it isn't a fit tale for a Sunday."

"Oh, that would be wonderful, Miss Romeyn—" Layla broke off, startled, as a thunderous stampede of feet shook the front stairs and stormed across the porch to the door. There was a pause, filled with heavy breathing, and then the unmistakable thud of someone getting hit in the head. "WillanBird?" squealed a child.

"It's the Lloyds," observed Willa.

"And Lottie and Myra and Mary-Shore," said the little voice helpfully. "Come on out when you're done, okay?"

"What're you playing?" called Bird.

"Capture the flag."

Bird pushed back her chair, muttering, "M'I please be excused?" and galloped down the hall without waiting for an answer. Willa rolled her eyes and followed more sedately. The three grown-ups laughed softly.

"I guess some things don't change," Emmett said.

"They don't seem to break as many bones as we used to," Jottie said.

"That's because Felix and Vause aren't in charge," said Emmett, smiling.

Jottie shook her head. "Jun Lloyd is just as bad as Felix and Vause ever were. He was trying to get Bird to jump out a second-story window last week. And of course she was perfectly happy to do it."

"Who's Vause?" Layla asked.

They turned toward her. Emmett said, "Vause Hamilton. He was my brother's best friend." He stood. "That was a fine supper, Jottie."

In the kitchen, Emmett picked up a plate and scraped a few carrots into the can.

Jottie stared at him. "When did you start that?"

He scraped another plate. "How do you think my dishes get done?"

"I guess I thought you left them for—what's that girl's name—Ota?"

"No. Ota comes to clean house. I cook and wash up for myself."

Jottie whistled softly. "A pearl of great price, that's what you are."

"Thanks." He stacked the dishes by the sink.

She watched his back. "You should get married."

"I could say the same to you."

That wasn't fair.

"And who'd I marry, anyhow?" he went on.

"Plenty of girls would jump at the chance," said Jottie. "Stella."

Emmett spun around, outraged. Jottie laughed. "All right, all right. A lot of men think she's real pretty."

"I'd rather talk to a bread box."

"Don't you go with anyone?" she asked, daring.

He frowned. "Remember? I'm the one that doesn't answer all your questions like you were God Incarnate."

"I don't think I'm God Incarnate," sputtered Jottie.

Emmett smiled at the plate in his hand. "Sol sent you his best, by the way."

"Oh," she said, disappointed. "That's all he said?"

"That's exactly what *you* said!" Emmett exclaimed. "If you'd said something more, he would have done the same."

"What should I have said, if you're so smart?" Jottie asked.

"How about Sorry I don't talk to you," he suggested.

"I do talk to him!" she protested. "I said hello to—"

"Or," Emmett continued over her, "Sorry Felix won't let me talk to you."

"That's not true!" Jottie said. She turned to scan the kitchen for her cigarettes. "And besides, I *do*—"

"Or, Sorry I do every single damn thing Felix says and Sorry I can't go anywhere and Sorry I can't see anyone and Sorry I'm stuck in this house forever because I'm too much of a coward to leave it."

"Stop that!" She snatched her cigarettes from the table. "That is just not true! I go places—"

He snorted contemptuously. "Oh, that's right! You go to scenic downtown Macedonia. To the New Grocery and Krohn's Department Store. Yes, it's quite a life," he said. "You'll die young from that kind of excitement." He set a bowl on the drainboard with a crack. "I can't believe Sol still cares," he said bitterly. "How many years has he been trying to get your attention? Twenty? Jesus. I hope he gives up. I hope he finds himself someone nice and gets married. Hell, *Sol* can marry Stella, and they can have themselves a pile of babies. Better than him spending the rest of his life waiting for you to get out from under Felix's thumb."

Jottie tried to steady herself. He was mad about Felix and Miss Beck, that's all. He was jealous. "Emmett," she began, "honey. I know you're upset"—he glared at her—"but you're not being fair. You're not seeing Felix's side. What Sol did, it wasn't something Felix could forgive." She looked up, into his eyes. "Imagine what it was like for Felix after Vause died. It was like the end of the world. And then to have Sol say it was Felix who'd done it, that it was his fault—"

"That's not what Sol said." Emmett shook his head. "He only said it *seemed* like something Felix would do."

She tried to explain. "But that's just it. Don't you see? It was just an idea, and then people started to believe it because they wanted to. Everyone had been waiting for years to see Felix fall off his high horse, and nobody wanted to think anything bad about Vause. Everybody loved Vause." She sighed. "I don't hold it against Sol, I really don't. I think he was beside himself with grief. But Felix? Felix almost went out of his mind. He can't forget it." She looked up at him. "Don't you see? After finding out that Vause had betrayed him——"

"Vause betrayed *him*?" said Emmett. "What about you?"

And there it was: Betrayed. Lied to. Abandoned. Not loved. Never loved. All of it, a lie. A joke. Shame squirmed inside her, an awful worm. *"Don't,"* she said. "Just don't." She brought a cigarette to her mouth with trembling fingers. "It was terrible, and Felix stood by me. He didn't leave me and he didn't lie to me and that's all. That's all there is."

For a moment, Emmett stood, watching her fruitlessly strike match after match. Finally he sighed and took a match from the box. "I'm sorry, Jottie," he said. "I'm sorry, honey." He held out the lighted match and she bent over it. When she straightened, he said, "You paid." He gestured to the tired kitchen. "You gave up college, you stayed home with Mama and Daddy, you're raising the girls. You paid like it was your fault, and I don't understand why."

She tried to smile. "I paid for being stupid, I guess. For being so in love with Vause that I couldn't see what he was like."

He frowned. "Nobody saw it. Not Felix, not you, not anybody."

"I should have known," she murmured.

"What? How could you?"

"If I'd known, I could have stopped it from happening. If I had seen it, I could have saved"—she hesitated—"all of us."

"Hold up. Are you saying you think it was your fault the mill burnt down?"

Her eyes darted toward him and away. "Maybe a little," she admitted. There was a silence. "One time, it was right after Vause got back from the war, when he was still so worn down with the flu, we went to the river, the two of us. He fell asleep, there in the shade, with his head in my lap"—she flushed—"and I watched him. For hours, I looked at him. I didn't stir. I didn't want to wake him. I just looked at his face, and all I thought was how beautiful he was, like something in a picture of heaven. Golden." She lifted her eyes to Emmett's. "Remember that about him? Like there was gold under his skin?" He shrugged and she dropped her eyes. "But that was my weakness, you see? If I had looked *better,* I would have known what he was inside, and I could have stopped him. I could have told him to leave, and"—she smiled at herself—"oh, it's silly, I know, but I always think that then he'd still be alive, and Felix would be the president of the mill, and everything would be fine."

"Fine," he repeated, and then cocked his head quizzically. "And what would you be doing?"

She took a long breath of smoke. "That's a good question. I don't know. I don't ever get that far, I guess. Maybe I'd have finished college." She laughed. "Maybe I'd be like Caroline Betts. A pillar of rectitude."

"Maybe you'd be married to Sol."

"Puh. Sol would be married to some nice lady." She glanced down at herself. "Someone stylish. Someone who plays canasta."

"Canasta?" He paused. When she said nothing, he went on. "You're nuts. The whole thing's nuts. You couldn't have known what Vause was going to do. Nobody knew."

"I guess." She nodded, unconvinced. "Will you go call the girls?"

He went out in the twilight to find them while she set the last of the cups in the dish drain. Listlessly, she wiped the table, the counter, the stove, and moved to the pantry for the broom. When he came back, the weak wood of the back porch cracking under his shoes, he was carrying Bird under one arm, like a library book. "She dared to resist," he said to Jottie.

"Carry me upstairs!" Bird ordered.

"Carry yourself upstairs," Emmett said, setting her gently on her feet.

"Get in the bath, honey. Church tomorrow," Jottie said.

The door wheezed again as Willa came in. She stopped still, looking at her aunt with narrow eyes. "What?" she said. "What happened?"

Jottie lifted her head and blew smoke in Willa's direction. "Nothing happened. Did it, Emmett?"

✻

It was pretty late by the time we got into bed, almost ten o'clock. "You-all go to sleep," Jottie said. She flicked the light out and made to close the door, but she sort of faltered as she brought it to, like she knew she wouldn't get away with it or maybe didn't even want to. We knew we had her then, and Bird pounced. "Tell us a story."

She tried to sound stern. "One story."

One, we agreed piously, and Jottie came in and settled herself against Bird's pillows and waggled her empty arm for me to snuggle into. Jottie asked what kind of story did we want.

"I want one about me," said Bird. Like she always did.

"No. Father," I said. "I want one about Father when he was little."

"Something bad he did," commanded Bird.

"Well," Jottie said, "that makes it easy. You want the one about Slonaker's barn? Or the polo ponies?"

"One we haven't heard."

She was quiet for so long that I thought she'd gone to sleep. I was preparing to jostle her when she sighed and began to speak. "Now. Listen." I loved her voice when she told a story, so low and round. "We had an uncle—he wasn't even our real uncle, just someone Daddy liked for some reason—Uncle Dade. He was just a horrible man. He gave the boys presents all the time—never a thing for us girls, but he'd bring the boys all sorts of grisly things, like knives and cap guns. One day, he showed up with a bow-and-arrow set for Felix—not a toy, a real one, with genuine deadly arrows, all knife-sharp points on one end and feathers on the other. Felix was about twelve at the time, and Mama was itching to take those arrows away, I could see she was, but she couldn't do it in front of Uncle Dade, so Felix said thank you and whisked off before she could stop him. I followed him, like I generally did, and together we fixed up a wonderful plan. Felix was going to shoot an apple right off my head, like William Tell. We figured that once we'd practiced it a couple of times, we could sell tickets. Who wouldn't pay a penny to see Felix shoot an apple off my head?"

"I would," said Bird.

"But that's terrible!" I said. "What if he hit you by mistake? Weren't you scared?"

Jottie laughed softly. "No. I was excited. I thought it was thrilling. And, besides, after he shot the apple off my head, I was going to shoot an apple off his. Sounded fine to me."

"Huh. And you're always telling us we don't have any sense."

"Well, I did begin to feel a little flimsy once I was backed up against the barn with an apple resting in my hair. Felix kept squinting and pulling the bowstring and flexing his arm. He said he had to get in the right mood or his hand would shake, which didn't make me any easier in my mind. But right about then, a couple of his friends came climbing over the fence. They saw what he was doing, and one of them told Felix to stop."

"Who?" I asked.

"Sol. His name was Sol, short for Solomon."

My eyebrows practically hit my hair, but no one saw in the dark.

"Sol. Sounds fat," observed Bird.

Jottie laughed. "He wasn't fat. He was small, then, and pale, because his mother made him stay inside and play the violin."

"Eww," Bird said.

"I know," she agreed. "Anyway, he started yelling, but Felix paid him no mind, just kept squinting and aiming, so Sol ran over and yanked me away from the barn. I acted real indignant, but inside I was relieved—and then Felix said Sol had to take my place or he'd shoot at me anyway, and he'd *aim* for my head, he said. Poor Sol didn't know what to do. He looked from Felix to me to Vause—"

"Vause Hamilton?" I asked quickly.

"Yes. Vause was there, too. After a moment, Sol stood up against the barn."

"Golly," I said. "Just like Sydney Carton in *Tale of Two Cities*."

Jottie gave me a funny look. "Maybe. Once Sol was standing there with the apple on his head, Vause started to laugh. 'Stop fooling,' he called to Felix. 'You ain't really going to do it and you know it. You never were.' Oh Lord, I knew just exactly what would happen next, and it did. That arrow flew through the air and went straight through the apple into the side of the barn, about a quarter of an inch above Sol's head. Any closer and it would have killed him."

"What did Sol do?" asked Bird.

Jottie's voice slowed. "He stepped away from the barn and looked at the arrow. Then Felix said—oh, he could be so awful sometimes—he said, 'Missed.'"

We were quiet. It was an awful thing to say. "Then what?" I asked.

I could see Jottie's eyes glittering in the dark. "Then Sol picked up a rock and threw it at Felix as hard as he could."

"Did it hit him?" Bird asked.

" 'Course not. You know how fast your daddy can move. But Vause, he was quick, too, and he lit out after Felix. He was mad. Only time I ever saw him mad at Felix."

"Is he the one that burnt up?" asked Bird.

"He didn't burn up, he smothered," I said quick, so Jottie wouldn't have to say it. I glanced at her, to see if she looked sad. But she didn't. She looked regular. "What happened then?" I asked.

Jottie stroked my hair. "Oh. Nothing much. Felix came home a few hours later with a bloody nose."

"What? Why?" Bird asked.

"Vause caught him and hit him," Jottie said. "But they were thicker than ever, afterward."

No one said anything for a long time. I heard Bird fall off, her breath coming smooth and even. "What about Sol?" I asked quietly. "What happened to him?" But Jottie was asleep, too, by then, with her arms circling us. I stayed curled up against her, but I wasn't asleep. I was thinking about that story and how it had ended. Jottie had stopped telling it, but it wasn't really finished. Afterward, something else had happened with Mr. McKubin, something that made Jottie turn pink when she saw him. And afterward, Jottie had liked Vause Hamilton especially. So the story wasn't over. No story was ever really over.

17

The next day, Sunday, we went to church. Jottie said that getting us cleaned up enough for Sunday school put her soul in such mortal peril that she had to go to church afterward, but I think she liked to go. She walked between me and Bird, holding a hand apiece. Hers was thin and strong. My hat was from the summer before and too small, so that the elastic dug into my throat and I couldn't turn my head. I looked straight ahead, like a soldier.

Jottie's church dress was rose-colored, with little white feathers floating on it and a cloth rose at the neck. She looked pretty. She stepped along, nodding and saying hello to people I couldn't see.

"Well, look here, if it isn't the lovely Misses Romeyn," called a voice I knew. It was Mr. Bensee. He didn't sit in the grape arbor. He sat on the porch, reading the Macedonia *Sun*.

I yanked off my hat so I could say hello. "Hey, Mr. Bensee!"

"Miss Willa, I have just finished reading a story about you in this very newspaper here," he said, flapping the *Sun*.

"What does it say, Mr. Bensee?"

He frowned at the paper. "It says you're planning to go to church this morning. It says Miss Willa Romeyn plans to wear a pretty yellow-checked dress and Miss Bird Romeyn plans to wear a pretty blue-checked one. It's rare these reporters get their facts straight. Let me look at you."

We stood in front of his porch, side by side.

He nodded. "That's a relief. A reliable newspaper is a fine thing. Well, Jottie, pray for me."

"Won't do a lick of good, Spencer," said Jottie.

He laughed, and we walked on down High Street toward the church.

Father didn't go to church. According to Jottie, Father and Reverend Dews had discussed it, and Father had promised to go to church every day of the year in 1952, so Reverend Dews said it was all right if he didn't go until then. We knew better than that. Father liked to sleep late on Sundays.

Someone fell into step next to Bird, a grown lady, I could tell from her shoes. "How-you, Jottie?" she began. Jottie said "Fine" kind of distantly, but the lady went right on. "Who *was* that girl I saw Felix with yesterday? Mary Car said it looked like that cousin of yours from Moorefield, but I bet her a nickel it wasn't."

It was Mrs. Combs. Her boy, Bobby Combs, was in my class at school. He was all right.

"June," said Jottie. "Are you asking me to aid and abet in gambling on the Lord's Day?"

"Now, Jottie, you know I'm as stubborn as a mule," sang Mrs. Combs. "You just have to settle my bet with Mary Car."

"You won," Bird broke in. "That was Miss Layla Beck. She lives in our house."

"She does?"

"She boards," said Jottie. "She's writing a book about Macedonia. You should buy me a cup of coffee with that nickel, June."

"Daddy was showing her places for her book," Bird explained.

"Is that so?" Mrs. Combs's voice rolled out rich and fat. "Ain't that nice of him. They looked so cozy I didn't reckon they were doing business."

Cozy? What did that mean? I looked at Jottie, or I would have if I could have turned my head all the way. Her hand closed around mine, cool and tight. She didn't say a word.

"Well," said Mrs. Combs after a bit. "I knew it wasn't that cousin of yours. What's her name? Florence?"

"Irene," said Jottie.

"Mary Car said she saw Emmett yesterday, too."

"Mary Car sure had a busy day, didn't she?"

"Oh, you know Mary. She likes to keep an eye out."

We had come to the stairs of the church by then, and Jottie did some chatting with Mrs. Tapscott and Harriet while I stood quiet and thought. I thought about cozy and about Waldon and Mae and about how pretty Miss Beck was. Even Emmett thought so, and he hadn't taken her specially to Dolly's Ford. I remembered what he had said: "How is it that Felix gets everything he wants?" Maybe Miss Beck was the thing Emmett meant, the thing Father wanted.

Miss Cladine came out and rang the bell, and we all trooped down to the basement to hear Bible stories.

I loved Miss Cladine. In real life, she was an algebra teacher over in the high school, but she was crazy about the Bible. Not in a preaching way, though. She never talked about being good or bad. Instead, she told the Bible in stories, acting out all the parts, with yelling and wailing as necessary. Even the very worst boys, like Harmon Lacey, sat as quiet as mice during Sunday school. Miss Cladine had her favorites—not in the class but in the Bible. She thought Daniel was a sourpuss and a know-it-all, and she didn't like Paul, either. She called him a busybody. The one she loved was Samson. She had a colored picture of him knocking down the pillars, pinned to the walls of the basement. The Philistines were scrambling around with their mouths hanging open in terror. "Serves them right," Miss Cladine said. "The sneaks."

Today she was telling about Joshua and Jericho, but I couldn't concentrate. I kept looking at the picture of blind Samson and the scattering Philistines. Maybe the roof fell on them, but it fell on him, too. I didn't think that was such a happy ending as the Bible made out. Beautiful Delilah had sold Samson down the river. She had stroked his head until he got sleepy and told her the secret of his seven locks. I pictured my father with his head in Miss Beck's lap, her little fingers coiling in his hair as he told her everything about himself, everything he had never told me.

✳

Academy Street drowsed under its Sunday afternoon spell. Time softened on Sundays; it stretched itself out in vast rubbery lengths, and by two o'clock, there was more of it than would ever be needed for anything. There was no point in reading a book, writing a letter, or playing a game, because time was too flaccid ever to proceed to the moment in which the plot would twist, the letter would be sent, or the game would be won. House by house, all activity ceased. Only the tinny radio preachers raved on, unaffected by the lethargy.

Through the open window of the Romeyns' front room, a sermon billowed out onto the porch: "Feel His love! Feel HIS love! When you FEEL His love, though you be a-crawling-crawling-dragging-dragging across the dusty plains of sin—" Abruptly, the radio was shut off.

Sitting by the window in a saggy porch chair, Layla exhaled. "Whew." Once again she attempted to concentrate on the pamphlet in her hands, *The Christian Mission in the False River Environs.* "The Eel River Council of 1821 influenced the Commission of Disciples in the following ways . . ."

Her thoughts slid away. Only six days. A week ago, I had no idea that Felix Romeyn existed. One week ago, I was miserable about coming to Macedonia. One week ago, I couldn't imagine that I would be so interested in this town. And in this family. Not just Felix, but all of them. Are they prominent? The house is grand. And they seem educated, especially Felix and Jottie and young Mr. Romeyn. Funny how they're so dark and the twins so fair—

The radio flicked back on. "You, SINNERS, when your hour comes and you repent, will Jesus hear your cry? Will Jesus bend down from Heaven and pull you from the flames? Will he pour the balm of His tears on your blistered FLESH? Your burning FLESH?"

Layla heard Bird giggle. "Hey, Jottie!" she yodeled from the front room. "That lady preacher is talking about flesh! She says it's going to blister in you-know-where!"

Even more distantly, from the kitchen, came Jottie's voice. "Just turn that right off! She shouldn't be talking about flesh on a Sunday!"

The radio went off. Layla listened to Bird chortle for a few moments. "Bird?" she called through the window.

"Yeah?"

"Where are Mrs. Saubergast and Mrs. Odell this weekend?"

There was a pause, and then Bird stuck her head out the window. "At their houses."

Layla blinked. "I thought they lived here."

"Only during the week."

"Oh." Another pause. "Where are their houses?"

"Mae's out at Hampshire Downs, that's her farm, hers and Waldon's. And Minerva's just over there." Bird pointed up the street. "She's got a big old house. She just got purple drapes, and Jottie says it looks crazy, but Minerva likes purple."

"Purple. My," said Layla. "Who's Waldon?"

Bird frowned at her obtuseness. "Mae's *husband.*"

"Oh! I didn't realize!"

"What?"

"That she was, well—married."

Bird squinted. "She's called Mrs."

"Yes, but, I just didn't know," stammered Layla. "Does Mrs. Odell have one, too?" she asked cautiously. "A husband?"

"'Course she does. Henry," said Bird. "We like Waldon better, though. Waldon lets us jump from the loft into his hay wagon. And he let me watch one of his cows have a baby. He thought I'd faint, but I didn't. I liked it. Henry doesn't let us do anything."

"Now, that's enough of that." Jottie's voice, much closer. "Henry's always been real nice to you, even when you don't deserve it, which is most of the time." Layla listened, smiling, as a discussion about the relative merits of Waldon and Henry ensued—mostly, on Bird's part, a recitation and evaluation of favors bestowed and presents given, mostly, on Jottie's, a remonstrance, until finally Bird was declared to be no better than a gold digger and sent off to pick weeds.

There was a long silence.

Then Jottie's voice came from the front room. "You can ask why, if you like."

Layla burst out laughing. "Oh, Miss Romeyn! Are you a clairvoyant?"

Now Jottie appeared in the window. She settled herself comfortably on the wide sill, facing Layla's chair. "You know," she said, "this Miss Romeyn business is wearing me out. I'd take it kindly if you'd call me Jottie."

Friends at last! thought Layla. "Only if you call me Layla instead of Miss Beck."

"Delighted."

They smiled at each other companionably. "I'm trying to summon the spirit to make a pie for supper," said Jottie. "You like peach pie?"

"Yes, of course," said Layla. "But will you—I mean, may I ask about why Mrs. Saubergast and Mrs. Odell—"

"Oh Lord, just call them by their first names. They won't mind. You want to know why they live here during the week instead of with their husbands."

"Not that it's any of my business," Layla said apologetically.

Jottie laughed. "That never stopped anyone before. The two of them can't stand to be apart, is the real reason. They got engaged to Henry and Waldon at about the same time, got married in a double ceremony—prettiest wedding you ever saw—and went dancing off, Mae to the farm and Minerva to Henry's house, just as happy as clams. For about a week. Then they found out they were miserable without each other. They had never spent more than a few hours apart before, and they didn't know what it would be like. You should have seen them: They were gray as ashes inside of a month. So they came home."

"But—don't their husbands *mind*?" Layla asked.

"Waldon never minds anything, bless his heart. Easiest man on earth. Henry, well, you'll probably run into him sometime, and you'll see what he thinks. He don't like it much. He used to try to keep Minerva home, but she'd give him the slip. She'd tell him she was going to run over here to borrow a cup of sugar, and then she'd stay. Around nine o'clock, he'd come for her. We'd hear him stomping up the front stairs, him and his little mustache." Jottie chuckled reminiscently. "Once he came in and recited their wedding vows aloud in the middle of the front room. Minerva lay on the sofa and listened just as meek as a dove until he finished, and then she said, 'Isn't it funny how "cleave" means two opposite things?' Henry stormed out of the house, mad as hops, and I thought that was going to be the end of them, but they managed to patch it up." Jottie smiled into Layla's wide eyes. "Funny, isn't it."

"Well, it's unusual," said Layla, striving to reconcile truth with tact.

"Yes." Jottie nodded. "Henry's an odd one."

"Henry?!" exclaimed Layla. "I would say Minerva!"

"Oh, *Minerva*," said Jottie affectionately. "I could have told you she'd get tired of living with Henry day in and day out. Henry never was much fun. He wanted to be a banker when he was five years old, can you imagine? He used to try to lend us children money at interest. The snake." She paused, remembering. "There was one day Felix caught him at it. He tied Henry to a tree and put up a big sign saying he was a usurer."

Layla giggled. "Poor Henry."

"Puh. It was the most exciting thing that ever happened to Henry Odell. Best day of his life. He spent the next ten years hanging around here trying to get someone to pay that much attention to him again. Henry's been real fond of Felix ever since. Won't hear a word against him."

Layla smiled. "Who would say a word against Felix?"

"I can think of a couple people," said Jottie carefully. "Henry's aunt Augusta, just for example. Her daughter Sylvia was married to Felix there for a while."

"But she's dead, isn't she?" blurted Layla. Instantly she blushed. "I mean—I don't know where I got—I just assumed he was—a widower."

"A widower?" Jottie smiled. "No. Divorced."

"Well!" said Layla, digesting it. "Divorced. It's not uncommon these days, is it? Plenty of people get divorced. Personally, I think it's fine." And she did, she decided. "If people are unsuited, well, then, there's no shame in admitting it."

Jottie nodded noncommittally.

"Were they—Felix and his wife—unsuited? In your opinion?" Layla probed.

Jottie felt in her pocket and withdrew a box of cigarettes. "They didn't know each other very well." At all, she added internally.

"Really? Why not?"

Jottie opened the box and looked inside. "They eloped three weeks after they met." How much should she tell? How much would be enough to make this girl wary?

"They did?" Layla's voice rose with enthusiasm. "How romantic!"

Jottie tried again. "Sort of. They were both engaged to other people at the time."

"Oh!" Even more romantic, really, Layla thought. Love over discretion.

"Then they got found out, and they more or less had to run off and get married," Jottie said flatly. "Felix was . . . fickle."

Fickle? That seemed unfair. He was romantic. "Well, a fickle youth!" Layla said lightly. "Is he still fickle?"

"Yes," said Jottie. Her eyes held Layla's. "Very."

Layla recoiled. How terribly cold. Poor Felix, condemned for following his heart, just as she herself had been punished for refusing Nelson. Did Felix's kindness, his warmth, his obvious affection for his family count for nothing? It wasn't right. "He certainly seems very devoted to you. And to the children," she said icily. "I've never seen such a devoted brother, actually."

Jottie looked away. It was true. "Yes," she said after a moment. "Yes, of course. Very devoted. No question about that." She sighed. "Do you have a brother?"

"Yes," said Layla guardedly. "Yes. One. Elder brother."

"That's nice. Are you close?"

"Close?" Layla repeated, as if she didn't understand the word. "Well. A bit. Some. He's very . . . intelligent."

Jottie smiled. "You're no dummy yourself."

Layla flushed with pleasure. "Thanks."

"Where does your family live?" asked Jottie conversationally.

"Washington," answered Layla. She rose. "I'd be glad to help you with that pie, Jottie."

Jottie slid the pie into the oven, closed the door, and stood. Her fingers crept into her pocket and withdrew a cigarette. She had tried. Nobody could say she hadn't tried. "He certainly seems very devoted to you." And he was. He had taken care of her when she had lost everything. She couldn't deny it.

"I can't."

"Sure you can," Felix insisted.

"Felix." Jottie shook her head. "I just—just—maybe next week. Not now."

"Come on, honey." He ducked his head to see into her eyes. "Button your coat and pull your hat down a little." When she made no move, he reached up and tugged it for her. "See? You look fine. No one can tell about your hair. It looks like you got it bobbed, that's all."

She could feel the perspiration on her forehead. "I can't, Felix."

There was a swish of cloth as their mother entered the room behind them. "Well!" she cried, catching sight of her daughter. "It's about time!" Felix sent her a warning glance. "Don't you give me that look, Felix Romeyn! I'm just saying it's about time Jottie got over the whole thing and stopped acting like a widow or something!"

"Mama," he said. "Drop it."

"It's not like it wasn't an awful shock for me, too. Or for your daddy!"

"I said to drop it."

If his mother noticed the change in his voice, she gave no sign of it. "And you, too! When I think of how you and Vause were friends, why, I could just scream!"

Jottie steeled herself as Felix's fingers closed tight around a squat bronze figurine from a nearby table. "Get out of here," he said to his mother.

His mother's eyes dropped to the figurine. There was a moment's calculation before she said, "How can you talk to me like that?"

"Easy. Get out."

Mrs. Romeyn took a step backward. "You're so harsh with me, Felix. You were the sweetest baby." Her eyes filled. "But now you're just cruel. Maybe it's the shock, but honestly, anyone would think I was the criminal, the way you talk to me."

Felix smiled, and the whiteness of his teeth was startling.

Mrs. Romeyn swallowed pitifully to allow time for an apology that didn't come. Then she said, "We'll see you at supper?"

"Maybe."

She gave a theatrical sigh and rustled away. Felix set the figurine down and turned back to Jottie.

"Thanks," she whispered.

"My pleasure."

"Don't leave." If he left, she would die.

"Remember what I said? I'll stay by you. You'll see. Now, let's us go for a little stroll." He studied her, frowning, and then fastened the top button of her coat. "There. Let's go."

"It's just that—that everyone knows—" She broke off, shaking and helpless.

He waited. When she said nothing, he urged, "Everyone knows what?"

"Everyone knows"—her voice sank to a whisper—"that I believed him. Everyone knows he made a fool out of me. They're going to look at me and feel sorry for me and I can't—I can't—"

Felix looked at the floor and nodded. "I know. But he did it. Not you. You didn't do anything wrong." He lifted his eyes to hers. "Vause lied. He did wrong. Not you. Got that?" She shrugged. "Come on." He picked up her hand and drew it through his arm. "Here's what: You don't have to look at anyone. You just hang on to me and I'll stare 'em down for you, okay? Because neither of us did anything wrong. Okay?" He wheeled her around to face the mirror. "Okay?"

"I loved him."

"I know. Me too. Come on."

As they stepped off the front porch, her trembling fingers dug into his sleeve. He looked down at her and smiled. "See how nice it is out here?" he said. "Smells like spring."

Jottie took a long, glad pull on her cigarette and waved the match out. Then she swung around to look at Layla. "Wasn't I going to tell you about Reverend Goodacre this afternoon?"

Layla smiled. "I certainly hope you are! Let me get my notebook."

18

Father came home from his business with Clayton V. Hart on Tuesday, but he had to leave again after a few days, to go to Columbus, Ohio. He said he had been hired by the town fathers of Columbus, Ohio, to inspect their statuary. It wasn't true, of course. He was joking. But I wondered what he was really going to do there. Was he going on business for Cooey's Red Apple? I couldn't decide, and I couldn't ask him, either. I watched his face and thought he probably was. A minute later, I thought he probably wasn't. I was in my room, trying to figure it out, when I heard his car crunching down the dirt alley behind our house. He was gone. I decided to go over to Capon Street to see Geraldine. I wanted to throw some plums.

Mrs. Lee pushed back the rhododendron branches and found us. "Thought I heard something."

Geraldine was trained for capture. "We're just sitting here, Mama. Just talking about holy baptism."

"That right?" Mrs. Lee peered at me. "Who's that?"

"That's Willa, Mama. You know."

Mrs. Lee looked doubtful. "Willa Romeyn?"

"Yes'm," I said.

"Whoo. You sure don't look like your mama, do you?" I didn't answer and she turned away, wiping her hands on her faded dress. "Romeyn through and through." She made it sound nasty.

Geraldine waited until Mrs. Lee was back at the clothesline. "You don't have a mother."

"I do, too," I said. I hated this conversation. "She's sick." I waited. I knew what was coming, but there was no reason to hand it to her on a silver platter.

"What's she got?"

"Leprosy," I said, shaking my head sadly. I'd recently read *Ben-Hur,* and leprosy had struck me as exactly the right kind of sickness for my mother. People who had it were sent away, far away, where no one had to see their falling-off noses. This was the first time I'd used it.

"I never heard of it," said Geraldine.

"Oh, it's just awful," I said. "Your eyeballs hang down over your face, and your skin gets all scaly, and your limbs twist around backward. Sometimes." Ben-Hur's sister got holes in her lips, but I didn't want to overdo it.

"Nuh-uh," said Geraldine.

"It's true. Haven't you ever read *Ben-Hur*? You'd like it. It's a real religious book."

"Your mother's eyeballs hang down over her face?" Geraldine stared at me. I began to think that maybe leprosy was not the perfect sickness. I wondered should I go back to smallpox.

"No. No. She has a mild case of it. But she had to go to a leper colony all the same. That's where they keep them, all together, because they're the only ones who can stand to see each other." Really, my mother lived in sin in Grand Mile with Mr. Parnell Rudy. Mr. Rudy was married to someone else, a lady who would never ever let him go, according to my mother. But I wasn't going to tell Geraldine about that. That was none of Geraldine's beeswax.

"If my mother had leprosy, I'd stand it," Geraldine said proudly. "I wouldn't let them take her away."

"Yes, you would. Otherwise, you'd go crazy. That's what happens if you see a leper. It's a known fact."

"Jesus healed the lepers," she said.

"I know. That's in the book, too. But that's Jesus." I looked at her sternly. "Jesus is God. I don't set myself up to be as good as Jesus."

I had her there. She unbent a little and said, "Let's practice spying."

I didn't feel like it. And I didn't want to run afoul of Mrs. Lee again, either. "I got to go home now," I said. "I have to scrub the floors."

Geraldine nodded sympathetically. "Okay. Tomorrow, then?"

"Maybe," I lied.

I turned down Blooding Avenue. The name sounded like butchers, but it was a real pretty street, with trees all along, and I enjoyed walking in the shade. I got cooler there and stopped fussing. I didn't care what Mrs. Lee thought, not about anything, and especially not about my mother. Twice a year, Bird and I had to go to Grand Mile to see our mother. We hated those visits. She gripped us too tight and moaned about how we were lost to her. One time I said, "You're the one who left, aren't you?" but that only made her moan louder. And she always made Monte Cristo sandwiches for lunch. She called it a treat, but it was the only thing she knew how to make, and Bird usually threw up on the way home. Sometimes, if I held her hand real hard, she didn't, but mostly she did.

I came to an old bridge made of yellow stone and stood still for a bit, watching the cloud of bugs that hung over Academy Creek. Geraldine's army hadn't been as much fun as I'd expected anyway. I slipped round the end of the bridge and made my way down the soft, rot-smelling banks to walk along the water. I liked being alone. There was a chance I'd be a hermit when I grew up.

I hadn't been down there long when I saw Father, walking along the sidewalk about twenty feet above me. He wasn't in Ohio any more than I was! I almost called out, and then I thought better of it. I wasn't sure he'd be glad to see me. For a couple of seconds, I stood there, thinking maybe I should let well enough alone. But as Father walked away, I decided to follow him. It would be almost like we were on an adventure together.

So I trailed behind and below him, keeping on the lookout for branches and nettles and, at the same time, watching as he moved along, quick and sure. Then, from one second to the next, he disappeared. I scrambled up the dirt banks as fast as I could, wondering where he could have gotten to. Then I saw. I'd come up in back of Mr. Russell's house, the Tare Estate. It was one of the biggest houses in town, a real mansion, with real gardens, too, like the ones you read about in books—flower beds tidy inside low boxwood hedges and a fountain with a naked cherub boy in the middle. All that grand place belonged to little Mr. Russell, who mostly just sat on his veranda and drank ice-tea.

Jottie paid Mr. Russell a call now and then, and it looked like my father did, too. I stood behind the stone wall and watched Father skim through the garden, twisting and turning among those boxwood hedges as if he did it every day of his life. He was so fast. In no time, he reached the house, and then he did a thing that surprised me. He didn't follow the path that led to the front porch, the way you'd go if you were visiting; instead, he turned the other way, toward the back of the house, with its towers and porches and the conservatory that bulged out. I squinted, watching him stop at a small black door that was in the bottom of a tower. He didn't have a key, so far as I could tell. He just opened it and went in.

✳

Five blocks east of Willa, Jottie proceeded along Prince Street, keeping step with Inez Tapscott as they retreated from the home of Mrs. Sloan Inskeep, where the Daughters of Macedon had been edified by a towering cherry cake and a demonstration of Mrs. Inskeep's tapestry work on international themes.

"Those tapestries were real interesting," Inez observed. "She must be busy as a bee, making all those."

Jottie nodded vigorously. What could she say? "I liked the one about Argentina."

"Oh, my, yes! So exotic, with all those—things!" Inez exclaimed. "Though I can't say I like those little pencil mustaches. Do you?" She sent an inquiring look at Jottie.

Pencil mustaches? What on earth was she talking about? Gracious and pleasant, Jottie reminded herself. She took a stab at it. "I guess I like them better than those great big ones that look like a weasel taking a nap."

"A weasel—" Inez began to giggle. "Jottie Romeyn, you just *slay* me!"

Abruptly, Jottie came to a halt. "Oh, Inez! I almost forgot! I promised I'd get the girls some ice cream! I'm just going to run in here! Such a good time! So interesting!" The words streamed from her into Inez Tapscott's pleased face. "Thank you kindly for letting me come along! I sure will look forward to the next meeting!"

Once inside Statler's, she leaned against the door, inhaling the candied air of freedom.

"Jottie! How-you? Been a long time!" Armine Statler, big and pink, lay a meaty hand on his counter. "What can I do for you?"

Refuge came at a price; you couldn't expect otherwise. "I'll have a chocolate soda, thanks, Armine," she said.

As he busied himself with scooper and glass, Jottie pressed her hip against the cooler. If only she could press her whole body into the chill of the metal. Her head, ensnared in her best hat; her hands, ensnared in white gloves; and her bowels, ensnared in a girdle borrowed from Mae. "Stupid," she muttered under her breath.

"Beg pardon?" shouted Armine Statler. His head was inside the cooler and he couldn't hear a thing.

"Nothing. I didn't say anything," Jottie said.

"Oh. Thought you did." He pulled his head out. "Chocolate, right?"

"Yes. Chocolate." Chocolate, indeed! As if she needed a chocolate soda at four-thirty in the afternoon! At a cost of ten cents! Perfectly good money thrown away because she couldn't think of one more thing to say to Inez Tapscott. Loyal, good-hearted Inez, who had never once failed to greet Jottie like a long-lost sister—and how had Jottie repaid her? She had run away. She was ashamed of herself.

Jottie set her purse on a little white table and sat down. When Armine Statler brought her soda over, she looked with distaste at the brown bubbles foaming up the sides of the glass. She didn't even like chocolate sodas. Vause had liked them; that's what it was. When, long ago, she'd come to Statler's with her friends, after school, she'd waited for him—not in a way that anyone else could see, but with her ears alive for his voice, her skin open to the heat of the bodies that flocked around him each afternoon. Felix came, too, of course, and usually Sol, and a pack of other boys and girls, but Vause was the center. Vause, separated from her in public by two years and his various forms of celebrity, would eventually see her, or Felix would, and she would glory in the brief acknowledgment: "Josie!" Sometimes one of them would come to her table and talk for a moment.

"Ain't you going to eat it?" Armine Statler said.

Jottie jumped. "Oh! I'm woolgathering, Armine."

"Gonna get real hot in all that wool, Jottie. Ha!" Armine slapped himself in merriment.

"I was just thinking about how we used to come here when I was in high school. Back when your father ran the place."

Armine nodded. "Uh-huh. I worked out in the back then, but I remember."

Impulsively, Jottie said, "Do you remember Vause Hamilton? He used to have a chocolate soda pretty near every day." It didn't matter if she talked about him to Armine. Armine was in the business of being agreeable. He wasn't likely to point out that Vause had burned her father's factory down.

"Sure. Vause—he spent a lot of nickels in here." Armine smiled warmly. "All the kids did then. Not like now." His good humor vanished. "Ice cream is the first thing folks stop buying. The first thing." He frowned at her soda. "Ain't you going to eat it?"

Jottie picked up the glass and took a long, obedient sip. Milky bubbles filled her mouth. "My, that hits the spot, Armine," she said.

He nodded complacently and moved away as another customer came in. Jottie looked at the reflection of her hat in the window. She looked like a lady. But she wasn't a lady; she was a coward. All the flower-arranging in the world isn't going to make Willa safe if you can't be gracious and pleasant for one afternoon, she scolded herself. But I don't understand what they're talking about half the time, she pleaded. Doesn't matter, the scolding voice snapped. Pretend.

The door slammed and a man in shabby trousers came in. "I need another doggone carton of vanilla, Armine."

Armine smiled. "That's fine. I'll get that right up." He called over to Jottie. "Bill, here, his wife likes her vanilla ice cream."

"She's expecting," explained Bill.

"That's nice," said Jottie.

"Every day, she eats ice cream," Armine added. "It's good for you, see?"

"I reckon so," said Bill. "Costing me an arm and a leg."

Jottie turned again to the window. Everlasting's out, she observed, as Prince Street filled with tired-looking men. Great eddies of people surged by and fetched up around Coca-Colas, around lampposts, around jokes that made them laugh hoarsely.

And there, suddenly, was Sol, walking on the sidewalk opposite, more impressive than he ever was in her memory. Stately, even, in a dark-blue suit. Concealed behind a drooping curtain, Jottie allowed her eyes to follow him, to read him like an illicit book. He was dignified. When had that happened? Her default Sol—dancing with fear, his fingers gripping hers, his eyes on Felix and Vause far, far above, *They're going to fall, I know it, I know it!*—had disappeared, and in his place was a man grown solid and calm and admirable. And he had done it without her, without Felix or Vause or her, when once he had sought only their approval.

"I can't believe Sol still cares," Emmett had said. Did he? After all this time? Her thoughts moved back to the parade, to the plea that had appeared on his face: Can't you forgive me? Can't we be friends again?

But the Sol walking along Prince Street made no such supplications. He was no beggar. She watched him, mesmerized by his steady tread, the casual lift of his hand, the brief laugh, the slapped back—the serene recessional of the well liked and universally respected. Faces turned toward him in anticipation as he approached, looked after him with friendly regret as he passed. Hungrily, Jottie gleaned every detail.

Before she could stop herself, the thought came: If Willa had a father like Sol, she'd be safe forever. And then, even more unthinkable: If I married him, I could make her safe. It was a shocking thought; it was a heady thought. It would mean instant respectability, instant freedom from the past. Instant pudding, she jeered at herself. It's going to be a real trick, marrying someone you haven't talked to in eighteen years.

Emmett said he still cares.

She assessed the possibility while Sol strolled on. No. But, then again, maybe. He had cared, once. How watchful he'd been, trying to see what she thought before he spoke, trying to slip into the chair beside hers before anyone else did, trying to take her away from the others with questions: *Is that a new dress? What're you reading? I can help you with that geometry if you want.*

Imagine being married to Sol. It would be so easy, pressing shirts and passing coffee cups, nothing more, nothing hard. And in exchange: an honorable estate, the sweet peach of unimpeachability, safety without end, amen. Jottie pictured it in longing detail: Willa and Bird, immaculate skirts swishing as they came up freshly painted front stairs, carefree and ignorant. And there she was herself, at the door, with a plate of cookies in her outstretched hand, her smile simple and straightforward, nothing more or less than what could be seen. The girls will be fine, she reminded herself halfheartedly; I joined a club, didn't I? She studied Sol through her eyelashes. The small, milky boy had disappeared; he'd become almost handsome. Better than handsome. Assured. The suit had something to do with it. Did Violet pick out his clothes? They picked them out together, probably. In Washington, maybe. She was willing to bet they went to Washington to shop. Not Krohn's—she'd put a nickel on it. Imagine going to Washington to buy clothes.

Across the street, Sol lifted his hat to a lady passing, a lady she didn't know—and there, he smiled, too. He was happy. Sol's face never lied. He was perfectly happy. She was a fool. He didn't care about her, not anymore. He probably had a girl. He was probably in love with some sweet little twenty-year-old girl. He had his own life.

It hurt.

She sat at her table for a few moments longer, until Sol turned up Council Street. Then she stood, fumbling her purse over her arm. "Thanks, Armine," she called as she made for the door. She stepped outside, gulped a breath of sodden air, and turned right, in the direction of Academy Street.

19

June 24

Dear Ben,

Pursuing history of Macedonia with zeal and enterprise. Went to jail Wednesday. Nearly starved Thursday. Wore hole in shoe Saturday. Will WPA reimburse?

Layla

June 24, 1938

Darling Rose,

I beg your pardon in advance—this is going to be a short letter because my fingers are practically paralyzed from all the writing I've been doing. How I wish you could see me pounding away at the typewriter keys in my slip, with a pencil behind my ear. My industry (and the state of my slip) would move you to tears. It's so steamingly hot up here that I shed my dress and hose the instant I walk through my bedroom door and work in my unders, but I live in mortal terror that I'll forget to put my dress back on when I leave—the WPA expressly forbids its employees to engage in indecent behavior. Also to shoot or willfully incinerate one another (Ben is safe for now).

I am diligently writing Macedonia's history, though I've plenty more interviews to conduct with leading Macedonians and assorted natural wonders to visit. My supervisor advised me to complete my research before commencing to write, but I simply haven't the time, for the town fathers are demanding their book by September 24, the anniversary of the incorporation of Macedonia. It seems to me that I could solve the problem neatly by changing the date of the anniversary in the book, but the town fathers are a fussy bunch and therefore I'm working frantically to meet their deadline. I'd make better progress if I wasn't forced to squander hours in writing letters to Mother, promising her that I'm not starving, coal mining, or coarsened by contact with low minds. How I wish that Mother had never read *Tobacco Road*. No matter what I say, she thinks that I'm working in the fields, bending over rows of turnips in a ripped cotton dress while lascivious farmers eye my youthful form and squirt tobacco juice between their front teeth. The truth disappoints her, which, I suppose, is why she doesn't believe it.

I was glad to get your letter about Georgette and Nelson, but, really, honey, I couldn't possibly care less and you don't have to say she looked like a cow in her dress (though everyone *does* look like a cow in those shirred necklines). They would be a splendid couple, those two. Georgette could stop dragging herself over the dance floors of Washington and settle down to a lifetime sitting at a corner table of the Pall Mall Club, which is what she truly enjoys. And Nelson could say, "My wife—one hundred percent North Carolina thoroughbred filly, heh-heh!" Really, it's a match made in heaven.

As for the rest of your letter, if you hate all of it so much, why do you go? Now that I have the vantage point of eighty-five miles and thirteen days, those parties seem like an awful waste of time. I feel as though I've spent the last seven years dancing with men I don't like. Nelson, for example, and Louis Yards and Harry and, well, all of them. Dressing and smiling and dancing and pretending to laugh at weak jokes. Why do we do it? I know what you'll say— that we don't want to be old maids—but do we really want to marry Louis Yards or Nelson? I honestly believe I'd rather not marry at all. And, then, there may be other men, in other places, whom we'd like better.

In Macedonia, for example.

That's a hint.

I know I told you I was boarding with the Romeyn family, but I believe I neglected to mention the specific existence of Mr. Romeyn—Felix, I'm to call him now. He lives here with his two daughters (he's divorced from their mother). His sister takes care of the children and keeps house while he works. I'm not certain what he does, but he travels for his business frequently. He is certainly the kindest person I've met in Macedonia; just last weekend, he took me touring round to historic sites for my book. Wasn't that sweet? We had a lovely time, too—unlike Nelson, he actually *converses*. On topics other than himself! And expresses interest. In me! And my ideas! He's cultivated and gentlemanly and charming. Not precisely handsome but terribly attractive, with dark eyes and hair and a smile that made me feel faint the first time I saw it. There's something electric about him, something slightly mysterious and very, very alluring—oh dear, I'm making him sound like the desert sheik, and that's not it at all.

I don't want you to get the idea that I've lost my heart indiscriminately. Just as Miss Telt advised us lo these many years ago, I have not submitted my affections to the buffets of superficial attraction but have withheld my esteem for that one who will prove himself worthy of my virtue(!), a friend to the downtrodden and model of humility to the great, a consolation in adversity and a companion in joy, upon whose bosom I might lay my perplexities both great and small. Darling Miss Telt! Do you think she ever met an actual man?

I know, I know, I'm being flippant, but I'll admit—to you alone—that I am a little taken with Mr. Felix Romeyn. I wasn't expecting anyone like him in Macedonia, West Virginia, which shows, I suppose, how small-minded I am. I was expecting, not lascivious turnip farmers, exactly, but something close. Bumpkins, anyway. Instead, I've found a small town that looks like any small town, with wide streets, old elms, white houses, and a tattered, dead-quiet town square—all seething with white-hot passion and Greek tragedy. You would faint dead away if I told you about the first Baptist minister in these parts, a saga that includes two seductions, an empty coffin, and a snake! I'll send you a copy when I've finished writing it up, but you must be sure to keep it hidden from your mother and Margaret. They're too young for such shocking fare.

I must run, darling. It's time for supper, and I have to put my dress back on. I remembered!

Love,
Layla

June 27, 1938

Dear Layla,

WPA is glad to reimburse: sending newspaper (under separate cover) to stuff in shoe.

Ben

The twenty-two pleasant churches that today grace the streets of Macedonia betray no hint of the religious turmoil that roiled the town in the late 1820s and early 1830s, during the tenure of Reverend Caymuth Goodacre. The tribulations began in 1828, when young Reverend Goodacre arrived in town to establish a Baptist ministry, accompanied by his sister, a mute, who acted as his housekeeper. Goodacre's rhetorical and spiritual vigor were much admired and drew many converts to his faith, but his earthly attributes evidently aroused the attention of Macedonia's womenfolk. The favor of his presence at dinner was hotly contested, and one parishioner, Mrs. Elizabeth Shanholtzer, wrote to her cousin Glorvina that the reverend was "the most wonderfull of God's Works." Whatever the source of his appeal, it seems clear that by the spring of 1829, Goodacre was enjoying a successful mission: out of a total population of 785, approximately 390 souls had been confirmed in his church, proving their faith with baptism in the icy waters of the False River.

But Goodacre's triumph proved fleeting, and it was none other than the admiring Mrs. Shanholtzer who was the rock upon which his ministry foundered. In late 1829, this lady disappeared from her home, leaving a letter announcing to her husband that she had found her "Soul's true Helpmeet" and had decided to "travel by his Side in Life." On March 21, 1830, Reverend Goodacre comforted the bereft Mr. Shanholtzer with a sermon on the subject of female perfidy.

In October of 1830, another young woman from Goodacre's congregation—her name is unrecorded—disappeared during a stormy afternoon. Though her corpse was not found, she was presumed to be a victim of a rapidly rising river, and her empty coffin was the first to be buried in the cemetery behind the newly built Baptist church (N. Mentor St. at Sattlebarge Ln.). Goodacre's eulogy on this occasion was said to be stirring.

Imagine the surprise of the congregation when, in late October, as Reverend Goodacre intoned the Declaration of Faith, the church door opened and Mrs. Shanholtzer herself stalked down the aisle, a baby at her breast, shrieking accusations as she approached the reverend: He was the helpmeet! He had spirited her away to a secret hiding place, where he fed her with promises of undying love, only to betray her, after she had borne his child, by announcing that he was tired of her and suggesting that she return to her husband.

The quick-thinking Reverend Goodacre was more than a match for Mrs. Shanholtzer, whose hysterical denunciations he dismissed as the ravings of a madwoman. Deploying the rhetorical force that had always served him so well, he prayed for her swift recovery from the foul hallucination that he had been her seducer and begged the Lord to reveal the identity of the true villain.

After a volley of prayer that lasted over two hours, Goodacre claimed to get his answer. Mrs. Shanholtzer had been led astray by one Jervis Offut, a middle-aged bachelor about whom little has been preserved, except for the salient fact that he was a Presbyterian deacon. Goodacre's silver tongue ensured that this accusation was quickly adopted as truth, and a detachment of burly Baptists was dispatched to bring Mr. Offut to justice.

Mr. Offut unwisely took to his heels at their approach, which confirmed his guilt in the public mind. According to The Tattle-Tale, an early Macedonia broadside, Mr. Offut was finally captured in the tannery and brought not before the courts but before the pulpit

*of the Baptist church, where he met his accuser face-to-face on No-
vember 3, 1830.*

*Reverend Goodacre shook the very rafters with his rage as he
charged Mr. Offut with seduction, adultery, and fornication, and
called upon the constable, a Mr. Sayle, handily present, to arrest
him. Goodacre's fiery speech brought the congregation, now swelled
to twice the usual number, to its feet, crying for more immediate vengeance. Mr. Offut would have been tarred and feathered within the
hour had it not been for an unlikely intervention. At the peak of the
frenzy, mute Miss Goodacre stepped forward to place herself between Mr. Offut and his foes. Disconcerted, the vigilantes drew back
and looked to the reverend for guidance. But he, too, appeared
shaken by the sight of his sister, and when Miss Goodacre put a letter
in the hands of the constable, the reverend grew pale. As well he
might, for the letter provided evidence that Mrs. Shanholtzer had
spoken truth and moreover offered to take Constable Sayle and any
other interested parties to the reverend's new retreat, where his second mistress, the supposed victim of the storm, would be discovered.*

*Thus it was that Goodacre found himself in short order receiving
the very punishment he had called down upon Mr. Offut. Constable
Sayle—assisted, one hopes, by the outraged Mrs. Shanholtzer—
clapped Goodacre behind bars in the Macedonia jail, where he lan-
guished, with no recorded repentance, for two weeks, before he was
transported to Richmond to stand before the Court of Virginia the
following spring.*

*A grateful Jervis Offut quickly married Miss Goodacre, and the
pair lived to a ripe old age. Their later lives were, alas, touched by
tragedy: Their only son died at the age of fourteen from the bite of a
copperhead, which Mrs. Offut insisted was an incarnation of her
brother.*

*Word of the reverend's infamy spread like wildfire through the re-
gion. Churches of various denominations saw clearly that Macedonia was a fertile ground for spiritual sowing, and within weeks,
Methodist circuit preachers, Congregationalists, Presbyterians, and
legitimate Baptists descended through the mountain passes to fill
the religious void.*

Miss Betts glanced over the rim of the paper at Layla, who
sat at a table, leafing through a collection of clippings on the

American Everlasting Hosiery Company. Miss Betts pushed back her chair and clicked across the library floor.

"Well?" asked Layla, at once eager and anxious.

Miss Betts smiled. "Miss Beck, I don't believe I've ever read a more interesting account of Goodacre's ministry." Layla blushed with pleasure. "But," Miss Betts continued, her mouth wary, "your claims are . . . provocative. There is another side of the story, of course, and many Macedonians will object to finding that this is to be the official version."

Layla frowned. "What other side of the story?"

"Well." Miss Betts drew out a chair and sat, smoothing her neat skirt. "There are some who believe that Goodacre was, well—wronged."

"Wronged?" repeated Layla.

"That Mrs. Shanholtzer was indeed a lunatic and her accusations were false." Miss Betts laid her hands on the table. "And that Reverend Goodacre was innocent of wrongdoing."

"But he was arrested!" exclaimed Layla.

Miss Betts gave Layla a sharp look. "Surely you don't believe that imprisonment is identical to guilt?"

"No," admitted Layla. "But Mrs. Shanholtzer—she did leave her home and come back with a baby."

"No doubt about that."

"And the other girl did disappear."

"There is no record that she ever reappeared."

"But—his own sister said he did it," Layla protested.

"Yes. But there could be reasons a sister would say such a thing even if it were untrue. She did receive a proposal of marriage from the man she defended."

"Jottie said that everyone in Macedonia knows about Goodacre's philandering."

Miss Betts nodded. "True. And most of them enjoy the story a great deal. However, the Baptists—understandably—deny it, and there are a number of others who dismiss the tale as lurid sensationalism."

Who? Who dismisses it? Layla thought resentfully. Dullards. People who want everything to be as bland and boring as possible. People like Parker Davies. She looked up at the shaft of dusty sunlight that flowed from the windows above her and thought, I don't care. I'm not going to change it. If I change it, it'll be ruined. It'll be dull, and no one wants a dull history. He probably did it, too, the goat. And nobody knows for sure. Why shouldn't I choose the version I think is the most interesting? "I think," she said to Miss Betts, "that if history were defined as only those stories that could be absolutely verified, we'd have no history at all."

"My." Miss Betts slid back in her chair, seemingly nonplussed by this resistance to judiciousness. After a moment, she said, "Perhaps you are right. But—be prepared." Her eyes strayed to the yellowing scraps of newspaper on the table. "Are you finding what you need here?"

"I don't really need anything special, I guess," said Layla. "I've got an interview with Mr. Shank next Thursday, so I'm studying up on American Everlasting." She pointed to a clipping. "I had no idea that Mr. Romeyn was the first president of the company."

"There have been two presidents. Mr. Shank is the second."

"So he must have known Mr. Romeyn."

"Oh, of course. Mr. Shank was a sort of protégé of Mr. Romeyn's."

"I see. I wonder why Jottie didn't say she knew him? I had her go over my list, you see—the list of interviews I'm to do—for introductions, you know? She must know Mr. Shank, but she didn't mark him."

Miss Betts inhaled and her glasses slipped down her nose. "An introduction from Jottie would not be likely to endear you to Mr. Shank."

"Whyever not?" Layla asked, surprised.

"Mr. Romeyn was . . . much beloved. Mr. Shank tends to suffer from comparisons."

Layla chuckled. "Very diplomatic, Miss Betts." She paused. "Tell me about Mr. Romeyn."

"He was a very kind man. Very benevolent," Miss Betts said. "Generous to a fault. His employees worshipped him."

Layla smiled politely. Miss Betts's description was insipid: A benevolent man was anything and nothing. An empty coat. Not like Jottie's Goodacre. Not like the Joe Dolly that Felix had summoned up. She tried again. "Do you remember him yourself?"

"Me?" said Miss Betts, startled out of grammar.

"Yes. Did you know him?"

"Well. Yes. I suppose I did." Miss Betts pushed her glasses up her nose. "My father—Anderson Betts was his name—had the greatest admiration for Mr. Romeyn. My father ran a funeral parlor, and Mr. Romeyn on several occasions paid the funeral expenses for workers whose families couldn't afford them. It was very generous of him." Miss Betts gazed into the dusty sunlight. "And, too, I remember a time he came to our home—above the parlor. He gave me a penny for candy." She smiled with long-ago pleasure. "I treasured it for weeks before I spent it. Because Mr. Romeyn had given it to me."

"He came for a worker's funeral?" Layla asked. No wonder they liked him.

Miss Betts's smile faded. "No. No. He came because one night Felix and—and a friend of his slipped into the funeral parlor, climbed into two satin-lined coffins, and fell asleep. My mother found them the next morning and was quite . . . undone by the sight." Layla laughed, and, after a moment, Miss Betts managed a weak smile. "I suppose it is funny. My mother did not find any humor in it."

"I can see why she wouldn't," giggled Layla. "Did she think they were dead?"

"Yes," said Miss Betts. She looked down at the papers in her hand. "And there in a nutshell is the problem of history, Miss Beck. Two boys sleeping in coffins. To you—and to Felix, I suppose—it's an entertaining episode. To my mother, it was an outrage. To me, it was held up as an example of youthful depravity, and I considered it a very grave offense. I have never, until this moment, found it amusing. Which proves my point with regard to Goodacre. All of us see a story according to our own lights. None of us is capable of objectivity. You must beware your sources."

Layla frowned. "If none of us can be objective, then the problem is intractable, and all history is suspect."

Miss Betts regarded her carefully. "You are a very astute young woman," she said. "But consider: Perhaps it is only the claim of objectivity that is suspect. In that case, the question becomes what do you want *The History of Macedonia* to be?"

"Me?" said Layla. "Why, I have no stake in the matter. There's nothing particular I want it to be." The moment the words left her mouth, she realized they were false. She wanted *The History of Macedonia* to spurn the dull and to amuse the witty, to advance the Romeyns and to trounce the Parker Davieses, and to announce that she, Layla Beck, had perceived all that they had been blind to.

"Really?" said Miss Betts. "Then you have the advantage of us, Miss Beck, and the truth shall prevail." She tapped the papers straight and held them out.

20

Father had been gone for almost a week. Bird wrote him a letter telling him he'd better come home soon or she'd loose her flea-circus fleas in his bedroom, but we didn't know where to send it. Miss Beck's high heels tapped up and down the stairs, and her little fingers tapped out her book, with a ping at the end of each line. I took comfort from knowing that wherever Father was, he was just as far from Miss Beck as he was from us. The days slipped by, Mae and Minerva smoked and laughed and listened to the radio, and I found *Jane Eyre,* which was the best book in the world. I read it three times straight through.

I was heat-addled by the end of the third time. When I'd picked up the book that morning, I'd been in the shade, but as I closed the cover, I realized that the sun had been burning down on me for a long time. I lifted my eyes, and all I could see was a blue rectangle the size of a page.

I got up and went inside, thinking I should get into the cool. But the kitchen was hot. Not as hot as the outside, but hot. And quiet. I felt my way to the refrigerator and stuck my head inside, because Jottie wasn't there to tell me not to. The motor rumbled in my ear, and when I came out, nice and chilly, I could see again. I saw there was money underneath the sugar bowl on the kitchen table. I didn't count it—didn't touch it, even—but I knew what it meant. Father was home. That's where he always put it, there under the sugar bowl. "Father's back," I called to whoever might hear.

No one answered.

"Jottie?"

Nothing. Where was she, anyway?

I licked my finger and stuck it in the sugar bowl, making sure not to muss the money beneath it.

"Father?"

The whole world might have dropped away, that's how quiet it was in the kitchen. I sucked on my finger for a minute, and then I snatched a dustrag out of the cupboard and sidled up the back stairs without making any sound. Miss Beck's room was near the back of the house, next door to the one Bird and I shared. Jottie had the big room way up in the front. Father's door was closed—he could be inside, sleeping. He usually slept for a long time when he came home from business. I walked silently to Miss Beck's room and listened carefully at her door for a minute before I scratched on it. "Miss Beck," I murmured. If she answered, I was going to say I was there to dust. I'd go ahead and do it, too, if I had to. You have to make sacrifices if you want to get anywhere in life.

I swung the door open and relaxed. She wasn't there. I stepped in and shut the door behind me. I had promised God I wouldn't touch anything. I'd just look at what was lying around. If Jane Eyre had only looked around a little, she might have saved herself a lot of heartache.

I looked. She'd made her bed, but she hadn't tucked the sheet in. It hung below the bedspread, and my fingers itched to twitch it right. I turned away, so as not to succumb, and went to her dresser. She'd put out a silver brush set on the top, and there was a squirting perfume bottle in a silver holder beside it. I couldn't get my nose high enough to smell what kind it was. She'd put three photographs up there, too. One showed her family, I supposed, because she was in it. A father with a big stomach, a mother wearing a frilly dress, a man who must have been a brother, scowling, and Miss Beck herself, holding on to her curls. There was another picture of the brother, too. He was still scowling. The third frame showed a beautiful young lady—she could have been in the movies; that's how beautiful she was. She was wearing an evening dress and she looked surprised. Underneath her face was writing: "For darling Layla with love, Rose."

Miss Beck had left one of the drawers hanging open. Jottie

always said that was the sign of a sloven, but, to be fair, that dresser had sticky drawers. I didn't touch a thing, but I looked. I figured it was nightgowns I was looking at—I couldn't really tell without holding them up—because there was lace and slippery pink stuff, all tumbled together. I caught sight of a piece of satin, too, with embroidery. Suddenly I thought that maybe this was what she wore underneath, and I blushed. It was just exactly what seductresses wore underneath—lacy, satiny things. The picture of Mae and Waldon flickered through my mind, even though I didn't want it to. I turned away, but not before my stomach squeezed a little.

Miss Beck's table wasn't slovenly atall. There was a type-writer standing in the middle of neat stacks of paper, some typed on, some clean. I almost forgot my promise to God and touched the stack of fresh white onionskin, I loved it so. Just at the last second, I pulled my finger back. I turned my head side-ways to read the paper on top of the stack:

~~Mr. and Mrs. Arwell Tapscott (know Jottie)~~
~~Mr. and Mrs. John Sue~~
Mr. and Mrs. John Lansbrough
Mrs. Hartford Lacey (knows Jottie)
Mr. Tare Russell (knows Jottie?)
Dr. and Mrs. George Averill (hospital?)
Mr. and Mrs. Tyler Bowers TUESDAY, 3:00
Mr. and Mrs. Baker Spurling
Mr. and Mrs. Ralph Shank (Amer. Everlasting)
    THURSDAY, 2:00
Mr. and Mrs. Sloan Inskeep
~~Mrs. Alexander Washington~~
Mr. and Mrs. Eugene Silver

Pretty boring, I thought. But then I looked again. Someone—Miss Beck, I figured—had drawn an arrow next to Mr. Shank's name, an arrow pointing to a note: "Why no job fr Felix, Amer. E? When?" That was easy to figure out—she wondered why didn't Father have a job at the mill. Mind your own business, I sneered. And then I thought about what I was doing and I had to bite my mouth to keep from laughing out loud.

I turned to the other things on the table: ink, a red fountain pen, a few pencils, a dictionary, a notebook I was too honorable to open, and a stack of letters. She got a lot of letters. "Get thee behind me, Satan," I whispered, and he did. I only bent down and blew a tiny bit, no more than a breeze might have done. The stack of envelopes shifted, and a thick creamy one slid off and fell to the floor. On the back of it, in dark-blue printing, it said "Senator and Mrs. Grayson Beck, Hillyer Place, Washington, the District of Columbia."

I straightened up and peered at the father in Miss Beck's photograph. Could he be a senator? His stomach looked like a senator's, but he didn't seem old enough otherwise. I looked at Miss Beck's table once more and my heart flopped. There, where the stack of envelopes had fallen sideways, I could see the edge of a piece of paper peeking out from beneath, and on that paper was my father's writing. It was just three words I could see, but I could tell his straight up-and-down writing anywhere. The words were: "you're alive. F."

Oh, then temptation did come up and nearly crush me. *What* "you're alive. F."? I could think of a million things but only one that was important: "I'll love you as long as you're alive. F." Never mind that it was impossible to imagine my father writing such a silly thing; in that moment, torn to pieces as I was, I could see him doing it. No, no, no, I told myself. It's just something you made up, like thinking Miss Beck was royalty. I saw him walking away with Miss Beck on his arm. No, I said to myself, you made it up and it's not real. There's one way to find out. No there's not, I said. God will strike you down if you do. God will understand.

My hand crept out, all on its own.

I heard the screen door slam. "Anyone home?" called Jottie.

I was halfway down the stairs before I knew where I was. Jottie would save me.

✳

Felix appeared suddenly as they were eating dessert. One moment, the door was an empty square, and the next, he was leaning against the door frame, smiling at them all. Minerva, lifting a forkful of pie to her mouth, squeaked.

Jottie raised an eyebrow. "He is risen."

"Daddy!" squealed Bird. She squeezed out of her chair without bothering to push it back and threw her arms around him.

"Hey, Birdie," he said, cupping his fingers along her cheek. He smiled at Willa. "Hey, sweetheart."

"Hey—" she began, but her soft voice was drowned in Minerva's.

"I don't know why you have to *creep* up like that, Felix!"

Hooking his arm under Bird's, he pulled her along with him into the dining room. "Anything left for me?" he asked. "Or did Layla eat it all?"

She looked up, smiling, to protest, and he dropped her a wink.

"Want some pie?" Jottie asked.

"Sounds all right," he said, pulling out his accustomed chair. "Come on up here and sit in my lap," he said to Bird. "You can be my napkin."

"Don't spill pie on me," warned Bird, hoisting herself up by his belt. "This is my fourth-best dress."

"Mm," he said. "Good thing. I'd probably go blind if you were wearing your first-best." He took the plate Mae handed him. "Thanks. Any coffee in that pot?"

"How was your business trip?" asked Layla.

"Fine, fine." He glanced at Jottie. "These girls behave themselves?"

She passed him a cup. "They weren't as bad as they usually are."

"Any news?" His eyes circled the table.

Mae sighed. "Nothing much. Hot as can be, but that's not news."

There was a short silence.

"Miss Betts and I had quite a discussion about history today," offered Layla. She glanced at Jottie. "She recommends that I beware my sources."

"Oh, she does, does she?" said Jottie.

Layla nodded, her mouth full of pie. "And"—she swallowed—"I heard about a certain incident in her father's funeral parlor." She gave Felix a conspiratorial smile. "Something involving coffins."

He did not return the smile but merely lifted one eyebrow and reached around Bird to stir his coffee.

Flustered to find she had miscalibrated, Layla swerved to a new subject. "Yes, well, we were discussing your father, really. And American Everlasting. I've got an interview with Mr. Shank next Thursday, and I thought I should do some research." She looked around the table hopefully. "Miss Betts said your father was very popular. Much beloved, she said."

"Much beloved," said Felix. "Is that right?"

"He was!" Minerva said. "He was much beloved, Felix."

Felix laughed. "Depends who you're talking to, I guess."

Layla glanced at him in confusion. "Miss Betts remembered him fondly. He gave her a penny for candy once."

"Ah," said Felix.

"That's *just* the kind of thing Daddy would do," said Minerva. "He was always doing things like that."

"He sure was. Handing out pennies to the friendless night and day," said Felix.

"Miss Betts wasn't friendless," Layla said. "He just gave her a penny."

"Maybe she said she was friendless," suggested Bird, "so he'd give her a penny."

Jottie laughed. "I bet you're right," she said to Bird. "She's crafty like that, Miss Betts is. I can see her now, lurking on a street corner, waiting for Daddy to come by so she could say she was friendless and get herself a penny."

Felix glanced up from his coffee. "If she did a clog dance, he'd give her two pennies."

"Daddy couldn't resist a clog dance," Jottie said, shaking her head. "It was like strong drink to him."

"You don't see much clog dancing anymore," offered Minerva.

"It's a shame," said Felix. "Miss Betts clogged with the best of them."

"Where'd she get the clogs?" asked Willa, looking between her aunt and her father with sparkling eyes.

Felix looked pained. "I'm sorry to say it. She stole them."

Jottie grimaced. "Don't tell me. Just don't tell me anything about it."

"From a child."

"A little Dutch child?" asked Jottie. "A little lost Dutch child?"

Felix nodded. "Took 'em right off her purple feet."

Mae choked, and Jottie reached out to thump her on the back. Mae nodded, her eyes watering, and Jottie glared around the table. "Now, don't you-all go passing judgment on Miss Betts."

"Clog dancing exerts a powerful fascination," Felix murmured.

"None of us is beyond it," Jottie said sternly.

"If a lady like Miss Betts can fall, what hope is there for the rest of us?" asked Felix.

"Prayer is my armor!" cried Jottie.

Felix dropped his face into Bird's curls and laughed.

Jottie smiled. "I win."

He nodded, acknowledging her victory, and turned his eyes to Layla. "See, now, I wouldn't trust that Miss Betts as far as I could throw her."

"How could I?" Layla giggled. "Now that I know her secret vice."

No, thought Jottie, watching Layla's dazzled face, you win, Felix, as always. Tired of her brother's invincibility, tired of her own lack of it, she scraped her chair roughly away from the table and stood. I wish Sol had seen me the other day, she thought. I wish he'd come into Statler's and seen me. Then I'd know if he still cares. As the circle of eyes turned to her, she slid Willa's plate beneath her own, placed the forks on top, and made a decision. "I'll take you over to the mill on Thursday, Layla. If you like."

Felix's eyebrow rose, questioning.

Jottie looked away.

Layla pushed back her chair and began to make a replica of Jottie's neat stack. "That would be grand, Jottie. Thanks."

Felix watched the two of them for a moment and then pulled his cigarette case from his pocket and settled himself back in his chair.

Willa, too, remained at the table, watching the women move competently from the table to the kitchen. She waited them out, ignoring their slim arms reaching and worn heels tapping back and forth; she waited until there was nothing left for Layla to carry and then she waited as Layla put one foot on the bottom stair and turned back to see if Felix was looking. She waited until Layla slowly climbed the stairs, and then she waited for Felix to draw a cigarette out of his case and glance at her. She waited for the swift scratch and the waft of sulfur and the smoke coiling upward, and then she pushed back her chair and stood. "Guess I'll go out and play now," she muttered.

Felix laughed quietly. "I guess you will."

She stopped at his chair and bent swiftly to kiss his shoulder. Then she went out into the falling blue evening.

21

July 2, 1938

Layla Beck
47 Academy Street
Macedonia, West Virginia
Layla,

I ran into Denton at Fiske's last night—it was a seat-of-the-pants party in honor of Larry's latest, *Noose around the Moon* (real stinker of a title, I think, but he insisted). In between diatribes about the Non-Intervention Committee and the decline of Amalgamated Meat Cutters, Denton let loose a headline about you. He claimed that you were an *employee of the Works Progress Administration* (italics mine, of course; Denton loves only meat-packers). He didn't know anything else—or, if he did, he was too pickled to convey it—so I telephoned Lance from the party and asked him where the hell you were. He didn't want to tell me, the old protective-brother routine, but he didn't stand a chance against the Antonin bloodhounds and I got it out of him.

My god, Layla, has the Earth stopped in its gyre? When you said your dad was tired of supporting you, I figured he'd land you a cozy little sinecure with one of his bureaucratic toadies—Secretary to the Delaware Perfume Board, something along those lines. But the WPA? Is it a plot hatched by Senator McNary to kill your father? Are you a mole for Father Coughlin? What are you doing down there? Lance told me you were on the Writers' Project and said something about a history book. I said, That's preposterous, Lance. Layla doesn't know enough history to carve on the head of a peanut. He got sore and told me you were a fine writer. He might be right about that. You can write—it's *what* you write that's absurd.

I've been practically living in the office while Teutzer's in court. They've brought out every damn argument in the book, including moral turpitude and providing aid and comfort to the enemies of the state, but he's going to get off. It's free speech, and even the fascists at the D.A. can't find a way to get around that. The upshot is that I'm writing almost every issue of *Unite!* single-handed and spending most of my nights here, on the sofa. I can't remember what my apartment looks like, but perhaps that's just as well. At least the windows here open and—maybe you remember?—the sofa is accommodating.

Nonetheless, I'm due for a few days off and I want to get out of the city. I'd travel a long way to see you on relief, my luscious Layla. What say I come down to take in the sights of West Virginia, including that one? I'd like to get a firsthand look at how FERA is organizing coal-worker relief, and the Arthurdale settlement could be good for a laugh. If I get two stories out of it, Marlon may even pay expenses. Unlikely, but worth a try. Are you staying someplace where my presence would go unnoticed, or do you have an old lady in a lace collar barricading your virtue?

I've missed you. Remember those last two words I said to you? I want a retraction.

Love,
Charles

July 5, 1938

Charles Antonin
c/o *Unite!*
7 E. 14th St.
New York, New York
Charles,

Surprised to hear from you is putting it mildly. Didn't you issue an irreversible diktat of banishment at our last meeting? Or had the bourgeois fog that clouds my reason (a direct quote) got into my ears as well? Perhaps I am mistaken and you *didn't* say that our relations were founded upon decadent individualism and that I was nothing more than a whore of the upper class.

No, I remember it clearly. That is what you said. Those bourgeois fogs come and go.

How dare you write me such a letter? You, with all your cant about humanity and the elevation of mankind, are as coldhearted and inhumane as any of the fascists you claim to despise. If you really had one thought about me, as a laborer or a person, you would have been ashamed to mock my work and boast about your own. Your arrogant delusion that your motives are hidden from me is an insult to my intelligence. It's perfectly plain that you want to come here to go to bed with me, nothing else, but what I find most insulting is your assumption that the flyspeck of charm expended in your letter would be adequate to achieve that end.

It may be of some passing and, I hope, deterrent interest to you to learn that I have met a person so far your superior in manner, morals, and feeling that I can hardly believe you belong to the same species, much less the same sex. After I had been cast out—it's not too strong a phrase—by everyone I had supposed would stand by me, and I arrived here absolutely friendless and bewildered, he welcomed me, he helped me with my work (rather than ridiculing it), and he made me feel at home. All this without hidden object—he's gentlemanly and intelligent and considerate of everyone around him. In every little action, he achieves what you, with all your bombast and posturing, fail to achieve: He makes the world a better place for the people around him by showing them courtesy and kindness.

And now, to quote you once again and irrevocably, good-bye.

                                                    Layla

P.S. There are no coal mines in this part of West Virginia. Your presumption and ignorance are typical of the effete intellectual class.

                                                    July 5

Dear Ben,

If I murder a Communist, will I get acquitted for justifiable homicide?

                                                    Layla

                                                    July 5, 1938

Dearest Rose,

I'm so mad I could spit.

Charles Antonin has had the gall, the insuperable gall, to write me a letter inviting himself to Macedonia—after casting me out not two months ago on the grounds that I was a superficial, uncontrolled whore (that's the abridged version). And now comes a letter, laughing at me for working on the WPA, sneering at my ability to write history, bragging about his essential contributions to that rag *Unite!*, and then, *then,* suggesting that he come down here, provided he wouldn't be kept from my bed by an overscrupulous landlady.

I spent half an hour utterly incapacitated by fury. I just stood in the middle of my bedroom floor and shook with rage. Then I sat down and wrote a masterpiece of a reply, telling him exactly what I thought of him. I include a copy for your delectation—isn't it brilliant? I am beginning to think I have a knack for writing. Oh, I hope Charles is absolutely floored—he seems to think that all he needs to do is announce that his interest has revived and I will swoon with delight.

Unfortunately, I know where he got that impression. I blush now when I think of the way I trotted up to New York every time he whistled. You were right, Rosy, when you said he was incapable of caring for me as much as he cared for the proletariat—except substitute the word himself for the word proletariat. He likes to hear himself use such words, and he loves the idea of himself as a revolutionary, but if the revolution consisted of tedious, repetitive tasks performed before no one, he'd be a counterrevolutionary in a second. He wants attention and parties and fist-waving arguments more than he wants the classless society. It's all so painfully clear to me now. I don't know why I believed in him before. Yes, I do—I believed in him because, every few months, he condescended to favor me with his undivided attention for a few moments, and, desperate as I was, I'd pretend that those moments were a glimpse of our future. Delusion, delusion—I'm no better than a chambermaid in a Victorian novel, seduced by the rakish son's promises of respectability. I was led astray, first by Lance, who said Charles had a fine mind and was worth twenty of my usual swains, and then by Charles himself, who said I had a passionate—though latent—intellect. Could you withstand that? I couldn't. You've met Lance, so you can imagine what a heady thing his approval is. Being the sister of a genius is dreadfully thin gruel, I'll tell you. The last time Lance praised me outright was when I threatened to tell the newspapers the disgraceful wage Father paid the gardener. "Stupid," Lance said. "But brave." On the strength of those three words, I telephoned the Star and was immediately shipped off to Miss Telt for four years. So you can see how Lance liking Charles would turn my head—in fact, I expect that accounted for nearly two-thirds of his irresistible charm. The remaining third was lodged in that passionate-intellect line.

I've spent far too much time on Charles already. He doesn't deserve to occupy my mind or yours any longer. Thank you for your lovely letter, Rosy dear. I'm sorry to hear about Paris, but I think your mother is right. This Sudeten affair has everyone on edge, and no matter what Daladier says, it seems clear that France can't go on much longer pretending that Hitler doesn't exist. Get out a map and count the number of miles between Paris and the German border; there aren't many. Imagine how you—not to mention your mother—would feel if you found yourself in the middle of a war. Father's aunt Emily was caught out in Belgium in 1914 and had to come home via Shanghai with only the clothes on her back and a pair of opera glasses, her lorgnette having fallen overboard at Port Said. Father said she shook like a leaf for years afterward at the slightest mention of wurst. It was sweet of you to invite me to go on the lam with you, and for a moment I thought desperately of Montmartre, but I can't. I have a *job*. Until now I never understood what people meant when they said that. A job seemed to me something you'd want to escape. But I don't. I want to finish this book. It's true that Macedonia is lacking in cafés and brasseries, but I'm wrapped up in this odd little town and its history. I've encountered more lurid characters and strange doings here than I could possibly find in Paris, sewers included, and I'm beginning to think that I have a responsibility to bring them all to life.

Next item: Mason. I think you should listen to him. I don't think it's ridiculous to marry someone you've known since you were seven, not if you love him. Marrying someone who first saw you in a playsuit is only superficially different from marrying someone who first saw you in an evening dress. When I think of Mason, I don't think of him at seven (though I do remember Lulu's party, the one where he threw the ice cream). I think of Mason at twenty-two, when he found out you were sick. You should have seen him, Rose. You wouldn't have any doubts at all if you could have seen him that night. He didn't say one word about Louis or anything—he just wanted to know if you were going to be all right. I never told you how jealous I was, did I? When he left, I sat down and cried, because no one cared about me as much as Mason cared about you.

My Lord, look at the length of this letter! The last rays of sunlight are filtering through the leaves of the dogwood in the front yard, which means it must be nearly eight. Have I turned naturalist? No. I don't have a clock in my room, and I'm forced to rely upon trees to tell the time. When the moon rises above the maple across the street, I go to bed.

In preparation for which epoch, I herewith set my seal. Plus love.

Layla

P.S. Don't forget what I say about Mason. Unlike Paris, he's not eternal.
P.P.S. Are you, with your keen powers of detection, able to discern the identity of a certain mysterious person mentioned in the final paragraph of my letter to Charles?

July 7

Dear Layla,

If you murder a Communist, you'll probably get a Congressional Medal.

What's going on up there?

Ben

22

For weeks, I had been applying ferocity and devotion to the mystery of Father and Cooey's Red Apple, but I didn't get much of anywhere until I had a blazing flash of inspiration one afternoon in July. After I had it, I couldn't believe it had taken me so long to get it, but that's how inspiration is.

"Mrs. Bucklew wants me," I said to Jottie. I tried to look mournful, to throw her off the scent.

"She telephoned?" Jottie asked, surprised. I nodded, which was less sinful than lying out loud. "Well. All right. You go on over there and be nice to her."

I sighed heavily.

Jottie grinned at me. "My mama used to say that good works performed with a reluctant heart were an abomination to the Lord, but I never had much truck with that line of thought."

"Bye," I said sadly, and I made sure my shoulders sloped as I trudged down the hall.

Once I got out of sight, I stopped trudging and stepped briskly. Even though she was a grown-up—an old lady, even—Mrs. Bucklew was my friend. She and I had a secret, and we'd had it since I was ten years old. No one knew it, not even Jottie.

She lived at her daughter's house, Mrs. Bucklew did. It was a big, fancy house, and her daughter was fancy, too. Her name was Mrs. John Lansbrough, and people called her Mrs. John, all except for Mrs. Bucklew, who called her Wanzie. I don't think that was her real name, though, and every time she heard it, Mrs. John sucked her teeth hard. I had recently come to the conclusion that Mrs. Bucklew did it to be aggravating. That would be just like her.

When I stepped up to the porch, Mrs. John was sitting cool and straight and white in her chair, needlepointing. Inside her house, everything that could be needlepointed was needle-pointed, including little cushions with sayings on them stuffed under all the doors to keep out drafts. Not that there were any.

"Afternoon, Mrs. Lansbrough," I said, real polite. "It's hot, isn't it?"

Her needle cracked through her canvas, and then she looked up. "Did Mama call for you?"

"Yes, ma'am, she did," I lied aloud. There wasn't any way around it.

Mrs. John sighed. I think I aggravated her, too. "Well, I sup-pose you'd better go on up, then, hadn't you?"

"Yes, ma'am." I thought I might aggravate her less if I looked a little downcast, so I thought about grisly things until I was inside the cool of the house. Then I scuttled up the stairs and knocked on Mrs. Bucklew's door. "It's me," I called low. "Willa."

"Willa?" She sounded startled. I'd never before come with-out her asking for me. "Wait a titch."

I heard a couple of thumps.

"Come," she said.

She was sitting up in her chair, but she couldn't fool me. I could see the little red bumps on her face where she'd been pressed into her bedspread. "Willa. How-you?"

"I'm fine, Mrs. Bucklew. How-you?"

"You grew."

"Jottie says I'm growing like a weed."

Her old dark eyes scraped over my face. "Getting pretty."

I shook my head.

She nodded. "You are. Nothing you can do to stop it." She sat up straighter. "I used to be pretty once. If you can believe that." She pushed herself out of her chair and lurched over to her bureau to take a look. One of her legs was shorter than the other, and when she walked, it was like two half-people who had been sewed together. Two half-people who didn't like each other very much. She looked at herself in the mirror and then turned around and smiled at me. "And this leg of mine was part of it. I tell you, Willa, if you ever happen to have your leg run over by a freight train, don't you repine. The men'll line up to tote your teacup for you." She giggled. Even though she was old, she sounded young. "Now, miss, I hope you came to tell me some news." She measured off a little stretch of her finger. "I'm this far away from going crazy and running raving mad down the street in my underdrawers. She'd just love that." She nodded at her floor, but what she meant was Mrs. John.

Mrs. John didn't exactly keep her mother locked up, but she didn't take her anywhere, either, and with her short leg, Mrs. Bucklew couldn't walk far. Jottie and I saw her one day, trying to get downtown. It was a pitiful sight. She'd get up and take a dozen steps and then she'd have to stop, leaning against a wall or sitting right on the curb. She was red in the face, too, and breathless. Jottie went to get the car while I sat on the curb with her, and then we drove up Prince Street and out to the Race Street Bridge and back. Mrs. Bucklew didn't say much, but she looked and looked, while Jottie told her things about the people we saw, including some things that she'd never tell me, such as what exactly Irvin Weeks had done that got him sent to the penitentiary. When we were done, Mrs. Bucklew said it was the best time she'd had in years, but she wouldn't let Jottie bring her home. She said Mrs. John would have both their hides. She and I got out at the corner and I helped her hobble up the street. Mrs. John wouldn't pay any mind to a little girl, Mrs. Bucklew said.

Now we sat down on her bed, and I told her all my news, about the Reds coming up State 9 and Mr. Vause Hamilton burning his boot and Miss Layla Beck and her research. She nodded and nodded, her dark eyes on my face. She wanted to know what weapons Geraldine planned on fighting the Reds with, how long Mr. Hamilton's boot burned, and especially how Miss Layla Beck looked.

"She's pretty," I admitted. "She wears real stylish clothes."

"Does she have any callers yet?" asked Mrs. Bucklew. "Any beaux?"

"No," I said. Father was not Miss Beck's beau. No one would

say so. I decided it was time to come to the point. "Mrs. Buck-lew?" I said. "You want me to go see Mr. Houdyshell for you?"

She looked at me sharply, and then she heaved herself up and hobbled over to her sewing basket. I could hear coins rat-tling as she reached inside. "I only got five dollars and eighty-six cents," she said.

"Still. That's two."

She nodded. "And that's two more than none."

"Well, then." I waited. I didn't want to get her suspicious.

She held out the money. I quick bustled around the room, pulling out Mrs. Bucklew's big straw basket and some clothes from the closet. "Now, look," I said. "I'm putting everything blue on top, so I'll only need to get one spool of thread, all right? No sense in wasting money."

"What are you up to, Willa?"

I drew myself up. "I just thought I'd offer. If you don't want me to go, I won't."

That did the trick. "No, honey," she said quick. "You go. I— well, you go on."

I went, closing the door softly behind me.

This was our secret. I had to go to the five-and-dime first, so everyone could see that I'd bought blue thread for Mrs. Buck-lew. But that was just for show. After that, I went past town square and up Unity Street until I got to G. Houdyshell Tack and Saddle. It was a dirty old building, and the door almost fell to pieces in my hand when I opened it, but I knew how to go. I wove between the old pieces of bridles and dusty saddles until I got to another door, and I opened that.

"Mr. Houdyshell?" I called.

Nothing.

"Mr. Houdyshell, I'm here for Mrs. Bucklew," I said to lure him out.

"Cheese it! The cops!" cried someone behind me, and I al-most shed my skin. I couldn't even begin to imagine what Jottie'd do to me if I got put in jail. But there wasn't any police behind me. There was a man I'd never seen before, sitting on Mr. Houdyshell's stool. Next to him, Mr. Houdyshell was sunk down in a deep chair that seemed like it should be in some-one's parlor. It had little flowers all over, and in it, Mr. Houdyshell looked like grim death. He had never looked real good, but now he was awful—his face was yellow and his eyes were red and he was slumped over like he couldn't straighten out.

"Never mind him, Willa," croaked Mr. Houdyshell. "He's been sampling the wares. Thinks he's real smart."

The other man talked right over him. "What do you want, little girl?" He kind of sang it.

I hadn't figured on a stranger. I said, real prissy, "I'm running an errand for Mrs. Bucklew, if you please."

"If you please," he imitated me in a high voice. "Running an errand. What else you running, sister?"

I looked at Mr. Houdyshell, but his eyes were closed, so I said, "I don't know what it is. Just what Mr. Houdyshell always gives her. Two of them." I lied through my teeth. I knew what it was: Four Roses whiskey. Macedonia was a dry town in a dry county, which meant that the grown-ups had to drive to the ABC store in Martinsburg for their intoxicating beverages. Poor old Mrs. Bucklew couldn't even walk down the street, and Mrs. John sure wasn't driving her to the ABC, so she was obliged to seek the services of Mr. Houdyshell. And me.

The man on the stool smirked. "Innocent as a baby, ain'tcha? How much money you got?"

"I got five dollars and eighty-two cents." I'd spent four cents on thread.

He sniffed loud and wet. "Six dollar for two, sister."

"Give her two, Brennus," rasped Mr. Houdyshell, with his eyes closed.

"Thank you, Mr. Houdyshell," I said, and then I believe I smiled triumphantly at the man on the stool, because his face got real red.

"George, you're a sucker," he said.

"Two," Mr. Houdyshell moaned.

The man on the stool cleaned out his throat good before he stood up and shuffled to another splintery old door and disappeared.

"Mr. Houdyshell!" I hissed.

He nodded without opening his eyes. He could hear me.

"Mr. Houdyshell, I'm sorry you're poorly, but I have to ask

you something." I chewed at my lip, worried. He looked like he might die any minute. "Is my father a bootlegger?"

Mr. Houdyshell's eyes flew open. He blinked and shook his head, but he didn't look at me.

"Mr. Houdyshell, please," I begged.

"No. He ain't," he gasped.

"Who's your daddy, sweetheart?" crooned Brennus, coming through the door. He'd been listening. "I'll tell you. Who's your daddy?"

I hated him. "I wasn't talking to you," I said.

He set two bottles on the counter and peered at me. "Let's see if I can guess." He stretched out a finger toward my face, but I jerked away. I'd sooner let a rat crawl on me than let him touch me.

Hurriedly, I laid out Mrs. Bucklew's money. Mostly dimes and nickels and one soft dollar bill.

He paid no mind to it; he just kept looking at my face with his head cocked a little to one side. I could smell his sour sleep smell, he was that close, and I could see the yellow stain on the side of his mouth that meant he chewed tobacco, and inside me I shivered, but I couldn't break away from his pale eyes.

Finally, slowly, he said, "I'll be goddamned. She Felix Romeyn's kid?" He swung round to Mr. Houdyshell like he couldn't believe it.

"Go on, Willa," wheezed Mr. Houdyshell. "Get."

I quick lifted away the blue cloth and put the bottles into Mrs. Bucklew's basket, but Brennus was shaking his head in amazement. "Felix and Sylvia's kid. Jesus. Your mama was the most beautiful girl I ever seen. That hair," he sighed.

I'd heard that plenty. My mother had had long golden hair, and people fell all over themselves telling me how beautiful she was. Usually they finished up by staring sorrowfully at me.

"You don't favor her much," Brennus said, as if he was breaking the news to me.

"I know. I look like my father," I said proudly.

"Psssh," he sneered. "Nothing to brag about. Your daddy."

"Shut up, Brennus," Mr. Houdyshell said. He sounded stronger now. Or louder, at least.

Brennus straightened up and looked behind him at Mr. Houdyshell. Then he leaned close to me. "Listen, you give Sylvia my regards, all right? When you see her? Say Brennus Gower sends his regards, all right?" He rubbed his hands together.

"But I'm not going to see her—" I began.

"But when you do," he insisted. "You say Brennus Gower was asking after her. Okay?"

"My mother dyes her hair," I said. "It's not golden anymore. It's gray. So she dyes it."

He drew back like I'd spit on him.

"Go, Willa," Mr. Houdyshell said wearily. "You got to go."

I gathered up Mrs. Bucklew's basket. "I hope you feel better, Mr. Houdyshell," I said, zigzagging between sawhorses to the door.

As I pulled it open, Brennus Gower started to yell, "Your daddy's a bootlegger all right, girlie! And everybody in town knows it! He been running whiskey for years, and that ain't all. He's as crooked as a barrel of fishhooks, for all his high-class airs, and you can tell him I—"

I slammed the door so hard I was surprised it didn't fall off.

Mrs. John turned her smooth face in my direction as I came through her screen door. "If she wanted thread, all she had to do was ask," she said. Her needle cracked through her canvas again.

"Yes, ma'am. I'm glad to help," I said.

It was the wrong thing to say. "I *help* her," Mrs. John sniffed. "I spend every blessed minute helping her."

"I'll just take this upstairs now," I said, mealymouthed as could be.

She shrugged. "Fine."

I was proud of how slow I walked across the porch and up the stairs. "It's me," I said, tapping on Mrs. Bucklew's door.

"Thought you'd got lost," said Mrs. Bucklew, and I went in. She was sitting on her bed, waiting. "Bring them here."

I took her the basket, and she quick rustled underneath the thread and the cloth and brought out a shiny bottle of Four Roses. "Praise the Lord," she said, and snapped the paper that held the cap on. "You'll excuse me," she muttered, and tipped the bottle right up to her mouth. I watched. Those roses looked like tulips, I'd always thought. She brought the bottle down and wiped her lips. "Got to check George ain't watering the product," she explained. I nodded and she drank again. "Oh my," she sighed when she had swallowed. She peered into the dark glass. "That had better settle my hash for now. Got to make it last, don't I?" She lifted her hand and patted my cheek. "Thank you, honey. I don't know what I'd do without you."

"Is Mr. Houdyshell a criminal?" I blurted.

"George?" She looked up, surprised. "No. He just sells a little liquor under the table."

"But it's illegal," I pressed. "Won't he get in trouble if he gets caught?"

She pursed her lips. "I guess he might. Everybody knows he's doing it, though, honey. Everybody in town knows it already, including the police chief."

I nodded, feeling better. "So where does Mr. Houdyshell get it? Does he go to the ABC? Or does he," I made my voice casual, "get it at Cooey's?"

She frowned. "Cooey's Red Apple? What do you know about that?"

"I know it's a bootlegger's," I said airily.

"You do, do you?"

"Why do you go to Mr. Houdyshell?" I asked. "Whyn't you send me to Cooey's?"

Her fingers closed over my arm. "You listen, Willa. Cooey's is no place for you. You hear me? You just keep out of there."

I swallowed. Mrs. Bucklew had never seemed to think twice about sending me to Mr. Houdyshell's, but there was something about Cooey's that spooked her. And that spooked me. "Why is it different, what Mr. Houdyshell does and what they do at Cooey's?" I asked, kind of nervous.

"Cooey's is for—well, it's just different, that's all." She looked at me. Her eyes were bloodshot already. "You stay out of there, you hear?"

I nodded. I didn't want to go there, anyway. "Are they criminals? In Cooey's?" I thought of the man in the white hat.

She folded her lips tight and unscrewed the cap again. "No," she said, and took a gulp. Then she winked at me over the top of her bottle. "Glass houses," she said, and giggled.

*   *   *

I walked home slowly, thinking it out. Mr. Houdyshell said my father wasn't a bootlegger. Brennus Gower said he was. I liked Mr. Houdyshell. He'd always been nice to me. I'd never seen Brennus Gower before, and I hoped I'd never see him again. He'd been mad at me. Why did I believe him and not Mr. Houdyshell? Because I'd seen Father come out of Cooey's Red Apple with my own eyes. Because Father's special case was locked. Because Mr. Houdyshell hadn't been able to look at me, and Brennus Gower had.

I stopped walking and practiced thinking it: My father is a bootlegger. Oh, my father? He runs whiskey. He runs whiskey out of Cooey's Red Apple. I remembered Mrs. Bucklew's face and felt nervous again. He probably didn't spend much time there, at Cooey's. Maybe it was just the once. It was jumping to conclusions to think he worked for whoever was inside there. Maybe they wanted him to but he wouldn't. I started walking again.

Was he a criminal? I made my mouth shape the words: My father is a criminal. Then I tried to say it out loud, but I couldn't, not even in a whisper. He didn't seem like one, anyway. The only criminals I knew were the ones in movies, who talked without moving their mouths and fired guns out of car windows. Father wasn't like that. I thought of how he stroked my hair sometimes and how he laughed so low and soft. He wasn't bad, no matter what. "Criminal" was the wrong word. He was more like an outlaw. Like the Three Musketeers and Robin Hood. Suddenly it occurred to me that some people would say that I was an outlaw, too. After all, I was Mrs. Bucklew's bootlegger, in a way. Runs in the family, I thought, and felt better. We were practically an outlaw band, Father and me, even if Father didn't know it. Maybe someday we would go into the bootlegging business together. He'd have to tell me all his secrets then. Right now I just knew the one, but I'd take good care of it. His secret was safe with me.

23

Layla looked sideways at Jottie. Was she wearing lipstick? She was certainly more dressed up than usual. To go to a mill? Well, Layla thought, perhaps it does count as an outing, in a town like this. Again, a sideways look. Really quite attractive, with those enormous dark eyes. Attractive for a middle-aged woman, anyway.

A shadow fell over them as they turned on to East Main Street. It was the mill. Its vast expanse of red brick stretched out for the length of two city blocks and up, too, into the hot-metal shimmer of the sky. They passed a wide yard boiling with trucks and approached the only vaguely ornamental portion of the edifice—a wide stairway leading to a pair of shiny wooden doors.

Jottie hesitated at the foot of the stairs. "It's been a long time since I've been here," she said apologetically to Layla. "Kind of gives me the willies."

Layla nodded, her eyes on a sign above the door: American Everlasting Hosiery Company, Est. 1900 The Socks That Keep America on Its Feet.

"The socks that keep America on its feet," Jottie repeated. "Sounds like something that came to Ralph in a dream."

"Better than the socks that bring America to its knees," said Layla.

"You're right there," agreed Jottie. She took a deep breath. "I'll just walk you in."

They stepped through the door into a cavernous space with the proportions—though little of the furniture—of a lobby. Around them, the heavy throb of machinery welled from a hundred invisible sources. "Hello?" called Jottie, approaching an empty desk. "Anyone home?" Her voice was lost in the din.

"Is there a bell?" yelled Layla.

Jottie shook her head. For a minute they stood, waiting for something to happen. Nothing did.

"Honestly," Jottie said at last. "This place has gone to hell in a handbasket. Come on!" She whirled around and strode confidently to a corner where, Layla now saw, a hallway led off the lobby. Clearly in familiar territory, Jottie breezed past several glass-paned doors and pushed open a metal one. Inside was a broad staircase of shining wood. "President's office is on the second floor," Jottie said over her shoulder.

After the lobby, the second floor seemed hushed and serene. Layla followed Jottie along a bank of windows until they reached a sober paneled door, unmarked and considerably more dignified than those flanking it. Jottie looked at it for a moment, snorted, and pushed it open.

"Good afternoon—why, Jottie!" From behind a desk strewn with papers, a woman stood up, smiling broadly. "Jottie Romeyn! I haven't seen you in *years*."

Jottie held out her hands. "Mrs. Tay!"

"Call me Margaret, honey. You're all grown up now." They clasped hands.

"And Daddy isn't here to give me the dickens for it," laughed Jottie.

"Puh. Wish he was," muttered Mrs. Tay. "How you been keeping, Jottie? You're looking fine."

"Can't complain," said Jottie. "And you? How's Quincy?"

"Oh Lord, Jottie, didn't you hear? He went off to Florida, thinking he'd find some work down there, which I told him he wouldn't, and very first thing, he meets some trashy girl in the burley-cue." Mrs. Tay rolled her eyes suggestively. "Next thing I know, he's calling me collect to tell me he's gone and married her! I swear, Jottie, I don't know where that boy was when they were passing out the brains!"

"Well," said Jottie, attempting to keep afloat under this deluge. "Isn't that something?"

"Who's this?" said Mrs. Tay, pointing her chin at Layla.

Chagrined to find her stature so thoroughly dwarfed by Jottie's, Layla said loftily, "I am Layla Beck. I've an appointment with Mr. Shank at two o'clock."

Mrs. Tay resumed secretarial coolness. "I'll let Mr. Shank know." She stood and opened a door behind her. "Mr. Shank, Miss Beck is here."

"Miss Who?"

Jottie and Layla exchanged glances.

"Miss Beck from . . . well—" There was a pause, and Mrs. Tay stuck her head around the edge of the door.

"She's writing *The History of Macedonia,*" called Jottie. "Don't you want to be in it, Ralph?"

"Jottie? Is that you?" Sol pushed out of Shank's office, past Mrs. Tay, and stood before her.

It had happened. "Sol." She lifted her chin and smiled at him. It was much easier than she had expected.

He looked at her in silence, the usual anxious question on his face. His unease steadied her, allowed her to captain the craft. "I was just showing Miss Beck here the way," she explained. "She's interviewing Ralph. For her book. *The History of Macedonia.* The sesquicentennial."

Layla watched curiously as Sol nodded without removing his gaze from Jottie's face. She certainly is the apple of every eye at this mill, thought Layla. She's like the visiting countess. It was intriguing. It suggested a childhood of privilege similar to her own. Layla pictured the worn kitchen on Academy Street, Jottie's endless round of housework. What had happened?

"Miss Beck," called Mrs. Tay. "Mr. Shank will see you now."

"Thank you," said Layla. She touched Jottie's shoulder. "Thanks, Jottie. I'll see you at supper."

"Yes, indeed," said Jottie, a little breathlessly. "See you then." The door closed behind Layla, and with Sol still disconcertingly silent, Jottie turned to Mrs. Tay. "Well, Margaret, I guess I'd better let you get back to your business. I hope I see you again real soon. . . ." She took a preliminary step toward the door.

This seemed to jolt Sol into action. "I'd better show you the way out, Jottie," he said. "Otherwise you'll probably get lost."

Suddenly he was smiling. "Don't want you to get lost! Can't have that, can we, Margaret?"

Mrs. Tay smiled indulgently. "Sure can't, Sol."

He opened the door with a flourish. "You just come with me, Jottie. We'll have you out of here in no time. I know a secret way." He whisked her out into the hallway. "Yessir." He seemed to be talking to himself. "I know a secret, secret way." He walked rapidly down the hall, half a step ahead of her, and then swung sharply to the right and proceeded down another corridor.

"Where on earth are you taking me, Sol?" Jottie panted, nearly running to keep up with him.

"Downstairs!" he said gaily, swinging around a corner. "Here we are!" He yanked on a nearby door. "Come along."

It was a stairwell, a different one than she had taken with Layla. It was dingier and narrower and it smelled of dust. The pounding of the machines grew louder. Sol stopped on the landing and turned toward her, his face glowing. "I can't believe you're here, Jottie. I'm awful glad to see you."

She knew he was. His gladness frightened her. "Me too," she said, and it sounded spare. Spare and mean. She pushed Felix away and said boldly, "I've missed us being friends."

His eyes seemed to widen with his smile. "You have? I thought you—well, I thought I was public enemy number one."

She shook her head. "No. That's not what I think."

He dipped his head to look into her eyes. "So, all this time, you've just been toeing the line? Felix's line?"

Suddenly a sea of weariness lapped at her. Maybe she didn't want this, after all. "Oh, Sol. Don't let's begin on all that." She put her hand to her head. "Let's pretend we just met. Let's pretend we met a week ago."

"A week ago?" His forehead wrinkled. "Doesn't give me much to go on, a week."

"Sure it does, Sol. Why—you could show me this fine mill you work in. I hear you make socks."

"Socks?" he repeated, frowning, and impatience bloomed up her spine. But then he understood. "How'd you like a tour of the American Everlasting Hosiery Company, Jottie? As my distinguished guest."

"That would be grand," she said.

✳

He was actually chomping on a cigar, Layla noted, just like a cartoon magnate. She suppressed a smile and moved on to her next question. "When I was preparing for our interview, I noticed that American Everlasting employed over nine hundred and fifty people in 1928. What is the current number of workers you have here?"

"I've built the company up plenty since then," he replied irritably. "I thought you wanted to know history. I wrote out some notes—"

Layla assumed an affronted expression. "I'd like to ask you some questions first. Mr. Davies particularly asked me to give an account of the state of local industry."

"Parker doesn't want you bothering me with frivolous questions, miss. Let's just say that American Everlasting is the leading industry in Macedonia. Hell, you can say it's the only industry in Macedonia if you want to. Pretty near true."

"There's Leland Brickworks," she challenged. "United Lime and Stone. The Equality Mill. Spilman's Nail and Wire Foundry."

"Jew business," he observed.

She raised her eyebrows.

"Well, it is. And Equality's a small operation. Doubt he has more than two hundred guys. Nothing like this." He waved his cigar at the floor, indicating all below him.

"Why, then, we've come right back to my original question: How many people do you employ here at American Everlasting?"

He looked at her coldly. She could see that he thought well of himself; his thinning hair was carefully combed, his nails were trimmed to scrupulous evenness, and his tie sported a lavish Windsor knot. She straightened in her chair and gave him a dazzling smile. After a moment, he smiled reluctantly in return.

"You're a persistent gal, aren't you? One thousand and sixty. Give or take."

She noted it on her stenographer's pad. "I understand from an article in the *Sun* that Interwoven Mills made an offer to buy American Everlasting several years ago. Do you have any plans to sell the company?"

He scowled. "I don't care to answer that question, miss. If I want to sell the company, I'll take the matter to the board, not to you."

Mentally, she sneered. You think I'm scared of you, Mr. Ralph Shank? You never met my father. "It certainly would be a blow to Macedonia if the company were removed to Martinsburg."

"It's not going to happen," he said. "They don't have the capital anymore." He showed his teeth in a smile. "And I take the interests of my employees to heart, of course. They're like part of my own family. I will never let them down."

"And yet there's no union here, is there?"

He flushed. "I treat them right, and they don't have to pay a union to tell them so."

"But weren't a number of men recently let go?" she asked. "I would think that would give rise to—"

"You some sort of Socialist?" he broke in roughly.

"Pardon?"

He eyed her suspiciously. "There's no need for a union at American Everlasting," he said. "And that's all I have to say about it."

She dropped her eyes to her paper. "Have you changed the operations of the company much since you became president?"

He gave a short laugh. "Yeah, we make a profit now."

"It didn't before?"

He shrugged. "Sometimes yes, sometimes no. St. Clair was—well, he wasn't a modern businessman, let's put it that way."

"St. Clair?"

"Romeyn."

Wickedly, she said, "I understand he was much beloved. Mr. Romeyn."

Mr. Shank crossed his legs. "Much beloved. Sure. But what they really love is having enough money to put food on the table, right? That's what I give them, and they respect me for it. You can't say the same about St. Clair. He ran this place like Santa Claus. Psht." He gestured disparagingly with his cigar. "In the long run, people don't care about anything but putting food on the table. All that other stuff fades like—like an old photograph. Sure, you look at it every once in a while and you think of the good old days, but after a couple of years you can't even remember who the hell it's a picture of." He smiled, luxuriating in his metaphor. "St. Clair's gone, and everyone thinks, Ah, those were good times—but did he have a Depression on? No, and he'd have run the place into the ground by 1933 if he had. You mark me, miss. He would have. People just don't like to think about that. They say I'm a hard man. Let 'em. They'll thank me later, when American Everlasting is still around in 1950. Then they'll thank me."

Layla smiled, hoping he would continue, but he didn't. "Well. Mr. Shank, can you tell me any other changes that have occurred during your tenure here?"

He nodded decisively and reached for a closely written sheet of paper that lay on his desk. Setting it in his lap, he began to read: "When I came to American Everlasting in the year 1922, it was in the humble position of . . ."

Let the history commence, she thought, her pencil recording his words almost before he said them.

✳

Jottie felt shrunken, engulfed in the giant noise of the looms. Nothing could be heard over their monstrous rhythmic gnashing. Next to her, Sol smiled and waved his hands toward one gyrating contraption that seemed to have a particular significance she couldn't discern. Maybe it was new. Her father had always announced the arrival of a new loom as if it were a new baby, until it became a family joke and he stopped. She noticed a few of the men looking at her curiously—did they maybe think she was Sol's girl? Puh, she reproved herself; they're thinking, Who's that old lady? She stood up straight and smoothed her skirt, glad that it was a nice one. Her mother had gone to the mill sometimes. At Christmas, of course, and to have lunch with her father every once in a while. It was something a married lady did, visiting her husband's place of business. She started a little, noticing the precipitous turn of her thoughts.

Sol touched her elbow and led her into a room lined with sample cards. "Reinforced toes," he commented. "That's our biggest line. 'Twice as durable.'" He leaned close. "Tell you a secret." She looked up, waiting. "I like the plain kind better. Don't tell Shank." They looked at the advertising office, the box room, the docks, and the thread warehouse. They sidled past the accountancy office—"They'll talk your ear off in there," Sol said—and then they came to a large room containing many tables but only three men, clustered in a tight knot of conversation. At Sol's entrance, they turned to face him.

"Hi, fellas," Sol said. "You looking for Mr. Dailey?"

"Hey, Sol," said one of them, a shoulderless man with deep creases in his face. "Yeah, we couldn't find him nowhere. Order here's all bunked up." He held out a crumpled pink paper. "Dunno what he means."

Jottie gazed politely into space while Sol scrutinized the paper. "It says purple," he said after a moment. "That can't be right."

A second man scratched his neck. "That's what we thought." His faded eyes rested on Jottie. "Say, you're Mr. Romeyn's daughter, ain'tcha?" He smiled. "That's nice. Nice to see you here, ma'am."

"Thank you," she said, warmed.

The shoulderless man nudged the third man, who stared first at Jottie and then at Sol. "You sister to Emmett, miss?" he asked finally.

"Yes, that's right," she said. "Are you a friend of his?"

"Yeah. Charlie Timbrook's the name." He nodded thoughtfully. "He's a real sharp one, Emmett. He's got lots of interesting ideas."

Sol's head jerked up, and he gave Charlie Timbrook a penetrating look but said merely, "Wish I could say the same for Dailey." The three men chuckled. "Okay, can you fellows get started on the Kenneshaw now? I'll find Dailey and shake it out of him later this afternoon."

"A-yup, will do," said the shoulderless man. "Thanks, Sol."

Jottie nodded good-bye, and Sol swept her away, through yet another corridor to the dye shop. But that was the end; the dye shop led to the lobby, with its still-empty desk.

"Is there someone supposed to sit there?" Jottie asked.

Sol frowned. "I don't know."

Jottie turned to him, holding out her hand. "Well, Sol, thanks for touring me—"

"Jottie," he said quickly, "can't you and I ever—say hello?"

She smiled. "Hello."

"No," he said impatiently. "That's not what I mean. Can't we see each other? And don't say we're seeing each other right now."

His frustration made him seem childish. Feeling adult, she said, "What kind of seeing do you mean?"

"Could we—well, we could go to the pictures, for instance."

She wanted to laugh: The pictures, a harmless amusement. And she wanted to flee: The pictures? In public? Where everyone would see? What was he thinking? He's irreproachable, she reminded herself. He doesn't have any idea what it's like not to be. She took a breath. "Yes. We could."

"Really? I can call you?" he asked, his words stumbling in eagerness.

Now that was hard. Not harmless at all. She closed her eyes for a second. "What if I call you? I could telephone you, couldn't I?"

"But will you?" he said, shaking his head, knowing the answer already.

They had reached it so quickly: the moment she would have to turn back. This very second must bring the idea to an end, the point at which her freshly painted stairs, her carefree Willa, her simple platter of cookies, all of it would be forced to return to the primordial dust of her imagination. It was a daydream, nothing more, and she had been a fool to carry it so far. Because Sol had told a terrible lie about Felix, and Felix would never forgive him. And what she owed Felix could only be paid in loyalty.

She glanced up at Sol and saw him readying himself for disappointment; his eyes were steady but guarded. There wasn't any sweet twenty-year-old, she saw. He was lonely. Pity pressed on her heart: At least she wasn't lonely, not most of the time. Felix would never have to know. She had every right. It was just the picture show. It was just friendly. Before she knew what she was going to say, she was saying it. "Listen, Sol. How about I meet you at Sprague's Palladium next Tuesday for the eight o'clock show? I think it's supposed to be Rosalind Russell in something or other."

For a moment, he was speechless with surprise. And then, quickly, "Yes! Sprague's Palladium next Tuesday. Eight. Yes, I'll meet you there." He seized her hand and gazed at her delightedly.

He was too glad; he shouldn't be so glad. She said, "If it turns out to be that Andy Hardy, we'll have to go buy some whiskey off George Houdyshell and get drunk before the show."

He laughed immoderately. "Oh, Jottie, I've missed you! You promise you'll be there?"

"Yes," she said, and meant it.

"Even if Felix finds out?"

"I can go where I please," she said. "It's a free country." It wasn't. If Felix found out, she'd pay.

"Good," he said, squeezing her hand. "That's good."

24

"A vigorous Mr. Shank avers, 'American Everlasting will be here next year and the year after that. Why, I fully expect that we'll be going strong in 1950!' The second president in the history of the company, he is known for—"

"Your Co-Cola."

Layla nodded to the doughy girl on the other side of the counter—"Thanks"—and returned, frowning, to her pad. Vigorous. Honestly. She penciled "obnoxious" lightly over "vigorous."

"Miss Beck?"

She looked up. "Mr. Romeyn! Please! Sit down!"

"But you're working." Emmett glanced at the papers in front of her.

"I'm stuck. You'll be doing me a favor."

He eased on to the stool next to hers. "What are you stuck on?"

She grimaced. "The charming Mr. Shank."

He grinned. "Dazzled you with his charisma, huh?"

"I had been warned," she said. "I wasn't surprised."

The waitress reappeared. "Something for you, Emmett?" she asked eagerly.

"I'll have the same as Miss Beck here, thanks, Mab."

Layla's eyes followed her as she trundled away. "Her name is Mab?" she asked under her breath.

Emmett nodded, permitting himself a small sideways smile. "So. You're having a hard time capturing Ralph on paper."

"Oh, I can capture him on paper, all right. . . ." She tilted her pad so he could read what she'd written, and he laughed. "What I don't understand is how he gets away with no union."

He glanced at her sharply. "You going to put that in your book?"

She shook her head. "I don't think it's exactly what the town council had in mind. It's just—I don't understand. They're textile workers, aren't they?"

"Shank makes them sign—" Emmett broke off as Mab slid a spoon and a brimming glass his way.

"I put some peanuts in for you."

"Oh, that's real nice of you, Mab. Thanks."

"Now, drink it all, Emmett. You're looking mighty thin."

He nodded heartily. "I sure will."

She gazed at him with a satisfied air and then turned back to the kitchen.

Layla's eyes followed her. "Must be nice to have people fuss over you like that."

"Trade you," Emmett said instantly.

She snickered. "All right, I guess it could get a little close sometimes. But still."

"No one fusses over you?" he asked, carefully making wet 8's on the counter with the bottom of his glass.

"Not now," she said. "Not anymore. Shank makes them sign what?"

He watched her as he explained, absorbing her understanding, her indignation. "But that's ridiculous!" she exclaimed. "That's completely ridiculous!"

He raised one eyebrow. "There are plenty of people who think like you, and you'd be surprised who they are. But there's plenty more who need a job too bad to argue."

She sat up very straight. "Maybe I will put something in my book. Just a little description of the hiring policies at American Everlasting."

He smiled. "Would you? Brave girl."

She gave him a troubled look. "That's funny. The last time someone called me brave, I got in a big mess."

"What did you do?"

"Nothing, really." She bounced her pencil against the counter, thinking. "To tell the truth, it was a lot like this. Only not so important."

He frowned with concern. "Be careful, Miss Beck. Don't go losing your job over this."

She smiled at him. "Good. I got someone to fuss over me."

After the sweltering walk home, Layla dropped her handbag and notepad on the bench below the stairs and went straight to the kitchen. She leaned against the sink, relishing the almost-coolness of the tiles through her thin dress, and cupped her hand under the spigot. She bent and greedily lapped at the water in her hands, sighing with relief as it touched her lips, her tongue, her throat. She splashed her face with water and tipped her head back, letting the drops run where they would. "My God, it's hot," she whispered, running her wet fingers through her hair.

The cellar door banged open, and Felix strode into the kitchen with an apple in his hand. He stopped, and she saw his eyes widen at the sight of her. It was the first time she had ever seen him surprised, the first time she had ever had the advantage of him, and she felt a sudden tingle of power. She smiled at him, shaking her wet hair back, flirting. "I'm just getting a drink of water," she laughed.

He crossed the space between them in some unimaginable fraction of a second and kissed her. His mouth tasted of apple, and his hand was warm against her cheek. He broke away slowly and smiled, and then, to her astonishment, he bent his head and she felt his tongue in the hollow of her neck, where the drops of water had pooled. "I'm thirsty, too," he murmured against her skin, and the light movements of his lips made her giddy.

She was panting, she could hear it, and she wanted more and more of him. When he straightened again, she put her arms up around his neck, and he bent her back easily and opened her mouth with his.

The porch door slammed, and they heard Willa's voice: "—needlepointing the whole time, like that Madame Defarge."

Felix stiffened. He dropped his forehead to Layla's shoulder and rested it there for a moment. "Goddamn it to hell," he said under his breath.

"Felix," she whispered, and, briefly, his fingers curved around her hips and pulled her hard against him.

"Awful small drink of water," he murmured, and stepped away from her.

"At least knitting is useful," Jottie's voice came closer. "Needlepoint never did anyone any—oh." She stopped in the kitchen doorway, her eyes darting from Felix to Layla and back again. "Willa," she called quickly, without turning, "run get my purse. I left it on the porch."

"What? You did?" Willa's voice moved back down the hall.

It's not as if there's anything wrong about it, thought Layla defensively. She glanced at Felix for reassurance and found his eyes on Jottie, his expression unreadable. He's divorced, isn't he? Just because she's an old maid doesn't mean that I can't kiss someone if I want to.

"You're back," Felix said softly.

"I sure am," Jottie replied, her voice cool. "Attending to the household gods."

"Keeping the home fires burning," he agreed.

Her eyebrow shot up. "Keeping some fires burning, putting some out."

He chuckled. "You're a regular one-woman fire brigade, aren't you?"

Layla watched them, confounded. How could they joke? It wasn't—gallant, that was the word—it wasn't gallant for him to joke. He should be consumed, like she was. He should be wanting what she wanted. She blushed, thinking of what she wanted.

"Do you know," Jottie said, "I've heard about firemen going to fires for fun, on their days off, just for entertainment. Sometimes they even start fires themselves, I've heard."

Felix tilted his head. "Is that right?"

The screen door slammed. "Jottie! It's not on the porch."

"Well, what do you know? It's right here under my arm," called Jottie.

"Your aunt Jottie's losing her marbles," called Felix so Willa could hear.

"Father!" Willa clattered into the kitchen. "I didn't know you were here!" She caught sight of Layla and recoiled a little, her face falling.

"'Course I'm here, honey," he said. "Look at Jottie's purse, right under her own arm."

"Pooh," said Jottie. She dropped the purse on the counter. "You're older than I am, Felix. You'll lose your marbles before I will."

Willa looked happily between them, obviously subtracting Layla from the scene. "I'll take care of you both. When you both go crazy, I'll take you out for walks."

Jottie and Felix laughed.

"I think I'd better go write up some notes," said Layla. Holding herself very erect, she stalked out of the kitchen.

✳

In the dark wasteland of night, Jottie kicked her sheet away and rolled to her side, seeking a cool patch of pillow. There wasn't one. She lurched up to look at the clock again; it claimed, ludicrously, that only ten minutes had passed since her last look. Sol, Sol—what had she been thinking? She wasn't supposed to speak to him. She was supposed to toss her head and look away. But she hadn't. "Oh, Jottie, I've missed you!" She knew it was true. She sighed, rolling over in the other direction. For so many years, he had been part of the inner circle, had been, in fact, her guard. *Don't you dare go up on that roof! I'll tell your mama, I will!* How many times had he dragged her, raging, to safety? Dozens, and she had hated it. But now? Now safety was the pirate treasure, long ago stolen and buried and gone. And Sol had it. Sol, so eager and glad. Sol, so safe and happy that he couldn't imagine a movie would keep her awake half the night. She'd do it. She'd go. She would. She'd do it, for Willa and Bird. *Pooh,* sneered her sly enemy. *It's for yourself, as well. Been a long time since anyone asked you to a movie. Vause never did. No movie theaters back then, back when he was alive. When he was alive*—stop it, she warned herself—*we never even thought about safe. Only cowards thought about safe. We did anything and laughed about it* afterward. Even when I almost killed him, Vause laughed. Stop that. Don't go thinking about him. Stop it—

"Come on out of there, Josie!" It was Vause, standing at the barn door. *"You don't know how to drive."*

She'd been eleven; she'd been running away from home. She'd planned it all out: Vause and Felix were going to drive her to the ferry. She'd given them a dollar, even, to do it, and they'd promised. And then they'd forgotten, or pretended they had. And then they'd laughed at her.

"Go away! I hate you!" She wished she had something to throw at him. *"You better get out of my way or I'll run you down."*

"Josie—"

"Shut up! I hate you, and I hate Felix, too! I don't need you anyway!" Heaving herself to the very edge of the seat, she stomped on the pedal she thought was the right one and whacked the self-starter as hard as she could. The engine coughed.

Somewhere behind her, Felix hooted. *"You can't even get it started!"*

"I'll get it started!" she hollered. *"And then I'm going to kill you!"* Praying that she had it right, she jammed the stick shift into the reversing hole, hit the self-starter again, and lifted her shaking foot off the clutch. *"You better watch out!"*

The car shot out of the barn with shocking speed, flinging her backward on the seat so that her feet no longer touched the floor. She was glad to hear Felix's laughter turn to a grunt of surprise.

"Step on the brake, Josie!" It was Vause yelling, but he was in front of her now. Alarmingly. *"The brake!"*

Using the steering wheel for leverage, she pulled herself forward on the seat and tried to peer through the windshield, but all she could see was rain, drops and splashes flooding her vision. Where was Vause? Where was anyone? She didn't care. Angrily, she kicked at the pedals—she'd hit one of them, anyway, and drive away as fast as she could; they'd never catch her, they'd never see her again, they'd never pick on her again, they'd never—

There was a shuddering crunch, and the car thumped to a halt, tossing Jottie sideways like flotsam. What? What? She scrabbled upward and saw, directly behind her, where the back of the car normally was—the maple tree.

On the front lawn, Felix was doubled over, laughing.

Jottie erupted into tears of rage. "It's your fault!" she cried. "I hate you!" She flung herself out of the car, seized a branch from the ground, and rushed at her brother.

But he was too fast for her. Laughing, shouting, he danced away. "That sure was a short trip!" he yelled over his shoulder.

She whirled around, swiping her sleeve over the mixture of tears and raindrops on her face, seeking Vause. Sometimes she could catch Vause. There he was, by the barn.

"I hate you!" she cried, rushing at him. "I hate you, Vause Hamilton! It's all your fault, and now Daddy's going to kill me!" Raging, she flailed at him, hoping to hurt him at least a little before he ran away to laugh with Felix.

He caught the branch as it hit him and pulled it away from her. Now she was defenseless. He was so much bigger than she was; he'd probably knock her down, but she'd get him good before he got her—she raced forward and kicked him as hard as she could in the ankle.

"Ow! Josie!" His arms came around her, tight. "Stop that."

She struggled, trying to bite his shoulder. "No! Let me go! I hate you!"

"Shh," he whispered, holding her. "Shhhh."

"I'll kill you," she sobbed. "You took my money and then you wouldn't drive me to the river and it's all your fault and I'll kill you and Felix both." She tried to jerk her arms free so she could hit him, but he gripped her tighter.

"Hush, shhh," he crooned, rocking her.

He wasn't mad, she realized. He wasn't getting ready to punch her. He was just holding her arms. Even though she'd tried to run him over, he wasn't mad. It surprised her into wonder and then reflection. Why was he holding her so? Why? In spite of herself, she let him soothe her and fell quiet in the cradle of his rocking. But as her rage ebbed, her fear grew to take its place. What had she done? What madness had come upon her? The enormity rose until it towered over her. She had smashed the car. She had smashed her daddy's car that she wasn't even supposed *to touch. No one was supposed to touch it, not even Felix, though he did. She began to sob again, against Vause's shoulder.*

"Daddy's going to whip me," she wailed. "He's going to, he's going to—"

"Hushup, you," Vause murmured in her ear. "Your daddy ain't going to whip you. I'll tell him I did it. 'Cause I practically did, didn't I?" He shook her gently. "My Lord, it's no wonder you lost your temper, with me and Felix taking your dollar and making fun of you and not driving you to the ferry like we said. I'll tell him it was me that did it, and your daddy won't whip me because I'm not his boy, so he can't."

A sob came out in a burp. "But your daddy will. Won't he whip you?" she asked anxiously, lifting her tear-mottled face to look at him.

"Oh, him," scoffed Vause. "He's so skinny and feeble he can barely lift up the switch and bring it down. I don't hardly feel it."

She sniffled thoughtfully. "Vause?"

"Huh?"

"Why would you say you did it when you didn't?"

"Well." He glanced at her and burst into a grin. "I sure liked seeing you mad, Josie. I've never seen such a sight in my life."

She found herself smiling back at him in the dark. Oh my dear, she thought gently. My dearest. It was a minute or two before she pulled herself free. He didn't care, she recited to herself. He never loved me. Still, though, she felt herself rocked in the warm cradle of his arms.

The morning pall hung heavy on the kitchen. At the table, Willa, Bird, and Minerva sat, stunned and lumpen, while Jottie stepped about, stirring and pouring.

"Coffee, please, honey?" muttered Mae, dropping into a chair. Jottie poured a cup of steaming black and pushed it gently toward her.

"Families in magazines are always laughing while they eat breakfast," Bird observed. "Nobody around here laughs."

"Anybody laughs, I'll shoot 'em," muttered Mae, leaning on her hand.

There was an interval of chewing.

Willa looked up from her bowl. "Mrs. Roosevelt suggests calisthenics," she said. "To combat torpor."

"Mrs. Roosevelt wouldn't know torpor if it came up and bit her," yawned Minerva.

Bird glugged her milk and stood. "I'm going over to Berdetta Ritts's house. I bet they laugh at breakfast."

Bird passed Layla in the doorway. "Morning, Bird," Layla said cheerily. "Good morning, everyone!"

This was met with grunts. Mae flapped her hand wearily. Jottie smiled. "Morning. Coffee?"

"Grand." Layla sat down and scanned the table for the sugar bowl. "Looks like another hot one."

"They're all hot this time of year."

"Hey, everybody!" It was Emmett, outlined against the back screen.

There was a flurry of attention—Willa sat up and smiled—and Jottie bustled over to let him in. "Emmett! Honey! What're you doing here?" She reached to touch his shoulder. "What's in the poke?" He was holding a sack.

"Got some apple butter and things."

"Mmm," said Layla. "I love apple butter."

"Do you?" said Jottie, but she was looking at Emmett. "You came all this way to bring us apple butter?"

He put the sack down on the table. "And some bacon. And a couple other things. I'm meeting someone in town." He drew out a jar of apple butter and set it in front of Layla. "Here you are."

"Thank you very much." She smiled at him. "Do I have to share it?"

"No," he said. "I brought another jar. They can have that."

"Good," she said, and closed her hands around the jar. He laughed.

"Good God. What is this, old home week?" said Felix, coming into the kitchen. "What're you doing here, Emmett?"

"Just stopped by," said Emmett.

Jottie looked at Felix. "You're up early."

"Too hot to sleep. Coffee, coffee."

"It's right here," Jottie said. "Just keep walking."

"Mm." He tapped Layla on the shoulder as he passed her,

and she lifted her face to smile at him. At the stove, he fumbled with the pot, groaning mildly as he poured himself a cup.

Emmett watched him for a minute. Then he said, "I brought you a book, Miss Beck. In case you want to know more about what we were talking about yesterday." He reached into his sack and brought out a little brown book. "It's a history of the mills in the Eastern Panhandle."

She took it up. "Why, thank you, Mr. Romeyn! That's kind of you. It'll come in real handy, I'm sure." She opened the front cover and glanced over a few pages. "Looks like just exactly what I need." She smiled. "Apple butter *and* history. What more could a girl want?"

Felix turned around swiftly. "You got apple butter? You'd better give that here, miss. I like apple butter."

"You can have the other jar," she said. "This one's mine."

"Uh-uh," he said. "Don't be greedy." He reached over her shoulder and picked it up, unscrewing the lid with a pop. He scooped out a fingerful and ate it with relish. "Mmm."

"Felix, you are undoing the work of years," scolded Jottie. "You want your children to behave like pigs? Willa, ignore your father. Pretend he isn't here."

Felix laughed. "Fine. I'll leave." He went out of the kitchen with the jar in his hand.

"That's *my* apple butter," said Layla, following him. "Isn't it, Mr. Romeyn?" She looked at Emmett over her shoulder.

"It is," Emmett called, but they were gone by that time. He leaned against the counter. Mae slid down in her chair, her eyes closing.

"Well," he said, after a minute or two. "I guess I'll be on my way."

Jottie looked up quickly. "Oh, sweetheart—" she began, but he was already pushing himself off the counter.

"Bye, girls. Bye, Willa."

With one hand, Jottie pushed aside the limp curtain at the window to watch him walk, tall and straight, to his truck. The other hand curled around Willa's shoulder. Was there no one she could protect?

The little brown book lay, unwanted, on the table.

25

Layla waited patiently on Mrs. Lacey's silken love seat for the old woman to emerge from her reverie. She didn't mind. Alone in all of Macedonia, Mrs. Lacey's parlor was cool. The cool was old, like its mistress, a relic of long-ago gusts that had curled through the house and been captured and preserved by the heavy drawn curtains and never-opened windows. When Layla had stepped over the threshold into the grand, gloomy room, she had even, for one moment, shivered. But perhaps it wasn't with cold, she mused. Perhaps it was with fear.

For Mrs. Lacey was terribly old, frighteningly old, slumped with time, knotted and lined and half belonging to another world. Jottie had called her "the last of the great ladies," and Layla saw what she meant. There was something monumental about her, a dignity of endurance, of being the only one left.

Mrs. Lacey lifted her bowed head and turned her cloudy eyes on Layla. "It was covered with soldiers," she said suddenly. It wasn't, as Layla had thought at first, that Mrs. Lacey was confused; she was simply indifferent to the triviality of the present. "Covered," she muttered again.

Mrs. Lacey's maid, Sallie, standing slightly behind her chair, leaned forward. "You mean the lawn, ma'am?"

Mrs. Lacey smiled at her. "Yes, the grass. They died there, before they could get in the house."

"The hospital was inside, wasn't it, ma'am?" said Sallie.

"Yes, inside." Mrs. Lacey nodded slowly. "Mama's room was for the operations, the cutting, but everywhere else was soldiers, without an inch between them."

"Were they Confederate or Union soldiers?" asked Layla.

"I don't know," said Mrs. Lacey. "I don't remember."

"Blue or gray uniforms?"

"Bloody uniforms."

"Both, miss," said Sallie softly. "Both sides at different times."

Mrs. Lacey nodded. "All bloody."

"Yes'm."

Mrs. Lacey spoke. "Mama buried all the silver under the big branch of the hickory, and she didn't take it out no matter who was winning. She said she wouldn't trust those South Carolina boys with a toothpick." She paused. "We had a New York boy died here one day and they buried him up on the creek, where the dirt was soft. He was a long way from home." She gazed at Layla without seeing her. "Mama took off his shoes so I could have them. Then they carried him away, and I saw his poor bare feet joggle out from under the winding sheet. It was a terrible sight, his feet joggling like that. I couldn't even cry out, I just gripped his shoes tight against me." There was a long silence. "Mama got after me—why didn't I wear those shoes, they were good shoes. I told her what I'd seen and she got Clarence to dig him up. So I could see he was dead."

Another hypnotic silence fell. To break the spell, Layla ventured, "Did your mother favor one side or the other?"

Mrs. Lacey lifted her head, returning from wherever she had been. "Favor?" she said slowly. "I can't say I know. We didn't know who was winning. The boys who came here didn't know. They fought up in the mountains, in the trees, and they couldn't see three feet ahead of them. They didn't know anything." Mrs. Lacey nodded slowly to herself. "There came a boy," she sighed. "He'd got turned around and shot at his own. He'd killed his own. The poor boy was so frightened, he burned his uniform." Pause. "Sauk Reston said he could tell which side they were on by their noses. Secesh had thin noses, Sauk said, with points at the end. Yankees had soft red noses." Mrs. Lacey smiled. "After he told me, I could see it clear as day." She mused for a time. "Sauk's dead now. He died on a fence."

Layla lifted her eyes to Sallie, inquiring.

"Blood poisoning, miss," whispered Sallie. "From the barb-wire fence."

Mrs. Lacey nodded. "But that was after."

✳

Miss Beck was walking real slow along Winchester Street, just inching along, and when I caught up close behind her, I saw why. She was peering into her notebook, reading what she'd written. I'd spent practically my whole life trying to read and walk at the same time, and I knew it was a perilous endeavor. "Hi, Miss Beck!" I yelled, hoping she'd fall over and maybe break a tooth.

She didn't. She turned around and gave me a big smile. "Willa! How're you?"

She didn't seem to realize that I didn't like her. "Hot," I said.

"I've been visiting Mrs. Lacey's this afternoon, and my goodness, her parlor is just as cool as an icebox."

"I know," I said grumpily. "I've been there plenty of times."

"Have you?" she looked at me, real interested. "Why is that?"

"She was my grandmother's friend," I said. "We go to see her."

"Ah." There was a silence. I was thinking about telling her I had to go somewhere, when she spoke. "Was this grandmother Felix's mother or your mother's mother?"

Oh! I was just about speechless with surprise. Calling him Felix, to me! You didn't call grown-ups by their first names to children! And how did she dare talk about my mother, as though she knew anything at all? The sneak, trying to weasel tidbits about Father from me. The Delilah! I could have kicked her, with pleasure. But then I got a better idea.

"Well, I was talking about Grandmother Romeyn, but I'm sure Grandmother Peal knows her, too." This wasn't even a lie. She probably did know Mrs. Lacey. Everyone old knew Mrs. Lacey.

She fell on it like a duck on a June bug. "Does your, uh, Grandmother Peal live here in Macedonia?"

"She did. She lives in Grand Mile now, to be near my mother. To comfort her broken heart."

"Her broken heart?" She was practically gulping.

"Yes, my poor mother is just heartbroken. About Father." I didn't mind lying to Miss Beck atall. She deserved it. "And of course, Father is brokenhearted about her, too." I shook my head sadly.

"Really?" said Miss Beck. Her voice had gotten a little distant. Good.

"Oh yes! Even though they divorced, they're brokenhearted about each other," I said. "You see"—I leaned in, like I was confiding in her—"I think it was all a terrible misunderstanding, due to my mother being so beautiful. She was the most beautiful girl in town—everyone says so—and she had so many boyfriends, or admirers, I mean, that I think Father got jealous."

"Jealous," repeated Miss Beck. She was looking at me hard.

"Yes, but it wasn't her fault! She only ever loved Father. And he only loves her," I said. "And I expect they'll be reconciled any day now."

Miss Beck nodded. "Any day now," she said. "And you'll be happy then, won't you?"

She was taking it too calmly. "Yes!" I said, loud. "Yes, I'll be happy because Father will be so happy. If you think you've ever seen him happy, you haven't."

Miss Beck stopped still. "Listen. Willa"—she put her hand on my shoulder—"I think I know what you're trying to say—"

I snatched my shoulder away. "Good."

We walked the rest of the way home without talking. A couple of times I peeked sideways, and I was pretty sure her face was etched with despair. I'd blighted their romance and saved Father, even if I'd had to lie through my teeth to do it. That's ferocity and devotion, I thought proudly.

And just the way teachers are forever saying, my pride went before a fall. We came through our front door and there stood Father with a newspaper under his arm. "Hey, honey," he said to me. "Where've you-all been?"

"At Mrs. Lacey's," I answered. "For her book." I jerked my head at Miss Beck.

He looked up and smiled at her, and my heart shriveled some. He'd thank me in the end. I glanced, kind of stealthy, at

Miss Beck, expecting to see her turn away from him in anguish. And do you know what she did?

She shook back her curls and spoke so easy and sure I almost gasped. "Felix, she was utterly fascinating!" Hadn't she listened to a word I said? She stepped up beside Father. "Look at this." She opened her notebook, and he bent close to read over her shoulder. "Her *mother* was the surgeon. Can that possibly be true?" She lifted her big brown eyes to his, and he nodded. "The woman deserved a medal. Mrs. Lacey said she tried to manufacture her own anesthetics, from a recipe she got from some old Indian, but Mrs. Lacey said it didn't work too well, no better than whiskey, so she made that, too." She chattered on and on, not caring a bit if my mother was beautiful and my father was still in love with her. I hadn't turned her at all. Father didn't help, either. He didn't look like he was pining for anyone; he looked interested, maybe even fascinated. For a moment I was angry at him for not being tragic and heartbroken, the way he was in my lie. But that was silly. Father was fine. It was Miss Beck who was terrible and heartless.

✳

Sol was waiting outside Sprague's Palladium as Jottie approached. "It *is* Andy Hardy," he called when she was a few steps away, and he pulled a silver flask halfway out of his coat pocket.

She laughed. "George should set up a stand out here."

Smiling, he reached to take her arm, but she veered away. Didn't he have any sense? Her eyes circled the sidewalk. No one was watching. Stop that, she told herself. Stop cringing. Just a pair of old friends going to the show, that's all it looks like. That's all it is. She tried to attend. Sol was speaking: "I almost called—you know, to see if you wanted to change, but then I thought Felix might—"

"Felix is out."

"Oh." He raised his eyes to scan the street.

"Out of town," she amended.

He smiled. "Ah. Well. Do you want to see something else? We could go to the Marquee."

Warmed by his solicitude, she shook her head. "It's all right. Let's go see what old Andy Hardy is up to."

They passed through the cheap, palatial glamour of the lobby, inhaling its butter-and-dust scent. "I got us seats on the balcony," said Sol, guiding her up the stairs, laden with popcorn and jujubes.

"The high life," murmured Jottie.

"Nothing but the best for you," he said.

She blinked, unsure whether he was joking. The balcony was nearly empty, just a few old couples down in the front row and a pretty, nervous-looking girl sitting alone in the center.

They settled into their comfortable seats, Jottie carefully removing her gloves to cover her silence. She wished they were down below, in the regular rows; she could hear the boys and girls talking and squealing and the low, repressive murmur of grown-ups telling them to behave. A single dapper usher stood at the lonely door to the balcony, while the scrape and shuffle of a half dozen of his fellows welled up from below. But then again, Jottie remembered, Felix would never in a thousand years turn up in the balcony. It occurred to her that Sol had made that calculation already. This is what it is to be taken care of, she thought, and glanced at him with quick wonderment.

He caught her eye. "What?"

She shook her head. "Nothing. I'm glad we're here."

"Even though it's Andy Hardy?" he whispered, as the lights dimmed.

"Just you get that flask ready," she replied.

He smiled and patted his pocket. They sat sedately through the travelogue—"This is Pat Fitzpatrick and Fitz Fitzpatrick bidding a fond farewell to the sunny Seychelles"—and the cartoon—mice slamming cats on the head with giant hammers—and the newsreel—"Four quiet burgs make the ultimate sacrifice for modernity as the construction of the Quabbin Reservoir begins"—and the trailers for next week's picture—"Bette Davis is Dixie's Daring Enchantress, Half Angel, Half Siren, All Woman." Finally, with most of the jujubes consumed, the feature began.

"Will you, Polly?" gasped Mickey Rooney.

Ann Rutherford lowered her eyelashes demurely. "Why, of course, Andy."

"GOSH!" he yelped, leaping to his feet.

Jottie tapped Sol's arm. "Hand it over."

He gave her the flask and she took a long pull. Silently, their eyes on the screen, they passed the flask back and forth.

Andy crouched disconsolately before Judge Hardy. "Dad, I don't understand these modern girls. Polly won't let you kiss her at all, but this Cynthia, she'll let you kiss her whenever you want, all the time. She won't go swimming, she won't play tennis, she won't go for a walk, she just wants to kiss you all the time." In the center of the theater, the pretty girl and a young man who had joined her at some point began to neck passionately.

Jottie leaned over to whisper in Sol's ear, "A little tennis would fix those two right up." He gulped and then began to shake with laughter, and after a moment she joined in. Together they choked and sniffled and wiped tears from their eyes, each succeeding scene sending them into a new fit of strangled gasps. Finally, as the lights rose, they dropped their heads back against the prickly velour, exhausted. The pretty girl and her date reeled from their seats, rumpled and dazed, and the old couples staggered with their canes to the door, and still Jottie and Sol kept their seats, tears drying in streaks on their faces.

"My God, I haven't laughed that hard in twenty years," Sol said at last.

"Eighteen. Only eighteen years," she said. "I think I'm drunk."

He lifted her hand to his mouth and kissed it.

"Gosh!" Jottie said indistinctly.

He laughed and rose. "Come on. I'll take you home."

Deep within the chasm of a dream, Jottie felt a nudge. "Hey. Hey, Jottie." Felix was standing beside her bed, fully dressed. "Wake up."

"No. Go away." She hadn't slept nearly enough for it to be morning. Had she? "What time is it?"

"Don't know. I got a cut and I can't find the iodine."

"Oh for God's sake, Felix." She sat up, blinking, and saw two glints of moonlight where his eyes were. "Let me see." She flailed weakly until her hand collided with her lamp, and she switched it on. "Oh," she said, taking his hand in hers. Two of his knuckles were split and bleeding. "What happened?"

"Cat scratched me. Where's the iodine?"

"You never could hit with your left," she said. "You should know better."

"Shut up. Iodine."

Her mattress creaked as she rose. "Come on, I'll wrap it up."

In the bathroom, they squinted against the blare of light, and Felix sat on the edge of the bathtub, watching her as she rummaged in the medicine cabinet. "There's the iodine, right where it always is," she muttered, settling herself beside him. "Did you wash it?"

He shook his head.

"Wash it."

Smiling slightly, he got up and washed it.

"There." Jottie watched in loopy fascination as the yellow medicine invaded his wound. "See how it follows all the little lines?" she whispered.

"You smell like a still," he said. "You been drinking?"

"Yes." She wasn't used to having something to hide.

He looked at her with mild surprise. "Lush. Where'd you get it?"

For a second, she imagined saying, Sol gave it to me. It was almost exhilarating to think of the crater. No, it wasn't. "George Houdyshell." She'd have to get better at covering her tracks.

Felix laughed. "Patronizing the competition, huh?"

"I forgot about you."

His eyes crinkled with amusement. "No loyalty. No family feeling."

In silence, she circled gauze around his hand and tied a neat knot over his knuckles. This was why he'd wakened her, she knew. He wanted her to tend to him. "Who'd you hit?"

"A punk. A rube. Tried to skim." He made a face. "Stupid."

"You're getting kind of old to be fighting."

"You're telling me." He rubbed his forehead. "I got mad."

"I wish you wouldn't."

"What? Get mad? Me too."

"No. I wish you would do something different."

He gave her a dark glance. "Stop it."

She nodded.

Still watching her, he said, "I heard there's a strike brewing at Everlasting."

Her head jerked up. "Soon?"

He shook his head: He didn't know.

"Daddy would have been heartbroken," she said, picturing her father before a crowd of workers, his grin ebullient, his hands spread wide.

"Daddy's heart broke pretty easy," Felix said indifferently. He stood and stretched. Jottie could hear his bones crackling. There was a silence, and then, to her surprise, she felt a single finger resting on her head. "Don't drink alone, Jottie. If you want to get drunk, tell me, and we'll drink together." He left the bathroom.

Alone on the edge of the tub, she thought, That's the most he'll ever say. That's the most he'll ever take care of me. But she was touched, too. Sometimes Felix seemed like an empty house, but he wasn't really. It was just that he kept all his possessions in a locked room. And when, once every few years, the door cracked open for a moment, she felt strangely moved to see herself within.

She tilted the little brown bottle of iodine and peered into its murky depths. She would need to get more. Why would it kill you, Felix, to be known? "Safety for ALL . . . with Johnson & Johnson," she read, yawning, and thought of Sol.

26

July 15, 1938

Mr. Tare Russell
58 Fayette Street
Macedonia, West Virginia
Dear Mr. Russell,

   I hope you won't think me presumptuous in introducing myself to you. I am Layla Beck, and I have been retained by the town council of Macedonia to write a short history of the town. My landlady, Miss Romeyn, assures me that no history of Macedonia would be complete without the ornament of your considerable knowledge of the events that occurred here during the War Between the States. If, without inconvenience to you, I might come to your home and interview you on the subject, I am certain that *The History of Macedonia* would be the better for it.

Sincerely,
Layla Beck

July 16

Dearest Layla,

   Did you get those hose I sent up last week? I have the most awful feeling that you're wearing darned hose, which a lady simply can't, even if she's off in the middle of nowhere with just farmers and things around.

   It's been boiling here, just awful, but we're going up to

the shore next week, Papa's promised, though you know
the House will probably send up a bill at the last minute,
I think they do it to be mean. I hope it's cooler where you
are, dear.

To come to the point, I'm writing to you because your
brother *insists* on marrying that insignificant scrawny little
Alene, despite arguments that any rational man would
consider, like how's he going to feel when people think his
children have tapeworms. Your papa said it was my duty to
treat her like my own daughter, so I won't say another
word, but honestly, I don't know how he can sit in the same
room with her after he was almost engaged to Belinda. I
practically cry every time I think about it.

Nonetheless, I'm going to turn the other cheek and
throw the biggest engagement party anyone ever saw, after
we get back from the shore. Raymond is almost certain
that we can have the club on August 20th, and I hope we
can, because otherwise it's the house in Dover. I'll write
you the very second that I know, but you have to be there
whether you're done with that pamphlet or not. At first I
thought I'd have a tea, but then I thought it would be more
fun to have a dinner dance. And you know Alene—she
folds her hands and says she'll be content with whatever I
plan, which she'd better be. I just know she's going to wear
some dreary dress. Don't tell anyone about the dinner-
dance plan. Papa is being the most awful stick-in-the-mud
about it—he keeps talking about sleeping under railroad
bridges—but you know Papa, once he's at a dance, he's the
happiest man for miles around.

Darling, Mattie found your white bathing suit when she
was going through the trunks, and I'm sending it up. There
must be a club somewhere around there.

Love,
Mother

July 18, 1938

Dear Mother,

Yes, I received the hose, thank you very much, though your dark presentiments have no foundation, because I couldn't darn a pair of hose if I tried. I hope I won't harrow up your feelings too much if I tell you that there are days when I wear no hose at all, for fear of dissolving into a puddle of sweat and hair before noon. I spend most of my time shut up in my room, writing, with my naked legs decently hidden, and I simply don't have the moral fiber to put on a pair of hose for my own edification.

Now, about Lance and Alene, Mother, you really must cultivate a more Christian spirit. *He loves her.* I confess that she doesn't strike me much one way or the other, but she's a perfectly nice girl and she worships the ground he walks on (as if he didn't think well enough of himself already). I thought she was just a handy all-purpose girl— his usual better-than-no-one date—the first time I met her, until I overheard Lance actually ask her about the events of her day. With genuine interest! And give his opinion about her concerns! I almost fainted dead away. Anyway, it was obvious to me from that moment that he loved her, and if he loves her, so should we. That means you, too.

Of course I'll come to your dinner dance, though I detect you taking a certain pleasure in planning the most agonizing possible occasion for shy Alene. You know she'd much prefer a tea. However, if you are determined to torture her, I will come and lend her and Lance my sympathetic support. I suppose I can bring a man for myself? You and Father will like him.

I must close, as I have several years of the Civil War to commit to paper before sundown. Today I had tea with a lady who swore that Stonewall Jackson lived in her mother's root cellar for two months in the spring of 1862. She showed me the exact spot, currently housing potatoes.

Love,
Layla

P. S. Please do have Mattie send the suit. I can wear it while I type.

◆

July 18, 1938

Miss Layla Beck
47 Academy Street
Macedonia, West Virginia
Dear Miss Beck,

I trust *The History of Macedonia* is proceeding with all due speed. We have been so pressed here, with submitting final copy of the tours to the Local Advisory Committees, that I have been content to attribute your silence to diligent toil. Please inform me at once if my contentment is misplaced, most particularly if your silence indicates a deadline in danger of being missed.

In a separate matter, I have with some difficulty persuaded the Farm Security Administration to loan us one of their photographers for the illustrations in *The History of Macedonia*. The photographer in question, Miss Colleen Echols, has agreed to stop in Macedonia on her way to Washington next Monday, July 25, and take the pictures you require. As Miss Echols is, I am warned, excessively busy, I suggest that you select the subjects in advance. I anticipated your agreement to the extent that I engaged you to meet Miss Echols at noon in the town square (Macedonia doesn't possess more than one, I believe).

Yours sincerely,
Ursula Rookwood Chambers

◆

July 18, 1938

My Dear Miss Beck,

I have been twiddling my thumbs for weeks waiting for you to come and pay me a call. I thought to myself, Why would that girl give a hound like Parker Davies a hearing and not me? My heart was just about to crack in two when

I got your note. If you come over on Friday afternoon, we can have a nice visit. Tell Jottie to come along, too. I haven't seen her in a coon's age.

> Your obt. servant,
> Tare Russell

One afternoon around four, Jottie swept into the front room. "Let me see your knees."

I rolled over on my back so she could look at them. She had a hat on. "Where're you going?" I asked.

"*We're* going to Shepherdstown, more's the pity," she said. "Brush your hair, will you?"

I hopped off the couch. "How come?"

"Because it's sticking up on one side," she said, clomping down the hall.

"No!" I called. "Shepherdstown!"

She didn't answer. She was hollering for Bird from the front porch. I went to brush my hair. It was sticking up something awful.

When I got back downstairs, Jottie had Bird by the collar and was giving her what we called a spit bath. "Oh Lord, have mercy on me, a miserable sinner," Bird squalled, twisting this way and that.

When we were finally clean enough to suit her, Jottie made up a plate for Miss Beck, covered it with a napkin, and then hustled us into the car. We sped off down Academy Street, pretty near killing Grandpa Pucks's rooster in the process.

"How come we're going to Shepherdstown?" I asked again.

"Because," said Jottie, "your daddy, for inscrutable reasons of his own, left his car in Martinsburg and went off to Shepherdstown without it. And now he needs a ride from the one to the other."

There was a pause while we thought about that. "But how did he get to Shepherdstown without his car?" Bird asked.

"I don't know," said Jottie, sounding disgusted.

She didn't stay disgusted. Once she'd pulled up in front of the Court House Hotel and my father had appeared out of nowhere and slid into the front seat, we started to have fun.

He turned around to smile at Bird and me. "My, you girls are looking pretty." He looked at Jottie. "You, too."

"You'd better say that." She shook her fist at him, but she was smiling now. "Making me come all this way." She started the car.

He put his hand on the steering wheel. "Is the house on fire?"

"Not last time I was there," she answered.

"Well, then," he said, still holding the wheel, "what's your rush? See America first. Let's go out for supper."

She laughed and shook her head at him. "I thought you needed your car."

"I do. But not this minute." He glanced over his shoulder at Bird and me. We assumed our most pleading expressions. Bird even put her hand on her stomach to show how famished she was.

"Please, Jottie," I whispered.

"Hm," she said, not quite ready to say yes. "We've got perfectly good food at home."

"They've got perfectly good food at the Bavarian Restaurant, and you don't have to cook it and wash up afterward," said Father.

"The Bavarian Restaurant? Kind of fancy, isn't it?" She looked over her shoulder at Bird and me.

"I'm rich," he said. He took out his wallet and waved it at her. "I'm a tycoon."

Then she said, "Can you girls behave yourselves?" and we knew that meant yes, so we said Yes ma'am, yes ma'am and didn't bounce in the seat, to show her how perfectly behaved we could be.

The Bavarian Restaurant was dim and cool, with fans in the ceiling and white tablecloths and two different kinds of glasses at each place. Father said we could get anything we wanted, and of course Bird tried to get nothing but pie, but I ordered Roast Beef Lafontaine Style, which Father said was a famous Bavarian dish made out of old Frenchmen. I said I knew better than that, and he told Jottie that I was getting too smart and she shouldn't let me read any more books. He was joking.

We had soup first. It was white as cream and delicious, and

there were rolls with little curls of cold butter, too. My Roast
Beef Lafontaine Style was all rolled up with mushrooms on
top and it was wonderful, but I couldn't finish it. I was too
happy. Father and Jottie were laughing and talking as if they
went to the Bavarian Restaurant every single day of their lives,
and then Father looked around and said that all the other people in the restaurant probably thought that Bird was an heiress.

Bird was minding her manners so hard that she swallowed a
bite of Veal Escallope without hardly chewing so she could
speak. "Why?" Her eyes watered.

"Because," he said, "anyone can see that the three of us"—he
circled his finger to include me and Jottie—"are related. But
you? Big blue eyes and yellow curls? They're going to figure
we kidnapped you. And why would we kidnap you unless you
were an heiress?" He leaned over to wipe a tear off her cheek.
"Not to mention your table manners. You'd have me fooled if I
didn't know better." Bird smiled and sat up straight in her
chair. She liked being an heiress. It was fine with me; I didn't
mind being a kidnapper, if Jottie and Father were, too.

After dessert, which was Boston Cream Pie and which I got
even though I didn't finish my dinner, Father and Jottie pushed
back their chairs and drank coffee and talked about the farms
and Mr. Roosevelt and Swiss neutrality. It was the most boring
conversation imaginable, but I tried to look alert and interested
so they'd know they could take me to restaurants anytime. Bird
folded her napkin into shapes.

Father paid grandly, not even looking at the money, just laying it down on the little silver tray that the waitress had put on
the table. And when we left, the folks at the other tables nodded slightly to Father and Jottie, as if they were saying, We'll
see you at the next restaurant.

The sun was setting through the trees on Route 45. I watched
the sky turn orange and pink and blue and bluer. Starlings zig-
zagged through the colored light; I blinked and they were bats.
In Martinsburg, Father left us and got into his car, but he kept
just ahead of us instead of speeding away, and when we got
home, he came to Jottie's car to get Bird, because she'd fallen
asleep. He carried her against his shoulder, and I went right

behind him to pull back the bedspread before he put her down. Miss Beck's door opened a crack, and I saw her watching but Father didn't, because he was holding Bird so carefully. So there, I thought. I didn't think it meanly, though. I was too happy.

27

I was still happy the next morning. For a little while, anyway. We were at the breakfast table, Miss Beck and I, when Father steamed into the kitchen, kicking up a ruckus about where was his hat, he was late, he couldn't find his *hat*.

Jottie found it, of course, but as Father was leaving, Miss Beck asked, "Where are you off to, in such a hurry?"

"Got to see a man about a horse," he said, and laughed. Then he rushed off, happy and kind of fizzing, the way he got sometimes when he was going out on business.

Miss Beck watched him go. Then she turned to me. "What do you suppose *that* means?"

I gave her my blankest look. "Maybe he likes horses."

She nodded and went on chewing her toast, but her face fell into thoughtfulness. I didn't like it a bit. I was beginning to think that Miss Beck might be just as much of a natural-born sneak as I was.

Later, I went to gather up the mail. I was generally the one who brought the mail in and set it on the hall table. I saw this as an opportunity for a little mild snooping. I didn't read anyone's letters, of course. I just saw who got what. Not that there was much to see. Jottie got plenty of bills and some letters, mostly from cousins and her friend Raylene, who was a missionary in darkest China. Father got almost nothing, except letters from my mother asking to see me and Bird. Miss Beck got the most—letters from Washington, D.C.; from Delaware; from the Department of Chemistry, Princeton University; from

Cape May, New Jersey; from the West Virginia Writers' Project in Charleston; and from Mr. Tare Russell.

Mr. Russell's envelope was elegant, all creamy and thick. I stared at it, thinking of my father, stepping so quick and sure around Mr. Russell's boxwood hedges to let himself in the little black door. I was almost sure that was where he kept his bottles. I had gotten used to the idea of him being a bootlegger. I even sort of enjoyed it, especially when I thought of it running in the family and us being an outlaw band. But now, looking at that creamy envelope, I thought to myself that I didn't truly know why my father went there. I didn't truly know very much atall.

I knocked on her door. "Here's your mail, Miss Beck."

She opened it looking distracted, with a pencil behind her ear. "What?"

I smiled with all the teeth I could muster. "Your mail. I brought it."

"Well! Thanks." She was a little surprised, I guess. "Thanks."

She was turning away when I stopped her. "I see you got a letter from Mr. Russell." I wedged myself in the door. "You going to visit him?"

"Oh, good." She riffled through the envelopes until she found his. "Yes," she said, as she slit it with a hairpin. "I've heard that his house is full of wonderful artifacts, practically a museum . . ." She trailed off, reading.

"He's going to show you his house?" I asked. "The whole thing?"

"Uh-huh," she said, kind of absent. "At least, I hope so." Then she looked up, a lot sharper. "Why do you ask?"

She thought she had a right to know Father better than I did, because she was a grown-up. She thought I was just a silly child, but she was wrong. I knew his secrets, more than she did, more than anyone did, probably, and I'd guard them. I'd guard him. Honor among thieves, I said to myself, though of course we weren't thieves. All for one, one for all was a better saying. I decided to go see for myself just what was there, behind Mr. Russell's black door.

I practically cracked my head in two, smiling. "Oh, no reason."

* * *

I got through the creek pretty fast, considering the mud, and when I came up at the back wall of the Tare Estate, I peered around carefully. There wasn't a soul there, not in all that garden that stretched out as far as I could see, but I couldn't conjure up the nerve to stride through the paths like Father had. I edged my way around with the wall at my back. It just took longer, that's all. I still got to the house and the small black door. I stood in front of it with my heart thumping—I couldn't help but think of Bluebeard's wife. I'd always thought she must be a ninny, to barge in where she'd been told not to go, but I had more sympathy now. The door had a few steps in front of it, not leading up, but down into the ground. It was a basement door. Breathing fast, I went down and turned the handle, just like Father had done. And, just as easy, it opened. A gust of deep, cool air came up to greet me. I went in and closed the door quietly, though I needn't have. There was nobody there. The pounding in my heart began to subside a little. I was in a basement, all right, brick and dirt and cement, with shelves and long high tables—maybe workbenches—all around. I turned slowly, not looking for evidence, not yet, just getting used to the dim, greenish light and the rich, damp smell of dirt. If I had a place this cool and quiet in my house, I'd have spent every minute there. But Mr. Tare Russell didn't come there much, I could tell. There was a layer of dust on all the shelves and benches and tables, and not just a layer of dust, but a layer of dustiness, of left-behind-ness, that covered everything. A couple of trunks were stacked in a corner, and some cans of paint were lined up on a shelf. There was a broken-down velvet chaise propped up against a wall beside a cobwebby doorway. I began to look for bottles straightaway, but I soon stopped. Father was cleverer than that. He wouldn't leave them right out for people to see. He'd put them in something.

The trunks were disappointing—empty, and balky besides. I had to practically rip the lock off one, and it made a bad squeak when I opened it. That set my heart galloping again, and I looked up, above my head, hoping there wasn't anyone listening. After all that effort, I found only a bedspread, old and faded. Honestly. I inspected the few boxes on the shelves and looked behind the velvet chair. I even crawled around like a rat under the workbenches, but I found nothing. It was irritating work.

Ferocity and devotion, I reminded myself. So I swept the cobwebs away from a doorway and peered into another basement room. This one was smaller. Just as cool, just as dim. A few more trunks—this time with ladies' clothes in them—and lots of empty frames. The shelves in the next room were full—of boxes! For a moment, I thought I'd hit the jackpot, but every single one of those boxes held a pair of shoes. Men's shoes. There must have been forty boxes of men's shoes. I didn't have time to stop and ponder this mystery, because there was another doorway and yet another room. Considering the size of Mr. Tare Russell's house, I calculated that he could have a dozen rooms in his basement.

By the time I got to the seventh room, I wasn't nervous anymore. I still jumped a little when I heard a sound, but that's because I figured it was probably mice or worse, not because I thought someone was going to catch me. Above my head, the house was still as a tomb.

So I strolled into the seventh of the basement rooms and glanced around with what they call a practiced eye. Couple of trunks, *again,* and a row of terrible-looking jars of fruit on a splintering shelf. They must have been there for years to look as they did. There was a rag tucked into the corner next to the last jar. Nothing, I thought, and turned to the next door. But then I turned back. The rag. It was nothing, just a bit left by mistake, but it was the first sign of a presence I'd seen since I'd come in. I went to the shelf and picked it up. It was a handkerchief, yellowed with time.

I dropped down, squatting on my haunches to peer into the bottom shelf. Nothing. Nothing until I lost my balance, tipping over slowly but surely, and landing plump on my back. Cobwebs in my hair, I thought regretfully. I was on the verge of hoisting myself up when I saw what I had come for. They had been shoved under a workbench, three of them. Three black leather cases, identical to the one in Father's car. Scrabbling to my knees, I reached into the darkness and dragged them out, one by one. And there it was, F. H. R., stamped in gold beside the handle—on two of them, anyway. The third was plain, with no initials, and it was shabbier than the others. Older.

They were surprisingly easy to drag, and I soon discovered why. The first F. H. R. was empty. Not a thing in it. I suppose that was good news, but it made me grim. I was going to a lot of trouble to protect Father, and the least he could do was need protecting. The second F. H. R. case was even worse—ten glass bottles stood in a sort of harness, but they weren't whiskey bottles. They were small and carefully labeled: Bromine, Potassium chloride, Ammonium . . . Tucked in alongside them were some papers. I took one out. "DuPont Company: Better Things for Better Living . . . Through Chemistry!" Beneath that were descriptions of how wonderful and useful their chemicals were. I shoved the paper back beside the bottles and snapped the case closed. Suppose I'd got it wrong, and Father's job really was selling chemicals? But if his job was selling chemicals, what were the chemicals doing in Mr. Russell's basement? I didn't know what to think.

Discouraged, I reached for the third case, the old one. It was heavier than the others but not so heavy I couldn't drag it close to me. And it was locked. *Locked.* I twisted the button clasp back and forth and yanked on the strap that connected the two parts, but it was locked. Suddenly, something came over me. I was as angry as I'd ever been, and for the first time in my life I knew what people meant when they said they saw red. I was furious. I pounded on the case with all my strength; I bashed at the lock until my hand hurt. And then I rustled around in that damn basement until I found a piece of pipe and shoved it underneath the strap that held the lock. I stood up and stamped down on it as hard as I could. The strap popped up, quivering in the air.

I'd done it.

It was hard to stop being angry so suddenly. For a moment I just looked at what I'd done, panting. Then, gingerly, I reached down and pulled the sides of the case wide. At first I couldn't understand what I was seeing. Cloth. White cloth gone yellow with age. I lifted it out and discovered that it was a package. I unwrapped it and I found more cloth. Brown, this time. I stared at it, frowning, trying to figure out what it was. I didn't know until I held it up—it was a jacket, a man's suit jacket. Kind of old-fashioned. I checked the back, the front. Why would Father keep an old jacket tucked away here? I shrugged and was about to put the thing down when I looked at it again. It was too big, too long. Father wasn't that tall, I was pretty sure. Maybe it wasn't his. I checked the pockets. In a side pocket, I found a buffalo nickel, but I couldn't read the date on it. In the breast pocket, a handkerchief, yellowed like the other one, but neat and flat, like it had just been ironed. I flopped the jacket over. The other side pocket held a folded paper. I unfolded it— and there was Father's writing, straight up and down like always. "V," I read, "Talked him down to $200, but it'll need a new tire, so $250. F." V. Vause Hamilton? I touched the paper, glad to find a bit of long-ago Father, and put it back, refolded just as I'd found it. A little distracted, I reached into the inner pocket, the one that's hidden inside men's coats, and felt a small piece of heavy paper. A photograph?

Yes.

I stared.

It was Jottie. A long-ago Jottie, with her hair coiled up on the back of her head. Her face was tilted up and she was smiling sideways, almost laughing, so shining and beautiful and hopeful. I'd always thought Jottie was pretty, with her thick dark hair pulled into a neat knot at her neck and her smooth skin and her eyes so round and deep and bright—but this was Jottie more beautiful than I'd ever seen. She looked like Father, just exactly like Father, but lighter, more delicate, like she was floating.

I spent a long time looking at that picture. I wanted it. I wanted it with all my heart. But it was too precious, I could see that. I put it back, very carefully, in the pocket where I'd found it. There were so many things I didn't understand—why Father had kept the jacket, why it was inside the shabby case, and why the photograph of Jottie was in its pocket—but I understood that my father held it dear and no damage could come to it. I folded the jacket perfectly, so that every crease was exactly as it had been, and wrapped it back in its yellowed cloth just as tender as I could manage. It seemed wrong to set that bundle on the dirty floor, though I couldn't have said why. I blew dust off a shelf and set it there before I turned back to the case. What I saw wasn't very exciting, just envelopes, the big brown kind. Five of them, lined up. I drew one out. Printed along the top, in faded black ink, was American Everlasting Hosiery Company, and then below, in spidery handwriting—I twisted my head to read it—September 2, 1920. Old. I lifted up the flap to peek inside—and almost shed my skin: In that envelope there was a pile of money, a stack of bills thicker than I'd ever seen. I gasped, and the sound scared me worse than anything that had happened that afternoon. My heart commenced to thumping, and I quick dropped the envelope back in the case and slammed it shut. For a second, I sat still and frozen, and then my hand crept out and pulled the two sides open again. Very, very slowly, I drew out the envelope again and looked inside. It took my breath away. I reached to pull out a few bills. Ten-dollar bills. A thick bundle of them, more than I could count. Some of them looked funny—old, I guessed, and brown with age. The words "wages of sin" popped into my head, but I pushed them away. I swallowed hard and stretched over the case to pull out another envelope. Twenty-dollar bills, divided into three packets. The next one held five-dollar bills, a mess of them. Then one-dollar bills, jammed and stuffed into their envelope any which way. I dug in and plucked out a handful, just to see what it would feel like. The last envelope was the thinnest. Fifty-dollar bills, eight of them. I'd never seen even one before.

All of a sudden I stopped, appalled, and looked at the money lying on the floor around me. Father would know. If the money was mixed up, if the stacks weren't right, Father would know I'd been here. He could be here any minute. He'd gone out on business, hadn't he? He was probably going to come right over with the money he'd got. I felt sick. I had to put it back, quick, just like it was before. I was shaking as I put the money in the envelopes, shaking so hard I couldn't get the bills straight and then shaking harder because I couldn't. It was real. It was real. My father was a bootlegger, a real one. I hadn't made it up. Somehow I got it all in, the bills in the right envelopes the way they had been before, or close enough, I hoped. I was panting as I set the envelopes in order on the bottom of the case and put the yellowed cloth bundle on top. Then I closed up the sides of the case and tucked the clasp back into the lock. It wasn't fast, but it stayed. I rubbed it a little with the old rag. If you didn't look close, you couldn't see the scuff mark I'd made. Father would never know. No one would ever know. I pushed the cases deep under the workbench and walked out of that basement fast.

28

Up on the screen, Charles Boyer arched his worldly brows and shrugged. "All women have eyes," he purred, and Sol's hand closed over Jottie's.

It was their third movie in two weeks. Jottie was growing accustomed to the prickly velour seats of the balcony, to the tribute of jujubes and popcorn, and to Sol's hand holding hers. As Hedy Lamarr powdered her lovely nose, Jottie stole a sideways glance at the hand that rested on hers. Wide, masculinely hairy, with clean, blunt fingertips, it covered her own small hand completely. He wasn't nervous; his palm was dry. The hand of an honest man, she thought, and smiled. Stealthily, she watched him watch the movie, his face open and attentive, enjoying himself as much as he had expected to enjoy himself.

He looked at her suddenly. "You bored?" he whispered in her ear.

She shook her head, and his fingers tightened around hers.

He lifted his chin at Charles Boyer and murmured, "Reminds me of Felix."

She looked. She could see what he meant. "Thank God Felix doesn't have a French accent," she said pensively.

He chuckled, his eyes on the screen. "The streets would be paved with the fallen."

She laughed. He made it seem so simple.

After the show, Sol suggested a walk along Prince Street. His serene supposition of normality was contagious, and Jottie found herself casually agreeing. Men lounging and strolling greeted Sol, touching their caps, ducking their heads.

"They like you," Jottie whispered, between salutations.

He glanced around in puzzlement. "Who?"

"These men. They work at the mill, don't they?"

He nodded. "Yeah, sure. That was Tommy Boyes. You know him, don't you?"

She shook her head, smiling. "No. Never seen him before in my life."

He shifted uncomfortably. "I should've introduced you."

"No. Sol, that's not what I mean. I'm just—I noticed that the men who work for you like you, that's all." It was the same respectful admiration her father had enjoyed—had lived on, really—and where she had once believed it to be a bounty as endless as sunshine, she knew better now. It was earned, so it could be lost.

"Oh." He smiled, pleased. "I guess. They liked your father, too. They're good fellas, most of them."

She nodded. A young couple, sleek and smug, approached on the sidewalk. "Mr. McKubin," murmured the young man, touching his hat. His wife, clearly in pursuit of a good impression, smiled coyly at Sol. Jottie watched her, warm with nostalgia. How many times had she waited on her father's arm while the same plot unfolded?

Sol smiled. "Brady," he said, and nodded to the simpering wife. "Good evening."

Look, she told herself like a visitor pointing out a monument, look what Sol has. He has Macedonia in the palm of his hand.

They moved on, passing the New Grocery, Pie Dailey Barbershop, the Pickus Café, Columbia Hardware. The crowds dwindled as they progressed, and in the gloom outside Krohn's Department Store, Sol slipped his arm through hers. Nervously, Jottie broke away, pretending to inspect the windows, but they were too dark to offer much more than her reflection, with Sol's face shadowy behind hers. She turned and scrutinized his lapels. "Did you buy that suit here at Krohn's?"

He looked down at his suit. "This suit? No."

She put her hands on her hips. "Do you buy any of your suits here?"

"Why do you want to know?" he asked, bewildered.

"I just do."

"Well." He gazed over her head, struggling to recall. "No. No. I don't think I've ever bought a suit at Krohn's. Do you think I should?"

"No. Do you buy them in Washington?" she demanded. "Your suits?"

He squinted at her. "Yes."

"What store do you go to?"

He shrugged. "Woodward & Lothrop. Garfinckel's. Why do you want to know where I buy my suits?" He put his hand on her shoulder.

"Just because," she persisted. "Does Violet go with you?"

He nodded. Tentatively, he put his other hand on her waist and drew her farther into the darkness. "I got some suits in New York last year," he said.

"New York!" she exclaimed. "You went to New York for a suit?"

He nodded yes and then shook his head no. "I was going, anyway," he said, and then added, "Business. Jottie?" He leaned down and kissed her gently.

"What?" she said. It came out muffled because he was kissing her again. New York for a suit! she thought. And then: Felix is going to find out. It was at least ten seconds before she thought of the last time she'd been kissed. *I have to go, Josie. Give me a kiss for luck. Uh-huh, but why do you need luck? I don't, I guess. Just kiss me, all right?* Ten seconds isn't bad, she thought, ignoring the twist of longing. I really must be over him, just about. She took a step away. "What?"

Sol smiled. "I was going to ask you if I could kiss you. But then I figured you might say no."

"I might have," she admitted. Go away, Vause. And you, too, Felix. Neither of you is an honest man. Go away and let me live. She smiled up at Sol. "I'm glad you didn't ask," she said.

Sol let out a relieved breath. "Me, too." He reached for her again.

29

"Whoo," Jottie said softly.

"What?" Layla asked.

"You ate lunch, I hope?"

"Yes. A sandwich. Why?"

" 'Cause you're not going to get a bite here." Jottie surveyed the yellowing grass and weary shrubs before her. "Twenty years ago, he had three gardeners working year-round on this yard. One just to clip the trees."

Layla followed Jottie's gaze. "Not anymore."

"No. Depression hit him hard. Used to be servants crawling all over this house. The Tare Estate, he called it."

"Isn't Russell his last name?"

"It's his mother's line he's proud of. That's the Tare part. Russell was just money. Not enough of it, either." Jottie clicked her tongue. "Poor old Tare."

Together they climbed the steps and walked up a broad flagstone path through the depleted garden, passing a dry fountain and a plaster cornucopia on a pedestal. From within a deep, shadowy porch, a voice called, "As I live and breathe, if it isn't Jottie Romeyn!" Tare Russell, small and freckled in a seersucker suit, waved to them from within the gloom. "And you must be Miss Layla Beck!" he sang as they stepped inside the screen door. "You'll excuse me if I don't get up, won't you? Asthma."

"Of course, Mr. Russell. I'm delighted to meet you," said Layla, leaning down to shake his hand.

"Tare, I must be going." A thin woman in a green hat rose swiftly from a tattered wicker chair.

"Anna! So soon?" he said wistfully.

"Yes," she said, putting on her gloves.

"Well, if you must, you must."

Nodding curtly to Jottie and ignoring Layla completely, the woman threaded her way between the chairs and pushed open the screen to disappear in the white sunlight.

No one said anything for a moment, and then Jottie turned to Tare Russell and glared. "Did you do that on purpose?"

He giggled. "I was hoping it would be more exciting than that. She's a bore."

"You're a devil, Tare."

He giggled again.

"What happened?" asked Layla, looking from his face to Jottie's.

Jottie lifted her eyebrows. "Tare?"

"Well," he said cheerily, "that was Anna May Bowers, who once hoped to be Anna May Romeyn."

"She was engaged to Felix," Jottie explained.

Layla flushed. "Oh."

"He jilted her," snickered Tare Russell.

"Tare! Stop that!"

"He did! He ran off with Sylvia, and she swore vengeance."

"She did not. She had every right to be—upset," said Jottie. "She behaved fine."

"Did she or did she not spit on your shoes?"

"That was a long time ago."

"Well. I was hoping for a fracas."

"You would."

Tare made a little sound in his mouth and sat back in his chair, smiling at Layla. "Aren't you a pretty thing, dear."

"Why, thank you, Mr. Russell."

"Oh, call me Tare. Everyone does." He waved his hand elegantly. "Now. I have some macaroons inside and I'll get them in a minute, but first let's us chat about your book. Your *History of Macedonia.*" He popped his eyes at her. "The War Between the States. It was a stiletto in the heart of Macedonia. A wound, you see, from which we have never recovered. Families torn apart like the Union itself, nobody left unscathed. Why, there are still places where the blood flows on certain days." He paused.

"Pardon?"

"Some things can't be laid to rest," he said ominously. "If you're ever standing on the Race Street Bridge on the seventh of March, you'll hear a gunshot. It'll nearly knock you out of your skin, it's that loud, and you'll think, Lord, someone's been killed. And that's God's own truth, because it's the echo of Ridell Fox shooting his brother Carson on March 7, 1863. Ridell was Union and Carson was Rebel, and they were both mixed up in the raids around here because they knew the land like their own selves. That day, Ridell comes down out of Pownall to steal fodder for the horses, and he's riding along the bridge when he hears a clattering. Uh-oh, he thinks, Rebs coming; I'd better get me underneath this bridge. Under he goes and in the nick of time, because along comes a pack of Rebel raiders, whooping and laughing about how they just got a good load of guns off a boxcar. They pull up on the bridge, and Ridell thinks he'll scare them away and get the guns back for the Union. Be a hero. He whips out his pistol, pokes his head over the bridge bed, and takes a shot—right into the brain of his own brother. Ridell sees that, and he don't wait, he starts running, with the Rebels on his heels, leaving poor old Carson to die alone there on the bridge, cursing his brother with his last breath. On that very day, the seventh of March, you can hear the shot that killed him. I've heard it myself." He sat back, triumphant.

"How do you spell Ridell?" asked Layla, writing breathlessly.

"And then this very house here is haunted," Tare Russell went on, ignoring her. "*I* should write a book."

"How do you know that it's—haunted?" asked Layla.

He looked at her sternly. "What would you say if I told you that I have a picture that bleeds real blood?"

Jottie crossed her legs. "Does it do that still?"

"Well," he said. "Not for a few years. But. It has. Bled real regular for a long time. It's a photograph of my great-uncle Major August Tare, and on anniversaries of big battles he was in, blood flowed right out of the glass." He nodded. "And that's not all. The spirits of war are unsettled. Things *move*. Why, I'd set down a sword or some such thing in a nice place and then come back a day later to find it across the room. If that isn't a ghost, I don't know what is." He glanced at Jottie for corroboration.

"Maybe more than one," she murmured.

"Wait." Jottie paused at the top of the wall. "This is Tare Russell's house."

"Uh-huh," Felix said, swinging his leg over.

"What are we doing here?"

"You'll see." He jumped down lightly and held his arms up for her. Inside the garden, rows and curlicues of hedges formed something that was almost but not quite a maze. The air was cold and fresh; every branch, every stalk, was vibrating with coming spring. Crouching low, Felix ran to the nearest hedge and gestured to her to follow. In relays, they raced from cover to cover—after the shrubs, they had to find protection behind tree trunks. Jottie lunged for shelter behind a beech tree and found Felix there before her. They scuffled, each pushing the other to gain more cover. "Shh, shh," he warned as she began to laugh. He shook his head somberly. "If we get caught?" He drew his finger across his neck.

"I thought you said it wasn't going to be dangerous!" she hissed in alarm.

He smiled. "I said I didn't think it was dangerous."

She slapped him on the arm, and he laughed. "Look," he said, turning to the house. "We want that door there." He pointed to a narrow black door at the base of a brick wall. "It's open." He turned to grin at her. "Last one there is a girl." Away he flew.

Inside the cavernous basement, they balanced like storks, removing their shoes. "We need to get to the parlor," Felix whispered. "That's where he keeps most of it."

"Felix, I'm not going to steal anything," she whispered.

He drew himself up. "Who said anything about stealing? I'm not stealing."

"What are we doing, then?" She bounced up and down on her toes anxiously.

"We're making Tare Russell's life more interesting," Felix

said, and ran up the cobwebby basement stairs two at a time.
She glanced around the dim, silent basement. It was peaceful.
She could stay down here and be at peace. But she'd be alone.
Felix cared nothing for peace. He annihilated peace wherever
he went, destroyed it as easily as he'd walk through a cobweb—or
something less, even, something he wouldn't feel at all.

Jottie ran up the stairs after him.

"You get them sheets," said a rolling Negro voice.

"Lavender water!" called someone in a high-pitched cry. "I
forgot it!"

The Negro sighed. "Bring Mr. Tare his lavender water there,
Wesley."

Felix's arm held her against the velvety wallpaper. She tried
to breathe without sound. He turned his head toward her and
nodded. Together, they scampered across the wide hall and en-
tered Tare Russell's parlor. Felix pulled the well-oiled door shut
behind him.

It was a room of splendor, stretching long enough to accom-
modate four tall windows shielded with velvet curtains. At one
end, a rosewood mantelpiece loomed over a vast hearth, and at
the other, a large portrait of a man in a blue uniform glowered.
In between were small clusters of silk chairs and sofas, leavened
with shining tables and glass cases. Jottie stepped onto the lush
expanse of a pale silk rug. "Look at that," she whispered. On a
satiny table, a silver vase held a profusion of starry white lilies.
She took another step and sniffed with quiet rapture. "Heaven
must smell just like this." She reached out to pull him closer.
"Smell."

He smiled and bent over the flowers obediently. "Nice," he
said. "Now. Jottie. Listen. Tare Russell thinks he's got a haunted
house, you know?"

She nodded. "Mama says it is haunted. She says he's got a
picture that bleeds real blood, and swords that move all by
themselves. He's seen 'em floating down the stairs."

Felix laughed silently. "He hasn't seen them. He's making that
part up."

"How do you know?"

"'Cause it's me," he whispered. "I've been moving things

around for years. I sneak in here and change his pictures and swords."

Jottie covered her mouth with her hand.

He nodded happily. "Yup. It's me. But I want to do something special this time." He glanced to a golden clock under glass. "First I got to take care of my old pal over here." He moved swiftly to a small table that held a large daguerreotype in a leather case. The case was opened to show a rat-faced boy soldier, his gray cheeks enlivened by two spots of rosy pink.

"He looks like he's about to kill someone," said Jottie, peering over his shoulder.

"Oh yeah, he's a big hero," muttered Felix, fumbling in his pocket. He pulled out his knife and, before Jottie could protest, slashed himself lightly across the palm of his hand. A thin line of blood appeared; Felix tilted his hand, and the drops collected and splashed down on the gray soldier. "I always do that first," whispered Felix. He took out his handkerchief and wiped his hand. "I don't know why. But here's what I need you for, honey. I want to take that big picture down, and I can't do it by myself. I tried, but it's too wide."

Jottie turned to consider the enormous glowering portrait. "Let's not just take it down. Let's turn it around to face the wall."

A set of pistols gleamed in a glass case. "Let's cross them in the other direction," whispered Jottie.

"We've got to go," Felix said, looking worriedly at the golden clock. "I've never been here this long before."

"You a man or a mouse?"

Scowling, he lifted the top of the case, and Jottie reached in and turned the pistols upside down.

"You ain't gonna wax today?" a voice said loudly outside the door, freezing Felix and Jottie where they stood. "Ain't it Wednesday?"

From far away, another voice said something.

"All right, you tell him, though," the near voice said. "Ain't gonna be me."

Felix brought the glass lid down without a sound and pointed to a window at the far end of the room. Silently snatching up her shoes, Jottie followed her brother around the clusters of chairs.

Placing his fingers lightly on the sash, Felix eased the window upward, setting his teeth as it squeaked. Far across the room, Jottie saw a doorknob turn.

"Here!" whispered Felix frantically, pulling Jottie out onto the deep porch.

They careened around low wicker tables and chairs and nearly set a wooden seat swinging into a glass door. "Come on!" At the top of the front stairs, sure of victory, they looked at each other and cheered softly, and a figure working in the shrubs below straightened up. It was a young Negro man holding a long thin saw. For a moment, the three of them stared at one another. Jottie clutched Felix's hand and pleaded silently with the Negro. Finally, with a tiny shake of his head, he turned back to his shrub, and the two of them sprinted down the stairs like deer, heading for the path.

They almost made it.

"Is that Felix?" called a shrill voice. "Felix? You just come right back here, sir!"

"Oh God," muttered Felix. "Don't say anything." He wheeled around and, holding Jottie's hand firmly, retraced his steps up the path toward Tare Russell.

"Felix Romeyn! You haven't been to see me in ages!" said Tare reproachfully, coming down the stairs.

"Hey, Mr. Russell. This is my sister Jottie."

Tare glanced at her kindly. "Lovely to meet you, dear. Don't you look like young Felix here?"

"Nice to meet you, too, Mr. Russell," said Jottie, almost curtsying.

"Call me Tare, both of you. I'm not so very much older than you." He was thirty if he was a day, thought Jottie.

Felix did the talking. "I brought Jottie over to look at your sculpture. She didn't know what a cornucopia was"—Jottie shot him an outraged glare—"and I couldn't explain it right. So I brought her. That's all right, ain't it?"

Tare reached out a freckled hand and touched Felix's shoulder. "Of course it is. Didn't I say you could come anytime, anytime at all?" His hand traveled down Felix's arm to his wrist and patted it awkwardly. "Now. Wouldn't you like to stay for some—cookies?"

"Well, we'd like to, Mr. Tare," said Felix, "but Jottie's got a piano lesson in about five minutes. She's not very good at the piano, and she needs all the lessons she can get. So we have to go now."

"Thank you, though," added Jottie.

"Well," said Tare, bunching up his mouth a little. He looked at the ground and then jerked his head up in surprise. "You're in bare feet!"

Felix's eyes dropped as though he'd never seen his feet before. Then he looked up, smiling hugely. "The state of nature is a state of grace."

Tare gave a little start. "That is just exactly what I always say," he confided breathlessly. "The noble savage is—is something of an ideal of mine."

Felix laughed. "I figured it was." He turned away, toward the front gate.

"Wait!" gasped Tare, and his hand darted out to snatch hold of Felix again. Then he remembered himself, blushing, and plunged his hand into his pocket. Felix's eyes gleamed with amusement as Tare nodded apologetically to Jottie and patted his chest. "Asthma. Nothing to worry about." He gulped some air. "Now, you be sure to come back. And you, too, Lottie."

"We will," said Felix. "Me and Lottie, I promise."

Her feet were tingling with cold as they walked home. "Can I come with you again?"

"To tea with Mr. Tare?"

"No. To move things," she said.

"Told you it would be fun," he said smugly.

"I bet there's more upstairs."

"Yup. Lots. He's got a Rebel flag over his bed."

She giggled. "We could change it for a Union one."

He whistled in admiration. "Should have brought you in a long time ago." He nudged her arm, and she tucked it through his.

"Ladies, you've been delightful company," said Tare, hobbling alongside them to the edge of his porch. "You've spoiled me for all my other callers."

"Tare, thank you. I don't know when I've been so entertained," said Jottie, patting his sleeve.

"Yes, thank you, Mr. Tare, for sharing your wonderful collection with me," said Layla, gathering her notebook and hat.

"Why, you're certainly welcome, my dear. You just come on back anytime." He smiled benignly, but his grip on Jottie's hand was white-knuckled. "Tell Felix to come pay me a call," he said under his breath. "Tell him that."

"I will," Jottie said sympathetically. So many years of hopeless longing. Why didn't he give up? "I sure will."

He nodded, not meeting her eyes.

The two women parted at the corner. "See you at home," Jottie said, lifting her hand in a brief wave. "I'm going to the New Grocery."

"See you," Layla replied limply. She walked along, feeling steam accumulate inside her hat. The streets of Macedonia lay still and stupid under the flatiron sun. I may die, she thought, plodding up the shadeless wastes of Monongahela Street. I may die, and all they'll find is a little greasy spot where I dropped. Sweat slid from her arms and neck into her slip, wetting the lace trim.

A car rumbled past and stopped suddenly halfway down the block. With a grinding of gears, it whined into reverse and shot backward at the same speed with which it had proceeded.

"Oh, thank heavens," cried Layla. She held out her thumb. "Can I have a ride?"

Felix smiled. "You got to pay."

"Gladly. How much?" she asked, opening the door.

"I'll let you know." He took in her flushed face and damp dress. "You a little hot?"

"Yes, and I don't know why you're not. Why aren't you ever hot, Felix?" It sounded more accusatory than she had intended.

"I'm like to melt," he said cheerfully. "How about we go downtown and get us a Coca-Cola, nice and cold?"

And why don't you ever argue? she thought, disgruntled. "All right," she said. "That would be nice." She turned to set her notebook on the backseat beside a large black case. "What's that?"

"Hm?"

"What's that case?" She waited for him to evade answering.

He glanced over his shoulder. "That? Chemicals."

She blinked. "Chemicals? What do you mean? What kind of chemicals?"

"Mostly chlorine. Some salt-brine derivatives. Bromine. Magnesium. Ammonia." He looked over at her and smiled. "Didn't you know? That's what I do. I sell chemicals."

Something inside her that she wouldn't name relaxed suddenly. She leaned her head against the back of the seat. "You sell chemicals?" She almost laughed. "Who do you sell them to?"

"Don't they give you a test before they let you write books?" he said. "To whom."

"You know what I mean."

"Just barely. I sell them to the Armed Forces of the United States. Among others."

"Felix, why—" She broke off, too happy to continue.

He pulled neatly up to a curb. "Why? Why not?" They gazed at each other, and then he leaned across her to open her door. "Madam."

"Such service!" she said gaily, stepping out onto Prince Street. "The heat's not so fierce here, is it—" She faltered, noticing that a line of men arrayed across the front of Shenandoah Tobacco and Cigar had turned, in unison, to watch her approach.

Felix materialized at her side, and as she looked to him for protection, she found his dark eyes assessing the row of men. He nodded formally.

Chins lifted in response.

"Out already?" he asked, looking at a man whose gray hair hung lank over his collar.

The man lifted his lip over long teeth. "Remember? They got to shut down when it hits a hundred."

Felix nodded again, more easily this time. "That's right. Glad to see there's some humanity left in the old place."

There were several smirks. "Ain't for us, don't kid yourself," jeered a tall man. "Shank just don't want the double cylinders to melt."

"Ah, Sol'd shut it down anyway," the first man said. "He's got a heart, at least."

Felix lifted his hat, and Layla felt his hand at her back. As they turned toward Pickus Café, she said conversationally, "Sol? Now, isn't he the man I met when I went to American Everlasting? I think that was the name. He's a friend of Jottie's, isn't he?"

Felix hesitated for only a second. "I don't know. They seem like friends?"

"Yes. He came out to see her. Felix?" she ventured.

"Hm?"

"Did you ever work there, at the mill?"

"Me?" He turned to her with a flashing smile. "I sure did. I was a superintendent."

"What's a superintendent do?"

"I don't know about you," he said pityingly. "A superintendent superintends."

She giggled. "Why'd you leave?"

"I like chemicals," he said. "Let's get that Co-Cola, and I'll tell you all the chemicals it's got in it."

30

The clock struck ten, and Jottie glanced up from her book. Like a ghost, Felix was standing in the doorway.

She flinched. "Didn't hear you come in."

"Surprise." He glided past her and stood at the window.

She watched his back as he shifted the curtain with one finger and peered out into the night, a gesture so uncharacteristically wary that Jottie felt her stomach clench. "What?" she said.

He glanced at her questioningly.

"Is there something out there?" she asked.

"Wolves," he said. "Cutthroats. Indians." He turned his head for one more look and then dropped the curtain.

Jottie's heart began to thump nervously. Something had happened. Was about to happen. She examined her brother's restless, unrevealing face. "Where've you been?" she asked tentatively.

He swung around. "Let's go for a drive."

"Who? Us?" she stammered, thrown off.

He glanced around the empty room. "Yeah. I don't like any of these other people."

"What about the girls?"

One eyebrow flew up. "I was kidding about the wolves. Come on." He held out a hand.

"I guess they'll be all right." She took his hand, her mind racing. Had he heard something? About Sol? Now, stop that, she scolded herself. You're jumpy as a cat on hot macadam. He doesn't know a thing. Probably. Oh, what a tangled web we weave, she recited silently, when first we practice to deceive. Let this be a lesson to you. Oh, hushup. Hushup and calm down. "Where are we going?"

"We'll see," he said. "The Lord will provide."

As they slipped through the backyard to the alley where Felix kept his car, Jottie felt her worries recede a bit, as though she'd left them in the front room. She gave a little skip of excitement. It would never entirely die, the fun of going someplace with Felix. "Let's pretend we're going someplace good," she suggested as she settled into the front seat.

Felix laughed and put in the clutch. "How 'bout New York?" The engine juddered to life. "The Big Apple."

"That's fine. I've never been to New York."

Felix glanced her way. "It's not so much," he said kindly.

She cranked the window down to feel the false coolness of the passing air. Walnut, Kanawha, Locust, Maple . . . the streets notched by, white houses flaring up and fading back as they passed, easy and familiar, same as always. Jottie felt her hunched shoulders relax against the coarse cloth of the seat.

They were on False River Road when Felix swung the car sharply left, and the narrow beams of the lamps illuminated a startled world of greenery and bugs, followed by a broad swath of empty black. Beyond lay spangled water and the decrepit, tilting mass of a boathouse.

"Look at that thing," said Felix. "Dollar says it falls into the river by Christmas." He cut the engine, and the brief silence was engulfed by a riot of insects. He leaned back and closed his eyes.

Within the car, everything was quiet.

Still.

Jottie felt the silence thickening. Inside her shoes, her toes opened and closed.

Still.

Then his voice came, gentle and low. "I hear you went looking for Sol."

"No!" she exclaimed with a surge of small-animal panic. Trapped. "No, I didn't." But I did, she thought guiltily. "I just . . . saw him. When I went to the mill."

"So now you're reunited, is that it?" His eyes snapped open. "Now everything's just like it was in the palmy days of yore, huh?"

"Oh, Felix," she begged. "Don't be like that. Sol—" She broke off, chasing after words. I knew this was going to happen, she thought. I should have been ready. She wasn't. "Listen, please, just listen to me." She looked through the darkness and licked her lips. "I think it's . . . silly—for me, anyway—to hold a grudge," she said carefully, and paused, waiting for outrage. Felix said nothing. Fighting his silence, her words tumbled out in a rush. How she wasn't trying to change his mind—she knew he wouldn't change his mind—and she didn't blame him, but she didn't want to be angry anymore, she wanted to be friends, remember what a good friend Sol had been? Well, it seemed silly to be angry forever because of, well, a mistake. Just a terrible, terrible mistake—

"A terrible mistake," she repeated. She couldn't think of anything else to say. The silence stretched between them. "Felix?" she said anxiously into the shadows.

"That was no mistake, Jottie," he said.

"Yes! It was!" she cried. "He was confused, and—"

Felix made a disgusted noise. "Confused, nothing. He was excited. He saw his chance and he took it—"

"Chance? There was no *chance*," she cried. "Sol was heartbroken about Vause!"

"Don't be a sucker. Sol was the happiest man in Macedonia the day Vause died. He thought he'd finally be able to get his hands on you, and he wasn't going to let anything stop him."

"He did not—he wasn't—" she sputtered. Of course Sol had always liked her, but it hadn't been like that, it hadn't been a thing he schemed about. "That's ridiculous! Sol wasn't after me—"

"The hell he wasn't," Felix sneered.

"He idolized Vause." She was certain of that.

Felix shrugged indifferently. "Sure, idolized. Wished he could be just like him. That's why he wanted you, honey." He smirked at her. "Sorry. It's the truth, though. And that's why he hated me, too. Because I was Vause's best friend." He shook his head. "I don't know why you can't see it."

"He never hated you," she said, hearing the quaver in her voice.

Felix heard it, too. He patted her hand. "I know you like to think he was a friend. But he wasn't. He wasn't, ever. He wanted you and he wanted me gone—listen, you remember the night before we left for Camp Lee? For basic training? Remember the party?"

"I wasn't allowed to go to that party," she said.

"That's right." He nodded, smiling fondly. "Funny, Mama taking such a stand about that party."

"She said there would be fast girls and immodest dancing and no daughter of hers was going to keep such company," Jottie recited, recalling her fingernails pressed helplessly into the flesh of her palms. *Please, please, Mama, I'll never ask you for another thing as long as I live.* "How I cried."

"She was right, though," Felix said. "There were some real floozies there. Lots of booze, too. And you know who bought it?" He looked at her. "Sol. He must have spent a month's allowance on it."

"Sol?" She frowned. Sol had never been a drinker.

Felix nodded. "Wasn't for him, though. Sol never broke a law in his life—commandments, yes; laws, no. Nope, the booze was for us. Vause and me. He said we should tie one on. Last chance and so on. I thought it was kind of funny—coming from Sol, especially—but friendly; you know, a friendly gesture. Then I noticed it was Vause he was chasing around—he was trying to get him drunk. I couldn't figure out why, not until Vause left to go see you." He laughed. "You should have seen Sol's face. He looked like someone'd shot his dog."

She shook her head. "You're just making this up."

"Believe what you want," Felix said, unmoved. He snickered suddenly. "Poor old Sol. He thought if he could keep the two of you apart for a few more hours, he'd be in the clear. Vause would be out of the way, and Sol'd get what he never had in his whole life—the chance to edge out Vause Hamilton with a girl."

"But he didn't know about Vause and me. No one knew—not then," she said, low.

"Everyone knew it was going to happen sometime."

"I didn't know," she murmured. "When he knocked on the window, my heart almost burst."

Felix smiled. "Good thing Mama slept like a rock."

"She wouldn't have minded. She loved Vause. Remember how she loved him?" She turned to him hungrily, wanting more thoughts, more words, more of anything that brushed against Vause.

"Mm-hm." Felix nodded agreeably, and Jottie allowed herself to surrender. Side by side on the roof, they had hidden their twined fingers between them like a secret. Vause had talked and talked—how itchy his uniform was, how he hoped the war wouldn't be over before he got there, how he'd send her a postcard from camp—and she had watched him, listening enough to know every word he said but keeping one part of herself back, to exult in his moonlit handsomeness, to glory in all the places he could be and wasn't, to bask in the heat of his hand wrapped around hers. She could almost feel it now; it would be worth the pain, it would be worth anything, to be back at the beginning with him, she'd do anything for it—

Stop.

No. She wrenched herself away, unwrapped the clinging hand. No, Vause. You were only pretending. It was only a game.

"He should have left me alone," she murmured.

"What?"

She straightened up. "I don't know about any of that," she said. "I don't know about any of it. Can't we just forget it? It's been eighteen years since Vause died."

Felix made a low sound in his throat. "Eighteen years since Sol tried to have me thrown in the penitentiary. I wouldn't be out yet."

"He made a mistake, that's all."

"Right. His mistake was thinking he could get rid of me along with Vause."

"He didn't want to get rid of you." But she could feel herself losing ground, backing toward the precipice.

Implacably, he pressed forward. "Is that right? So he said I'd set that fire and killed Vause out of friendly interest?"

"No. No. That's what he *thought*—"

"He had no reason to think it, Jottie. Not one goddamn shred of evidence. He was just trying to wreck my life."

"Felix, listen." She put out her hand and touched his. "Listen, even if he did want—even if he was trying to wreck your life—which I don't believe—it didn't work, did it? Your life isn't wrecked, is it?"

"Sure," he said. "My life is swell, especially the part where everyone in town wonders if I burnt American Everlasting to the ground and killed my best friend."

It was true. She licked her lips. "Most people don't think that. Most people don't think about it at all anymore, I bet."

"Sol thinks about it," Felix said.

"No—"

He spoke over her. "He thinks about how he almost got what he wanted—missed it just by a hair. He must hate that. I bet it eats at him—if he had only kept his damn mouth shut, he'd have gotten you, after a while. And later he could have figured out a way to get in good with Daddy and take my job."

"Get in good with Daddy? What are you talking about?"

An impatient twitch of his shoulders. "Don't play dumb—he wanted what Vause and I had. You think it's a coincidence he's manager over there? Just like me?"

It sounded so right. He seemed so sure. Could it be? She gave ground, fumbling for a new position. "I don't know, I— you don't have to, but—Sol's been awful lonely, I bet."

His hand closed around hers. "Sol lied. He lied about me." His fingers gripped hers painfully. "And Daddy believed him. He believed him instead of me."

This, too, was undeniable. *"Thank you, Oscar. We'll be down tomorrow to clear this up,"* their father called resonantly as he closed the door behind the retreating, unhappy police chief. *For a moment, he stood with his head bowed over the door handle. And then he turned to Felix. "I wish I believed you were telling the truth, Felix. But I don't."* That had been the end of everything between them. "Such an awful, awful time," she murmured.

"Yeah. And Sol started it," he reminded her.

"Yes."

A minute passed in silence. "I stayed," he said quietly.

He had stayed. Jottie stared out into the shimmering water, thinking about her brother. He alone had never failed her. He had failed many others, but not her. He was the only one who knew what she had had, the only one who had acknowledged her suffering when she lost it, and the only one who had ever given up anything for her. And he had been wronged. By Sol. Sol had told a story that laid waste to Felix's life. She couldn't defend him, and she couldn't ignore what had passed. There was no possibility of ignoring what had passed. The past was the only thing that really existed; there could be no future that was not based on the past. She had to choose one side or the other, and the side she chose had to be Felix's. It had been a ridiculous idea—that she could make something new, without him.

She took a breath. "All right. I'll stop."

"Sol's a liar," said Felix, victorious.

She closed her eyes and nodded. "Let's go home." She pulled her hand from his and dropped her head back against the seat.

She heard him smile. "Okay. Let's go home." The key slid into the ignition, the gear thumped lightly into place, the cloth of his sleeve squeaked as he set his arm along the top of the seat and looked over his shoulder. He paused. "Sol hasn't been pining for you, if that's what you're fussing about. He's got a girl up in Cumberland."

Without opening her eyes, she said, "Sometimes I hate you, Felix."

"Pooh," he said amiably. "You do not."

❖

July 23

Dear Sol,

I can't see you anymore. I must have been crazy to think that I could have done with the past, and crazier still to think that it didn't matter what you'd said about Felix so long ago. It matters to him, and I suppose to me, too. I will always remember our childhood friendship and these last weeks. But I can't see you anymore.

I'm sorry.

Jottie

31

It was the hot middle of Sunday afternoon, and I was reading *Gone with the Wind* under the house. I had to. Minerva was mad at me for reading her book to shreds, and Jottie was mad at me for telling Bird about the soldier getting his leg chopped off without any chloroform, and altogether, discretion was the better part of valor, just like Jottie always said. So I was reading it under the house. Under the porch, to be specific. It was the only place that had light enough to read by, because there was a hole, partly made by possums and partly made by me. I despised possums, with their naked tails and their bleary eyes, but for Scarlett O'Hara and Rhett Butler and poor old Ashley Wilkes, I was willing to live and let live.

Scarlett was just telling a passel of lies, dressed up in her mother's old drapes, when I heard Father's footsteps over my head. I sat up straight, listening. You hardly ever heard him. Where was he going? I tracked his steps like a pointer dog. He came down the front stairs, and I could feel my ears twist, following him. Was he off to do some bootlegging? Suddenly he passed like a breeze along the side of the house. Pooh. He wasn't going anywhere, just to the backyard. I settled back with Rhett and Scarlett, but I couldn't concentrate on their doings anymore, so I crawled out and shook the grit off me, and then I stuffed *Gone with the Wind* up my skirt, just to be on the safe side. Last time Minerva had caught me with it, she'd hidden it, and Jottie had made me read Elsie Dinsmore instead. I thought I'd die.

I strolled real casual down the side yard and peeked around

the corner of the house into the backyard. There he was, Father, standing all alone at the far end of the grass in the shade of the red oak, smoking. I would just go and talk to him. That would be all right. It was a breathless afternoon, and the lawn was steaming as I came across it. He smiled at me when I came close, but I couldn't think of anything to say, so I reached to hug him—and *Gone with the Wind* came crashing out of my skirt onto his shoe.

He yelped and jumped, and I was busy saying I was sorry when he picked up the book and looked at it. "Any good?" he asked.

"Why, yes, of course," I said. "Ain't you read it yet?"

"No," he said, turning it over. The cover was just about to come off now. Minerva was going to have kittens. "I haven't gotten around to it."

"Oh, you'd like it," I said. "It's extremely gripping."

"Extremely gripping, huh?" He smiled and opened it to a place where the binding was broken. "How many times have you read it?"

"'Bout twenty. But don't tell Minerva."

"Why not?"

I looked at the book. "She's already mad, and she thinks I only read it four times."

That made him laugh, and I was proud. "Seems like you might need your own book," he said.

"It costs three dollars," I said cautiously.

He whistled.

"But it's got more than a thousand pages. It's got a thousand and twenty-four."

"Well. We'll see," he said. "We'll see what we can do." He handed the book back to me.

Then he went on smoking. I looked at him and wished I hadn't told him how much the book cost. I wished I'd said I didn't want it. I wished I could hug him without anything falling on his feet, and I wished I could say that I loved him. I'd read about daughters who did that—Elsie Dinsmore, for instance, but other daughters, too, in good books. Their fathers liked it. But my mouth wouldn't open.

There was the sound of a sash being pulled up. "Felix!" It

was Miss Beck calling him from her window. She leaned out over the sill with a paper in her hand. "Have you ever heard of something called the Knock-Pie Trail?"

Just like that, he was smiling. "'Course I have. You can't graduate from high school if you don't know about the Knock-Pie Trail."

She made a face, but it was a face that made her prettier than before. "I graduated from high school just fine, and I never heard of the Knock-Pie Trail."

"It's a sin and a shame what they call an education down there in Washington." He didn't really mean it. He was teasing her.

She laughed. "They just ramble on and on about George Washington and Abraham Lincoln, when we could be learning about the Knock-Pie Trail."

"That's right."

Then they smiled at each other and didn't say anything. I didn't exactly wish that her legs would be cut off without chloroform, but I wished something would happen to her. Maybe she'd get sick. But that wouldn't help—she'd just sit in bed until she was better. Maybe she'd get so sick she'd die. I looked at Father and wondered how sad he'd be if she died. He'd get over it.

Finally he said, real quiet, "You going to come down here or am I going to have to come up there?"

She got pink. "I'll come down."

"Good," he said. "Bring the map."

I noticed that my stomach hurt. Maybe I'd die myself. Wouldn't that be just like God, to kill me for wishing death on Miss Beck?

"My stomach hurts," I said.

Father stopped looking at Miss Beck's window and looked at me. "Did you eat green plums again?"

I shook my head.

"Better go tell Jottie," he said. He rubbed my back. "She'll fix you up."

He was watching me as I went, but once I was inside, I didn't go find Jottie. I went upstairs to the room I shared with Bird. She was there, on the floor, cutting her everlasting paper dolls from the Sears catalog. She cut out whole families, and then she cut out their furniture and their cars and their bicycles and then she stuck them in a shoe box. She never did anything with them; she just cut them out.

"I don't know why you waste your time cutting them out when you never play with them," I snapped.

She looked up at me with her big blue eyes. "I like to cut things out."

"Whyn't you chop off their arms and legs, then, if cutting's all you like. You can make yourself a whole amputated family."

"I don't want an amputated family," she said, peaceful. "I want a pretty family. Look." She held up a golden-haired lady in a brown suit. "She's the mother."

"She is not," I said. I wanted to smash something. "You want to see a mother? Just look down in the backyard at Miss Beck, because I think Father's going to marry her!"

Bird stared at me for a moment, and then—oh, I could hardly bear it—she smiled. "Really? You think?"

"Don't you care?" I yelled. "It's *terrible.*"

Bird shook her head. "I love Miss Beck."

"No you *don't,*" I said. I sat down on my bed with a thump, but it wasn't enough. I toppled over and smashed my face in my pillow.

After a minute, I felt Bird's hand on my back. She held it there. "If you don't want Daddy to marry her, I don't, either," she said. "All right?"

I rolled over to look at her. She was just little, really. She didn't know the things I knew—that if Father married Miss Beck, he would never be ours again. That he'd look at her instead of us and smile and never wait for us. That he'd tell her his secrets and we'd have to traipse around, digging through scraps to know anything atall. She didn't know that Miss Beck would make us beggars, not for money or food but for Father. She was my little sister, and it was up to me to take care of her. I nodded. "All right."

She picked up the golden-haired paper lady and the scissors. She looked at me, and then she cut that lady right in two.

I laughed. "Give me one." Bird gave me a girl in a satin slip, and I chopped her into pieces. We cut up nearly the whole box full of dolls.

✳

Felix stopped the car.

"This is it?" said Layla, scrutinizing the layers of greenery outside the window. "I thought it was in the mountains."

"Mm-hm."

She swung around to look at him. "Felix! Is this the Knock-Pie Trail?" Her eyes narrowed. "Or not?"

"Not," he admitted.

She opened her mouth and then closed it. With a tiny smile, she folded her hands in her lap, relaxed against her seat, and waited.

Minutes ticked by, and the only sound was the droning roar of insects. Then she heard the car door close. Startled, she glanced to her left. He was gone.

A minute later he reappeared. "Come on," he said, "there's a stream down there."

"You!" she spluttered, but she was laughing, too. At him, at herself, at her pretense of resistance, at how much she wanted to touch him. Holding hands loosely, they clambered down something that had once been a path, entering a wood of thin, close-grown trees. Their struggle for survival had left them pale and listless, and their leaves fanned out low, catching at Layla's hair as she went.

Felix swatted a branch out of his way. "There," he said with satisfaction, as if he had invented the stream himself. "Let's go wading."

"Wading!" cried Layla, but he was irresistible, and the water was dark and cool and alluring, bordered with flat boulders and fallen trees. She glanced down at her shoes. And her hose. "Turn around," she said.

Obediently, Felix turned to face upstream. She lifted her skirt to unhook her garters, and the silk fell away from her legs, leaving them free and light. Stepping gingerly out of her shoes onto the warm rocks, she rolled her stockings into a ball and straightened to find Felix watching her with amusement. "You're not supposed to look," she said. "Only cads look."

He chuckled and bent to take off his shoes. "I've been called worse."

The dark water was a shock of exquisite coolness, and they wandered along its edges in silence for a space of time. Treading slowly through the stream, Layla listened to the inexplicable noises of unseen living things and sighed with pleasure. "We're so far away," she murmured. She stooped to watch a skeeter balance on the water's surface.

Felix sidestepped a half-submerged tree. "Here," he said, stopping at a level spot in the water and holding out his hand. "Stand right here."

Layla stood where he directed her. "Why?"

"Because," he said, and kissed her.

After a minute, she began to tremble. "I'm going to fall," she whispered.

He pulled away and looked at her questioningly. "Are you really?"

She nodded, frightened, and he swung her up into his arms and carried her to a low rock jutting into the water. He set her there on its cool, shaded surface and watched her for a moment. "Lie down," he said, and she did, glad to feel solid stone beneath her. She closed her eyes, almost sleepy there in the buzzing silence.

"What happened?" he asked after a time.

"You," she said drowsily. "I feel like I'm taking my life in my hands, being with you."

"What?" His fingers snaked around her forearm and grasped her tightly.

She opened her eyes at the harshness in his voice and saw his face set and tense above hers. "I didn't mean—" she broke off, confused.

"What did you mean?"

"I mean," she stammered, "that you have an, um, effect on me. I get dizzy. When you kiss me."

His hold on her loosened and his face relaxed into a grin. "Oh. That."

"What did you think I meant?" she asked, curious in her turn.

He didn't answer. Instead, he bent over her, smiling. "There's only one cure, you know."

"What's that?"

"And you're already lying down. So you can't fall." He drew his hand along the curve of her hip.

"What's the cure?" she asked, watching him greedily.

"Practice," he said, and she felt his warm lips through her dress.

32

"Hello?"

"Jottie? Don't hang up!" Sol's voice rose anxiously.

"I can't talk to you," she muttered, pressing herself tight into the wall for reinforcement.

"I know, I know. Just listen to me for a second." He paused, waiting to be hung up on. After a moment, he exhaled. "Okay. Jottie, you're throwing your life away. I'm not saying you have to—uh, choose me, but choosing Felix is, is—it's nuts." He paused, but Jottie said nothing. "You know what he's like, honey. Everything he's ever said has been a lie."

"Everyone lies," she said softly. "Even you, once or twice. I can't talk to you."

"I know." He sighed. "Listen, Jottie, I want you to change your mind—"

"I won't."

"I know. But *if* you change your mind, call me. Or if you can't call me, just come down to the mill to see me. No one will think a thing of it, and I'll be there. I'll be waiting."

"No," she said. "I can't do that. And I have to go now. I'm helping Layla with her book."

He hung up.

For a moment, Jottie stayed against the wall, thinking.

Mr. McKubin came across the field, black as a crow.

She had been nine. Maybe ten.

Black as a crow, he marched slowly through the tall grass, his head bent. The children, arrayed in a line across the top of the fence, watched his patient progress. They had been expecting him.

"Solomon," he said when he was close.

Sol climbed down and stood before his father, his back straight.

"Am I to understand that this is your doing?" said Mr. McKubin. He held up a golf club, or what had been a golf club and was now a stick with no head.

Jottie lowered her eyes respectfully, but looking sideways through her eyelashes she saw Felix and Vause nudge each other, their mouths tight with suppressed laughter.

"Yessir," Sol said. His eyes slid toward the other boys to see if they were watching. "It was my fault. I did it."

Jottie's head jerked up. "No, you didn't," she blurted before she could stop herself.

Mr. McKubin eyed her gravely and turned back to Sol. "This is no light matter, son. You have broken a thing of value. I speak of my trust."

Sol threw back his head. "I'm sorry, sir."

Jottie thumped the fence in indignation. What was the matter with him? "He didn't do it, Mr. McKubin. He didn't. It was Felix—"

Felix gave her a disdainful look and jumped to the ground. "Yeah, Mr. McKubin, Sol's lying. I did it. I borrowed your clubs 'cause"—he shot a lightning grin at Vause—" 'cause we wanted to play polo."

Sol's face went white. "I'm not lying. It was me," he insisted.

"My daddy will buy you a new club," said Felix casually to Mr. McKubin. "Or I guess you might need two. There was another one got kind of bent."

"I did it," said Sol, his voice shaking. Jottie saw tears glittering in his eyes.

"Stop it!" Jottie hissed at him desperately. "Stop it!"

There was a silence. Vause watched the ground, his face stiff with pity and embarrassment. Felix met Mr. McKubin's eyes and shrugged. Frowning, Sol's father reached out to grasp his son's shoulder. At his touch, Sol started and looked around wildly. "I did!" he whispered.

Jottie could bear it no longer. She darted forward and kicked

Sol in the shin. Then she ran, bounding through the long grass like a hunted animal.

Jottie returned to the dining room and sat down beside Layla. Picking up a sheet of onionskin, she continued reading.

. . . Well hidden amongst the rocky crags northeast of town, the Knock-Pie Trail (4.6 mi. north on County Road 6, near the junction of Mount Heaven Road and DeBoult's Loft) holds a distinguished place in Macedonia's Civil War history. In the summer of 1861, Confederate Brigadier General Robert S. Garnett was ordered to clear the mountain passes north of the Shenandoah Valley of Federal troops. To achieve this, he was given forty-five hundred soldiers "in a most miserable condition as to arms, clothing, equipment, and discipline." Opposing him were twenty-two thousand well-ordered and well-armed recruits from Ohio and Indiana, under the command of Major General George B. McClellan. In this unequal struggle, Garnett exercised ingenuity in place of weapons and developed a strategy of duping his Union foes into the belief that he had many more, and better equipped, soldiers than he actually possessed. One such charade took place on the night of June 30, 1861. Upon learning that one of McClellan's brigades was planning a nighttime exodus south to Sapony Mountain along the Mount Heaven Road, Garnett ordered his men to a rough, ill-marked trail above that road, there to string themselves out in a sparse, long line. Instead of guns, each man was given a metal plate or pie pan and a spoon, collected from sympathetic citizens of Macedonia, and commanded to bang one against the other at slow intervals, thus giving the impression of a large advance of cavalry and cannon. All that night, fearful Union soldiers reported hearing the rattle and clash of wagons, horseshoes, and artillery. They arrived in the settlement of Bear Park, two miles east of Sapony Mountain, thoroughly unnerved. "There is no doubt that the enemy has been reinforced to triple our strength," McClellan wrote to General Rosecrans on July 1. "We must retire, or lose all."
General Garnett, who was to lose his life at Corrick's Ford twelve days later, wrote to his cousin General Richard Garnett, "I shall always esteem the bakers of Macedonia, for their pie pans saved our skins." The unnamed trail upon which Garnett's troops ranged themselves was ever after called the Knock-Pie Trail.

"That's real good. I think you just about covered it." Jottie squared the sheaf of onionskin and looked across the table at Layla.

"You like it?" Layla smiled, pleased. She tapped her pencil against the tabletop. "I still can't figure out where Jackson was that next March."

"In 1862?"

"Yes. Mrs. Tapscott swears he stayed in her mother's house, but everyone else says he was down in Romney."

"Pooh, Romney. The way they talk, you'd think the entire war happened on their courthouse lawn, including Appomattox and the assassination of Lincoln. Inez Tapscott wouldn't tell a fib."

"All right." Layla scribbled a note on her paper. "Maybe Miss Betts has something in her file drawer."

"She might. She does love her clippings."

Layla glanced at the clock and stood. "I have to be off. I'm to meet that Farm Security photographer at noon."

Jottie nodded and swept imaginary crumbs off the table.

Layla hesitated, watching her. "Do you want to come along, Jottie?"

Jottie looked up and smiled. "Can't. I've got big plans to clean out the linen closet this afternoon."

She turned to the window and watched Layla hurry away along the sidewalk. She should get up, she knew. The linen closet wasn't going to clean itself out. She missed Sol. She missed his calm benevolence, his wondering regard for her, and the respectful looks that had followed them down the street. And maybe more than anything, she missed his belief in her allure. Dates! Movies! Holding hands! A woman's natural due. Well, she could read about it in books from now on. She should get up. She should get up and telephone Belle Fox and offer to bring a fruit salad to the next meeting of the Daughters of Macedon. I'm in a ladies' club, she reassured herself. My life is fine.

33

Miss Coco Echols, the photographer, did not have time to waste on Macedonia. Her presence was a favor to the Writers' Project, she explained, a gift from the Farm Security Administration, now gravely handicapped by her absence. She gazed stonily at Town Hall. The Writers' Project, Layla, and the populace of Macedonia, it was clear, were substantially in her debt.

"The mill's quite close," said Layla, after Town Hall had been disapprovingly immortalized. "It won't take long."

"It better not," said Miss Echols. As she swung around to her Oldsmobile, the whistle at American Everlasting let off its noon blast, and she jumped appreciably. "Jesus! What the hell was that?"

"The noon whistle at the mill," said Layla, hiding a smile.

Miss Echols made a sour face. "What kind of mill is it?"

Layla cleared her throat. "Socks. The American Everlasting Hosiery Company."

"Socks?" said Miss Echols contemptuously. "Jesus. What a dump. Come on, get in."

"It's right down the street."

"Still. All my stuff is in my car. We'll drive."

Obediently, Layla settled herself in the car and directed Miss Echols to the enormous brick expanse of American Everlasting. As the massive car docked at the curb across the street, the two women found themselves regarding an empty sidewalk.

Layla frowned. Wasn't it lunchtime? Did the workers eat inside? A thousand of them?

Miss Echols sighed heavily and opened her door. "Let's step on it, all right? I gotta be in D.C. at five."

Layla leaned forward to peer at the building. "Where is everyone?" She paused. "They can't possibly all eat inside, can they?"

Miss Echols, scrabbling with her black camera case, didn't look up. "Damned if I know."

In place of the expected crowd of mill workers, a black-and-white police wagon drove slowly down the street and parked in front of the entrance. Layla recognized the policeman named Hank behind the wheel. He did not appear to have any purpose; he simply sat in his car, reaching up occasionally to stroke his mustache.

Layla frowned slightly. "I wonder what's going on," she murmured.

Miss Echols looked up, a can of film in her mouth. "Huh?"

At that moment, the door opened. A man in a seersucker suit came out and slowly walked down the stairs. Layla cocked her head. Was it the man named Sol, the one she'd seen in Shank's office, the one who'd spoken with Jottie? Maybe. He approached the police wagon and leaned into the window, greeting Hank with easy familiarity.

While the two men bent their heads together, Layla noticed three other men drifting from an alley toward the sidewalk where the police wagon was parked. They were slightly down-at-the-heel, these three, and their faces were expressionless under their caps. Then two women turned the corner, one of them carrying a covered basket, their faces equally blank.

Mesmerized by the combination of determination and emptiness on their faces, Layla opened her door and stepped out. Four more men came to join the others. They didn't speak to one another. They just stood before the mill, their eyes on its brick front. She followed their gaze, scanning the building for information, and spotted a cluster of heads in an upstairs window. She couldn't be sure, but one of them might have belonged to Mr. Shank.

The sound of Miss Echols slamming her door brought Layla out of her reverie. "You want the front, right?"

"Something's wrong," murmured Layla. "Look at their faces."

Miss Echols surveyed the men and women on the sidewalk without interest. "I'll just do the front." She lifted her camera and snapped.

One of the men whistled, and Layla saw the man talking to Hank lift his head and glance quickly around. Their eyes met, and she was surprised to see him smile and shake his head.

"Maybe this isn't a good time to take pictures," said Layla uneasily.

"What?" The photographer sneered. "Don't be a sissy."

"Miss Beck?" It was the man who knew Jottie. She turned to him in relief.

"Yes?"

"I'm Sol McKubin," he said. "You and your friend—colleague—might want to go on your way. There's nothing going to happen at the moment, and your, uh, presence may be distressing some people." He nodded toward the straggling group of watchers.

"Who are they?"

"Bystanders. Friends, wives, you know."

"Friends and wives of whom?" she asked. "What's happening?"

His eyebrows lifted. "Strike. I thought you knew. I thought that's why you were here."

"No. No," Layla said. "I don't know anything." She nodded toward Coco Echols. "She's just taking a picture of the mill for my book. *The History of Macedonia.*"

He nodded. "Maybe you could come back another day."

"I think we have what we need." Layla looked at the silent mill. "It's a very quiet strike."

"Sit-down," he said. "God knows how long they'll go."

She felt a pang of sympathy for him, management or no. "Will there be trouble?"

"Trouble? I don't know. I hope not." He lifted his chin toward Hank. "He's the one I feel sorry for. Ralph's going to call him and Arnold in any minute."

"What about the National Guard?" said Layla, remembering the strikes she had read about.

He seemed to find the idea amusing. "The National Guard has bigger fish to fry, I expect. American Everlasting isn't General Motors."

She glanced up at the window. "No company goons, either, I guess."

He smiled. "Not unless you count Richie and me." He glanced toward the snapping Miss Echols and sobered. "Is there any way you can persuade her not to publish them? I'd like to keep the AFL out of this."

"Oh, don't worry," Layla assured him earnestly. "She hasn't noticed there's a strike. And I won't tell her."

He threw back his head and laughed. "No wonder Jottie likes you."

"She does?" asked Layla, pleased.

"Yes. She's spoken of you. Ah." His face clouded. "Don't mention I said that. Okay?"

Curious. She nodded anyway.

"And listen, Miss Beck?" For a moment, he looked mischievous as a boy. "When you get home, will you call Emmett in White Creek and tell him about the strike? Tell him I asked you to call. He'll understand."

"Why, all right." Curiouser and curiouser.

"Promise?"

"Yes, of course," she said.

He smiled at her and turned away, tossing her a look of extravagant alarm as he passed the clicking Miss Echols.

Back on Academy Street, Layla watched Coco Echols's vast car dwindle in the distance before she turned toward the house. In the shadowed, quiet hallway, she hesitated for a moment and then lifted the telephone receiver from the cradle. "Long distance, please."

"City, please?" the operator asked crisply.

"White Creek."

Layla listened to the telephone wires click. "White Creek, what number, please?"

"I'm trying to reach Emmett Romeyn." From the corner of her eye, she saw Jottie step into the hall, holding a knife.

"Hold the line, please." More clicks.

"Hello?" It was Emmett's voice, pleasant and distant.

"Go ahead," said the operator.

"Thank you. Mr. Romeyn?"

"Yes. This is he."

"This is Layla. Layla Beck."

"Layla! Miss Beck! How are you?"

"I'm fine, thanks. I'm calling to give you a message—"

"Is everyone all right down there?"

"Everyone's fine, but Mr. McKubin asked me to tell you that there's a strike at the mill started today, a sit-down—"

"What? A strike? *Who* told you to tell me?"

"Mr. McKubin. Sol McKubin. You know him, don't you? He said I should call to tell you and you'd understand why." Now Felix stood in the doorway, too, a newspaper in his hand, watching her.

Emmett's laughter rolled over the telephone wire. "Sol told you to phone me? And he calls *me* a rabble-rouser!"

"Pardon?"

"Never mind. Tell me about the strike. What were you doing there, anyway?"

"I needed a picture of the mill for my book, so I went down with a photographer," Layla explained. "When we got there, the place was dead quiet, even though the noon whistle had just gone. There was nobody anywhere, which was odd, I thought, and then a police wagon drove up." She recounted the scene at the mill, the strangely expressionless bystanders on the sidewalk, and Miss Echols's imperviousness. "She didn't pay any attention and started taking pictures, and then Mr. McKubin came and asked us to stop. That's when he told me there was a strike—a sit-down strike, he said."

"But it was quiet?"

"Yes, but he said that Shank—Mr. Shank—was about to call in Hank and someone named Arnold, and he felt sorry for them."

"The workers?"

"No. Hank and Arnold. Who's Arnold?"

"Another policeman," Emmett said briefly. "But you're sure he said it was a sit-down?"

"Yes."

"Good." She could almost hear him smile with satisfaction. "That's good news."

"Is Mr. McKubin—" She paused, distracted by a flicking movement on the edge of her vision. Felix was gone.

"What?"

"Is he on their side? You said I'd be surprised at who was."

"I should keep my mouth shut."

"So he is? That's rather—astonishing."

"Sol's not your average boss."

"Clearly."

There was another pause. "Well," Emmett said. "Thank you for calling me, Miss Beck. I'm obliged to you. Maybe I'll come down there and see this strike for myself tomorrow."

She laughed. "It wasn't much to look at."

"Got to hope it'll stay that way," he said. There was a pause. "Maybe I'll see you there."

"I don't think so. I'm supposed to be writing history."

"But it *is* history. Don't you want to champion the cause of labor in Macedonia?"

"Very tempting, Mr. Romeyn." She glanced at Jottie, leaning against the wall. "But it's not history yet. It's just a fight. It's not history until someone wins."

At suppertime, Felix's place remained empty.

"Where's your daddy tonight?" Layla asked Willa casually, lifting the butter dish.

Willa gave her a malevolent stare. "I don't know."

"He goes off, he could be in Timbuktu and we wouldn't know it," Bird expatiated helpfully. "Nobody knows where he is."

"Selling chemicals somewhere, I suppose," said Layla.

Willa said nothing, but Bird leaned forward. "He has one that could blow up the entire world."

"Bird," said Jottie, entering the dining room. "You lie like a rug."

The evening passed slowly. The porch was filled with excited talk of the strike and the rattle of coffee spoons, the dark perforated by cries of chasing children and creaking chairs, and when Layla excused herself and climbed to her room, she found it still and suffocating, the heat sheeting her slick with sweat. Listlessly, she bathed and made ready for bed, dabbling without interest in *The Rending of Virginia* for a few minutes before she tossed it aside and turned out her light.

Much later, she woke for no reason. There was a little breeze from the window. Sighing, she turned to receive it and saw Felix sitting on the windowsill, smoking. She stared at him for a moment, trying to understand if he was real.

Blue in the smoke, he looked toward her. "There you are."

"Felix," she murmured. "You weren't at supper."

"That's right."

"I wished you were."

He tapped his ash on the roof. "Sweetheart?"

There was a silence. "Is that me?" she asked finally.

He smiled. "Yes. That's you."

She nodded. Good.

"Don't go to the mill," he said.

She struggled to comprehend his meaning. "I already did."

"Again, then. Don't go again." He stood. "All right?"

She looked at him. Ever again? It seemed a strange request. Why? "Mr. McKubin already asked me not to."

"I don't care what Mr. McKubin asked you to do," he said. "I'm telling you not to."

"Oh, yes," she said, almost to herself. "You two had a falling-out."

"A falling-out?" He laughed softly. "Did Jottie call it that?"

"Mm-hm. Felix?"

"He's a liar, all right? Just stay away from him."

She shook her head sleepily. "He seemed so nice. Friend of Emmett's."

He stubbed out his cigarette with a sigh and came to stand beside the bed. For a moment, she watched him watch her, and then he bent to kiss her. "Sol or me?" he murmured.

She smiled. "Hard decision."

He kissed her again, his tongue tracing her lips. "Sol or me?"

"Can't decide."

He swung one knee over her and lowered himself over her

body. "Sol or me?" She could feel the heat of him as his hands closed around her, and she arched up to meet his mouth.

"My God. You."

He set her down and smiled. He rubbed his thumb along the line of her jaw and then over her lips. "Good," he said. He lifted himself off the bed. "See you tomorrow."

She stared wide-eyed as the door closed behind him.

34

The next afternoon, Emmett rose from his chair as she climbed the front steps. "Miss Beck."

"You came!" In the shade of the porch, she pulled off her hat. "Did you go to the mill? Is it still going on?"

Emmett grinned. "Yes and yes. Have a seat. Jottie's just gone in to get some ice-tea. I'll get a glass for you, too."

She nodded, watching his straight back as he retreated into the shadow of the hallway. He seemed exhilarated. By the strike, she supposed. And younger, too, much nearer her own age than she had thought. It was impossible to understand how she could have mistaken him for Felix. They were nothing alike.

He returned with two glasses. "What?" he said, seeing her eyes on him.

"You're the last holdout. On Miss Beck," she said.

"Excuse me?"

"No other Romeyn calls me Miss Beck now." She tipped back her head to see his face. "Will you call me Layla?"

He hesitated. "Emmett. Please."

She held out her hand, and he took it. "Delighted to make your acquaintance, Emmett."

"The pleasure is all mine, Layla." He bowed slightly.

"Finishing school, I see."

He laughed. "Jottie. Jottie and my mother."

"Me and mama what?" Jottie came out with a beading pitcher, Willa close behind, bearing a plate of cookies. "What'd we do?"

He smiled at her. "Taught me manners."

"You!" she scoffed. "You were born with manners. Your uncle Emmett," she said, turning to Willa, "used to stop ladies on the street and tell them how pretty they were. When he was three years old, he did that."

Willa giggled.

"They *were* pretty," said Emmett. "I thought they were all so pretty and they smelled so nice."

"You never saw a child get so much candy." Jottie smiled at him. "Used to send Mae into fits."

"Emmett," Felix said, coming outside. He slapped his brother lightly on the shoulder and dropped into a chair beside Layla.

"Remember when Emmett used to tell all the ladies how pretty they were?" Jottie said.

Felix nodded. "Got so you couldn't hardly carry all your candy."

"You helped," said Emmett pointedly, and Felix chuckled.

Look how wonderful he is, thought Layla, her eyes on Felix. Comfortable. Normal—better than normal. Lance never jokes with me, probably can't remember a thing about me as a child. Doesn't know me, doesn't care. I wish I had a real brother, one like Emmett. I wish this were my family. Maybe it will be.

Jottie handed a cookie to Willa and then turned her attention to Emmett. "Tell," she said. "How was it at the mill?"

"Well, like you said yesterday"—Emmett nodded to Layla— "it's pretty quiet. About two dozen men and a few women standing outside, a couple of signs saying things like We Support the Right to Unite. But quiet. Charlie Timbrook's wife— you know Cecile?" he asked Jottie. She nodded. "She says they're mostly sleeping."

"Where?" Willa asked.

He smiled at her. "At the looms, some of them. But mostly on the floor."

"What's Shank going to do?" asked Jottie.

"He called in Hank and Arnold yesterday afternoon, and they arrested five men for trespassing and then said they didn't have room in the jail for any more." Emmett's smile flashed.

"Said they couldn't release Winslow, because he was a menace to the community."

"Poor Miss Betts," laughed Layla.

"Another hope dashed," Jottie said.

"So they left the rest of the fellows where they were and went back to the station. Now Shank's got to figure out what to do—bring in strikebreakers or just wait it out or what." Emmett leaned forward in his chair. "Sol thinks he's going to wait it out." Layla's eyes darted toward Felix, and she saw Jottie's do the same. Felix, however, was gazing evenly at Emmett. "He thinks Shank's too tight to hire strikebreakers."

"What're strikebreakers?" asked Willa.

"They're people who come to a place where there's a strike," explained Felix, "and beat up the strikers and take their jobs."

"Ohh." Willa recoiled. She looked from her father to Jottie. "Isn't that bad?"

"Yes," said Jottie. "That's bad."

"I bet Sol's right," said Felix. He smiled blandly at Jottie's startled expression. "I bet Shank won't do it. He wants to be liked."

"Ah, he doesn't give a damn," said Emmett.

"Oh, he does," Layla assured him. "You should see the portrait of the benevolent industrialist he dictated to me when I interviewed him."

Emmett raised his eyebrow. "Fairy tales."

"Yes, but also proof that he wants the town to love him," she said. Felix nodded in agreement, and she felt a surge of pride. Straightening professionally in her chair, she said, "Is Shank still there, at the mill?"

"Yup. Sol and Richie and Arlen and the rest of management, too. They sent the salesmen home."

"How long could they go?" asked Jottie.

Emmett shrugged. "Food's the problem, I guess. The fellows brought in extra, of course, but it won't last forever. Hard to figure how to get more in."

"Can't they pass it through the windows?" said Willa.

"No. Trespassing. Easy to spot."

"Roof?" asked Jottie.

"No," said Felix authoritatively. They turned toward him.

"Management offices are below the roof," he explained, "except on the Unity Street side, and that's no good because of the drop from the skylight." He rubbed his face thoughtfully. "And that boiler room is pretty hard to get to, especially if you've got a lot to carry." Layla saw Emmett glance at Jottie and smile. "But there's the trucks—are the trucks still at the dock?" Emmett nodded. "Okay. Easy. There's a panel in the back of the cab; it's just held on with a few screws and it'll get you into the wagon. They're backed in, waiting to fill, right?" He nodded to himself. "That'll get you into the warehouse inside of five minutes. And last time I looked there was no wire at the top of the fence, so it's just an easy up and over—" He looked up as Emmett and Jottie began to laugh. "What?" he asked innocently.

Emmett shook his head as Jottie leaned back in her chair, laughing.

Layla glanced in puzzlement between Felix and his siblings. What was the joke?

But Felix was grinning himself now. "I've always been a friend to the working man," he said loudly. "Always."

———※———

July 26, 1938

Dear Layla,

Close inspection of today's *Star* disclosed that Macedonia is "rent asunder by labor discord" and "the malcontents' call for blood may not long go unslaked." Et cetera. After four paragraphs of this drivel, I managed to deduce that there's a sit-down strike at a hosiery mill in town. From the sound of it, the strike is a pretty quiet affair, and I doubt you've even noticed it (unless there have been stocking shortages). Nonetheless:

My dear niece,

If you feel the slightest disquiet I herewith order you to abandon your post *at once* and return to Washington. There is no book in the history of the project that compares in value with your safety.

And you can be assured that I have made a copy of that

paragraph for the Central File. I doubt Gray will peruse the *Star* with sufficient attention to discover the story (as far as I can tell, he only reads the articles that are about him), but if the invaluable Miss Kogelshatz brings it to his notice, he will fall on me like a ton of bricks, and I want to have my defense ready. I know you understand.

Hope you're enjoying yourself up there. And keeping on deadline.

Ben

P.S. On the off chance that the strike turns dirty, be sensible and get out of town. That's an order. A real one. B.

July 28, 1938

Dear Ben,

You couldn't get me out of here with a buttered shoehorn.

Layla

P.S. I was at the mill when it struck.
P. P. S. Workers, unite! You have nothing to lose but your chains!

July 30, 1938

Layla,

Are you trying to get me fired?

Ben

August 1, 1938

Yes!

35

Out on the porch, Bird flopped down on a wicker chair and hoisted one knee over the armrest. She brought the newspaper close to her face and read, ". . . Mr. Shank, president of American Everlasting, disputed the statement. 'I am a patriotic American. I've done more than anyone in this town for the workers, and I'm not going to sit back and let foreigners and Communists tear down what I've built.'"

Built? Bird frowned. Mr. Shank *built* the mill? That didn't make sense. Maybe one building, but he couldn't have built all of it. Still, she comforted herself, she was reading the newspaper. Not many nine-year-olds read the newspaper. She's a very sophisticated child, she imagined Minerva saying. *A prodigy,* Mae agreed in hushed tones. Fortified by this hypothetical admiration, Bird redoubled her efforts. "Mr. Charlie Timbrook, leader of the prospective"—what did that mean?—"local, took issue—"

With relief, Bird noticed a figure standing outside the screen door. A lady—a thin shadow of a lady—leaned in, shielding her eyes, and spotted Bird. "Afternoon, miss," she said.

Miss! Bird liked that. She rattled her newspaper ostentatiously. "Good day," she said.

"Is your aunt Jottie at home?"

"Yes," said Bird, wishing there were a longer word for yes.

"Will you ask her to step out, please, miss? You can tell her it's Zena here."

"Okay." Bird went inside and found Jottie, in the kitchen. "Someone named Zena is on the porch."

Jottie frowned in puzzlement, wiped her hands on her apron, and moved swiftly down the hall. Bird watched to make sure she was gone, and then she set the newspaper down on the kitchen table, licked her finger, and put it in the sugar bowl.

"Why, Zena!" exclaimed Jottie. "How-you? It's been a long time. Have a seat." She gestured to a chair, trying to look pleased instead of curious.

Zena tucked a wisp of her no-color hair under her hat and bobbed her head. "No. No thank you, Miss Jottie. I come—"

"*Miss* Jottie?" asked Jottie incredulously. "Zena, don't. We've known each other for thirty years."

Zena licked her lips. "I guess. If you say so."

"Come on and sit." Jottie sat and patted the chair next to hers. "Sit down and tell me what's on your mind."

Zena sat with the tiniest of creaks on the edge of the chair. "Thank you."

Jottie saw that her dress was limp with sweat. Surely she hadn't walked all the way from her house, not in this heat; it had to be three miles. "How about I get us some ice-tea, all right?" she said. And as many cookies as I can fit on a plate, she thought, eyeing Zena's thin arms. I wonder if she'd take a sandwich. "I'll be right back, and then we can have us a nice—"

"No! No thank you! I ain't thirsty!" Zena said nervously. "Please"—she held up her hand—"I just got to say something." She pulled in a breath, preparing to speak, but the breath fractured into a hiccup, and a pair of tears trickled into the hollows of her cheeks. She gave a long sniffle.

Filled with pity, Jottie watched her shuffle in her bosom for a handkerchief. Zena had never had a chance. There was Zena at seven, with her matchstick legs and her ruffled, too-big dresses. Zena at thirteen, at the American Everlasting picnic, squealing, *I done it, I done it,* as she tossed a horseshoe. Zena at twenty, walking along False River Road, freighted with a big baby in her arms and a sunken, silent husband at her side. "What is it, Zena?" Jottie said gently. "Don't cry. Just tell me."

"Jerry lost his job," Zena choked. "Down at the mill."

Jottie sighed. "I'm sorry to hear that. Real sorry."

"We sold everything we could and now all the money's gone

and we're down pretty low, Jottie, and"—her words rushed out—"I thought maybe you could ask Mr. McKubin. I bet if you asked him he'd give Jerry something; it don't have to be the same job as before, but just something, he'll do it. He'll do anything—"

Jottie's eyes widened. "Wait, Zena. What?"

"You could ask Mr. McKubin," Zena repeated. "Anything, Jottie. Like you said, we've known each other thirty years, and I wouldn't come if—we just got to have something, Jottie. Please."

"But Zena." Jottie swallowed, trying to select an obstacle that Zena could understand. "You know there's a strike on. They can't hire anyone during a strike—"

Zena broke in, "Yeah, that's what I mean! Jerry don't want a union, anyway. He'd be glad to go in and work if they don't wanna. You can tell Mr. McK. that Jerry hates Charlie Timbrook and always has done!"

Jottie licked her lips. "But I can't, Zena," she explained. "I'm not in a position to ask Mr. McKubin for anything."

Zena smirked. "Tell me another. I seen you two. Just the other day, there you was, drinking milk shakes. Been a lotta years since I had a milk shake." She laughed mirthlessly. "People say you're going around. He'd do whatever you wanted."

"That's not true, Zena!" Jottie said quickly. "None of what you're saying is true. Mr. McKubin and I are—well, I've known him as long as I've known you, I guess, but that's all. We're acquaintances." She swallowed. "I have no *influence* with him. Jerry should talk to Mr. McKubin himself."

"You think we ain't tried?" Zena snapped. "He said he can't do nothing. Says it's Shank who decides when to hire."

"And have you tried asking Mr. Shank?" suggested Jottie helplessly.

Zena snorted. "Pff. He don't talk to no one, and, anyway, from what I hear, he ain't gonna be there much longer. That's what Ceecee Timbrook says."

"What?"

"You ain't heard?" asked Zena, enjoying her rare authority. "The unionizers said they wouldn't—ah, whaddaya call it?— *negotiate* to anyone except Mr. McK., and now him and the big shots in New Jersey are talking all the time, and everyone says they're gonna get rid of Shank and make Mr. McK. president."

Jottie stared at her, speechless. Sol, president? Sol, in her father's place? Could it be true? She considered the source. No. Zena had probably misunderstood. Or exaggerated. Or made it up to sound important.

"So could you ask him?"

Jottie returned to the present. "Zena," she said, "you're mistaken about Mr. McKubin and me. I have no more—"

"Just ask him. Please."

"Zena, I don't—I can't—"

"You could if you wanted; you just don't want to," said Zena bitterly. "You got your milk shake."

"Listen—"

"No, you listen to me, Jottie Romeyn," snapped Zena. "You think you're so high up you don't have to treat someone like me right, but you'll find out different. You Romeyns always did think you were better than anyone." She rose and stood over Jottie. "But you ain't."

Jottie tried again. "It's not that I don't want to help you—"

"I don't need your charity!" Zena spat, her voice rising. "The big Romeyns ain't so almighty high anymore, huh?" Her eyes raked over the shabby porch. "That Felix, he's going to get caught any day now, is what Jerry says." She yanked the top of her dress straight. "He's a two-bit bootlegger and a thief. He set that fire at the mill, too, and stole the money. Everyone knows he done it and he killed Vause Hamilton, too."

Jottie lifted her chin. "Get off my porch now, Zena."

"You won't be so uppity when he's in jail, will you?" Zena went on gladly. "You'll be needing a job yourself then, uh-huh?" She grinned. "Ask Mr. McK. Maybe he'll pay for what he's getting."

"Get off my porch now, before I turn the hose on you."

Zena gulped up some air, her hollow cheeks inflating with spite. "And if those snippy little girls're anything like their mama, you're gonna run yourself ragged pulling them out of every barn in town. Those apples won't fall far from the tree, I bet."

Jottie rose and went to the screen door. Without a word, she proceeded to the hosepipe that stood against the steps and un-furled the coiled brown hose that lay beneath it. "The good thing about that furniture," she called over her shoulder to Zena, "is that when it gets dirty, I just hose it down. Like a dog." She turned the spigot and placed her thumb expertly over the opening, dousing the rhododendrons in a curving arc of water. She turned toward the porch, spraying water in a vast circle as she did so.

"Hey!" Zena cried, taking cover behind the screen door. "Cut it out! You can't turn the hose on me." She cracked open the door and craned her neck around it.

Jottie lifted one eyebrow. "Can't I?"

"I'm wearing my good *hat*," protested Zena.

"I don't care," said Jottie.

Water rained merrily into the rhododendrons while Zena gnawed the inside of her mouth, assessing the odds. After a minute, she tossed her head. "I ain't scared of you," she pro-claimed, thrusting the door wide. "I ain't scared of you, Jottie Romeyn." She took a flouncing step down and stopped. "You turn off that water," she called.

Jottie threw the hose on the grass and waited, watching, as Zena took another step, and then another, her eyes darting from the hose to its owner and back again.

As Zena arrived at the front walk, twitching her narrow hips, Jottie held up a hand, stopping her in mid-flounce. "Never come here again," she said. "Never speak to me or about me or anyone else in my family again. Or you'll be sorry."

"I'll be sorry? What're you gonna do—arrest me?" sneered Zena. "Last time I looked, you don't run the country."

"I'll tell everyone I know that you went to bed with Shank and gave him the clap and that's why he fired Jerry. I'll say Jerry's just a few months away from turning idiot—syphilis does that, you know. I'll say that's how come he limps."

Zena's eyes widened. "But you can't—it ain't true. I ain't—Shank—I don't have no syphilis and you know it. And Jerry's not—it's his foot. He had it since he was a kid—"

"Who are they going to believe?" said Jottie coldly.

36

Jottie had told Bird and me to stay right away from American Everlasting, that a strike was no place for gawkers, especially not children, and even more especially not us. We obeyed her, though we knew for a fact we were the only children in town who hadn't gone to look. Jun Lloyd said he'd crept down to the mill in the night and seen the blood seeping out from under the door and that's how he knew mill workers were being killed one by one in cold blood. He said Mr. Shank did it with a switchblade, because the folks outside would hear a gunshot. He said his own uncle worked inside the mill and told him that there was blood everywhere. His uncle had crouched down so Mr. Shank wouldn't get him.

Of course, I didn't believe a word of this, even though Jun Lloyd was a Boy Scout and supposed to be trustworthy on top of being clean, kind, and patriotic. He wasn't any of those things, either. "You lie like a dog, Jun," I said. "Ain't anybody stabbing anybody."

"All you know," he sneered. "You got any family down there at the mill?"

I was obliged to shake my head.

"Then you don't know," he said. "*My* uncle is on strike."

"My grandfather was president of it," was all I could say.

"Well, he's not now, is he?" said Dex Lloyd. And then he stuck out his tongue.

The next afternoon, I was at the library, as I was nearly every day in the summer. The rule was you could take out five books each week, but Miss Betts made an exception for me. She let me take two books a day, which was enough, but just barely. My selections were generally based on thickness. I was pushing out the door with my new books in hand when I saw Jottie down the street on the front steps of the bank. She was standing there frozen in place, and she looked like she'd been lightning-struck, but I knew better: She was doing math in her head. Jottie couldn't walk and do math at the same time—I couldn't, either—and when she came out of the bank, she always had to hold still for a bit, subtracting. I scurried down there, fast as I could, and she didn't notice a thing, she was that busy with her subtracting. "Forty-two!" I hollered. "Six! Twenty-seven!"

She jumped, but when she saw it was me, she began to laugh. "You are the worst child I ever met, Willa." She came down the steps and took up my hand in her little cool one. "We have either seventy-nine dollars or seventy-nine cents, and now only the good Lord himself knows which it is."

I shifted on my feet and looked down the block. I could just see the edge of the mill. "Jottie?" I began.

"Don't ask me for candy, you sinful child."

"I wasn't going to," I said, and it was the truth. "What I want is free."

"Good thing," she said. "What is it?"

"Let's you and me go look at the strike. Please?"

She frowned. "We've got no business there."

"Everyone else in town has gone to look, 'cept me and Bird," I said in plaintive tones. "Jun Lloyd's been four times, once in the dead of night, and he says there's blood oozing out from under the front door, because Mr. Shank's stabbing everyone—"

"That's ridiculous," Jottie interrupted. "I hope you have more sense than to believe that."

"I didn't believe it," I said. "But Jun Lloyd said I didn't know anything because I didn't have anyone in my family at the mill."

Jottie lifted her eyebrow.

"It's practically the only thing that's ever happened in Macedonia, and I'm missing it."

Jottie shook her head, but her face was sympathetic at the same time. "I'm willing to bet that it'll be a lot less exciting than watching a train back up, but all right. Let's go see the strike. Just for a minute."

Off we went, down Prince Street toward East Main. And Jottie was right: Once we'd turned the corner, it didn't look like much. There was the mill, a big long stretch of red brick, the same as ever. Out in front, in a straggling line, were about thirty or forty men and women. Some of them had signs, but since they were waving them at the mill, I couldn't read more than a few words, only To Unite! and The TWOC Supports the Rights of. I wondered who they were, these men and women, since the strikers were inside. Maybe relatives, I was guessing, when I saw that one of them was Emmett.

"Hey! Emmett!" I yelled, and he turned around, his face lighting up the way it did.

He came over to where we were standing, a little apart from the crowd, bringing with him a man I'd never seen before. There was the usual grown-up business of greetings and introductions, to which I paid little heed, as they never included me. The man was someone called Mr. Bryce with the TWOC.

"And this is my niece, Willa Romeyn," Emmett added, which brought me around a little. Emmett, I reflected, was politer than most grown-ups. It was probably because he was the youngest child himself and he hadn't quite forgotten the indignities of youth. Yet.

He and Jottie and Mr. Bryce talked. After a bit, I deduced that TWOC was the same thing as Textile Workers Organizing Committee and felt pleased with myself. Mr. Bryce had come up from Washington to see the strike, and he was real happy about it. According to Mr. Bryce, the union was confident that Macedonia was just the tip of the iceberg. The problem, according to Mr. Bryce, was that they had started too far south. Dalton was the wrong place to expect progress, he said. He talked on and on, Mr. Bryce did. As he talked, my eyes caught the big front door of the mill opening. Mr. Shank came through that door and stood on the top step, his eyes shooting over the line of men and women on the sidewalk and coming to rest on Mr. Bryce. I hadn't seen Mr. Shank so very many times, but when I had, he'd been stiff and cold, in fancy clothes. Today, though, he wasn't wearing a coat, and his face was pink and angry. There was kind of a ripple in the crowd at his appearance, and all the folks stopped talking. The only person who didn't notice him was Mr. Bryce, who was still going on about the tip of the iceberg.

Suddenly Mr. Shank yelled, "You people are damned fools! You're damned fools if you listen to a Communist agitator!" He swiped his hand in the direction of Mr. Bryce. "You want to pay for his supper with your hard-earned money? You want to throw away your paycheck on a bunch of Reds? We've got a good American shop here; I kept you working all through this Depression, and here you are turning on me. I kept you fed, I kept your children—"

Mr. Bryce was paying attention now. He swung around to face Mr. Shank. "I am not a Communist!" he shouted. "I am an American citizen, and I uphold the rights of all American citizens, including the right to unite!" Somebody near us cheered.

Mr. Shank was yelling, too. "And let me tell you one other thing—if someone by the name of Romeyn feeds you a line about how you need a union, it doesn't mean a goddamned thing!" He made a nasty face at Emmett. "This mill and its operation are not their business, and we don't need any Romeyns here."

Two or three things happened then, almost at once. A man booed. Jottie grabbed my hand and stepped backward. Emmett and Mr. Bryce both started yelling, one about free speech and the other about the right to assemble.

And someone hit Mr. Shank in the face with a peach.

For one second, everyone froze, breathless, staring at the shocking sight of Mr. Shank with juice and bits of peach dribbling down the side of his face. The whole street was perfectly still. For one second. And then another peach splatted against his shirt.

"Union! Union!" hollered someone. I saw a white face pressed up against one of the long weaving-room windows, looking out. It wavered, and I knew it belonged to a man standing on someone else's shoulders so he could see out. "Sit down now for the TWOC!"

"Dirty cowards!" yelled Mr. Shank, and more fruit flew. "Reds!"

The door banged open and another man came out. He looked real stern at the line of men and women, and the fruit stopped flying. He didn't stay there beside Mr. Shank; he marched right down the stairs. Just as I realized that he was heading toward us, I also realized who he was—the man from the parade, Mr. McKubin. All the people parted respectfully to let him by, and he walked right to Jottie. "You all right?" he asked, real grim.

"Hey, Sol," she gulped. Her cheeks were pink.

"You go on home now, Jottie," he said. "This is no place for you. This is no good." His eyes flicked over me and then he scowled at Emmett. "I don't know what you're thinking, Emmett."

"It's not his fault. We're going!" said Jottie hurriedly. "Right now!" She yanked on my hand, and I followed, but slow and draggy. I wanted to see what would happen next.

Mr. McKubin turned to face the crowd. "Now, listen, you-all, that is enough of this ruckus," he said firmly. "There's no sense in this kind of thing. Negotiation is what makes sense. Negotiation is the way we're going to—"

"You've got nothing to say about it, McKubin!" Mr. Shank broke in, real loud. "Sol McKubin does not represent the management of American Everlasting!" he barked. "As of today, he no longer represents the management and may not conclude any negotiations on its behalf!"

Mr. McKubin looked up at him, frowning, like he didn't understand.

"I will have a word with you in my office, McKubin!" Mr. Shank bellowed. His face was redder than ever, and his eyes were glittering. I'd never seen anyone seethe before, but that's what he was doing. "*My* office!" He flicked some peach from his shirt, pulled open the door, and stalked inside.

There was a pause. Everyone looked at Mr. McKubin, and he looked at the door. Then he blinked and kind of shook himself and took a step after Mr. Shank. The men nearest him patted him on the shoulder as he went, but he didn't seem to notice. Emmett put out a hand like he wanted to stop him, but then he took it back and stood, crestfallen, beside Jottie, watching him go.

When Mr. McKubin got to the top of the steps, he looked back, right at Jottie. She stood up real straight and waved to him. He nodded and went inside.

Everyone held still for a moment. Then Emmett let out a long breath.

"Well, I'll be goddamned," said Mr. Bryce. "Think that's the end of him?"

"We'll be going now," said Jottie real quick, and she grabbed my arm and frog-marched me right out of that place.

Well! I thought, as Jottie rushed me home, I had finally witnessed a dramatic episode! And we Romeyns had certainly been at the center of it. But what exactly had happened, I couldn't say. What had Mr. Shank meant? What had he called Mr. McKubin into his office *for*? Mr. Bryce had said it was the end of him—but how could that be?

"Jottie?" I asked—or gasped, really, because of how fast we were walking. "What happened?"

Jottie groaned. "We just lost Sol McKubin his job." She looked positively miserable, so I didn't ask any more.

It wasn't until the next day I read in the Macedonia *Sun* that Mr. Shank had fired Mr. McKubin for "colluding with the union."

37

Cresting the hill, Layla stopped to gaze at the dispiriting prospect before her. Zackquill Avenue was long, dilapidated, and featureless, its houses perched like molting birds high on either side of the street. She sighed. A strike was pulsing in the center of town, and she was on Zackquill Avenue. She had promised Felix. As a reward for her docility, she permitted herself to revisit his secret fingertips, brushing lightly along the back of her leg the night before. Right in front of everyone, too, but they hadn't noticed. They'd chewed their conversational cud, oblivious to the torrent of heat pouring from her body, streaming out over the porch, flooding across the grass, the yard, the street—

Layla gave herself a little shake and glanced down at *Warriors of Western Virginia*. "Generals John B. Imboden and William E. Jones harassed Macedonia throughout the winter and spring of 1863, raiding the town and the surrounding region for supplies and burning the homes of known Federal loyalists. Though Pace records that these guerrilla troops beat a tactical retreat to Mount Edwards when Union forces under General Benjamin Roberts showed themselves in the town, other sources suggest that the raiders went to ground in Macedonia itself. Lieutenant Calvin Rylands (CSA) later noted 'a cozy winter bivouacking on Zackquill Avenue, with a most gracious hostess, Mrs. Kerns.'"

Cozy? Layla scanned the glum dirt yards and listless houses for a shred of coziness. It was probably a fool's errand, anyway. What did she expect to see? Imboden's handprint on the side of the house? She frowned at her great expectations. Delusions of grandeur, meet Zackquill Avenue, she thought, and sighed again.

A single bolt of color jerked her eyes upward. High above the street, a red-haired woman in a violent purple kimono leaned over a porch rail, watching her avidly. As Layla affected ignorance, the woman reached a businesslike hand inside her kimono, scooped her enormous breasts upward, and rewrapped herself more securely, all without interrupting her scrutiny of Layla.

Well, really! Layla thought, insulted by the professionalism of the interest. She's got some nerve! A cheap floozy like her, giving *me* the once-over?

A deafening wolf whistle erupted above her. "Oo-whoo, baby!" sang a falsetto, followed by more whistles. She turned to find the source and saw a band of young men splayed over a sagging porch.

"Oo-ooh, lookit her! Wanna come up, honey? We're good company!" they caroled together, grinning appreciatively at themselves, plucking at their undershirts.

Layla lifted her chin and stepped briskly across the street, at once ignoring them and watching for them at the edges of her vision.

"Now, miss"—one of them had jumped down to the side-walk, blocking her path—"you oughta be more friendly." He ran his eyes over her insolently. "You know?"

Before Layla could respond, a deep voice rumbled from the house above: "You leave her alone, Bobby, you little shitbird, or I'll tell Mavis you're chasing tail behind her back." It was the woman in the kimono.

"Shut your pan, Della. This here's my new girlfriend," Bobby yelled. He slid closer to Layla, and she flinched a little at the smell. He grinned, sensing weakness.

"Yeah-huh," snorted the big woman. "Don't look like she likes you much." She considered Layla. "You want to come up here, girl?"

For a moment, she hesitated. Then Bobby leered, "Didn't know you were that type of gal. How much you asking?" Layla turned haughtily on her heel and climbed the mangled stairs to Della's porch, taking a bit of vengeful pleasure in imagining her father's face if he could see her current predicament. Wasn't this all your brilliant idea? she needled him. But now she had arrived at the porch and Della.

Layla dropped her eyes. "Thanks," she said.

"Yeah." Della nodded. "He'll go pretty soon. He's a twerp." She ran her small white hand over the purple effusion of her kimono. "I'm-a get dressed. Be back in a sec."

Layla waited, shifting on her feet. There were no chairs on the splintering porch, no signs of ease, nothing. Well, what do you expect? she asked herself. It's a whorehouse. People don't exactly come here to sit on the porch. She glanced at the tattered screen door. She'd always assumed these places would be a bit luxurious—tawdry luxury, to be sure, but still luxury. Garish silken sofas, for instance. Frayed garish silken sofas. A sidelong glance through the screen door revealed a hallway bare except for an umbrella stand and a small mirror, hanging crooked on the pale wall. Circlets of dust lay limp in the corners. As Layla leaned forward for a closer look, someone inside yawned, a slow, stretchy, intimate yawn, and she drew back hastily.

Della's return was announced by a cloud of Jungle Gardenia. She wore a flowered dress that followed the flesh of her body closely until it blossomed over her enormous chest. Her lips were a red surprise in the white-powder O of her face, but she was irretrievably pretty. She gave Layla a short nod and thumped over to the porch railing. "He's still there." A pause. "You want some ice-tea?"

Inside a whorehouse? Layla was mustering a dignified refusal when she noticed Della's guarded expression and felt an unexpected prickle of shame. "That would be nice, thanks. I'm just about parched."

Della's smile was quick and surprised. "Well! Come on in, take a load off!"

Layla followed her down the nondescript hallway into a dreary kitchen. There, Della moved from a peeling icebox to a peeling cupboard and set their bounty on a peeling table. "Have a seat," she said, sitting heavily herself. Layla perched on a worn chair and took an experimental sip of sin-steeped tea. It was good. "So," said Della. "Whatcha doing here?"

Layla sighed. The goose she chased seemed more cooked than ever. "I'm looking for a house," she began. "The Kerns house."

Della's eyes narrowed slightly. "For what?"

Layla attempted to explain. "You see, I'm writing a book about the history of Macedonia, and this"—she tapped the cover of *Warriors of Western Virginia*—"suggests that the Confederate general Imboden and his men were guests at the home of Mrs. Kerns here on Zackquill Avenue during the winter of 1863. But it's never been certain, and I was thinking that perhaps I might answer that question if I found the house . . ." She trailed off. "I don't know what I expected to find, really."

Della frowned. "I don't get it. You wanna know for a book you're writing—what?"

Layla tried again. "Whether General Imboden stayed in Macedonia in the winter and spring of 1863."

Della's frown deepened. "General who?"

"Imboden."

"You wanna know where he was?"

"Yes. I want to know if he stayed at Mrs. Kerns's house or not."

"Why?" asked Della blankly.

Layla licked her lips. "Well, historians argue about it. It's a historical question. People like to know what the generals were doing."

Della waited until it was clear that this was the extent of the explanation. Then she snorted. "This is it. The Kerns house."

Layla looked over the rim of her glass.

Della shrugged. "It is. Daisy Kerns. She ran this place back in the day. Did a real good business, too, during the war, the one between the states. The Kerns house." She flicked her fingers toward the wall. "This is it." Involuntarily, Layla's eyes circled the ugly kitchen and returned to find Della watching her. "Not good enough for a general? Yeah, well, he didn't mind none, I'll bet."

"It was—back then—a—um—Mrs. Kerns was a—" Layla stammered.

"How 'bout lady of the evening?" said Della. "That always sounds nice."

A most gracious hostess, Mrs. Kerns. General Imboden's whereabouts. A historical question. A giggle bubbled up in Layla's throat. "Men!" she exploded.

Della broke into a smile. "You said it, sister! You wanna know what the general was doing? Same as they all do! No historical question about that!" Jungle Gardenia billowed from her as she laughed.

Layla couldn't stop giggling. "I'm going to put it in my book," she gurgled. "Most gracious hostess! General Imboden! Mr. Davies will just love it!"

"Parker?" chortled Della. "You're writing a book for Parker?"

"You know Parker?" hooted Layla.

"Honey, I know everyone," said Della. She settled herself comfortably in her chair, watching Layla wipe her eyes. "'Cept you. You ain't from here."

"No. No, I'm from Washington. I'm on the WPA. Federal Writers' Project. I'm just here to write the history of Macedonia."

Della made a disbelieving sound. "You're on relief?"

Layla nodded.

"Yeah?" Della eyed Layla's dress, dubious. "Huh. Where're you staying?"

"On Academy Street." Seeing Della's expression, she added hastily, "I board."

"Ohh. Who with?"

"A family by the name of Romeyn."

"'A family by the name of Romeyn,'" mimicked Della. "I know the Romeyns, honey. Remember, I know everyone." She gave Layla a combative look. "I grew up here."

"Oh. I see," said Layla, primly uninquisitive.

Della crossed her arms. "Yeah, I was a kid once, just like you. Just like Felix and that sister of his with the funny name. Kids are kids. They don't care about what your mama does; they just want to play. Don't have a heart attack, sister, but sometimes I even played with Felix. Him and Vause Hamilton." She smiled suddenly. "Those two were the devil's own, I'll tell you."

"Oh yes?" In spite of herself, Layla leaned in.

"Yeah-huh. Things they'd do! Once I saw 'em in the middle of the night climbing up to the roof of the pool hall. Felix, he saw me watching and yelled down how they was going up there to pray. I almost died laughing." Della shook her head in happy memory and added conversationally, "I don't think he killed Vause. That never made no sense to me. Why would Felix burn down his own daddy's mill and kill his best pal?" She caught sight of Layla's face. "What?"

38

<hr>

After the dramatic episode at the mill, I was prepared for some excitement to ensue. But it didn't. I had to make my own fun. One hot afternoon, I was out on the porch, pretending to read *The Master of Jalna* but really listening to Miss Beck tear around the house in a frenzy.

Finally she burst out the screen door, wild-eyed.

"Why, Miss Beck!" I said, glancing up from my book in surprise. "You look fit to be tied."

She gripped at her curls. "Oh, Willa, I am! I'm supposed to be at Mrs. Lansbrough's and Jottie's gone and I can't find my map!"

That was because I'd hidden it.

"I'll show you the way," I said, positively dripping with loving-kindness. "I've been there plenty of times."

"Bless you," sighed Miss Beck. "I don't know what I'd do without you."

It was a bear of a walk in the dead heat, but I didn't really mind. I was willing to suffer as long as I could make Miss Beck suffer, too. When we got to Mrs. John's house, I decided to take the opportunity to torture her as well, and I kept right next to Miss Beck while she rang the doorbell.

"Miss Beck? So glad to meet you at—" Mrs. John broke off and frowned at the sight of me plastered right up against Miss Beck's side. "Did Mother call you?"

"No, ma'am."

Miss Beck put her hand on my shoulder. "Willa is my Indian scout, Mrs. Lansbrough. She showed me the way here."

"Isn't that sweet?" said Mrs. John, sucking her teeth.

I smiled like a big crocodile. "May I pay a call on Mrs. Bucklew, Mrs. John? I'd feel real bad if I was here and I didn't visit with her."

She couldn't say no, right there in front of Miss Beck, but I could tell she wanted to. "I'm sure Mama'll be thrilled to bits," she muttered. "You run on up there." She waggled her hand in the direction of the stairs. "Now, Miss Beck, why don't we set right down here in the parlor?" That was where she kept all her needlepoint cushions and things.

"Lovely," murmured Miss Beck. She drew off her gloves and turned to look through the arched door. "Such a lovely room! Don't tell me you made all these?"

Mrs. John tinkled a laugh. "I confess to a passion for needlework!"

Miss Beck tinkled right back. "I'm all admiration, Mrs. Lansbrough. My word! Look at these wonderful cushions!"

They were exclaiming away when I reached Mrs. Bucklew's door and knocked. There wasn't any answer, but Mrs. John wouldn't've said to come up if her mama wasn't there, so I knocked again. Still nothing. After a few more tries, I put my hand on the knob and turned it gently.

Mrs. Bucklew was lying across her bed, fast asleep. She was even snoring a little. I deliberated. Normally, I wouldn't dare wake a grown-up—except Jottie, who was always real nice about it—but Mrs. Bucklew was different. She could sleep anytime, and she didn't get much company. I leaned over and rocked her shoulder a little. She didn't so much as stir, but now I knew why. She smelled of Four Roses whiskey. I looked around for the bottle, but I couldn't see it. I drifted over to her bureau. It had a mirror on it, also a little paper box of Coty's powder, and a picture of a man I figured must be Mr. Bucklew. He was seated next to a marble column and he looked real put out about it. I wandered around—I didn't open any drawers, but I looked at the things she had. There wasn't much. A Bible. A cane, though I'd never seen her use one. A dusty candy box.

Mrs. Bucklew let out a long, snorty sigh. I watched her for a while, thinking about all the people who wished they could stay alive but died instead and how Mrs. Bucklew was alive but probably wished she was dead. It wasn't fair.

When I opened the door, it squeaked a little, but I heard no pause in the conversation below. I walked as quiet as I could to the stairs, and then I edged down until I got to the last step they couldn't see from the parlor. I sat.

Mrs. John was talking. ". . . can't take it up in any serious way, what with the press of business, but he's just as interested as he can be. He reads all these big old books and collects— why he's just a pack rat, that's what he is! I say to him, John, honey, you're going to have to move me out if you buy one more book, but he just does it anyway."

"It's quite a collection," said Miss Beck.

"We had a professor from West Virginia University to dinner not two months ago, and you know what he said?"

"What's that?"

"He said he hoped John would bequeath his books to the library there! I thought it was a tiny bit *morbid,* but John was as pleased as punch."

"I'm sure."

"Now, these are the books—and other things—about Macedonia, right over on this side. The newspapers are such a nuisance, falling to bits, and who ever wants to read an old newspaper? I say, John, it isn't news once it's old, but, well—he doesn't listen to me!"

"What's *The Hellene?*" asked Miss Beck.

"Oh, those. Those are yearbooks. My husband's high school yearbooks. I don't know what happened to mine."

"Really? How fascinating!"

"Mine would be much later, of course."

"This one is—what? Oh, 1917. My. Can I peek?"

"Yes, of course."

"Now, show me. Which one is Mr. Lansbrough?"

"Well. Let's see. John was secretary of his class that year—I guess he's always been interested in things like history, isn't that funny?"

"Mmm."

"Here he is."

"Oh, yes. Doesn't he look dashing?"

"And he played football, of course. Let's see." Pages riffled. "Ah. Yes. Is this him?"

"No. That's Tyler Bowers." Mrs. John giggled. "He's just as fat as a roll of butter now, isn't that something? John's that one."

"Oh, yes, I see." Then Miss Beck's voice went up a tiny bit. "Who's this?"

"That? That's Vause. Vause Hamilton."

"Vause Hamilton." Her voice was still high. I listened hard. "Seems to me I've heard that name a couple times before." She was lying. She was pretending that she didn't know who he was, when she did.

"Well, I reckon you would. General Hamilton was the founder of Macedonia, of course."

"Yes," Miss Beck said in a hurry. "Yes, of course, but Vause Hamilton—I've heard of him."

"His father shares his name. Poor old Mr. Hamilton. He's still alive, but you know—" I imagined she was tapping her head. "He's a little *touched*," she whispered.

"Is that right? Why is that?" She was still lying, I could tell. She wasn't like me. She wasn't a natural.

"Vause—this one here—died, and he just never got over it. Poor old thing."

There was a pause. "He looks like a handsome boy." What was she after?

"Oh my, yes, he was handsome as a god. I was much younger, of course, but I knew easily a dozen girls who were crazy about him."

Miss Beck had a smile in her voice. "Good athlete, I suppose?"

"Oh, goodness, Vause took one record after another! Football, basketball, track, *everything*. And he was the nicest boy, just the nicest boy in the world."

Mae and Minerva had said that exact thing about him. Mrs. Fox, too. Vause Hamilton must have been pretty nice. For a while, anyway.

"I bet he had lots of friends, then, didn't he? Was he a friend of your husband's?"

"Well . . ." Mrs. John paused. "*Yes*. Vause was the president of the class, so of course, he and John had a lot to do with each other. For dances and things." She paused again. "Of course, Vause spent a great deal of time with your—I don't know what you'd call him. Landlord?" She laughed. "Anyway, Felix. They were old friends."

"Oh, do you know Felix?"

"Not really. I was so much younger. I knew *of* him, of course."

"Famous, was he?"

Mrs. John kind of laughed. "Yes. Of course. Felix and Vause, Vause and Felix. They were inseparable. Until—well, you know."

"What?"

"Until Vause died."

"Oh? How did he die?"

Mrs. John gave a little groan that sounded real. "He died in a fire. The poor boy."

"Why, that's just tragic!" Miss Beck said, real sympathetic. "Was it his house that burned down?" The liar! She knew he'd burnt down the mill, because I'd told her so.

"The mill. The fire was at the mill. He came back from the Great War—he and Felix had signed up together, but Vause caught flu while he was in France, so he was late coming home. But he came back and he was home for—I don't know." Mrs. John sounded like she was telling it to herself. "And then he died. He got caught in that fire and *died.*" She groaned again. "I wailed when I heard. I just wailed."

"Terrible," said Miss Beck softly.

"Terrible," Mrs. John agreed.

"Did he work at the mill?"

Mrs. John snorted. "Vause? Vause was no *mill worker.*"

"I thought maybe in management." Miss Beck spoke smooth as butter.

"Oh. No. That was Felix."

"What was he doing at the mill, then? You know, when it caught fire."

"*Supposedly* he was stealing money from the safe," Mrs. John snapped. "Which is ridiculous, because Vause wasn't any kind of *thief.* He just wasn't."

"But he was there? When it caught fire?" pressed Miss Beck.

"There were plenty of reasons why he might be there! Honestly. He and Felix were like *this*."

"Oh; was Felix there, too?" Miss Beck's voice went up. She wanted to find out something about my father. I held my breath. "At the fire?"

I could hear Mrs. John hesitate. "No. No, apparently he wasn't. *I* don't know. There was a big to-do about it. He was at Tare Russell's playing pool that night."

"Tare Russell's?" Miss Beck sounded surprised. Why would she be surprised? People played pool. Lots of people did.

"Have you met Tare? He's a funny old thing, but oh my, you should see his house! That man has I don't know *how* many historical things. He collects them."

"Yes, but tell me—what, exactly, was the big to-do?"

I could have told her she was pushing too hard, trying to make Mrs. John talk about things she didn't want to talk about. "Oh. Well, after the funeral"—Mrs. John sounded vague—"lots of people didn't believe that Vause had been up to anything, you know, *wrong*. There could've been a perfectly good explanation for him being there—maybe he was trying to put the fire *out*. And the money, too: Maybe he just found it. And it didn't even matter. To plenty of people, it didn't matter. It was just too bad." She sighed. "There were hundreds of people at the funeral. John was one of his pallbearers. There were twelve. Pallbearers."

"Twelve," repeated Miss Beck.

"The church couldn't hold all the people. We didn't care, nobody cared what he'd done—and it didn't make *sense*. Everyone went anyway . . ." Her voice drifted off. "Because it was *Vause*."

She was talking to herself again.

"It must have been heartbreaking," murmured Miss Beck. "Did he have a girlfriend?"

"A girlfriend?" Mrs. John's voice stiffened up. "Vause Hamilton? No. Well, some people said he was going with Jottie—"

"Jottie?" Miss Beck squeaked. I thought of the picture of Jottie inside that jacket, and my heart beat fast.

"But that was just a rumor," said Mrs. John in a hurry. "He

was at her house all the time because of Felix, that's all. Vause could have gone with anyone, anyone he wanted. The girls at his funeral—how we cried! And not only girls, either. Sol McKubin was like to die, I never saw a man cry like that in my life."

"What about Felix?" asked Miss Beck quickly.

"Wasn't there," said Mrs. John. "Did not attend."

"Oh. Well. I guess since the mill belonged to his—well, it must have been a shock."

"I suppose so." Mrs. John sounded hard. She was back to normal. "Now, how did we end up on *that*? Goodness! Talk about history! What I *wanted* to show you is right over here. John bought it last—oh, I guess it must have been March—off one of those Spurlings—they've come down in the world, let me tell you. See?"

"Mmm," said Miss Beck. "Is it—isn't that Prince Street? Oh, I see—Spurling Square."

"Painted in the year 1872." You'd think Mrs. John had painted it herself.

"How interesting," Miss Beck said.

"I knew you'd think so!"

I slipped back up the stairs and stood outside Mrs. Bucklew's room, trying to figure out what Miss Beck wanted. Something about Father, it was clear. Something about him and that fire. What was it? She'd asked whether he was there. Why would he be? If he'd been there, he would have stopped Vause from starting it. Miss Beck was a tricky one. Sometimes I thought she was in love with Father, and sometimes I thought she suspected him of something. She was devious. Father was lucky, though, because he had me, and I was keeping watch over him.

I opened the door. Mrs. Bucklew was still asleep, stretched out on her bed, but she had rolled over so that her face was pressed into her bedspread. I slipped into her room and sat down in her chair, to think.

39

On the other side of town, Jottie passed expertly among the gravestones of the cemetery, weaving through names she had known all her life, until she arrived at her own. Romeyn. James. Forrest. Helen Arantha. St. Clair. Caroline. Charles Loy.

Footsteps squashed the grass behind her. Sol was always punctual. She turned, making an effort to smile.

He was—effortlessly—beaming. "Sweetheart."

"I'm so sorry," she began, as she'd rehearsed.

His face fell. "Why?"

"About your job," she said. He frowned. "You got fired," she added, as his expression remained cloudy. "It was my fault. And I'm sorry. Awfully sorry."

His face grew cloudier still. "Is that why you called me?"

"Well. Yes," she said. There was a silence. "I'm apologizing," she explained.

"For what, exactly?" he asked.

"Because you came out to—uh, tell me to go home. Didn't you?" she asked, suddenly unsure.

He nodded.

"And Ralph fired you. And now you don't have a job," she clarified, as though he might have forgotten. He looked like he had forgotten. "I'm sorry to have caused you such trouble, Sol."

For a moment, he said nothing. Then he lifted his face to the fan of leaves above. "The lady tempted me," he said at last.

"What?"

His blue eyes dropped to hers. "I lost my job because of you."

"I know," she said guiltily. "I can hardly bear it."

He reached for her hand. "You owe me."

She regarded him in confusion. He seemed awfully cheerful about it.

"You have to comfort me," he went on. He lifted her chin with his forefinger and kissed her.

"Sol!" she sputtered.

He shook his head. "The truth is that Shank was spoiling for a fight all week, ever since the strike committee told the board they wanted to negotiate with me. If looks could kill, I'd be dead already. I'm glad to get shut of the place."

"But it was your *job*. What'll you do?" Jottie asked.

"Oh, I'm taking a little time off," he said casually. She searched his face for anxiety and found none. Time off? But what about money? Nobody just took time off. "I expect I'll get another job pretty soon," he added.

What job? "Where?"

He shrugged.

Could Zena have been right? "President of the mill?" she whispered.

He laughed lightly. "Yeah, president of the rumor mill." His evasion was well oiled and utterly out of character. I'll be damned, Jottie thought. Sol's going to be president.

Instantly, a thousand doors to a thousand hallways flung themselves open in her mind, and she gazed through all of them. *I could have it all back again* met *Sol's crazy about me* met *Felix would never speak to me again* met *Would he take the girls away from me* met *He can't take care of them himself* met *Am I going to let Felix rule my life forever* met *I'd be able to give them anything they wanted* met *Daddy would be happy* met, at long last, *I want to be wanted—*.

She lifted her face and smiled at Sol. "You were real chivalrous to come out and rescue me from those peaches."

"I couldn't believe it when I saw you there in that mess," he said, scowling at the memory. "Of all times to pay a visit to the mill." He brightened. "But I was chivalrous, wasn't I?" He picked her up and set her atop James Romeyn's grave. "So what's my reward?" He bent to kiss her.

"I can't kiss on my own grandfather's dead bones!" she protested.

"Fine," he murmured, close to her ear. "Let's go kiss on my grandfather's bones. He's around here somewhere."

"No." She smoothed her skirt, flustered. "Only teenagers neck in cemeteries."

He grinned. "I'd be glad to neck somewhere else. You name it."

She put her hand on his chest. "Sol, if we are going to see each other again, we have to be . . . discreet."

His face darkened. "Why? Because of Felix?"

"A little," she admitted, wondering how she would ever bridge the chasm between them. It would take more than tact, more than diplomacy or honesty or memories of long-ago friendship, to reconcile them. Maybe they would just settle for a non-aggression pact, she thought hopefully. Like Poland.

Sol flushed. "I don't want to be discreet. And you know what? I'm not afraid of Felix. You know that, right? I'm not afraid of Felix."

"You should be," she said grimly.

"Goddammit." He turned from her with an angry movement and then wheeled around again to face her. "Don't you mind, Jottie? Don't you want to have what other people have? Just the regular things, you know, like a date or a kiss or a marriage?"

"I have some things." She sighed. "And haven't you ever noticed, Sol? Nobody Felix cares about has what other people have."

"He doesn't care about me, so I should get what I want," said Sol petulantly. "Which is you."

"Oh, he cares about you," Jottie said, feeling as though she were a hundred years older than he. "Felix cares plenty about you."

"Yeah, I know. He spends his leisure moments thinking up new ways for me to die. Listen, Jottie"—he took her purse off her arm and dropped it on a grave marked *Baby*—"let's get married. Right now. Today—I guess we can't today, but, okay, soon. Let's just say the hell with it and get married." He bent down to look at her. "Felix'll come around. Or maybe the shock'll kill him. No"—he caught the look on her face—"I'm just kidding. Don't mind me. Just—marry me, will you, Jottie? Please? Aw, hell, you're not crying, are you?"

"No," she whispered, wiping the tears from her face with the heel of her hand.

Sol examined her. "You sure look like you're crying, honey."

She shook her head violently.

"Josie?"

No, she pleaded. I can't bear it.

Vause propped himself up on one elbow and smiled at her. Dreamily, she watched light and shadow play on his face. The only sound was the river, slapping itself arrhythmically against the stones, and the faint creak of the trees above them. Vause bent over her again.

"Stop that." Felix's shoe prodded at Vause's shoulder. "Stop that, or I'll call you out."

Vause pulled away reluctantly. "I'm going to put a bell around your neck, Felix."

"He's just jealous," said Jottie, sitting up. She smoothed her hair and patted her kiss-disordered mouth. "He's jealous because there's not a girl left in town who'll go to the corner with him."

"Back numbers," said Felix briefly, dropping to the grass. "There's not a girl in town I'd want to take to the corner."

"We thought you'd be along before this," said Vause.

"That's because you don't know how important I am," said Felix, shrugging off his jacket. "I'm a linchpin in the machinery of prosperity."

Jottie giggled. He was quoting their father. "I always knew you were a linchpin," she began, but he closed his eyes and shook his head. He was pale, she noticed. For him, he was pale. "Was it so bad today?" she asked softly.

"All is vanity and a striving after wind," he said without opening his eyes. "Yours of the fourth inst. received and contents noted. We take pleasure in sending you six pair of finest ladies' woolen stockings, pale, under separate cover."

"I can see how you might take pleasure in that," said Vause

sympathetically. There was a silence. "At least you're not working for my father."

"Son, I'd like you to see to these accounts. Yessir." Felix's eyes popped open. "Got anything to drink?"

Vause sat up and shuffled in his pocket. A silver flask arched through the space between them, and Felix caught it neatly in one hand. Jottie thought, They've done that a thousand times.

"I'd rather be in the army again," Felix said, eyes fixed on far trees. Absently, he rubbed the flask back and forth against his knee. "I'd rather be stuck in mud up to my waist with a German coming over the wire to blow my brains out."

"Oh honey," began Jottie. She couldn't think what to say next. "Why don't you . . ."

"Why don't I what?" he said roughly.

"Quit. Leave. You don't have to stay at American Everlasting, or in Macedonia, either. You could go anywhere."

He smiled at her. "Smart girl, my sister." He unscrewed the cap of the flask and took a swig. "Why didn't I think of that?"

Her eyes narrowed. "Where're you going?"

He laughed. "Vause?" he inquired.

Vause eyed Felix thoughtfully for a moment. "We had a—a sort of a plan, Felix and I. When we were decommissioned. We thought we'd light out pretty soon. Take off to someplace else."

"Where?" she asked quickly.

They exchanged glances, and Felix shrugged. "Chicago, Ottawa—"

"Ottawa? Why Ottawa?"

Vause snickered. "That's what I said. I think it's some girl."

Jottie started up to her knees. "California!"

Felix burst out laughing. "Listen to her! She's dying to get rid of me. You want my room, is that it?"

"No, no." Her voice rose in excitement. "All of us, the three of us—let's go together! Vause, let's! Think how much fun we'd have!"

The boys exchanged looks again. Felix said, "You're the reason Vause wouldn't leave."

She swung around to Vause, withstanding the momentary percussion of his handsomeness, the split-second disbelief that after all those years, he loved her back. "I can go with you."

"You're supposed to go to college next month," he said, frowning.

She leaned forward to curl her fingers around his lapel. "I don't care about college!" She did, of course. College was hard-won. It was her theater, her chance to make herself new, the one step she could take that might lead her someplace else. But against lighting out? With Vause? It couldn't hold its power. Lighting out, a brilliant cataclysm of light, eclipsing everything. She grabbed Vause's other lapel. "Take me with you! Please, please, Vause, let's go together. All three of us!"

His eyes slid to Felix and back to her. "We weren't thinking about a vacation, honey."

"It's forever, Jottie," Felix said simply. "No coming back. If we go, they'll write us off. Daddy and Mama and everyone. They'll hate us."

She could see that satisfied him. He wanted them to hate him, or at least, that's what he thought he wanted. Even more, she knew, he wanted them to see that he hated them, that he could throw away everything they'd given him without a backward glance. He wanted their father to crumble under the blow. "Maybe they won't," she said. "Hate us. Why should they? We're going off to seek our fortunes. Maybe they'll think we're plucky. Maybe."

Felix shook his head. He wouldn't have it. "Scion of Local Family Bolts," he said.

"Two scions," said Vause. He squeezed her hand. "And girl, eighteen." He frowned again. "You're only eighteen, honey."

"Take me," she said breathlessly. "I've never been anywhere. I want to see orange groves and—and—all those other things in California." She couldn't think what they were, but she wanted them. She was desperate for them. She plunged on. "And we'll be together, the three of us, and it will be new. It will be filled with people we don't know—people we haven't known all our lives. I'm so sick of Macedonia and all the folks watching and talking and tattling every time we see each other." She squeezed the cloth of his jacket in her fist, the idea growing larger and larger inside her. To see Vause every single day and to see new places and to be with him and Felix—she was sick with longing.

What if they wouldn't take her? What if Vause wanted her to be a lady? What if he left without her? She would die of it.

Felix watched her closely. After a moment, he said, "I think she wants to go, Sam."

Vause was quiet, his blue eyes searching hers. Finally, he said, "Your daddy told you to forget about me."

She could take that. "Your daddy said worse about me. And you're still here."

"He can go to hell," Vause replied automatically. He was still watching her. "You'd go? With me? Leave everything behind?"

"Yes." If she made him laugh, he'd take her. She knew it. "As long as we're going to California. I don't want to stop in any old Kansas or someplace."

He laughed. "So it doesn't have anything to do with me? You'd go with anyone, long as he'd take you to California?"

She nodded. "That's right. I'd go with Porter Spurling, except he hasn't asked me."

"Porter Spurling," said Vause ruminatively. "Fair enough. What about Nels? Would you go with Nels?"

She nodded again. "If he gave me a blindfold."

Chuckling, he caught her in his arms and pulled her into his lap.

"Jesus, wake me when it's over," said Felix, dropping onto his back and pulling his hat over his eyes.

"Would you do this with Nels?" asked Vause, kissing her slowly.

She nodded. "It's my dream!"

She could feel the smile on his lips when he kissed her. It meant yes. Electric with joy, she pressed her body into his to make him want her more, and he kissed her harder, opening her mouth with his. This was thrilling—nobody had ever done it before, not that she had heard of, and it made her tremble with excitement. Vause put his mouth against her ear. "If Nels Donag ever so much as touches you, I'll kill him."

She giggled weakly.

"If anyone besides me ever touches you, I'll kill him," he said. "You're mine."

She nodded, hoping he'd kiss her again.

"Say it."

"I'm yours," she whispered. *"I'll always be yours."* There was nothing, nothing but him in the whole world.

He lifted her up to meet his mouth again. *"I don't see how I can love you so much when you're so little,"* he murmured, his fingers opening in a brief, warm handprint against her belly. *"We'll get married in California."*

"California," she repeated, unable to attend to anything but the traces of his hand. *"California. That will be fine."*

"In an orange grove," Vause continued. *"Hey, Felix, will you be my best man?"* he called over his shoulder.

"Sure," mumbled Felix from under his hat. *"I don't think you're going to make it all the way to California, though."*

Vause looked at Jottie and grinned. He found a pebble and tossed it, hitting Felix square in the chest. "Wake up," he said. *"We've got plans to make!"*

Felix brushed the pebble off his shirt and propped himself up on his elbows. For a moment he watched them, smiling affectionately, and then he rose to his feet in one fluid movement.

"Where're you going?" Vause asked.

Felix stopped in mid-step and half-turned. "We got to get a car, don't we?"

"Yeah," said Vause. *"You going to steal one?"*

"Certainly not!" Felix recoiled, insulted. *"I'll buy a car like anyone else! Honest to God, I don't know where you get your ideas,"* he said with dignity. *"I'm going to go earn some money, is where I'm going."*

Vause and Jottie watched in respectful silence until he was gone. Then Vause dropped back against a tree trunk and let out a contented sigh. He closed his eyes as his long fingers sought Jottie's, and their hands wove together.

Sol's voice jerked her into the present. "I know he's your brother," he was saying awkwardly.

She gasped, "That's not—you can say anything you want about Felix. You've got the right."

Sol gazed at a cement urn overflowing with grapes. "I guess you don't want to marry me."

"Sol," she began, and stopped to catch her breath. The pain was terrible, like something being pulled from her body. Vause was gone; he was gone yesterday and today and tomorrow and next year and every day until she died, hundreds and thousands of days she was going to have to go through without him. She put her hand over her mouth to hold back the sound she was about to make.

"What?" Sol turned toward her hopefully.

She swallowed. "That wasn't very romantic."

For a moment, he squinted at her in perplexity. Then his face cleared and broadened into a smile. "Is that why you're crying? Jottie?"

"Some," she admitted. It was true. It was true, and she longed for Vause. Both things were true. It was all wrong. She had never imagined this part of it. She hadn't thought that the scar would open like that. She had pictured only safety, calm and nice—a stroll in the serene landscape enclosed by Sol's regard, not this bomb-cratered plain. She had expected warmth, and here, instead, was death again. She hadn't been prepared.

"Here," Sol said, gently brushing her cheeks with his handkerchief. He looked out over the graves and took a deep breath. "I never proposed to anyone before, and I didn't expect I was going to do it today—maybe you could tell?" He waited for her to smile, but she didn't oblige. "I guess I should have planned it better." He frowned. "I'm going to make it up to you, honey. Not now and not"—he winced—"here. All right?"

She nodded.

He leaned down to look into her face. "I'm sorry, Jottie."

40

Layla whisked through the library door and pulled it shut behind her. "My God," she exclaimed over the din. "How long have they been doing that?"

Miss Betts pushed back a straggling lock of hair. "This is the fourth day."

From below, the chorus welled. "Sit down, just keep your seat! Sit down, and rest your feet! Sit down, you got 'em beat! Sit down! Sit down!"

Layla grimaced. "Sounds like Winslow's joined the CIO."

"That John L. Lewis has a lot to answer for," said Miss Betts. She shook her head as if to clear her ears. "What can I do for you, Miss Beck?"

"Oh, nothing," said Layla breezily. "I just need to check something in the clippings file."

"Help yourself." Miss Betts nodded toward a metal file drawer and then glanced at the clock. "We close at five, you know."

"Fine, fine! This won't take but a few minutes," Layla called over her shoulder.

"When they tie the hands of the union man! Sit down! Sit down!" A passionate vibrato caressed the vowels. "When they give 'em a pact, they'll take them back! Sit down! Sit do-ow-own! SIT DOWWN!"

Miss Betts stood. "I'm going downstairs to talk to Hank," she shouted.

Bent over the drawer, Layla nodded inattentively. Hamilton was quite a large file. She flipped through it: Hamilton Elected to Virginia House of Delegates, Hamilton Purchases 200 Acres, Hamilton Dead at 67, Hamilton Builds, Hamilton Weds, Hamilton Lauded for, Bowers–Hamilton Nuptials, Hamilton Arrives, Hamilton Weds, Spurling Née Hamilton Weds, Hamilton an Investor, Hamilton Heir Accused, Hamilton to Visit Boston, Spurling Née Hamilton Dead, Hamilton Late of this Town, Storied Past of Pella, Hamilton to Lead Parade, The Great Macedonian, Twins Born to Nevius Family, EXTRA EDITION! AMER-EVERLASTING BURNS TO GROUND! VAUSE HAMILTON III FOUND DEAD IN CHARRED RUINS!!!—

Her eyes flew past the screaming headlines:

SEPTEMBER 4, 1920.

The American Everlasting Hosiery factory was destroyed in a great inferno beginning around midnight last night, and the calamity redoubled when the remains of Vause Hamilton III were uncovered in the smoldering ruins.

Fire Chief Halbert Leed declared smoke asphyxiation to be the cause of death and delivered the astounding intelligence that Mr. Hamilton was found with a sack containing $2,000, evidently taken from the company's safe, which though fireproof was discovered open and plundered of its contents in the wreckage of the company offices this morning. Mr. St. Clair Romeyn, President of the concern, attested that the safe held over $5,800 in cash money when he left the offices the evening before. Police Chief Oscar Whiting and Fire Chief Leed concurred that Mr. Hamilton had "cracked" the safe and robbed it, afterward setting an arson-fire to mask his crime. A second sack containing the remaining thousands was presumably lost during Hamilton's desperate attempt to flee the flames. The corpse was discovered under a partially collapsed staircase adjacent to the Unity Street door; a long corridor connected this part of the works to the company offices, where the safe was housed.

St. Clair Romeyn broke down at the news of the robbery, saying, "He was like a son to me. I can't believe Vause would do this." Young Hamilton was a close chum of Mr. Felix Romeyn's; they attended school together and embarked upon the

Great War in the same company. Felix Romeyn, a Superintendent at the factory, today confirmed Chief Leed's suspicion that Hamilton was in possession of the combination to the safe. "Of course he knew it. He knew the mill backward and forward," said Mr. Romeyn, his haggard mien attesting to the strains of the night.

The conflagration was the greatest ever seen in Macedonia. Fire-fighters were called in from Keyser, Leesville, and White Creek to assist Macedonia's three engines in subduing the fire, but the teams' manful efforts were overmatched by the dreadful power of the flames, and as dawn broke this morning, the factory buildings, including the offices, storerooms, warehouses, and manufacturing plant, lay in smoking ruins. St. Clair Romeyn twice attempted to rush to the aid of the fire-men in the course of the night and was restrained by his assistant, Mr. Parnell Rudy. Scores of bystanders watched the stormy battle from the . . .

But she already knew all this. This explained nothing. Frowning, Layla dropped the brittle paper back into its place and flipped to the next clipping, Death of Vause Hamilton III, featuring the same smiling face she'd seen in *The Hellene*.

She scanned the obituary: twenty years of age, of smoke asphyxiation, remains discovered in the aftermath of Saturday's fire at American Everlasting Hosiery Company, returned last year from the battlefields of France to the home of his parents where he resided at the time of his death, funeral services were held, pallbearers were, in addition to his parents he is survived by, interment in, Hamilton was probably the most outstanding athlete ever produced by Macedonia High School, numerous victories in, captain of, member of, manager of, president of, editor of, vice president of, known throughout the state for his—

Nothing.

She glanced over her shoulder and pulled open the drawer marked R–T. Romeyn was considerably slimmer than Hamilton. Forrest Romeyn to Wed, St. Clair Romeyn to Return Home Saturday, Miss Cappilanti to Wed, St. Clair Romeyn Opens American Everlasting Factory, No Panic at American

Everlasting, Twins Born to Mr. and Mrs. Romeyn, No Clouds of War at A-E Fest, Gov. Appoints Romeyn Textile Guild Pres., Mrs. Romeyn to Preside at Rose League Tea, Romeyn Denies Guilt—

Felix Romeyn, 19, of this town, yesterday denied accusations made Thursday by Solomon McKubin, 20, also of Macedonia, that Romeyn set the fire that destroyed the American Everlasting Hosiery Company on September 4. In a statement made at the Macedonia Police Station on October 14, Mr. McKubin charged that Mr. Romeyn was the instigator of both the robbery and the fire that occurred at American Everlasting, which resulted in the death of young Vause Hamilton, whose remains were found in the charred ruins of the company offices on East Main Street. Mr. Hamilton is presumed to have been in the process of robbing the company when he succumbed to the flames.

"I know Vause didn't do it, not on his own lookout, anyway. It's got Felix written all over it. I don't care what he says. He's lying," Mr. McKubin alleged on Thursday. "I want an investigation. They've got to investigate Felix. He can't just go free."

Mr. McKubin's accusation was yesterday denied by Mr. Romeyn. "I don't know what Sol [McKubin] means. Why would I burn down my own father's factory? Vause did it, I don't know why. I thought he was my best friend." It has been established that at the time of the fire, Mr. Romeyn was at the home of Mr. Tare Russell. "We were playing at billiards," confirmed Mr. Russell. "My servant showed Mr. Romeyn in at eight o'clock on the evening of the 3rd, and we played until two the next morning. He won."

Mr. Henry Odell, a friend of Mr. Romeyn as well as of the deceased and Mr. McKubin, speculated, "Seems like Sol's gone crazy. I don't know why he said all that."

Police Chief Oscar Whiting promises "a complete and thorough examination of the evidence" in the coming days.

Layla's head jerked up and the scrap of yellowed newsprint fluttered from her hand. She snatched it before it touched the floor and slipped it back in the file. Any more? Just one:

St. Clair Romeyn Dead at 59. Leaf by leaf, she sifted through the pile, carefully inspecting each frail piece of paper. There was nothing more about Felix. Then she looked in the Hamilton file again, finding no more about Vause Hamilton's death.

She straightened up, absently rubbing her back. For a long while she gazed at the dust motes waltzing through the streaming light. Then she pulled out the L–M drawer. There was no file for McKubin.

It had come to nothing. An accusation, never proved. Dismissed.

And now everything made sense. "Sol McKubin was like to die; I never saw a man cry like that in my life." He'd gone crazy and accused Felix of setting the fire that killed his best friend—no wonder Felix hated him. "He's a liar, all right?" And Shank had hired Sol, probably took a vindictive pleasure in hiring him, to be his right-hand man—a sort of slap in the face of the Romeyns. Maybe they even plotted it, to keep Felix from his rightful position. "And I'm sure the poor man *hoped* that Felix would take over the business, but, *well,* that was impossible after—" Because Shank and Sol McKubin had edged him out. It was an insult. It was a shame.

Something chafed, bothering her.

Emmett. Emmett was a friend of Sol's. Why?

She pondered the complexities of brotherhood. Hadn't she heard a million times of discord between brothers? Discord, mistrust, and, most of all, jealousy. Cain and Abel, for example! But Emmett and Felix didn't seem like rivals. They seemed, actually, to be fond of each other. But perhaps their strife was buried deep beneath the cordial surface. It was, sometimes. Perhaps befriending his brother's enemy was some kind of declaration of independence Emmett felt he had to make. Awfully childish, but, then, he was the younger brother. It was generous of Felix, the affection he displayed to Emmett in spite of his petulance. She wasn't sure she could be so generous, if it were her.

And there was Jottie, too. She'd greeted Sol at the mill. Didn't she realize he'd nearly destroyed Felix's reputation? Of course, Jottie had been staunch to her brother—after all, she'd taken care of him and his children for years—but still, it seemed disloyal, that casual greeting. And she'd called him fickle! Poor Felix was on his own. Instantly, Layla longed to stand between him and loneliness, to protect him with herself. He'd been betrayed by his best friend, and instead of receiving comfort, he'd been accused of stealing and practically murder. On a whim, if the paper was to be believed. And when? Six weeks after the fact! Didn't anyone wonder why Sol McKubin had waited six weeks to make the charge? It was ludicrous. Yet even now the idea persisted. People like Mrs. Lansbrough insinuated and gossiped. They were barking dogs, snapping at his heels. It didn't matter, not to her, what other people thought of him. She would stand by him. Let the dogs bark, Felix. You have me. I'll protect you.

41

Jottie's birthday was coming, and Bird and I were getting exercised about her present. When we were little, we'd generally made her face cream from aspirin and hand lotion or picked her flowers from her own garden, but this year we'd decided we were going to get her a real present, a bought present. Mae and Minerva were going to take us shopping. It would be an adventure, Mae said, a daring expedition into the throbbing heart of the city. We were going to Krohn's Department Store.

We got ten cents a week each, Bird and me. It wasn't much, and it was less after we'd coughed up a nickel for collection on Sunday. That was one ice cream a week, the plain kind, not even a double dip. It took us two weeks to save up for a milk shake. When I was ten, I'd succumbed to the devil and learned how to plump my hand fist-down into the collection plate and lift it up again real quick with my nickel safe and sound inside. But it preyed on my mind. So I gave up plumping my nickel and hewed to the paths of righteousness, and pretty soon the Lord rewarded me: I got hired to take ticks off dogs for a penny apiece. A penny apiece! I couldn't believe it. Mrs. Harvill was my first customer. Ticks made her weak at the knees, especially when they were chock-full of blood and stuck fast to her dog, Seneca (Mr. Harvill taught Latin). I made a lot of money on Seneca, and then Mrs. Harvill told Mrs. Fox and Grandma Pucks, and they hired me for their ticks, too. Then Harriet asked me to come fix up her Ruffles. He was a nasty dog with ticks all over, and by the time I was done with him, I was squeamish. But I didn't tell Harriet. She was a nice lady, and, besides, I needed the money. Altogether I had a dollar and sixty-eight cents, and I was willing to spend it all on Jottie's present.

I knew just what to get her. It was a pocketbook. It came in Autumn Leaf, Plum, Araby Green, and Dubonnet, and tucked inside it were a compact, a comb, and a tiny coin purse. There was a place inside for a handkerchief, too. It was one dollar and ninety cents at Krohn's Department Store, which struck me as a fair price for such a wonderful pocketbook, but I needed Bird to go in with me. Bird didn't want to. She had seen a Myrna Loy movie the week before and wanted to buy Jottie some lounging pajamas.

"Jottie wouldn't be caught dead in lounging pajamas," I argued as we walked. "Not in a hundred years."

"You don't know. She doesn't have any," said Bird, jingling her coins. She carried them in a paper bag.

"Well, I'm not putting in my money for stupid lounging pajamas. Wait till you see this pocketbook. Araby Green is the best."

"They have some of those faille gloves," said Mae to Minerva.

Minerva made a face. "Hot."

It was awful hot. Even ladies like Mae and Minerva had big circles of wet under their arms and across their backs.

"I swear, my kneecaps are sweating," Mae groaned softly. "Wish someone would give us a ride."

But no one came along, and we walked on down Council Street.

"Perfume?" said Mae.

"They have those Evening in Paris sets with powder and soap," Minerva said thoughtfully.

Mae wrinkled her nose. "Evening in Paris."

"Well. Coty's?"

"Maybe," said Mae. "We'll give it a sniff." She sighed faintly. "Remember when Vause brought her lily of the valley?"

Minerva patted the back of her neck with her handkerchief. "Uh-huh."

"Did it smell nice?" I asked.

"Mmm," said Mae, remembering. "Like a dream."

"I guess she threw it out," Minerva said, after a minute.

Mae nodded regretfully.

We were on Prince Street now, and Bird said that all she really wanted in the world was a tiny little bite of ice cream, but Minerva said we had to put our noses to the grindstone. "Krohn's before pleasure," she said.

"Pearls before swine," said Mae.

It was fun to shop with the two of them. We looked at everything—jabots, cuffs, hankies, gloves, scarves, hose, snoods, housecoats, bed jackets, nightgowns. They let me and Bird sniff all the perfume we wanted, and when Mae bought a new lipstick, she let me try it. Carefully, I smoothed it on, making sure I dabbed extra up on my top lip. It was called Cherry Pie, and when I looked in the mirror, I saw a grown-up lady, twenty years old at least, looking back.

"You have to blot it, honey," said Mae.

"No. I like it like this."

"Only hussies don't blot," said Mae.

"Floozies," agreed Minerva.

"Girls with anklets," added Mae.

"Let me leave it," I begged. "Just for now. Please. I'll blot before we go home."

Minerva laughed. "I guess nobody's going to take you for a floozy. Let's go look at the jewelry."

Mae thought Jottie would like a locket. "She could put in a picture of each of you girls," she said.

"Or two of me," said Bird.

"Yeah, one of the front of your head and one of the back," I said.

It took Mae and Minerva almost twenty minutes to persuade Bird that Jottie had no use for blue silk lounging pajamas, and it took twenty more for me to be convinced that Jottie'd rather have a locket than an Araby Green pocketbook. The locket was real gold and it cost four dollars and fifteen cents, so we all chipped in, and Minerva still had enough left over to treat us all to ice cream.

When we stepped out of Krohn's, it was past the middle of the afternoon, but the heat was still pushing down like hot bricks. The few people out were gathered under the store awnings, trying to keep to the shade.

"Speaking of noses to the grindstone," said Minerva suddenly.

Father was leaning against a stair rail, drinking from a sweating-cold bottle of Coca-Cola. Mae put her hands on her hips. "I swear, Felix," she said, "if you got any more relaxed, you'd be dead."

Father looked up and smiled. "Hey, girls." He lifted his Coca-Cola. "To your health and prosperity."

"Pooh to that!" Minerva said. "Buy us ice cream!"

Mae laughed and said something, but I didn't hear, because Father's eyes had moved away from them and come to rest on me. His eyebrow flew up as he looked at me. "What did you do?"

I felt a red-hot blush shooting up my neck and face. I'd forgotten to blot. "Mae let me try her lipstick," I mumbled.

"You look all grown up." He stared at me. "My God, I feel old."

"Don't be a wet blanket, Felix," said Mae. "It's cute."

He made a face. "If you say so."

"You'd better get used to it," Minerva warned. "She's growing up. Pretty soon she'll be going on dates. Dates and dances. It won't be long before you'll be walking her down the aisle."

"And after that, you'll be a grandpa!" crowed Mae.

They were laughing, but Father wasn't. His eyes came back to me, not in the usual way but kind of leery, like you'd lift up a rock and see what was underneath.

I quick rubbed the lipstick off with the back of my hand.

The sun went down, but the heat stayed put. It was too hot to eat. We all just picked at our food, until finally Jottie said, "Oh, let's give up." Out on the porch, we could hear the other rockers and chairs along Academy Street creaking, but no one called hey-you. It was too hot. Bird laid herself out like a dog on the floor. I plopped into a chair and then regretted it when my skin stuck in every ripple of wicker. Father was sitting next to Miss Beck on the far side of the porch, and the light from the front room was shining on the pair of them. Every once in a while, he'd bend his head toward her and speak softly, but I couldn't hear what he said. Minerva and Mae were fussing about how hot they were, and Jottie was just stirring pensively at her ice-coffee. I wondered if she was thinking about her birthday, about what her present might be.

After a while, Richie and Harriet arrived, and then my uncle Henry. And then silly Marjorie Lanz, with her sleeves stuffed full of handkerchiefs the way they always were. She plucked one out to wave it like a fan, and I thought of telling her it would make her hotter, but I didn't. I didn't feel like it.

Richie was talking about the strike, something about getting food in, and I was halfway listening. Richie had the deepest voice I'd ever heard. It was like a big boat on water. ". . . it's driving Shank loony," he was saying, and I saw Miss Beck reach over to touch Father's knee. He turned to her and smiled, so warm and soft that I almost groaned. Actually, I did groan, just a little.

Jottie set her glass down kind of sharp and cleared her throat. It was the quickest thing anyone had done that night, and we all turned to her, expecting something. "This here is Bastille Day, in France," she announced.

"No, it's not," said Henry. He was sitting in a rocker with both his feet planted on the floor so it wouldn't rock. "Bastille Day is the fourteenth of July."

Jottie ignored him. "Bastille Day is when the French Revolution began," she said to me. I nodded. "The poor people broke open the doors of the jail, and the prisoners surged out and chopped off Louis the Sixteenth's head." She glanced at Henry. "And Marie Antoinette's, too. She said, Let them eat cake."

"That's not what happened," Henry argued.

"Oh, *Henry*," sighed Minerva.

"Well, it's not." Henry never understood Jottie.

Jottie's eyes were sparkling. "It was something like the time the drunks broke out of jail and took over the library."

I loved Jottie. "I never heard that one. Tell."

Father's head dipped close to Miss Beck's. "I wouldn't put this in your book, if I were you," he said.

"Hush!" commanded Jottie, waving her finger at him. He laughed and sat back, away from Miss Beck. "Now," she said. "It all began because Mayor Tapscott thought the inmates were eating too much—"

"Which was true," Henry said.

"How much is too much?" Jottie said. "You've never been hungry a day in your life."

"Yes, he has," said Minerva. "He almost starved to death in Pittsburgh once."

"Well, *Pittsburgh*," scoffed Jottie.

Mae and Harriet choked on their coffee.

"You were saying, Jottie?" said Richie, real solemn.

"I was saying that Mayor Tapscott believed—rightly or wrongly, who's to know—that the indigents were spending all their relief money on hooch to work themselves up to disturbing the peace so they'd get a free meal in jail."

"One hundred percent true," said Henry.

"So he cut their food back to half a turnip and a piece of bread scraped with lard."

"That is just not so," said Henry indignantly. "They got—"

"No! I lie! They got a cup of water, too. Naturally, they were hungry as bears inside of a day, and after two days, they were chewing on the soles of their shoes. That's when they decided to revolt."

I swallowed a giggle. "How'd they revolt?"

"Well, first they overwhelmed the jailer, which wasn't too difficult, because it was Dale Purlett and he hasn't got but one foot, and then they charged on the library. They chased Miss Lucinda Mytinger into the lavatory and turned the lock on her, and then they took all the books off the shelves and mixed them up."

"Tell what you did," said Father, chuckling.

Jottie laughed. "I got a crowd of my girlfriends together and we decided to go sing hymns on the sidewalk below. We thought our angelic voices raised in song would cause them to repent of their sinful ways."

"Did they?" I asked.

"They threw books at us and told us to go to hell."

Everyone—except Henry—burst out laughing.

"This family is berserk," said Henry grumpily.

"Too late. You're in it now," Minerva said.

42

·─━◆━─·

"Bye, honey!" sang Harriet as she disappeared into the night, clinging to Richie's arm.

"Watch out there, now," his low voice grumbled.

Jottie closed her eyes and dropped her head against the back of her chair, listening to the click of Harriet's high heels recede down Academy Street. "She's going to break her ankle someday," she murmured.

"She is kind of large to wear such heels." Layla yawned. "I'll take the coffee cups in," she offered halfheartedly.

"Oh, sit for a minute," Jottie said. "I think I felt a breeze."

"That was me, opening the door." It was Felix, with his hat on.

"Where are you going?" Layla asked, trying to sound casual. In the gloom, she saw the white brilliance of his smile.

"Going to see some friends."

"Now?"

An eyebrow shot up. "Yup."

"You want some company?" She stretched a little to show off her legs.

"Nope." He glanced around the porch and then bent swiftly to kiss her. As she reached for him, he broke away. "A girl your age needs her sleep. Get on up to bed. I got to talk to Jottie."

Reluctantly, she stood, her hand lingering in his until the last possible moment. "I'm not even tired," she pouted.

"Too bad." He smiled and pressed his thumb against her lips. "Get." When she had gone inside the house, he turned to Jottie. "Wake up."

"I'm awake," she said, opening her eyes. "I'm just trying to keep the veil of decency drawn."

He laughed. "Think clean thoughts."

"My thoughts are plenty clean. Yours could use some work." She sat up. "What do you want?" Lightning flared silently, illuminating the shabby porch.

"How much money do you have?" he demanded.

"Fourteen dollars and eighty cents."

"Oh, hell. That's all?"

"That's all I have here. If you wait until tomorrow, I can go to the bank," she said.

"No. Can't wait. Give me ten."

"You can have it all."

He shook his head stubbornly. "No. Just ten."

That meant he didn't know what was going to happen. When he didn't want to leave her without money, that's what it meant. Her stomach tightened. "Don't."

He lifted an eyebrow of inquiry.

"Don't do something bad."

He smiled. "I never do anything bad."

She nodded. "Let me get my purse."

When she returned, he was standing, facing the street, his hands jingling in his pockets. "Thanks," he said as she handed him two bills. "I'll pay you back."

"I know." She hesitated, watching his dark head bent over his wallet. "Felix?"

He grunted.

"Can't you leave her alone?"

He looked up in surprise. "Who?"

"Layla!" she said, exasperated.

"Oh." He grinned. "I didn't know I was bothering her."

"Stop it. She's crazy about you."

"Is that right?" he snickered.

"Don't laugh. She's in love with you." Jottie wiped perspiration from her upper lip.

"She's pretty cute." He shook his head fondly.

"She thinks you're going to marry her."

"She's in for a surprise, then." Again, lightning, dead white and off again.

"Don't break her heart. Please, Felix."

His eyes widened. "I won't. I wouldn't do such a thing."

She nodded. "Good. What will you do, then?"

"Me? I'm going out."

"Felix! What are you going to do about Layla?"

He smiled and tipped his head close to Jottie's. "I'm going to get her into my bed as fast as I can," he whispered in her ear.

She seized his arm. "No! For God's sake, leave her alone!"

He stiffened. "What's it to you? Since when do you care more about her than me?"

He was getting angry, but she was beyond caring. "She's a nice girl. She doesn't deserve to have her life ruined. For once, Felix, have pity!"

"Pity?" His face was scornful. "She doesn't need pity. And let me tell you, Jottie, going to bed with me isn't going to ruin her life. You don't know anything about it."

"I do too know—my heart broke, I wished I were dead. I wouldn't want a dog to go through what I went through."

He drew a tight breath. "That wasn't me."

"I'm not saying it was you. It was Vause. But I know what I'm talking about. Please, Felix? Can't you leave her be?"

He turned away, toward the street. For a moment he stared into the massive dark, and then he reached for her and patted her shoulder. "You worry too much."

She had failed. Again. Always. "You don't worry enough," she said wearily.

"Sure I do," he said, and slipped away into the lightning.

"Be careful!" called Jottie. A flick of lightning revealed him, mid-step, on the sidewalk, before he was erased by blackness. Maybe that's the last time I'll see him, she thought, and felt a tiny, shocking tingle of relief.

August 9—no, 10—1938

Dear Rose,

You'll excuse my handwriting, darling, when I tell you it's not drink but love that makes my hand shake. My stomach is diving and swooping like a starling, and I can't eat a thing, though perhaps that's the heat. Do you feel this way around Mason? If so, I don't understand how you manage to play tennis the way you do. I couldn't hit a ball to save my life just at the moment.

Oh, Rosy, I had no idea, none at all, that I could feel as I do, connected in my blood to another being. It would be alarming if it weren't so wonderful—I feel him come into a room, my senses are suddenly magnified, and for the first time in my life I truly believe in evolution, because it's *instinct,* this feeling I have—I must have a wolf in my ancestry to feel this keenness, this awareness of his tiniest movement. And there's the tenderness, too, the ferocious desire to keep all harm from him. I think, dear, that I am learning—finally—what it is to care more for someone than for myself, and what it is to be cared for. He watches over me, so quiet and calm, so generous and forgiving of wrongs—you'll see how wonderful he is when you meet him. And you, you alone, will see how it is between us. For no one else knows, darling. Up on the surface, where the world watches, we're chums. But below, we're simmering. Our eyes meet, and it's a delicious secret between the two of us—no one else can see the invisible strings that are pulling us nearer and nearer each other.

I may die of excitement.

When I think of how I begged Ben not to send me to Macedonia, it makes me glad that he detests me, glad that Father cut me off, glad even that he wanted me to marry Nelson. Though of course it would never do to tell Ben or Father how happy I am. They disapprove of me being happy. I'm supposed to be in the school of hard knocks, facing stark reality, and pulling myself up by my bootstraps. So, for the next few weeks, you must keep my secret locked up tighter than the crypts of the pharaohs and eat this letter if anyone threatens to read it. Don't worry, I won't make you take it to the grave, for I have a marvelous plan to bring Felix to Lance's engagement party. (You know about that party, don't you? Mother swore she wasn't going to tell a soul, so I expect half of Washington—including you—has been invited already.) That way, you'll be able to meet him, and Father will, too. And I will have the divine satisfaction of watching Father realize that his plan to make me miserable has been a failure and that my happiness no longer rests in his hands—but in Felix's.

Oh my, look at all those dashes! Don't worry, they're indicative of my racing heart, not a new prose style. My book is coming along at a great pace, though my typewriter seems to be afflicted by a poltergeist. I assume it's a Confederate ghost offended by my Union sympathies; for all I try to be impartial, I let out a little wheeze of triumph whenever the Federal troops outfox the Rebel raiders that swarmed over this part of the state.

Is Cape May gloriously cool and breezy? I would envy you, except there's no Felix Romeyn at Cape May.

Love,
Layla

P.S. Can you picture me as a stepmother? I must say, I can't. Every one that I can recall attempted to poison her new children immediately, which seems rather high-handed. I believe I'll try a more measured approach.

43

Jottie's birthday was on Friday, so on Thursday, Minerva and Mae and Bird and I locked ourselves into the kitchen to make her a cake. The problem was that Jottie was the only one who could cook. Mae and Minerva smoked about fifty cigarettes apiece and pored over an old yellow clipping from a newspaper. Bird and I ran around pulling ingredients from the cupboards.

"Mix dry ingredients," read Mae. "With what?"

Miss Beck came in after a while, but she didn't know any more than we did. She said she thought we ought to turn on the oven, but Mae said it was so hot she was going to wait till the last minute.

It looked all right when we put it in, but something happened to it in the oven. The recipe said it would be "airy," but I don't think they meant it the way it came out. Minerva and Mae and Bird and I looked at the thing in the pan and Bird said, "Jottie likes ice cream better than she does cake, anyway," and Minerva and Mae busted up laughing. Then Jottie shouted through the kitchen door that we weren't going to get any dinner if we didn't let her in soon, and we decided that Minerva would give Bird and me money to go buy ice cream for Jottie at Statler's the next afternoon. Mae and Minerva would both be off at their own houses by then, but they said we were big girls and they trusted us not to run off and squander the money on chorus boys. Then they smoked about fifty more cigarettes and criticized the way Bird and I washed the dishes.

The next morning when I got out of bed, it was already hot, so hot and thick that there wasn't enough air to breathe. And it was still. I guess the birds were too hot to get up to much singing. It made me feel bad for Jottie that the birds weren't singing on her birthday, so I sang "Whistle While You Work" as I came downstairs. I could do the whistling parts, too. Jottie said I was an infant phenom.

It was still real early. Jottie had pulled the shades against the heat, but it came streaming in anyway, and the kitchen turned bright yellow, so you would have thought the world was on fire outside the shades. Jottie poured me some cereal and sat down to keep me company while I ate. I couldn't imagine how she drank coffee when it was so hot.

After a while, the others came along: first Bird, who kissed Jottie's cheek and said she felt sorry for grown-ups because nobody cared about their birthdays, and then Mae and Minerva, who yawned and sang Happy Birthday while they drank their coffee. Father was away on business; he'd left the night Jottie told about Bastille Day, after we'd gone to bed. Bird and I listened to everyone moan about the heat until we couldn't wait one more second and then we brought out the locket, all wrapped up in red tissue paper. Jottie said it was the most beautiful thing she had ever seen in her life and she put it right on, even though she was going to have to take it off again to put in our pictures. She said she knew exactly which pictures she was going to use, and then she hugged us all. Bird muttered a little about lounging pajamas, but even Bird could see that Jottie liked the locket. Miss Beck came in then, and she wished Jottie a happy birthday, too. She even gave her a present, a handkerchief with a rose on it, which was nice, I suppose.

We fussed over Jottie a while longer, and then the real day had to begin. Minerva went to take a bath, and Jottie poured cereal for Bird and Miss Beck. Henry put his head in the back door and said it was going to get up to one hundred and two degrees later in the afternoon. He'd read it in the paper, he said, along with a story about cows dying of sunstroke. He looked at Jottie. "Many happy returns of the day," he said, and then he got mad when we laughed.

After he'd stomped off, Mae lit her first cigarette. "This had just better be the hottest day of the year."

"Or what?" I asked.

"Or I quit," said Mae.

Bird and I hunkered down inside the house all morning, putting off the moment when we'd get hot for keeps. As long as we stayed in the dark and didn't move, we wouldn't come right out and sweat. We went into my grandmother's sewing room—I don't think I had ever before spent more than five minutes there—and lay on the floor. Then we tried the old dead parlor, full of black furniture and dust. It was cooler than the rest of the house, and when I put my cheek down on a little marble-top table, I had a solitary second of cold against my skin. Bird stretched out on the horsehair sofa, to see how long she could stand it without scratching. She said she lasted a minute, but she didn't.

We weren't sweating, but we got awful bored, so after lunch we went down the street to see what the Lloyd boys were doing. We were hoping it was something pertaining to a hose, but no such luck. They were digging a grave, Jun and Frank and Dex were. They were going to bury their baby brother, Neddie, alive. It made me pant to look at them, digging away in the stomped-over grass, heaving up big clumps of dirt. Not Bird. She thought it was wonderful, and she offered to be their sample, while I threw myself down in the pitiful shade of their beat-up old maple tree. I looked up through the branches and saw not one leaf stirring. Not one. The sky behind the leaves was whitish gray, like hot metal, and every colored thing had turned pale.

Bird skipped over, drenched in sweat. "Jun says he'll bury me alive!" She was thrilled.

Jun lifted his head and smiled at me.

"You're joking, aren't you?" I asked him.

"Uh-uh." He shook his head and scraped up another chunk of dirt.

I sighed and got to my feet, feeling drops trickle down my back. It was too hot to fight. "Jun Lloyd, don't you dare. She'll die of suffocation," I said.

"Oh, *Willa,*" said Bird. "Stop picking on us."

Jun was twelve, like me, but he was big. He'd probably give

me a black eye. My only hope was maybe his father had said he couldn't hit a girl.

"He gave me a glass straw to breathe through," Bird said. She held it up. "See?"

Oh.

For a minute I watched the boys' shoulders move up and down, turning dirt. They were enjoying themselves, even if it was a million degrees. And Bird, too. She was skittering around the hole, pointing out rocks they needed to remove so she could lie easy in her grave. They were all happy as could be, and it seemed like they were on one side of a window and I was on the other. I thought about it, there under the tree. Maybe this was what came of all the sneaking and spying I'd done. Maybe I was permanently a spy.

"Don't kill her, now," I said over my shoulder as I trudged back down the lawn. I walked slowly home. Inside it would be dark and still, and I'd be able to hear the afternoon ratchet forward on the clock's metal wheels. I clicked open the door quietly, so as not to disturb Jottie's sacred resting time. She was in her pink chair, eyes closed, one hand on a book in her lap. I tiptoed by so quietly she didn't even stir.

In the kitchen, I put my head in the refrigerator, and, since I was there anyway, I popped three ice cubes into my mouth. When I closed the door and turned away, I saw the money under the sugar bowl. A lot this time. Almost what you'd call a stack. I was happy then. Father was home, sleeping. And Jottie was sleeping, too. In all the house, I was the only one awake, watching over them.

Then the telephone rang.

✳

Jottie bolted upright in terror.

Oh. The telephone.

She was still panting when she answered. "Hello?"

"Happy birthday, sweetheart."

"Who's this?" she asked dazedly.

"It's me, Sol," he said. "Were you asleep?" She could hear the smile in his voice.

"No," she said. "Not me."

"You sound kind of sleepy."

"You calling me lazy?"

"Jottie. It's your birthday."

"How'd you find out?"

"I remembered."

"Really?"

"All these years, I always remembered, but this is the first time I've been able to do something about it. Happy birthday."

"Thank you." She closed her eyes, picturing him. "Where are you?"

"What? My study."

"You have a *study*?" Her eyes flew open in amazement.

"Well. Yeah. You remember the house. Don't you?"

Oh. His father's study. But still. Sol, in a study.

"Listen, Jottie—"

"You don't smoke a pipe, do you?" she asked suspiciously.

He sighed. "Jottie, listen. I got an idea. About you and me going on an—an excursion. For your birthday."

"An excursion?"

"A trip."

"A trip?" What was he talking about?

"I thought we could—maybe—go to Charles Town. The Horse Show is on, and I remembered how you used to like going to the races. Do you still?" he asked anxiously.

Jottie laughed. "The Horse Show! I haven't been in *years*." He'd remembered what she'd liked. He'd remembered and he'd planned for her. Sol was wonderful. And Felix was away. The mice will play, she noted, and admired her pun. Serves him right, anyway, she added, thinking of their last conversation. To hell with him. She could go. It was her birthday, after all—

Sol interrupted her thoughts. "I thought we could make it a real vacation. We could go out to supper and even spend the night, I was thinking. So I made us reservations at the Jefferson Hotel. Separate rooms, of course." He stammered a little and took a breath. "It's a real nice hotel, and I thought we could—have fun. Together."

She said nothing. He was going to propose again. She'd be ready this time. This time, it wouldn't hurt. She wouldn't think of Vause. Vause was a liar, and she wouldn't think of him. This time, she would think of Sol and be happy.

"Jottie?"

"Sol," she said softly, "it's real nice of you. I'd be glad to go."

"Really?" he asked, his voice pitching sharply upward.

The image of Felix came rushing toward her, but she pushed him away indignantly. What right did he have to tell her what she could and couldn't do? None. Sol had lied—not even lied, been mistaken—*once*. Felix had lied to every woman he ever met. "Really."

"I made sure Felix was away before I called."

"That was smart."

For a moment, they were silent. Then Sol said, "I'll be right over."

"You mean *now*?" cried Jottie.

"Well. Yeah." He hesitated. "Or we could go later if you want."

Listen to him, changing his ideas to suit her! She laughed. "No. That's all right. That's fine, but listen, Sol, I'll meet you. I'll meet you at the corner of Winchester Avenue and Morgan Street. By Maple Shade. Okay?"

"When?"

She looked at the clock, feeling the exhilarated racing of her heart. It was an adventure, an escape, a getaway. "An hour. I got to get the girls fixed up, and then I'll come."

She hung up with the sound of his smile in her ear. "Willa?" she began. "Bird?"

✳

I knew it was Mr. McKubin even before she said his name. She was talking softly to him, and she didn't talk that soft in general. And I knew she was going to leave, too, but of course that was because she said about the Horse Show. I wished I could go. I liked to watch the sleek horses thunder round the track and the jockeys in their bright silk clothes.

I went into the hall and leaned against the wall.

Jottie put down the telephone receiver and stood still. Then she whirled around and looked at me. She smiled in an excited kind of way. "Willa, honey, here's a secret, but you got to promise not to tell, not anyone."

I nodded, and then in case that wasn't enough, I said, "Cross my heart."

"I'm going to the Horse Show. In Charles Town."

"Why is it secret?"

She wrinkled her nose at me. " 'Cause I say so."

" 'Cause you're going with Mr. McKubin?"

She raised her eyebrows. "How'd you figure that one out?"

"I heard you call him Sol. That's his name, ain't it?"

"Yes. But don't tell anyone. Not that there's anyone to tell." She laughed like that was a joke.

I nodded, but inside I was remembering Mrs. Jungle Gardenia at the parade. "Good thing old Felix ain't here." Jottie thought Father was out. But he was home, and only I knew it.

"Here's what we're going to do, honey," she said busily, shuffling in the mess drawer for a pencil. "I'm going to write Minerva a note saying I've taken it into my head to drive to Moorefield and see Irene for a little birthday outing, and I want you girls to stay with her while I'm gone. You and Bird can just walk on over there—can you pack up your toothbrush and your nightgown and Bird's, too, while I get my things? Where is Bird, anyway?" She glanced up.

"Down at the Lloyds'. Can't I come with you? I won't bother you."

She swooped down and hugged me. "You don't ever bother me, honey. But not this time. Next time, though, for sure. This here is just a jaunt. I'll be back by tomorrow afternoon. When you and I go, we'll stay longer, and we'll bet on every race." She grabbed up my hand and swung it. "Let's us go pack our cases, and then I'll write to Minerva."

Suddenly I thought of something. I didn't say it, though. What I said was, "What about Miss Beck?"

"What about her?"

"Well." I looked as innocent as I knew how. "What about her dinner?"

Jottie gave me the fish-eye. "You're worrying about Miss Beck's dinner?"

"You're supposed to feed her dinner, aren't you?" I said, real prissy. "I'm just trying to keep you out of trouble."

"Good thing I got you around," said Jottie, grinning. She reminded me of Father, the way she was fizzing. "I'll leave her a note, too. Will that suit you?"

"I guess," I said. I was starting to get an idea.

She nodded, not really paying attention, and then she moved toward the stairs, almost dancing.

Slowly, I followed her upstairs and put a few things on my bed. Nightgown, toothbrush, and toothpaste. Jottie whirled in before I was half done and swept all of it into a little case, along with Bird's things. Then she pulled me downstairs. "Now," she said, handing me an envelope with Minerva written on the front, "when she asks what happened, you just say I got restless and called Irene. Minerva'll never think to telephone long distance. Tell her I said I'd come and get you and Bird tomorrow. Tell her it's a birthday whim." She looked at me closely. "And don't breathe a word about—Mr. McKubin, all right?"

"I said I wouldn't."

I watched her set another envelope on the hall table. Layla, this one said.

"You got your locket?" I asked. I wanted to hang on to her skirt, the way I used to.

She turned around and smiled at me. There it was, shining against the front of her dress. "You want to see?" she asked.

I nodded.

She sat down and slid her fingernail between the little doors. They opened, and she held the locket up for me to see. There was Bird with her chin sticking out, and there was me, too. I wasn't smiling. "I love that picture," she said, tapping my side of the locket.

"How come?"

"Because you look like you're thinking about something interesting. And, I guess, because you look like me, and that makes me proud," she said. She closed the locket and held out her hand. I took it. "It's lucky I got this locket today," she said, and stood up. "Whenever I miss you, I can just whip it out and look inside."

I looked away. "Maybe you won't miss me."

Her hand held me tight. "I will."

"You'll come back tomorrow?" My voice wasn't too good. I was used to Father leaving, but not Jottie. It was like the air leaving.

"I promise."

"You never went away before."

"I know it. So you have to depend upon my promise. Have I ever broken a promise I made to you?"

I tried to recall. She didn't promise much, except I'd be sorry if I did such and such. So far, she'd been reliable. I shook my head.

"All right, then." She bent down to look in my eyes. "All right?"

I nodded. I couldn't talk.

"I'm going to go now. You go get Bird and walk over to Minerva's, okay?"

I nodded again.

She put on her hat. Then she kissed me quick and went to the front door with her satchel in her hand. "My God," she said as the heat poured over her. "This *day*," she said, but she sounded happy. She smiled at me and then she was gone.

My handwriting was pretty, but it didn't look a thing like Jottie's. Jottie's was perfect, except you couldn't read it. She once told me that it was her revenge against a penmanship teacher she'd hated.

I practiced for a long time, making loops and curls like hers and driving sharp, meaningless crosses over the tops of the words the way she did. No matter how I tried, it was still legible, but maybe Minerva wouldn't notice.

I took my things out of the little case, leaving Bird's, and let myself out the front door, closing it carefully behind me to keep out the heat. On the Lloyds' front lawn, Jun and Frank were leaning on their shovels, looking down at what they'd dug. I didn't see Bird anywhere.

"Where's Bird?" I called when I got near.

Jun and Frank glanced at me and back to their hole.

"It ain't big enough." Bird's voice came from the grave.

"But it ain't for you," said Jun like he'd said it before. "It's for Neddie."

"I'm your sample. You said I was," Bird argued. "And I can't even stretch out."

"It's plenty big for Neddie," said Frank.

"You need to take out some more up here," Bird commanded.

"Whyn't you just shut up?" yelled Dex. He was sitting under a tree. He looked about melted.

"Dex," said Jun. He was the oldest, so he was in charge of their manners, such as they were.

"Bird," I called. "You got to go to Minerva's house."

"What?" she yelled. "Why?"

"Jottie and I are going to Moorefield to see Cousin Irene."

She sat up, her hair matted flat against her head with dirt and sweat. "Moorefield? Today? Why can't I come?"

"'Cause last time we went, you said you missed Minerva so much. Jottie thought you'd like to stay at Minerva's better." I closed my mouth and waited. This was one of the spots where my plan could smash to smithereens. If Bird got into a snit, I'd have to pretend it was all a joke.

Bird swiveled her head around the edge of the grave. It looked pretty deep to me. Poor Neddie. "Where's Jottie?"

"She went to the United Garage to get some gasoline for the car." I made that one up on the spot, and I was proud of myself.

Dex flicked a clod of dirt at the grave. It hit Bird on the nose. "Hey!" she yelled.

"You gonna lie down or not?" said Jun.

"Ashes to ashes," said Frank enthusiastically.

Bird stood up. "I ain't letting the likes of *you* bury *me* in a puny baby grave. You can just stick old Neddie in here and sample it that way." She flung one leg over the edge of the grave and hauled herself out. I had never seen her dirtier. "*I* am going to my aunt Minerva's house, who is named after a Greek goddess, so there!"

Dex flicked another clod of dirt at her. I picked up a rock they'd grubbed out and tossed it a little in my hand, looking at him.

"All right, all right," said Jun, holding out his hands. "It's too hot to fight."

"Let's turn it into a pool," said Frank, looking at the hole.

"Small-potatoes pool," huffed Bird. "Minerva will probably take me swimming in the river, won't she, Willa?"

"Maybe," I said, taking up her hand. "We'd better get you over there." We walked slowly, in the shadiest parts of the streets, but each step was like pushing through warm cream. It was the hottest part of the hottest day. I felt a drop on my cheek and looked up, but it wasn't rain. The trees were sweating, too.

I stopped at the corner of Governor Street and pulled my letter out of my pocket. "Here's a letter from Jottie to Minerva. Make sure you give it to her." I handed her the little case.

Bird tilted her head to one side. She didn't often care to, but when she tried, she could see through me like water. I smiled as blankly as I could. "Whyn't you coming to the door?" she asked.

"Jottie's in a hurry."

She tilted her head to the other side, her blue eyes so narrow I could hardly see their color. "Huh," she said.

"Bye," I said. "See you tomorrow." I turned and walked away, leaving her to stare at my back. It was another smithereen-smashing place, but nothing happened. I looked back when I got halfway up the block, and Bird was gone. For a second, I fussed because I hadn't actually seen her go into Minerva's house, but then I laughed. Bird wasn't the kind to sneak off. I was.

44

I slipped in the front door without a sound and took stock. What I really wanted was a bath, but I didn't dare go upstairs. Father was asleep in his room, and Miss Beck could very well be up there, too, writing away at her book. Sometimes she went out to interview folks, but plenty of times she stayed home all day, typing or scribbling notes on her big yellow notepad.

It was a little after three, according to the hall clock, and still as a tomb. For now, my only job was to be quiet. I tiptoed through the front room to the bookcase. They thought they could hide *Gone with the Wind* behind *The Decameron of Boccaccio,* but I was too smart for them. Suddenly it occurred to me that this was an opportunity to broaden my horizons, and I plucked out *The Beautiful and Damned,* which I wasn't even supposed to touch. Also *Private Worlds,* which Jottie said would give me nightmares, and *Crime and Punishment,* which she said I might as well hit myself over the head with as read. That's what you get for leaving, I told her silently. I walked without a sound like an Indian brave to the front parlor. I had noticed, that morning, that if you sat behind the door but left it half open, you could see right smack into the front hall. The wood of the floor was cool, even if it was hard. I opened *The Beautiful and Damned.*

I was on page 92 when the clock struck five. I couldn't see why they were damned, unless it was because Anthony Patch made nasty remarks about his grandfather. Or maybe it was the cocktails. Still, I liked it. I liked it that they all seemed so desperate.

A few minutes later, Father came down the stairs, patting himself on the face the way he did when he'd just shaved. "Hey!" he called, as he reached the front hall. "Jottie. I'm home!"

Of course I didn't answer. Nobody did.

He mumbled something—or maybe he was humming, I don't know—and looked at himself in the mirror for a moment. "Jesus," he muttered. Then he saw the envelope marked Layla. After a second, he slit it open with his finger and read it. Then he laughed. He stood at the bottom of the stairs, holding the note in his hand. "Layla!" he called. "You up there?"

A door opened upstairs. Good thing I hadn't taken a bath. "I'm here," she called. "Is that you, Felix?"

"Yeah, come on down a minute," he said. I could see him smile, standing there at the bottom of the stairs, looking up. I knew it was her he was smiling at, even though I couldn't see her.

"You're home," she said.

"Uh-huh." He waved Jottie's note at her. "Got some terrible news here, honey."

"Oh?" She sounded worried. "Oh, dear."

"Just terrible. Jottie's gone to Moorefield for the night. The girls are staying over at Minerva's house. Mae's at the farm." He got closer to the stairs. "It's just you and me."

I saw her hand on the banister. "Oh, that's terrible," she said. I could hear her smile. "Just you and me?"

"Come down here," he said.

She did what he said, and then I could see both of them. She laughed and then she stepped up against him and lifted her face to his. "That's terrible," she repeated. I felt a little sick. I hadn't really thought this part out.

He kissed her. "We might starve to death," he said. Then he tipped back her chin and kissed her neck.

She shook her head. "I can make toast."

He laughed. "That's breakfast food. We've got the whole night to get through."

She blushed.

"Mmm, you're pretty when you do that," he said. He was so

happy. He pulled her close and kissed her again. Then he leaned away and said, "Hey. I got an idea. Are you hot?"

"Of course I am. Roasting."

"Let's you and me go swimming."

"Oh, Felix, where? I'd kill to be cool for just one minute."

"You would, would you? I know a nice place on the river. Got some shade trees, too." He lifted her hand to his mouth and kissed her fingertips. "How 'bout that?"

She nodded. "I'll run get my swimsuit."

"No," he said.

She laughed. "It's a pretty snappy swimsuit. You'll like it."

"No, I won't," he said. I hid my eyes then. I didn't want to see what they were doing. After some time passed, he sighed. "Sure you want to go?"

"Yes. Please. It's so hot."

"All right, honey. Go get your snappy swimsuit, and I'll run around and get the car." He kept his car in the alley behind our house. He started off, but she didn't let go of his hand. He glanced up at her, his face a question. "What?"

"I'm glad you're back," she said.

He smiled. "Me too."

She skipped up the stairs and he watched her go. Then he turned on his heel and went out the front door without making a sound, the way he did.

Then I went back to being alone.

I took a bath. I could have read *The Beautiful and Damned* in the tub if I had wanted to, but I didn't. I just sat and looked at my legs. They stretched almost the length of the bathtub now. I could lean back against one end and stuff my washrag into the faucet with my toe at the other. When I scooched down, I had to bend my knees. There was no one to tell me not to get my hair wet, and it bobbled in the water against my neck.

It was impossible to know if what I thought was the truth. I thought Father would never choose Miss Beck instead of us. I thought she had bewitched him, made him not himself. I thought if I could recall him, show him the light, he'd thank me. But I wasn't sure. In books, even in books like *The Beautiful and Damned,* things were connected; people did something and then something else happened because of that. I could understand them. But outside, here in the real world, things seemed to happen for no reason that I could see. Maybe there was no reason. Maybe people just drifted here and there, aimless and silly. But no, people had been thrown out of the Garden of Eden for *knowing,* so there must be something to know, reasons, all the time and everywhere, for the way they behaved. Reasons I couldn't see yet, no matter how hard I tried. I had always hoped that Jottie would call me into her room and tell me the secret, the thing I needed to know to understand why people did the things they did. So far, she hadn't. When she called me into her room to explain where babies came from, I thought I was about to get wind of something good, but I was disappointed. What I wanted was bigger, a giant blanket that would hold the world. I had become ferocious and devoted so I could learn the secret truths, but I still didn't know them. Did Father love Miss Beck? More than he loved me? I couldn't understand why, I couldn't understand how, I couldn't understand if. It seemed so hard that I had to work out the answers on my own, but that's what I had to do. I had to keep at it, finding out, guessing what would happen next, fighting for the right ending, trying to save them all.

I didn't know how long Father and Miss Beck were going to be gone, so I got out of the tub and even dried it with my towel in case they checked. That was pretty clever of me, I thought. I was feeling kind of hungry by then, so I went to see what I could rustle up in the kitchen. If they appeared suddenly, I could slip down the cellar stairs. They didn't, and I ate some tomatoes and bread and butter, carefully wiping up my crumbs. I washed my milk glass and plate and put them away. Even Mr. Sherlock Holmes would be hard-pressed to find evidence of my existence. Frank and Joe Hardy would be stumped, too, but they stumped easy.

There was still plenty of light to read by in the parlor. I got a pillow to sit on and picked up my book. I couldn't believe how much fuss that Anthony Patch made about kissing Gloria in a taxicab. You should come around here, I told him. You'd go out of your mind.

* * *

It was almost dark when they came in; there was only a thin band of hot orange on the very edge of the world. I had gotten tired and was sort of stretched out on the floor. I was still behind the door, but they could have seen my foot if they'd looked toward the parlor. Which they didn't.

"You sure you're not hungry?" Father was saying as they walked in.

"Not a bit. I ate all that ice cream." I thought of the ice cream we were supposed to have for Jottie's birthday.

"Wasn't much."

"It was plenty."

"You want some coffee?" I could see him but not Miss Beck. He looked cool and clean.

"No."

"Want anything?"

I could hear her breathe. "You," she said, real low. He stepped away, toward her, where I couldn't see, but I don't think I would have wanted to anyway. I had thought that I would stop them, but I didn't. I didn't jump out and I didn't frighten her away. I didn't do any of the things I'd planned. I curled up and let my tears drip sideways over my nose and onto the pillow beneath my head. I did that without making a sound.

After a while, she said his name and he said, "Upstairs, all right?"

I could hear the stairs creak as they went, and then she sort of laughed and said, "Whose room?"

Father said, "I'm not doing it in Emmett's bed. Come on."

"Is that whose room I've got?" Her voice faded. "Emmett's?"

"Shh," Father said.

It was quiet a second and then she gasped.

Father laughed.

✳

Charles Town was bustling with jockeys, breeders, and racegoers. The track had closed at five-thirty, but that seemed only to spur the crowds to new heights of gaiety. They surged out of the clubhouse and descended upon the quiet streets to celebrate their wins, their places, and their shows, or, failing that, their prospects for tomorrow. Now, at eight o'clock, the orange sky was paling to blue, and the sidewalks were thronged with hoarse, ebullient men and ladies who'd been in the heat too long.

Sol stopped before a restaurant. "I'll just check," he said, ignoring the pack of humans within.

Jottie raised her eyebrows. "It looks full."

He pulled open the door, and a glad cry of "Chaaaar-lieeee!" escaped into the dusk. Through the plate glass, Jottie watched him shoulder his way toward a waiter like a man pushing through a blizzard. She tried to see him with stranger's eyes: his fair hair—too long—and wide-spaced eyes, his broad shoulders and straight back. He looked intelligent, capable, and calm. His feet were enormous. Good thing he worked at a sock factory. If she married him, she would roll his enormous socks into pairs, carefully peeling one back to cover its mate.

She shook her head to clear it. She should be thinking about how wonderful he was, not about his feet. And he was wonderful, Sol. Good. And honest. She hoped Willa was all right. Of course she was all right. There was nothing to fuss about. Willa probably had her head stuck in a book, there on Minerva's purple sofa. Probably hadn't given a thought to her since the moment she'd passed out of sight. There was nothing to fuss about.

"Look what I got," said Sol, appearing at her side. Smiling triumphantly, he produced a thick china plate upon which rested half a chicken and two buttered biscuits.

"The man returns from the hunt," observed Jottie.

He laughed. "Come on. Let's find us a bench. I got to return the plate before ten or that waiter's going to stick me with a knife."

"Let's go eat in front of where they hung John Brown. I like to think of him dangling."

"You're a Confederate?" he asked as they began to walk.

"Me? No. Union forever. I just don't like John Brown." She sidestepped a man walking unsteadily in her path. "He was a show-off. The old fool."

They entered a little yard between two buildings. This place, alone in the thronged town, was hushed and solemn. A bench had thoughtfully been placed before the site of the gallows, which was marked by three stones.

"Taken from his cell," said Jottie, settling herself on the bench.

"What?" he said, fixing the plate between them.

She nodded toward the stones. "Those stones. Taken from John Brown's cell. He wrote on them in blood."

She could see Sol smile in the deepening twilight. "Sounds like you've made quite a study of the old man."

"I don't like him," she repeated, feeling flat. Willa would have wanted to know what he wrote. Even Bird would want to know that. And Felix? He would have pretended that he already knew—he'd be quoting now, something ridiculous.

They ate without talking, silent amid the soaring chorus of cicadas. Jottie patted her mouth with her handkerchief and swallowed. "No cooler here than at home," she said. It was something to say.

Sol nodded.

"What did you tell Violet?" she asked.

"About what?"

"About—this." Jottie waved a chicken bone, indicating all of Charles Town.

"Oh. I told her I was going to talk to a man down at Interwoven." Sol chewed slowly. "She didn't care."

"How is it, living with her?"

He looked at her, surprised. "It's all right." He thought for a moment and added, "I wish she'd get married."

Jottie laughed. "Why?"

He frowned. "She's bored. Or something. So she fusses too much. She fusses around and makes up things to do."

"She needs a job."

He nodded. "You could be right. I was thinking a husband."

"Might be a little late for that," Jottie said.

He lifted his head and looked at her. "She's younger than you are, and I want to marry you."

Jottie nodded.

"Are you done with this food?"

"Yes." She held herself in readiness. She was prepared.

Sol picked up the plate between them and set it on the ground. Moving next to her, he said, "I sort of hate to propose at a gibbet, but I guess it'll do."

Jottie laughed nervously. "I got a soft spot for this gibbet."

He picked up her hand and pressed it between his own. "Jottie," he began. "That day last month when you came to Everlasting, that was the happiest day of my life. I'd thought, before, that you and I were going to start—talking—being friendly again. I'd thought that we'd run into each other; we'd see each other and talk. But you always looked away." He squeezed her hand. "Then, when you came in with that girl Layla, you—it seemed like you wanted to know me again. I was so glad, Jottie, you can't imagine. I can't put it into words. You seemed like your old self, back when we were kids, and happy to see me."

"I was," she said quietly.

"You don't know how that made me feel, honey. I'd been missing you for so long I'd got used to it. I was even thinking I'd maybe find someone else and get married. But then I'd see you—or even Emmett; he'd do it to me, too—and I'd feel hollowed out again. But then, I don't know what happened. I don't know why you came to Everlasting that day. I could hardly believe it, but—well, I'm going to go ahead and try to make it stick. Will you marry me?"

Jottie pressed herself hard against the slats of the bench, feeling his hand, dry and calm, around hers. "Sol?" she said tentatively.

Sol tilted his head, waiting.

"Why are you so set on me?" She looked sideways at him.

He smiled. "You fishing for compliments?"

"No!" She blushed. "But you could have anyone, a nice, pretty girl—"

"You're nice and pretty," he interrupted.

"A lot younger than me," she continued.

"I don't want someone younger than you. I've loved you as long as I can remember," he said.

She looked at him sharply. Could it be true? Don't be so suspicious, she chided herself. This is Sol, an honest man. Sol is wonderful, she repeated to herself. He loves me. If I marry him, I'll be a new woman. I'll be Mrs. McKubin. I'll start fresh.

"I remember thinking that I was going to marry you back when I was about twelve," he said reminiscently. "In my mind, it was all settled."

"You never told me."

"No." Sol took her face between his hands and kissed her, gently at first and then harder. With one finger, he smoothed a line down her throat. "You're so little," he said, almost to himself. "I didn't think you were going to be so little." He moved his hands to circle her waist.

"Felix says I act big," she said breathlessly, trying not to remember Vause doing the same thing.

He put one arm around her and lifted her onto his lap. "Felix ain't invited to this party," he said into her neck. There was a pause. "I always wanted to do this."

"Did you?" *If anyone besides me ever touches you, I'll kill him.* Go. Go away.

"Mm-hm. All along, this was how I wanted it to turn out." She touched his face experimentally and felt him smile. "I used to get so worried that something was going to happen to you before I could ask you to marry me. You-all did so many crazy things."

She lifted her eyes to the freedom of the deepening sky. Let me go, Vause, she begged. I'm so tired of the past. "How come you never said anything to me about it?"

Sol's hands tightened on her. "Because you were in love with Vause." He held her apart from him and looked at her. "And I'm not an idiot."

She nodded, sorry she had made him say it.

"Goddammit," he sighed, pulling her close again. "Marry me."

"All right," she said.

※

There was no way to sleep on the horsehair sofa, and of course I couldn't go to my own room. I opened the parlor window a little and laid some pillows out beneath it. It wasn't too bad. I woke when the clock struck one and a tiny breeze curled down from the window and ruffled the hair on my neck. I woke again later when I heard water running upstairs. Was one of them taking a bath? Was that part of it? Not having any answer, I fell asleep again.

✳

Jottie kicked at the thin, clean hotel sheets, waking herself up. For the first moment, she lay still, panting, dread flooding her veins until her fingertips tingled. She'd been dreaming of Willa and kittens. An awful thing, trying to pull Willa from a sea of kittens as they dragged at her with their tiny claws, their milky eyes unblinking. Jottie shuddered, dislodging the dream but not the dread. The dread stayed. Befuddled, she struggled to find its source: What's the matter?

Sol. She'd said yes; she'd agreed to marry him.

Her heart commenced to thump, to gallop. What is happening to me? she asked the dark. Cautiously, she lifted her hand to her breast and felt the wild beating inside. Like a bird breaking its wings on a cage, she thought. But why?

She'd said yes; she'd agreed to marry Sol.

Oh God, what have I done? she asked herself. She rolled to her side and drew her knees up to her stomach. It helped a little. The voice of reason, shrill as it was, could be heard in this position: What have you done? Why, you've done exactly what you set out to do! You got yourself a fresh start, a new name, a new everything! Sol loves you! And Sol's wonderful, you know he is! You're going to marry him and move into his house, and you're going to be so happy!

No, I'm not.

Of course you are! This is what you wanted!

I was wrong. I don't want it.

Yes, you do. You're loved. You're going to be married to the president of the mill! Everyone in town will smile when they see you coming! The girls won't have a care in the world! They'll swish up the stairs, and there you'll be, with a plate of cookies in your hand!

The scene had become lifeless through overuse.

And Felix would never speak to her again. He would hate her. She had broken faith with him.

Felix, she pleaded with him, I'm sorry. I was so worried that the girls would be hurt, and I couldn't change you, so I had to change myself. I needed to have Macedonia on my side, for Willa, and Bird, too, so they wouldn't be ashamed. I'm sorry. I have to stop being a Romeyn. I have to do it.

Felix didn't leave me. He could have, but he didn't. I owe him.

No, you don't. You don't owe anyone your whole life. Lie still and count your blessings. Sol's a fine man. Most women would be thrilled.

I think I'm sick.

Hushup. Breathe. Again. Again. That's right. Of course you're a little worried. It's a big change. But that's what you wanted, to change. *Felix put his hand over her shaking fingers. "You don't have to look at anyone. You just hang on to me and I'll stare 'em down for you."* Oh God, what have I done? I've betrayed my best friend.

She rolled over in her fetters of sheet and buried her face in the pillow. Nothing eased her, nothing helped. Vause? she called in desperation. Help me, honey, please. But he wouldn't come, wouldn't help, until she stopped trying, and then he appeared in a flickering picture from the last day of his life, when she'd loved him so much that there wasn't enough air in all the world for her to catch her breath. His arms taking her in one last crushing hug because he had to go, had something to do, he'd meet her later. *I have to go, Josie. Give me a kiss for luck. Uh-huh, but why do you need luck? I don't, I guess. Just kiss me, all right?*

No, this was unbearable. She sat up. She stared at the white hotel wall that separated her from Sol. She could bang on it— he'd said she should wake him if she wanted anything. But no. He'd come to her door in an instant, his face all lit up with hope, thinking that she wanted him in bed. Jottie hid her face in her hands. That's what other people want, she told herself. That's what's normal. And when I say, No, I've made a terrible mistake, I can't marry you, I'll have to watch the happiness drop away from him like bricks collapsing. I can't do it. I can't do anything. I can't go forward and I can't go back. I want to go home.

✳

Layla opened her eyes and lay very still. Outside the window, the night had turned from black to blue. Day was coming. But the important thing, she told herself, the terribly important thing, is the location of the window. The window is on the left. Which means I'm not in my room. Which means that I'm in Felix's room. In Felix's bed. She shifted slightly, onto her back, and smiled at the languor of heavy usage in her hips.

She turned her head to look at him. His back was to her, lean and brown, with his black hair curling on his neck. She watched one shoulder and the top of an arm rise and fall with his rhythmic breath. Moving carefully, so as not to wake him and destroy the opportunity, Layla turned. She wanted to look at him. There hadn't been a chance before, not for looking, not for becoming expert. Her eyes traced over the shoulder, the arm, the back, the delicate shoulder blade. There was a puckered scar on his shoulder, a dark, shriveled, almost perfect circle. It was odd that it was so perfectly circular. Curious, she stretched out her hand across the space between them. For a second, her finger hovered there, and then she touched it.

Without a sound, seemingly without moving, he was out of the bed. Blindly, he felt for the wall and put his back against it, facing the room. He stood there in silence.

Layla sat up. "Felix? Honey?"

He looked at her, his eyes fierce.

"Felix? Did I startle you? I'm sorry—I—um—I guess you're not used to having company."

Still, he said nothing.

She watched his chest rise and fall. "You're fast. I didn't even feel the bed move when you got up."

His eyes scanned the room and returned to her. "There's no one here," she explained. "I touched you. On your back. You have a scar there. And I touched it. That's what woke you up."

He let out a slow breath and nodded. His eyes went to the window, and the minutes passed as he watched the lightening blue. Finally, he turned back to Layla and saw her worried face. He smiled then and came back to the side of the bed.

Without speaking, he twitched away the sheet that she held against her body.

She relaxed and, smiling, settled herself against the pillows.

"I know why you woke me up," he said. "You don't have to lie about it."

45

I woke in the dawn. The sky was roaring orange and pink and gold, more colors than I'd ever seen before. I watched the black branches outside turn back into trees as the sky grew light. It was still more cool than not, but it wouldn't last long. The curling breeze of the night was long gone, and the day was still and waiting.

For the first time, I dared to think about how much trouble I was going to be in when Jottie got back. Maybe Mr. McKubin would distract her, but I doubted it. There was no possibility of hiding it; at least, I couldn't think of a way. I could buy off Bird but not Minerva. Well, I would take my punishment, whatever it was, but I hoped Jottie wouldn't tell Miss Beck that I'd been here all along; I would never be able to look her in the eye again. Not that I wanted to. The more I thought about it, the worse I felt. I got up and put my pillows back on the fancy parlor chairs. I should get my breakfast, I decided. Even though Father liked to sleep late, Miss Beck might rout him out of bed.

It was harder than the night before, because I couldn't make so much as a peep. I cut myself a piece of bread and threw the crumbs out the window. It must have taken me a full two minutes to open the refrigerator door silently, and then I stood there, torn with indecision. Eventually I drank some milk from the bottle and stuck my fingers in a jar of applesauce a few times. What Jottie didn't know wouldn't hurt her.

I tiptoed around a bit more, combing my hair and such, and then I just waited. The parlor was beginning to feel like a jail, so I stood inside the broom cupboard for a while and then I went to the back porch and wedged myself up against the washing machine. Nothing happened. I watched the sun come over the trees. The clock struck seven, eight, and nine. The telephone rang, but no one answered it. The heat began to gather in the sky, and the outside went limp. After a while, the clock struck ten.

I wished I had something to read, but the longer I waited, the more frightened I was to go back to the parlor, for surely they would get up soon. I waited and waited until the back porch was driving me crazy, and I decided to chance it. I edged through the kitchen and made for the parlor as quickly as I could. I was in the hallway on my return when I heard a door open upstairs, and my heart gave a big thump. I skittered right to the kitchen, but I was too scared to open the porch door, because it squeaked, so I dove toward the cellar. The cellar door didn't shut properly but hung a little open all the time, so there were no squeaks to fear. It was dark on the stairs, and soft threads brushed against my face, but it was a little cooler there, if I wanted to count my blessings. I sat down on the second stair, *The Beautiful and Damned* in my lap.

✳

Seven was the earliest she could wake him. At four, that's what she had decided. At four, seven seemed soon, just around the corner. Maybe she'd even sleep again, knowing she could wake Sol at seven. She'd knock on his door at seven, dressed, with her hat on, even, so he wouldn't get any ideas, and she'd tell him the truth. Seven was only three hours away.

At quarter of six, she didn't think she could stand it much longer. Sol, she would say, I can't marry you. I'm deeply fond of you—no—I love you. But I can't break up the family; I can't abandon Felix.

He'd get mad. He'd say, You promised me. He'd say, This is your last chance to be a real person, a regular person, and you are about to throw it away.

At ten after six, she got up and took a bath. The bathroom was cramped and dim, with a small window overlooking a light shaft. She scrubbed herself zealously and washed her hair for good measure. She peered in the mirror as she combed it out. She hadn't looked at herself so closely in years.

A heavy rap on the door startled her, and her comb clattered to the floor. "Just a minute!" she called breathlessly. After a moment of panic, she put her nightgown over her head and opened the door.

Sol slipped in, his face ablaze with happiness. "I couldn't sleep. I haven't slept a wink." He leaned against the wall and shook his head in amazement. "But I'm wide awake; I never felt better. I couldn't wait to see you, dear. Not another minute. I started thinking about when I could come over—at four, I started thinking about it. I thought I should wait till seven, but I couldn't."

She couldn't help smiling a little. "That's funny. That's what I was thinking, too."

"Were you?" He seized her hands. "Were you awake, too?"

"I was."

He didn't hear the grimness in her voice. He laughed. "You should have banged on the wall. I would have come over."

"You could have banged on the wall just as well as I could," she said.

He nodded. "I didn't want you to—well, to feel like, like I was, uh, importunate."

"Importunate?" She loved Sol, she truly did. "Importunate?"

He flushed. "You know."

She nodded, trying to keep a straight face. "You were being considerate."

He nodded eagerly.

"Makes a nice change," she said.

He smiled. "Can I kiss you good morning?" He reached for her. "In honor of how considerate I was at four?" She nodded and stepped into his arms. "Good morning," he murmured, pulling her close. "Good morning, sweetheart."

It was wonderful, the way he held her. As though she were something precious. She softened. Maybe she'd been too hasty. Maybe she could work it out somehow. Maybe she could marry him and live at home, like Minerva—

Sol's voice was gentle, next to her ear. "You want breakfast?

There's a café—what's it called? The Paddock or something. Anyway, it's across the street. We could get something to eat before the first race."

"The first race," she repeated.

"It's not until ten," he said. "We've got lots of time." He pulled away from her and smiled. "But I'm hungry now."

Her heart sank. "I guess I'd better get dressed, then."

He nodded. "Yeah. I'll go wait next door."

"Unimportunately."

He smiled. "You watch out. I'll be plenty importunate once we're married." He gave her shoulder a squeeze as he opened the door. "I can't believe you're going to be *mine*."

She nodded. Her head felt like a skull.

"Sol?"

He looked up and frowned with concern at her plate. "Don't you like your pancakes?"

"Oh, yes," she said. "They're fine." She looked down at the pool of syrup. "It's real luxurious to have someone else make my breakfast for me."

He nodded, satisfied.

"But, Sol?" she persisted. "I got to talk to you. About this"—she couldn't bring herself to say marriage—"wedding business. There's a lot of things that need figuring out." That was a good phrase, she thought.

He put his fork slowly down. "Jottie? You're not backing out on me, are you?"

She blinked. "No. No! That's not what I meant. I'm just fussing, is all."

"About?"

"About the girls," she said. She licked her lips. "I—I have to think of the girls. You see, I promised Willa I'd come back."

He cocked his head. "Come back when?"

"Well. Today. But she's—you know, I have to take care of her. Bird, too. I've been taking care of them all their lives."

His eyebrows met. "Felix works you like a convict."

"No!" She touched his wrist. "No, it's not him. I wanted it this way. They're my girls." She thought of Willa's dark eyes. "They're my children."

"They're Felix's children," Sol said. "And Sylvia's."

She twitched her shoulders dismissively. "Oh, *Sylvia*. I raised them. And Willa, she's something else. Smart as a whip, but she takes things hard, you know? She struggles. By herself, too; she doesn't ask for help. She wants to understand everything, wants to make sense of things, and God knows, plenty of things don't make much sense—"

"Especially if you're Felix's kid," Sol said, his voice harsh.

Jottie nodded. "Yes, there's that, but she adores him." She pressed her fingers around her temples. "I have to hold on to her, Sol. I have to make sure she knows she's not alone. I have to keep her—safe."

"What about the little one? Bird?"

Jottie smiled. "Bird. God bless Bird. Tough as shoe leather since the day she was born."

"So she's like Felix," Sol interjected.

He didn't understand. "I suppose she is. But Willa is, too. The way Felix really is—" She broke off, unable to finish, unable to express her unease.

Sol held out his hand across the table. After a moment, she placed hers in it. "Listen, Jottie. She can live with us, if you want. Both of them can. If that's what'll make you happy, that's what we'll do."

Her eyes dropped to their linked hands. He had no idea that his generosity conferred nothing, that she had never envisioned herself without them. She looked up at him and smiled. "You're sweet, Sol. You're awfully sweet." She peered across the crowd of tables to a wooden telephone booth in a corner and stood. "What time is it?"

He looked at his watch. "Almost nine."

"I'm just going to make a phone call."

He watched, frowning, as she wove between the tables.

Honestly, thought Jottie, listening to Minerva's phone ring for the eighth time. You'd think she could bestir herself a little.

"Morning." It was Henry.

"Henry. This is Jottie here. How-you?"

"Fine. I'm fine. Where—"

"I'll be coming along pretty soon, Henry. But it's going to take me a while. I'd better talk to Minerva."

"She isn't here. She and Bird got up at the crack of dawn and went off to the river with Mae."

"Well, it is awful hot, I guess. I'll talk to Willa, then."

"Willa?"

"Yes. You said Bird went to the river with Minerva."

"She did, but Willa's with you. Minnie said."

Henry never paid attention to anything. "Willa's *there*," Jottie said. "She spent the night there."

"No, she didn't. The two of you went to Moorefield, is what Minnie said."

Her brain refused the information. "No," she said to Henry. "She's there."

"*No.* She isn't," Henry insisted.

"Willa's not at your house?" Jottie whispered.

"No. Are you saying she's not with you?"

"No."

"No yes or no no?" Henry demanded.

Lost. Jottie closed her eyes tight, trying to find her.

"Jottie!" yelled Henry.

Where would she go? What would she want? Her mind wasn't working; there were no ideas, no pictures, no traction. Finally, who knew how long it took, there was an itch—where did it come from? Yesterday. Yesterday, what had she said? Something about Layla, about leaving her alone in the house. It had seemed so strange. As if she were worried about Layla— but she didn't care about Layla. It was Felix she cared about, and Felix wasn't home. He wasn't. Though she hadn't checked.

"Henry, I got to go. I'll call back later." Jottie held down the hook, her unseeing eyes fixed on a table of old men in front of her booth. Blindly, she fumbled for another nickel and dropped it in the slot. "Collect call, please," she said to the operator. "Macedonia again."

✳

Layla woke to the blaze of full morning, hot and heavy. She was trapped under the weight of Felix's leg, bound by his arm. She stirred restlessly, her sticky skin peeling away from his.

He didn't move.

She could wait. After all, wasn't she where she wanted to be? She smiled to herself, looking proprietarily at the mixture of their bodies. She'd surprised him, she knew. *That must've been some finishing school.* She giggled.

"Shh."

He was awake! She burrowed deeper against him. "We should get up," she murmured.

Nothing.

She kissed his neck. "Get up," she whispered.

His hand moved from her waist to her mouth and covered it.

She laughed against his palm. She wanted to exult with him. He needed to be awake so she could love him. "It's late," she urged. "Rise and shine."

He rolled off her and turned away. Far away, downstairs in the hall, the telephone rang.

"Telephone!" she called, hoping to rouse him.

Nothing.

She listened to it ring until it stopped. Then she examined the ceiling. She waited, her stomach gurgling. She was starving. He wouldn't want her to starve. She leaned over him and hesitated, remembering his strange, silent flight the night before. After a moment, she exclaimed, "It's after nine!" Silence. She tried again. "Do you know how many hours we've been in bed?"

He didn't move.

"Twelve!" she said. "Almost twelve hours."

"In bed isn't sleeping," he mumbled.

"I know. But aren't you hungry?"

He nodded, his eyes closed.

She could touch him now, she decided. She leaned over his shoulder, her hair falling in a curtain around his face. "We'll have years to sleep, Felix. Years and years of sleeping, you and me together. I'm too happy to sleep now."

His eyes opened then and slid sideways in her direction. He smiled. "You want to know something?"

"What?"

"Jottie's always right." He was almost laughing.

She shook her hair, tickling him. "Jottie?" She stroked his chest. "Pooh. I'm the one who's always right."

With a swift movement, he reached around, flipped her onto her back, and rolled over, pinning her hands down with his own. She felt a prickle of alarm as his eyes traveled over her speculatively. "What was Jottie right about?" she asked, subdued.

"Mm," he grunted.

"What?" She wiggled and his hands tightened. "What did she say?"

Finally he looked into her eyes. "I'll tell you later. It'll be a surprise." He released her and rose.

✳

"Stop," Jottie said as they drove through Martinsburg. "There's a drugstore. I'm going to call again."

Sol nodded and pulled the car up to the curb.

Inside an airless booth, she listened to her telephone ring fourteen times. She could hear its angry blare pushing at the walls of her house. Why didn't they answer?

Jottie swallowed. "Macedonia again," she said to the operator, and gave her Mae's number. It rang and rang.

"Guess nobody's home," the operator's voice came crisply into the fifteenth ring.

"Oh God," whispered Jottie.

"Ma'am," said the operator reprovingly.

"All right. Try this one," said Jottie. Please, Emmett.

"In Macedonia?"

"No, this one's in White Creek." Be home.

It rang only twice. "Hello?"

"Emmett!" she cried.

The operator interrupted. "Will you accept the charges from a Miss Jottie Romeyn?"

"Yes."

"Go ahead," said the operator.

"Emmett, can you go down to the house? Willa's missing, and I think—"

"What? Where are you? Jottie?"

She was crying. "Emmett, I'm—well, I'm in Martinsburg

now—I'll explain it all later, but I told Willa to take Bird over to Minerva's to spend the night while I was gone, and she never went, and I think she's in the house with Layla, but they don't answer the phone, and"—she caught her breath the best she could—"can you go over and see? I'll be another forty-five minutes at least, and I just can't—"

"Sure, yes, I'll go now. Where's Bird?"

"She's with Minnie; they've gone off to the river or something. It's Willa. She never went—"

"Okay, I got it. I'll go right down. I'll be there in about fifteen minutes."

"Drive fast."

"All right." He sounded calm and sure. "I'll find her."

"Please. Find her."

Out on the heat-choked sidewalk, Sol was waiting for her. Mutely, he opened the car door for her, and she slid into the seat and pressed her foot hard against the floor to push the car forward.

46

I heard Father come into the kitchen. "Coffee, coffee," he groaned, just the way he always did. My heart stopped racing and I felt a little cheered. Maybe I was mistaken. Maybe the world would drop back into its normal place after all. I leaned forward to look through the open door and saw that it wouldn't. I could see only a thin slice of the kitchen—the table, a bit of the counter next to the stove—but Father was there and he wasn't normal. He had a shirt on, but it was unbuttoned over his undershirt, the cuffs rolled up to his elbows.

"Coffee," he moaned, stepping around the kitchen. "Where do you suppose she keeps it?"

"Pantry?" said Miss Beck's voice.

"Maybe," he mumbled, moving away.

"Refrigerator?" she said. I froze, because the refrigerator was right next to my cellar door. She came to look herself, bending to see the shelves. She was wearing Father's dressing gown, his silk one with the golden belt. The cord was cinched tight around her little waist, and she was barefoot. "Here it is."

"Good girl. Now, coffeepot."

"Over here, I think. You know how to make it?"

"Sure. I'm an old hand. Camping."

"You camp?" Miss Beck laughed. "I can't picture that."

"Picture it, lady." He rattled around.

"I'll have to learn how to make coffee. Jottie showed me once."

"Jottie doesn't make it strong enough."

"She said it would put hair on my chest," Miss Beck said.

He laughed. "Let me see about that," he said, and Miss Beck squealed.

I jumped when the telephone rang, but they didn't hear me. They were jumping themselves, I guess.

"I'll get it," Miss Beck said, after three rings.

"No, you won't," Father said, kind of sharp. "Leave it."

I was glad. It wasn't her house.

We all three of us waited, listening to the telephone. Fourteen times, it rang.

"Didn't you say something about toast?" Father asked.

"Yes. I'll make some toast." Miss Beck went by with a package of bread in her hands. "How many would you like?" she asked.

"What?" He wasn't listening. I heard the half cough, half explosion that meant the coffee was perking. Father was listening to that.

"How many slices?"

"Oh. Two. No, three. I'm hungry."

For a while they were busy with toast and finding the sugar, and then she said softly, "Felix, I'll learn how to cook."

I could only see his back. He put the coffeepot carefully down on the stove and said, "Why would you do that?"

There was a tiny pause, and then she said, "Well. For us."

He turned toward her and took a gulp of coffee. "Ah. Us. The folks at home, you mean. And here I always thought senators kept cooks. If not butlers. Cooks at least."

"What?"

"You telling me your daddy doesn't keep a cook?"

"Wait," she said. "Wait."

"I *am* waiting. I'm waiting to hear why our senator from Delaware doesn't keep a cook. I'd hate to think it's because he's cheap."

"How'd you find out?" I don't know why she'd be ashamed of having a senator for a father, but that's how she sounded.

He took another gulp of coffee and sighed. "Layla. I believe I told you a long time ago that was a trade secret."

"Did you read my mail?"

He smiled. "I didn't have to, honey. It's printed on the envelopes. Senator and Mrs. Grayson Beck."

"Oh."

"You on a little research tour for the senator, sweetheart? Come to see how the other half lives?"

"No! Felix!" she gasped. "That's not it at all!" She moved close to him and put her hand on his shirt. "No. He threw me out, Father did. I really am on relief. Really I am. You have to believe me."

He smiled at her and shrugged. "I don't mind. Fine by me if you're slumming. I've enjoyed it. Especially the last"—he glanced up to the clock—"fifteen hours." He leaned down and kissed her lips. "I won't tell your daddy about that Red boyfriend of yours, either."

"Felix! What—how'd you know about that?"

He didn't answer.

"He's not my boyfriend; he's not anything anymore. It's you that—" She put both hands on his shoulders and took a breath. "It's you I care about."

I realized my hands hurt from gripping my book so hard. I loosened them.

He backed his head away from her. "Is that right?"

"I love you." Her fists bunched up the cloth of his shirt. "You must know that, after last night." She shook him a little.

He was quiet for a bit, and then he rubbed her cheek with his hand. "Poor little Layla. You don't know anything about me." She stepped right up against him and put her arms around his neck, but he pulled them away. "You don't know a damn thing."

"I don't care," she said, holding tight to his hands. "I know everything I need to know. It's true, Father's a senator, but what does it matter? It doesn't mean a thing about who I am or who we are or what we feel about each other."

"Very democratic," he said. "Very stirring."

She stomped her foot. "You're being ridiculous, Felix. How could you think I'd—how could I have"—she blushed—"done what we did if I didn't love you? I've known since the first time you touched me that we were meant for each other. Nothing else is important—not where I come from, not where you come from. You could be a—an Eskimo, and I'd still love you!"

He laughed. "Eskimos everywhere will sleep soundly tonight."

"Felix!" He was still laughing a little, but she put her hands on his face and made him look at her. She was pushy, that's what she was. "My past is unimportant. And so is yours. Nothing that happened before means anything to me. It's the future that matters." She lifted her face to be kissed. "Our future."

He didn't kiss her. He just looked at her. "Our future, huh? Yours and mine."

"Yes!" she said. "You and me together. Forever. A lifetime."

I stood up, not caring if I made a noise. She meant us. We were his past. She was telling him that we didn't matter, Bird and me. This was the moment I'd been watching for, the one where I'd face her down, where I'd prove myself. *The Beautiful and Damned* clattered away down the stairs, and I put out my hand to fling open the cellar door. "Father—" I started to say.

And then the screen door banged open and Jottie flew in, with Mr. McKubin right behind her.

I sat down again.

*

"Oh God," said Jottie. "You're here. Where's Willa?"

Felix took a step back, his glance flicking from her to Sol and back again.

"Willa!" called Jottie.

"Get out of my house," Felix said to Sol.

Sol's face was expressionless. "It's her house, too." He pointed his chin toward Jottie.

Felix wheeled around to Jottie. "What the hell is he doing here?"

"Felix," she babbled, "I sent the girls to Minerva's to spend the night, but Willa never went, she never went there, and I don't know where she's gone, I don't know—is she here? Did you—" She stopped as he seized her arm, his fingers closing tight around it.

"You went to Moorefield to visit Irene," he said, very quietly. "You sent the girls to Minnie's because you went to Moorefield."

"But it's Willa—" she said.

"Willa's just fine," he said smoothly.

"She's here?" Her voice soared with relief.

"She's upstairs." His fingers pressed hard into her flesh. "How about you tell me where you were."

Jottie looked down at her arm. "I wasn't in Moorefield."

"She was with me," Sol said loudly.

"No," Felix said, his face tight. "Not Sol."

"Felix," said Layla, frowning at Jottie's arm, "you're hurting her."

"You were with Sol?" He gripped her tighter and tighter.

"I came back," she said evasively. "Didn't I?"

Sol shifted on his feet. "Let go of her, Felix."

"Shut up," said Felix, without looking away from Jottie. "You promised me, Jottie. We made a deal."

"Some deal—she does whatever you say and you do whatever you want," said Sol, taking a step toward him. "Would you let go of her?"

"Sol," said Jottie, "just wait a second. Felix, let go."

He dropped her arm. "Don't forget, I stood by you. And I came back with the girls. Don't forget what I did for you."

Before she could speak, Sol exploded, "Goddammit, Felix, you act like you did her a favor—"

"Sol—" Jottie shook her head in warning.

"No, I'm not going to stop— You act like you did her a favor, you bastard, when what you did was come crawling back here with your children when your marriage fell apart and make Jottie your goddamn slave. You're full of shit if you think you did her any favors."

"Fuck you, Sol. You don't know anything and you never did."

"No, *you* don't know anything. You want me to tell you just one of the things you don't know?"

"Sol," Jottie pleaded, "could you—"

"No, I could not," he said, shaking his shoulders impatiently. "I'm tired of tiptoeing around Felix. Felix, I'm goddamn sick of you. And I'm not afraid of you, either."

Layla's eyes narrowed. "Afraid? I should think not—" she began, but Sol talked over her.

"Jottie and I are going to get married. She said yes. Do you hear me?" He leaned toward Felix, his eyes gleaming. "She said yes." Felix turned to Jottie and stared at her incredulously as Sol continued to talk. "We went to Charles Town yesterday, for the Horse Show, and when I asked her to marry me, she said yes. That's what she said." He gazed triumphantly at Jottie. "Didn't you?"

Briefly, she put her hand to her head. "That's what I said."

Footsteps hammered up the stairs to the back door. "You beat me!" called Emmett, looming dark against the screen. "Cacapon Road melted yesterday, and I had to drive around to State 9." He yanked open the door. "But now I'm here, I'll—" He broke off at the sight of Sol and, after a moment's hesitation, stepped inside, his eyes moving from face to face. "Well," he said at last. He backed toward the sink and stood against it warily. "This is unusual."

There was a short silence. Then Sol cleared his throat and said, "Jottie and I are announcing our engagement."

Jottie opened her mouth and closed it again as Emmett looked at her in mute astonishment. "Congratulations," he said finally.

Felix smiled brilliantly at his brother. "And Layla and I are announcing *our* engagement."

Layla's head jerked up.

Quickly, Felix stepped to her side and put his arm around her waist. "It's quite a coincidence, isn't it? Isn't it, Jottie?" She nodded, her lips tight. "While you and Sol were billing and cooing over there in Charles Town, Layla and I were doing the same thing right here in the comfort of home. Rapturous, wasn't it, Layla?"

She looked at him in confusion and nodded.

"Oh my God, you poor kid," Sol breathed.

"Shut up," Felix snapped, without taking his eyes from Jottie. "Let's us have a double wedding, Jottie, what do you say? Remember Minerva and Mae? That was real nice, I thought. We can go down the aisle together, kind of a last hurrah. And then we'll say good-bye. Good-bye and good luck. Shake hands. You can give the girls a kiss. You might see them downtown sometimes. Except I'm thinking of moving, to Chicago, maybe, the city of broad shoulders. Don't worry, though, because Layla here, she'll be a fine stepmother." He threw an appraising glance at Layla. "Well, she probably won't eat them or anything." He laughed.

"Felix, don't," Jottie said.

"What?" His arm tightened around Layla's waist. "You don't think she'll be a good stepmother? You doubt her? Won't you be a good stepmother, honey?"

She tried to smile. "I'll do my best."

Emmett made a sharp, frustrated movement against the counter.

Felix rounded on him. "What? You should find yourself a girlfriend, Emmett. I think you'd be happier."

"Felix," said Jottie, her voice rising, "you have to stop. We all know you're angry, but it's not right, what you're doing. It's not fair to Layla."

"Layla?" Felix gestured to her. "She's happy. This is everything she's ever wanted. She was just saying that. Weren't you, Layla?"

"Yes," she said, lifting her chin. "Of course, and I don't know what you're talking about, Jottie. It's no wonder that Felix is a little upset, with you getting yourself engaged to, well, a man who practically ruined his life with lies and slander." She glanced haughtily at Sol. "I don't know how you can do it. None of my business, of course, but I don't know how you can."

Felix's smile was radiant. "You hear that, Jottie? She doesn't know how you can. And neither do I." His smile disappeared. "Neither do I."

Layla put her hand on his and squeezed it comfortingly. "No one believes it, Felix. Everyone knows it was a lie. I mean," she looked around the room earnestly, "of course it was sad that that boy died, but obviously, *obviously,* you"—she pursed her lips at Sol—"were in some kind of, of—I don't know—delusion is the kindest word for it. I can't understand why anyone ever took you seriously. Six weeks after it happened. Ridiculous," she said contemptuously.

"He did it," said Sol. "No delusion. It was him. I know you were behind it somehow, Felix."

"You're crazy. I wasn't even there."

"Oh, *don't*," moaned Jottie. "Please. Can't we just—"

"No," snapped Sol, his eyes on Felix. "I don't know why or how, but I know you started it. I know you planned it; I know you lied. Because that's what you do."

"*I wasn't there.* It was Vause."

Sol's mouth curled. "Yeah, you'd say that. You never gave a damn about anybody as long as you got what you wanted. Anything you wanted, you took like it was yours. Hell, I saw you break into Everlasting a dozen times at least—along with half the other buildings in town. And you always got away with it."

"That's what gets under your skin, isn't it, Sol? That I did what I wanted and I never got punished. You always hoped I'd get in trouble—you were dying for someone to bring me down, and finally you decided to do it yourself. You always hated me."

Sol shook his head. "No, I didn't, and you know it. From the time we were kids, I wanted to be just like you. So smart and brave—the things you'd do. And then later, when all the girls were so crazy about you—I always wanted to be like you. Like you and Vause. I was so proud that I was your-all's friend, almost one of you. But not quite. Not really."

Felix sneered. "We felt sorry for you, that's why we let you tag along. God, there you'd be, tagging along and fussing at us, telling us not to do this or that because we'd get hurt. Yellow is what you were. You were always yellow."

Sol nodded. "I know. But I didn't hate you."

Felix said scornfully, "You were jealous."

"Yeah, I was, but mostly I just wanted to come along with you."

"You were jealous, so you lied about me."

"No." Sol shook his head. "I wasn't even thinking about you, really. It was Vause I was thinking about. The Vause I knew, he wouldn't have done it, not on his own. He wouldn't have stolen money and he wouldn't have set that mill on fire. He would have followed you there, I can see him doing that, but not without you making him."

"I didn't make him!" Felix snapped. "I didn't have anything to do with it. He did it himself!"

"No. Not Vause."

"He did," Felix insisted. "He knew how to open the safe, and he went there and stole six thousand dollars and then set the place on fire."

Sol shook his head. "It's not something Vause would have done." He appealed to Jottie. "Would he?"

She lifted her eyes to his. "I never—I didn't think so."

Sol was almost talking to himself now. "It couldn't have been him. Vause wasn't like that. He was so . . . clear, you know?"

She nodded. "And he didn't lie much. Hardly ever. Only to get Felix or me out of trouble." She turned to include her brother. "Remember?"

For a moment, he simply looked at her. Then he drew in his breath and began speaking softly. "That's what you want to believe, Jottie, but you know it's not true. You know the truth, honey. Come on," he prodded. "You know what he was doing. He was stealing that money because he had to get out of town. He'd gotten himself in too deep with you and he wanted to break it off. It'd started out as a joke—"

"Jesus, Felix!" exclaimed Emmett. "That's not—"

"Hushup, Emmett," said Felix. "You don't know anything. It had been a joke, you know, just a little fun before he moved along, but then he saw you were taking it hard." His words fell slow and gentle: "And you made it worse when you started talking about getting married—"

"No! It wasn't me," she cried. "Vause said it first!"

"Honey"—Felix shook his head—"I was *there*. It was you. Vause didn't want to hurt your feelings, but he didn't want to get married, either." He smiled. "He sure wasn't ready to settle down, I'll tell you—he had a couple other girls he was going with—"

"No," she protested, her hands rising to fend off his words. "That's not what—you never told me that."

"I never wanted to, but—" Felix shrugged, helpless. "Seems like today's the day. Honey, he lied. He wasn't in love with you. He told me. He was kind of worried about me being mad, but

I couldn't blame him much." His voice was warm and mes- merizing. "I mean, think about it; you know this, Jottie. Vause had been around, and you were just a small-town girl. That's why he had to have that money. He had to get out of here be- fore he got stuck with you—"

47

I stood up suddenly, like a rope had yanked me.

Father was speaking. "You made it worse when you started talking about getting married—"

And then I heard Jottie's voice. I couldn't see her, not from where I was, but her voice was awful. "No! It wasn't me. Vause said it first!"

I was so scared. I was so scared to hear her like that. Oh, Jottie—I put my hand over my mouth to keep from crying out. Father was talking and my heart was pounding in my ears, telling me to get to her, pounding so loud I couldn't hear all the words he said, but I heard some. I heard him say, "He had a couple other girls he was going with."

No, he hadn't. Vause Hamilton had carried Jottie's picture next to his heart, and Father knew it. He was lying; I could hear it the way you hear a tune and you know what the next note is; you know how it goes. I wondered how many times I'd heard him lie, to know so well what it sounded like.

Jottie whispered, "No." I dug my fingernails into my arm to take some of her hurt away. Father was breaking Jottie, and if she broke, I would split into pieces, too.

"He wasn't in love with you," Father went on, low and crooning. "He told me. He was kind of worried about me being mad, but I couldn't blame him much. I mean, think about it; you know this, Jottie. Vause had been around, and you were just a small-town girl. That's why he had to have that money. He had to get out of here before he got stuck with you. Let's face it, honey, you were never Vause's type—"

Jottie cried then, like she'd been hit, and I couldn't bear it. I suppose I made a choice between the two of them in that moment. I think I knew even then that I was making a choice, but in a way I was choosing myself, because if I had waited one more second, I would have stopped being who I was.

I banged open the door and flew into the kitchen. I'd been in the dark so long I was mostly blind, but I got to Jottie all right, and I was babbling as my arms slid around her, "He loved you, Jottie. He loved you, don't you cry, Jottie, don't, 'cause he loved you, I know he did. I found his coat, it's down in Mr. Russell's basement, in one of Father's cases, and he carried your picture right there next to his heart"—I squeezed her as hard as I could to make her hear me—"and it's a beautiful picture of you, too, and he carried it because he loved you and he wanted you right there, next to him. I wanted it so bad, but I knew not to take it out of the coat, 'cause I could see it was precious. He loved you and so do I, I love you, too, don't feel bad, Jottie. Father's lying, I can tell." Her arms came around me, but she was still shaking, and I said desperately, "Listen, Jottie, he loved you. I know he did, and Father knows it, too."

She held on to me tight. Then, in the distance, I heard Mr. McKubin say, "It's *where*?"

"Mr. Russell's basement," I said, wanting Jottie to stop shaking.

Some time passed, and then Mr. McKubin said, "*Vause's* coat is in Mr. Russell's basement? Tare Russell's?"

I lifted my head so he could hear me and stop asking questions. "Yes."

"And you said it was inside something?" he pushed.

"Willa." It was Father. I turned around and saw he wasn't looking at me. He was looking at Mr. McKubin, with a big smile on his face. "She doesn't know what she's talking about. She found something. Could be anybody's. Willa's got an imagination." He shook his head and chuckled.

He was trying to make me look like a baby, a fool. He was casting me aside, without even thinking twice about it. After everything I'd done, after I'd tried to save him from Miss Beck, after I'd kept his secrets all summer, after what I'd been through the night before. I came near to hating him then. "It's not anybody's," I snapped. "It's Vause Hamilton's coat, because inside another pocket there's a note from you. It says, 'V, Talked him down to two hundred dollars, but it'll need a new tire, so two-fifty. F.' It's your handwriting—you're F, so V is Vause Hamilton."

Emmett whispered, "Oh God."

Inside my arms, Jottie went still. "Wait."

I drew back a little to stroke her cheek. There were tears on it. "He loved you, Jottie," I told her again. I needed her to know it.

"Willa, *where* is this coat?" she asked.

More questions. "It's in a case of Father's," I said. "You know, those black cases he has, F. H. R. It's in one of those, in Tare Russell's basement."

"What the hell were you doing in Tare Russell's basement?" asked Father.

Even though I was mad, even though I almost hated him, I didn't betray him. I didn't say a word about bootlegging. "I was just there. Playing."

"What? You go creeping around in Tare's house without him knowing? That's trespassing!" he said, sharp.

"Chip off the old block," said Mr. McKubin.

"Shut up," said Father. He moved near me and put his hand on my shoulder. "Willa, we'll deal with you later. You get on upstairs and we'll—"

"No." It was Jottie. Her eyes were fixed on mine. "Tell me what else was in the case. With Vau—the coat." She stuttered like she didn't dare say his name.

I didn't mean to tell, but Jottie's eyes were in mine, and I couldn't look away and I couldn't lie. "Money," I said.

"How much?" she asked.

"Not much," I said. She put her hand on my cheek. "A lot."

"What else?" she prodded.

I shook my head. "Nothing. Just the envelopes."

Her hand against my cheek. "Envelopes?"

"Those big brown envelopes from the mill. You know. They say American Everlasting across the top, but these ones are old, because it says September Something, 1920, down below. The money's inside them."

"September 1920?" Mr. McKubin said, like he didn't believe it.

"Yeah." I tried to see the date in my mind, but I couldn't. I didn't know why it mattered, anyway. I turned back to Jottie. "But the picture," I explained, "it was right next to his heart, a picture of you."

Then Mr. McKubin said, "We've got you now, you bastard."

I spun around, and when I saw Father's face, I almost stopped breathing.

✳

The silence stretched out. Only the clock in the hall seemed to be living.

"Vause was running out on me, that's what you said."

Felix hesitated, then nodded.

"But he wasn't."

He shook his head.

"He wasn't," she insisted.

He shook his head.

"You lied."

He closed his eyes and nodded.

"Did he"—Jottie took a breath—"did he love me?"

He nodded.

She bowed her head.

"Well, well, look who was right all along!" Sol said, bringing his hands together. "What are we going to do?" He glanced around the kitchen. "We have to do something."

"Shut up, Sol," said Emmett.

"But we—"

As though she hadn't heard him, Jottie continued, "You were after the money—because we still needed two hundred dollars for the car. So you decided to steal it from Daddy, and then you decided to take it all, not just the two hundred but everything, because two hundred wasn't enough to hurt him." Her voice slowed as it came to her. "And then you decided to set the mill on fire because you hated it so, and you wanted to see it burn. And Vause, you made Vause come along—" She broke off, eyes widening. "He didn't know anything about it, did he?"

Felix looked at the floor. "He knew about the two hundred," he said hoarsely. "I said it was an advance on my paycheck."

She waited a moment. "This is the truth?"

"Yes."

"He didn't even know," she murmured to herself. "Give me a kiss for luck, but he didn't even know—oh God." She put her hand over her eyes.

Felix took an uncertain step toward her.

She drew her hand away from her face. "The things he said to me? Felix?"

An almost imperceptible nod.

"Felix?"

"He meant them."

She stood before him in silence, her eyes digging deeper and deeper into his, reaching far down into the past. Finally she said, "This time, you pay."

"Jottie—" he began.

She cut him off, implacable. "No. No. There's no way out of this. You were willing to do *that* to Vause? To me? All these years? You let me live like this, thinking Vause had thrown me away? It almost killed me, Felix." He flinched as she went toward him. "It almost *killed* me." She wrapped her fingers into the cloth of his shirt and scanned his face. "Didn't you care?"

He drew in a shallow breath. " 'Course I did, Jottie, but I had to—"

"No!" She pounded against him with her fistful of shirt. "No! You could have told the truth!" Harder and harder, she hit him, again and again and again.

"Jottie." His hands came around hers gently, and she stopped hitting him and dropped her head against his shoulder. "Jottie," he murmured. When she said nothing, he went on, speaking quietly, "This is bad. It's real bad, but it's not like when he died. That was the worst thing, and we made it through together. We can do this, too, I know we can, if we stick together. Huh?" She shook her head. "No? Okay, but listen." He bent his head close to hers. "I know it's bad. But you remember how it was, don't you? We only had each other. No one else understood. No one else even cared. And this is the same. You know it is. Everything that ever happened, we went through it together, didn't we?" He pressed her hands. "Didn't we?"

She said nothing.

"We can't stop now," he concluded. "We've got to stick together."

She drew away from him, her face empty. "No."

"Okay." He nodded, licking his lips. "Okay. I know you're mad, and I don't blame you, not for a minute, but you don't want to rush off and marry Sol. You don't want to do a crazy thing like that." He bent to look in her face and continued, "Sol's not what you want." He shook his head. "You think you want everything nice and pretty and normal, but you don't. All that's gone and done, and it's not worth having. It's not worth a nickel, Jottie."

"Not worth a nickel," she repeated.

"Haven't I always said so?" Felix prodded. "Isn't that what I always said?"

"Yes, you always said that, and I always thought you were wrong"—Jottie spoke sharp and clear—"but how could I be sure? I'd been so mistaken about Vause that I didn't trust myself. How can I know anything, I'd think, because I thought I knew Vause. You *swore* that you weren't there; you swore it on the Bible, remember?"

"I know—"

"And now you're trying to tell me I'd be better off without Sol? Better off with *you*? You *liar*," she spat, her face stiff with loathing.

"If you're thinking that you're going to get back at me by marrying Sol—"

"It has nothing to do with you," she snapped. "I know you can hardly imagine such a thing, but I wasn't even thinking about you when I said yes. I said yes because I wanted to!"

Sol made a vindicated sound they both ignored.

Felix glared at her. "Well, that's fine. Fine. Sauce for the goose, sauce for the gander." He slid toward Layla. "My betrothed," he said, laying his hand on her shoulder. Willa gave a muffled cry, but he didn't respond. His eyes were fixed on Jottie. "You like that?"

"No," Layla said, jerking her shoulder away. "No."

They had nearly forgotten her. All five of them turned to look at her flushed face.

"No?" said Felix quizzically.

"No." She took a jagged breath. "You—you—lied. About that poor boy. He was your best friend, and your sister loved him, and you let her think—you let her suffer so that you didn't have to." She put her hand to her cheek as if it hurt. "I can't believe—Jottie, I'm so sorry about—what happened. And you, too, Mr. McKubin; I'm sorry for the things I said before. I didn't know." She gazed at Felix. "All this time, people hinted about you and I thought they were lying. I never questioned— because I was in love with you—" Her eyes widened. "Oh God. You never cared about me at all, did you?"

"Sure I did. I'm crazy about you," said Felix.

"Don't." Jottie winced. "Don't do that, Felix."

He looked at her impassively. "Up to you, Jottie."

"You can't—" she began.

But Layla interrupted. "Jottie? Up to Jottie? It's not up to Jottie. You think that I'm such a—a—a *weakling* that I'd take you even if you're a liar and a thief? Even if you broke Jottie's heart? Even if I know you don't care about me? No, Felix."

He smiled at her mockingly. "Pretty easy to change your mind last time."

She flinched.

"Didn't even take five minutes."

"No," Layla said, backing away. "Don't."

"And it was fun," he went on. "Especially the last part. Re- member? When you—"

"Stop it!" she cried.

"Where do you think you're going?" Felix snapped as Em- mett took a step toward Layla. "Don't you touch her." Emmett froze.

"Stop it, Felix," Jottie said. She drew herself up. "I've had enough. You have to go."

"No," he said obstinately.

She stood stiff and straight. "Yes. It's over. I'm done with you."

"You can't," he said.

"I can. I am," she replied. "Out."

With a wail, Willa buried her face in her aunt's neck. Jottie cradled her head close.

Felix eyed the pair of them. "The girls. They're mine."

"No. Don't even try it. You know what I'd do." She glared at him. "They stay with me."

For a moment Felix stood, searching her for something he knew. She shook her head. "No, Felix. Not this time."

"Not this time," he repeated. Still, he didn't move but stood, rocking slightly on his heels, his face tilted upward as though he were waiting for something. He shook his head as if to clear it, and then he nodded. "Okay," he muttered. "Hang on. Okay." He took a breath and stepped forward to touch Willa's shoulder with a single finger. She didn't move. "Okay."

Without a glance at the others, he went out the door.

48

I heard him go. I felt him touch me and then I heard his footsteps, and I thought, He's making noise so I'll know he's leaving. He's saying good-bye. But I kept my head down. I'd been turned to stone. I couldn't look at him, I couldn't speak, I couldn't do anything. Finally, when I knew he was gone, I lifted my head from Jottie's neck. The minute I did, I began to pant, and then there were some minutes I don't remember very well, because the kitchen was tipping and spinning, lighter and darker and back and forth. My heart was racing. I have to go to him, I thought, I have to *run*. But when I moved it was only to put my hand out to steady myself against the table. I held on, trying to catch my breath. I ought to be in a hospital, I thought.

"Willa?" It was Jottie. She put her arm around me, worried. "Willa? Sweetheart?"

I blinked. Her face was rolling up and down, too.

"She should sit down," said Miss Beck, and she touched my arm. It was like a burn on my skin. I stumbled forward and scrambled, half running and half falling, across the room and out the back porch. I flung myself down the porch stairs and into the backyard, and then I raced to the gate, the one that led to the alley, and threw it open—and there was his car at the end of the alley, just turning out onto Walnut Street. I ran—my Lord, I'd never run that fast in my life—but the alley was so long, it was miles long, and by the time I got to the end of it, he was gone. I didn't even see his car in the distance. I didn't think to yell. I wonder if he would have come for me if I'd yelled.

Emmett picked me up off the ground. Just like it was nothing, he plucked me up and carried me back to the house in his arms. He didn't scold me, not a bit. In fact, he didn't say anything, which was a big relief. "Better take her up to my bed," Jottie's voice said, so he carried me up the stairs and laid me gently on Jottie's bed, like I was sick. Which maybe I was. I felt his big hand brush over my hair, and I started to cry. I thought I'd cried myself out the night before, but I hadn't.

"Sweetheart." It was Jottie's voice again. "Sweetheart, everything will be all right."

I wanted to tell her how I'd failed—how I'd meant to protect Father from Miss Beck, how hard it had been to watch them and keep quiet, how I'd tried to be devoted and ferocious and instead I'd destroyed everything, ruined everything, lost everything. But I couldn't. All I could do was cry.

✳

Jottie held Willa until there weren't any more tears left in her and she dropped off to sleep. Even after that, Jottie kept watch over her, noting the tracks of her tears, tallying the damage, laying it to Felix's account, and allowing the beautiful scourge of fury to clean her heart of him.

When, at last, she came downstairs, she found Sol waiting for her in the front room. He whirled around as she entered, his face glowing. "Sweetheart. Jottie. My God!" he said, moving toward her.

She lifted her chin proudly. "Starting now, I decide for myself what's right and wrong. Starting this minute."

"All right." He nodded. "That'll be fine." He slid his arms around her.

"Everything Felix stole from me, I want back," she said, pulling his arms tighter around her. "Everything." An entire life was owed to her. She pressed herself more closely against him.

"Jesus," he murmured after a moment. "Let's get married. Now." He drew back and grinned at her. "You're going to marry me!"

"That's what I'm going to do," she said, remembering her

agony for Felix the night before. "That's exactly what I'm going to do."

"Good," he said. His eyes circled the room. "Let's live here. It's bigger." He leaned in to kiss her.

"But," continued Jottie, not kissing him, "if you ever lie to me, I will end it. I will toss you out so fast your head will spin. And I will never let you back." She raised her eyes to his. "You hear me?"

"Yes, ma'am," said Sol. He butted her forehead gently with his. "I wouldn't lie to you. I wouldn't dare."

She nodded imperiously, acknowledging the promise.

Emmett's footsteps sounded on the porch. "I found 'em," he announced, coming into the front room. "They'll be along soon. Minnie's going to stop at her house first."

"Thanks, honey. How's Bird?"

"Cantankerous. You want some ice-tea?"

"Oh God, *yes*." She was so thirsty. Sol nodded, agreeing with her thirst. His agreement rankled. Agreement was the vanguard of pacification, and she would not—ever—be pacified again. She dropped into her pink chair, closed her eyes on him, and didn't open them until she heard Emmett return.

"Stick-tea," Emmett commented, setting down the pitcher and glasses.

She smiled, reaching for a glass. "I thought Felix was the bootlegger in this family."

Emmett lifted one eyebrow. "I got untapped depths."

For the first time in what felt like days, she laughed. "Thank God someone does. Emmett, honey, can you spend the night tonight? I think it would make Willa feel better, and I know it'll make me feel better."

"Be glad to."

"You want me to stay, too?" Sol asked hopefully.

She turned to appraise him and his hope. It was, she saw, a desire to be helpful, to come to her aid in her time of need, to perform the duties of a fiancé worthily. So, she said to herself, this is what safety looks like when it's in my front room. Ornamental. She smiled. "It's real nice of you, Sol, but I have enough to explain to Minerva and Bird without trying to explain you, too." She patted his hand. "And there's Willa," she added. "I'll need to be keeping an eye on her."

He nodded solemnly. "Okay. But we've got a lot to talk over, the three of us."

"No, we don't," she said.

"No, we don't," said Emmett at the same moment.

"Now, just hold on," Sol said, spreading his hands. "I know how you feel. Of course, he's your brother, and I don't say it's a case of bringing *charges*. But I'd like to find out what Tare Russell was up to—"

"Leave Tare alone," said Jottie, picturing his sad, freckled face. She hoped Felix had been honorable enough to repay him—in kindness, at least—for his lie.

"And then there's the money," Sol went on, as though she hadn't spoken. "You reckon he's been spending it all this time? She said there was a lot." He nodded thoughtfully. "I guess we got to get into that basement."

"No," said Emmett and Jottie together.

He looked up, startled. "But that's how we'll know!" His eyes moved between them. "You want him to get off scot-free?" he asked indignantly. "Think about Vause!"

Think about Vause? He was telling *her* to think about Vause? She stared in amazement at Sol's face, reading the story she found there. It wasn't a story about Vause; it was about Sol. It was about how he had been right all along. All these years, he had been fighting to win this particular piece of property from Felix. For eighteen years, Felix's version of the tale, unpopular though it was, had been the official one, the agreed-upon reality, and Sol's version had been wrong. It had been the hole in Sol's life, and it was now filled: He was now the rightful owner of the truth about Vause's death. And that's what he cares about, she thought, seeing his comfortable posture, his relaxed hands. Not about Vause himself. My poor darling, she mourned, my poor boy, they let you go. Their truth is nothing compared to yours, and I would let either story be true if it would make you live again. She turned to Sol, but there were no words to explain how terrible it seemed to her, that he and Felix should have lived so long on Vause's death. "You need to drop this, Sol. If you want to marry me, you've got to drop it.

I won't put Willa through it, nor Tare. I won't have it. You'll need to let it go."

Sol's forehead furrowed as he tried to comprehend her. "But that's—" He caught sight of her face. "Well, okay—if you're sure. I mean, do you think Tare knows the case is there? Don't you want to go see if—"

Emmett laughed softly. "If you think that case is still down in Tare's basement, you're crazy. He's had"—a watch-checking pause—"over two hours. It's long gone."

"Ah, *shit,*" said Sol.

When Sol finally, reluctantly, took his leave, Emmett saw him out. Returning to the front room, he found his sister standing still in a shaft of golden sunlight, brilliant golden motes spiraling about her. He watched her, seeing something years-ago gone restored to her face. Was it freedom? Authority? Love? No, he decided, it was her self.

She glanced up, suddenly aware of him. "Emmett," she said, stretching out her hand.

"There you are." He took her hand in his, and, reunited, they smiled at each other.

It was lucky there were so many bedrooms, she thought. That was a good thing. One for Emmett. Henry—who, Jottie admitted, had been genuinely worried about Willa—and Minerva in the room she usually shared with Mae. Mae off in Willa's bed. Layla in her room, of course. No one in Felix's. Bird had taken one look at Willa and refused to leave her side, and now the two of them were in Jottie's bed, packed tight together despite the heat. Jottie could just see Bird's silvery curls glistening beyond the dark breadth of Willa.

She was longing for a cigarette. Longing. But she wouldn't move. No, she wouldn't. Willa had purposefully wrapped her fingers in a handcuff around Jottie's wrist, and though her grip had loosened in sleep, Jottie would not free herself from it. When Willa awoke, she would find Jottie exactly where she'd left her. But between that moment and this, Jottie had time. Hours. She stared into the darkness and, diver on the precipice, looked down at the glittering blue. Now. Now she could. Carefully, schooled in starvation, she allowed herself to conjure

Vause. First, the whole of him, from a distance, then, closer, his shining eyes, his golden hair, and now his beautiful hands against her face. She dove, and the water closed cool around her. Oh, the luxury of it, the greedy joy of assembling him rather than banishing him, oh—and she was lost in it: He smiled with one side of his mouth first and he tucked his head like so when he ran and his legs were too long for his bicycle and there was that accordion he carried around for weeks and he was scared of babies and he wore that purple tie and he bit into oranges to peel them and one day in February he buttoned me into his coat—

"See how handy it is, me almost dying of the flu?" he was saying. "You wouldn't have fit before."

She burrowed, shivering, against him, breathing deeply of him.

"What're you doing in there?" he asked, his arms coming around the woolen lump that was her.

"I'm smelling you," she replied, muffled.

There was a pause. "Is it bad?" he asked.

"No. No, it's nice." She dug her chin into his chest.

"Hey." His arms tightened. "Stop that. Aren't your feet cold?"

"No. Yes. But I don't care. I like it in here." She stepped onto his shoes.

"Ow."

"I'm going to stay in here forever." Twin-tight against him, she listened to his heart, his stomach, his bones. Boldly, she untucked his shirt and slipped her freezing hands up along his skin.

"Jesus." He stiffened and then slowly relaxed as her hands warmed. She stroked his back, her fingers roving his ribs, smoothing his shoulders, traveling the rippled ribbon of his spine. "Mmm," he sighed. "I think your daddy would shoot me if he knew what you were doing right now."

"I'm not doing anything wrong," she whispered. She didn't tell that what she was doing was pretending she was him.

Jottie marveled at this lost treasure, this wonder now restored to her. Hers again. Hers forever, never to be taken from her. Faster and faster, she pulled him to her, all of him hers again.

It was a while before she noticed she was hearing something, and even when she did, she thought it was a cat. She returned to Vause. But there it was again. Must be a big cat. Then she changed her mind. A possum? Two? Fighting? Dying? Maybe it was a dog. She had once heard a dog without a voice box try to bark, and this sounded the same, only louder. A dying dog? How long did it take a dog to die? This went on and on. Could it be a horse? Maybe someone had shot a horse and it had run away to her yard to die. That'll be a diversion, she thought. A dead horse in the front yard.

On and on it went. The girls slept like they'd been enchanted. Finally Jottie couldn't stand it any longer. Quietly, she rose from the bed and opened her door, then quickly pulled it to when she realized that the noise was louder in the hall. Emmett stood motionless beside his door.

"Is it a horse?" she whispered.

Minerva appeared, a white shape. "What in God's name is that?" she whispered.

Henry peered around her. "Everyone all right?" he murmured.

"It's Layla," said Emmett quietly.

They all turned to look at Layla's door, tight shut and dark. Henry ran his hand over his face.

"That poor child," breathed Minerva. She looked at Jottie.

Jottie watched the dark door for a moment. Then she shook her head. "I can't. Not tonight." She glanced back at her own room, where Willa lay.

Minerva nodded and withdrew, Henry beside her.

Jottie looked at Emmett. "Tomorrow, I'll start again. I'll take care of her, I promise."

He nodded, and she opened her door and slipped inside. She knew he was still standing in the hall.

49

August 15, 1938

Dear Mother,

I can't come to your party for Lance. The deadline for my book is less than two weeks away, and I need to work every moment between now and then.

Kiss them both for me.

Love,
Layla

August 17

Layla,

Your mother's on the warpath, but I'm proud of you. Keep at it. There will be other parties.

Father

P.S. Check enclosed.

In 1898, Charles Canson Huddleston, plant manager of Columbia Woolens of Dunellen, New Jersey, sought a location for a new hosiery mill. Traveling west by train, he considered the relative merits of Hagerstown, Moorefield, and Cumberland before settling on Macedonia, which, as he wrote to the president of the company, im-

pressed him by its "modesty, sobriety, and freedom from the taint of the union." Huddleston's enthusiasm for Macedonia was soon

Layla looked up.

"Tested," said Jottie.

"Tested," wrote Layla, and looked up again.

"Oh, honey, give it here." Jottie took the pen from Layla's hand and began to write. For a time, the only sound was pen on paper.

Layla looked out the window.

Frowning, Jottie read what she'd written. "What's another word for garter?"

"I don't know," said Layla. She glanced at her father's letter. "The only time in his life he's ever been proud of me, and it's a lie."

"It's not a lie," said Jottie. "You're working."

"No. You're working."

Jottie put her hand on Layla's. "You already wrote most of it. I'm just filling in here and there."

Layla nodded. "Still. I'm lying. I'm pretending to be a writer."

"Oh, honey. I bet every writer thinks he's pretending, even Ernest Q. Hemingway."

"Ben and Father were right. I'm an idiot."

Jottie put down her pen. "You're not an idiot. It wasn't your fault. Felix was after you from the minute he saw you, and if there's ever been a woman who could resist that, I haven't met her. You have plenty of company, if it makes you feel any better."

There was a silence. Then Layla burst out, "Was he *trying* to make a fool of me?"

"No. No, honey. He just has no—no pity, I guess it is. He never has. I tried to warn you, but, well." Jottie folded her mouth tight. "I wish I could have stopped him."

"He didn't care about me, not for a second," said Layla bitterly. "He doesn't care about anyone."

Jottie sighed. "He does, though. He cares about the girls. He cared about Vause. He even cared about me. Just not as much as he cared about himself."

"Oh, Jottie, I'm sorry!" Layla squeezed Jottie's hand. "I don't mean to be so self-centered. It's only—I feel like I don't know anything about anyone."

Jottie nodded. "Felix has a real talent for making people feel that way."

Layla put her head in her hands. "I should be locked up for my own safety."

"That'd be a shame," said Jottie. "A real waste." She looked at the paper in front of her. "You think it's all right if I mention Daddy?"

Layla sighed. "He was the president of the company. You have to mention him."

"It feels like showing off, but I guess you're right." Jottie rubbed her nose and bent over the paper once more. "Twenty-eight years, he was there," she murmured. Layla stared out the window.

When Emmett came in, half an hour later, Jottie looked up with an absorbed frown. "Do you remember when they started making women's hose?"

"What?" His eyes darted to Layla and back again.

"American Everlasting. When did they start making women's hosiery?"

"1917."

"You're making that up."

He smiled.

"1917," she repeated, writing it down.

"Where're the girls?" he asked. "I brought a book for Willa."

She raised her eyebrows. "Don't expect her to thank you."

"I don't. I just brought it."

"She'll talk when she's ready."

"I know," Emmett said mildly. "All right if I take Bird to Statler's?"

Jottie nodded.

"Should I ask Willa if she wants to come?"

"You can try. Don't get upset if she doesn't answer."

"I won't, I told you."

Layla's eyes followed him as he left the room in search of his nieces. "What about *him*?" she asked suspiciously.

Jottie looked up. "Who?"

"Emmett. Is he like Felix?"

Jottie smiled. "No."

✳

They thought I stopped talking because of Father. Even Jottie thought that. But it wasn't true. I stopped talking because I was exhausted. Every day, I got a little bit farther behind everyone else, until I felt like I could just barely see them in the distance, their backs turned toward me, small figures I thought I'd known before. It was clear that I'd never catch up to them. I was too tired.

Jottie thought that what Father had done had struck me dumb: how Father had stolen money from the mill and set it on fire and then lied about it, lied even to Jottie, and broken her heart. And that was terrible, his stealing and lying. I knew that. I knew it. But inside my secret self, where I would never talk about it, even if I could, I understood why he'd lied. I understood what it felt like when he saw the flames and realized that Vause Hamilton was going to die because of him, how he must have put his hand over his mouth to keep from crying out and how he didn't know what to do, so he ran. I could understand how his heart had hammered, how sick he had felt, like he was dying himself, because in one moment he had lost everything. And he had lied, I knew, because he couldn't bear for Jottie to hate him, he couldn't bear to lose the one last thing he had. I knew because I had done it, too. I had lost everything, and I had ruined Father's life. I knew that if I had had just a minute more, I would have lied, I would have thought of a way, some way, to make Jottie know how much Vause Hamilton loved her without telling Father's secret. But instead I'd broken it all, and Father hated me, and every time I remembered his face when I told about the envelopes, I had to curl up into a ball, tighter and tighter, to make myself so small I'd disappear.

I tried to console myself by saying that at least I'd saved Jottie, that Jottie was better off because of what I'd done, but I wasn't sure about that. She told me that she was going to marry Mr. McKubin and he was going to come live in our house and everything was going to be grand. She kept saying that, over and over. How we'd have a wonderful new life, wonderful.

How Bird and I would have everything nice. Well, that was fine, I supposed, but I didn't care much about it, so I didn't say anything back, and after a week or so, Jottie stopped talking about our wonderful new life. She went on flying around like she always did, but sometimes I'd catch her standing stock-still, watching at nothing. Maybe she was thinking about her wonderful new life. Or maybe she was missing Vause Hamilton. I didn't know. I didn't ask.

Another thing I'd tell myself was at least Miss Beck didn't have Father any more than we did. But that was a poor scrap. He was gone, and I'd lost him.

I hated Miss Beck then. Oh, how I hated her. I knew it was my own fault he was gone, but I had to share out some hate. I already had too much for myself. I suppose I could have blamed Jottie, for she'd sent Father away. But I could never hate Jottie, I could only love her. So I settled on Miss Beck and hated her. I hated her so much I thought I might burst into flames, which sometimes happens, I've read about it. I sat at the dinner table with my eyes on my plate so I wouldn't look at her and die of my hatred. It was too much to expect that I would eat, too, but Jottie didn't know that, and she got more and more worried about me, piling my plate with spinach and beets and other awful things.

I couldn't explain. I was too tired.

The night Father left, I had a dream. It became a dream I had nearly every night, and that was why I was tired. I stayed awake, trying not to have it, and then I woke up after it with my heart pounding and couldn't go back to sleep. In my dream, Father came home. I could hear the soft thump of his hat falling onto the hook, even though I was up in my room. "I'm home!" he called, just the way he always did. And, along with knowing he'd come back, I knew he wouldn't stay very long. So I had to rush, rush downstairs to see him before he left again. I could hear Bird and Jottie, Minerva and Mae and Emmett, all coming out to greet him, surprised and happy. But then, in my dream, just as I was running out of my room, I looked down and saw that my dress was dirty or torn—something was wrong, and I didn't want Father to see me like that, so I had to change. My fingers fumbled at my bureau and slipped off the drawer handles, my clothes dropped off their hangers to the floor, and I scrabbled around to pick them up. "I'm coming!" I called. "Wait for me!" Sometimes I'd find a dress that looked all right and slip it on, only to catch a glimpse of myself in the mirror and find that it had turned to rags, that my hair was tangled, that there was lipstick on my mouth, that my face was dirty. And all the while I could hear him downstairs—usually, he was laughing. Every time, it was the same. When at last I got my clothes on, yanked the door open, and raced downstairs, I'd find everyone in the front room, everyone except Father. "Oh," they'd say, "Felix? He just left."

50

August 23, 1938

Mrs. Judson Chambers
Deputy Director, Federal Writers' Project
1013 Quarrier St.
Charleston, West Virginia
Dear Mrs. Chambers,

Enclosed please find the complete Editorial Copy of *The History of Macedonia.* I have submitted the same to the sponsor, the Town Council of Macedonia, for their approval.

Yours sincerely,
Layla Beck

"How about I take it to the post office for you?" said Jottie, eyeing Layla's crumpled dress. "I could use the walk."

A moment passed before Layla looked up. "Oh. Yes. Thanks. Thanks." She handed the manuscript in its envelope to Jottie and subsided back into her chair.

Jottie glanced through the back-porch screen to see Willa drifting across the yard toward the red oak tree. Jottie watched, frowning, as Willa placed one palm against the trunk of the tree and rested there, motionless. It's like living with a ghost, she thought. Two ghosts, she amended, looking back to Layla.

It was a relief to leave her haunted house behind, and, despite the soupy heat of the afternoon, Jottie dawdled along Academy Street, interesting herself in Grandma Pucks's hydrangeas, the dead-empty windows of the Casey house, and

Seneca the dog, currently sporting an abscess on his ear. "You shouldn't fight with cats, you dumb old thing," Jottie said to him. She passed over Academy Creek Bridge, leaning over the stone parapet to note the spot she and Vause and Felix had favored for digging worms to fish with.

Three ghosts, really.

For now Vause was hers again, and each night after she kissed Sol and waited to hear his shoes slap, slap away on the sidewalk, she flew upstairs to her bed so she could raise Vause from the dead and remember, unfettered, everything, every tiny thing, every beautiful thing.

It's adultery.

No, it's not, she argued. That's only if you're married. And I'm not, yet. Plus, he's dead. It can't be adultery if he's dead and I'm not married. I'll stop when I'm married.

It's deceitful. It's dishonest.

Yes.

Sol's an honest man, a good and honest man. He loves you. He's given you a new life. Everything you wanted. He deserves your love and loyalty. You should be ashamed of yourself.

Yes. I am.

Conscience-dogged, Jottie hurried down Council Street and then rushed up Prince to the post office. Feeling boiled, she plunged headlong through the massive doors and collided powerfully with a hard pink bosom.

"Well! Heavens! What on earth—" exclaimed Mrs. John Lansbrough.

"Oh my! Are you all right?" exclaimed Jottie at the same moment.

"Oh!" said Mrs. John, recovering herself quickly. "Jottie Romeyn! Goodness!" She put her gloved hand on her chest and trilled with laughter. "Aren't we a pair? John's always telling me, Watch where you're going, honey, and I guess he's right!" She gave Jottie a sparkling smile. "You all in one piece?"

Astonished, Jottie groped after her manners. "Why, I'm just fine, Mrs. John. It was only a bump. You?"

"Oh yes!" sang Mrs. John. She paused, turning her head

slightly to give Jottie a roguish look. "I heard a little something about you," she whispered.

Jottie goggled at her. "Oh, yes?" she said finally.

Mrs. John smiled. "Well, *I* wish you the very best. Both John and I do. We're old friends of Sol's." She gave Jottie a friendly tap on the arm. "We'll have to have you up to the house for a little dinner party, after the happy event. You know, to celebrate."

"Why"—Jottie swallowed air—"that'd be real nice. Such a nice thought!"

"We'd just be thrilled." Mrs. John wrinkled her nose, indicating thrilled-ness. Jottie felt her lips catching on her teeth as she smiled in response. Mrs. John leaned forward confidentially. "You heard what that Auralee Bowers wants for the next meeting?"

"Next meeting?" asked Jottie.

"Of the Daughters," explained Mrs. John. Then, seeing Jottie's blank expression, "Daughters of *Macedon*."

"Oh!" Belatedly, "What?"

"She wants to talk about that Mr. Gandhi." Mrs. John gave a little rippling shudder. "Which is all right with me, I said, as long as I don't have to look at him." She chortled. "He wears just about nothing at all!"

Utterly at a loss, Jottie found herself chortling back, and a wave of self-loathing washed over her.

"Well," Mrs. John's voice dropped to a piercing whisper, "don't you forget—John and I want to be the very first to invite Mr. and Mrs. McKubin to dinner!" Twinkling, she nudged Jottie and swept away.

"I'll look forward to it!" sang Jottie, hating herself more and more. I'll see you in hell first, Wanzellen Bucklew, she said to herself as, with numerous waves, she moved toward the counter. But even dire imprecations failed to comfort her. She had truckled to a known foe. She was a hypocrite and a liar. But the most loathsome thing of all was that she had attained her goal. She had been accepted. She was an eminent gentlewoman of Macedonia. Prestige had been granted, instantly, automatically, by virtue of her engagement to Sol. And it stung. Why? Because she hadn't earned it herself. Because she was being rewarded for seeing the error of her ways, for changing horses and choosing a winner, for shucking off her misguided loyalty to Felix. As though what she had been before was shameful.

Well, she said to herself, aren't you a one? You *were* ashamed. You *wanted* Sol's prestige. You were desperate for Sol's prestige. And now you have it, you're ashamed of yourself for wanting it? That makes no sense atall.

But she was lying to herself, she knew. It made sense. Because it made her no better than Wanzie Bucklew, who had cleaned herself of her dirty past when she married John Lansbrough, cleaned herself so thoroughly that she kept her mother locked away so nobody could see what she had come from and by doing so made herself far, far dirtier than her childhood had ever made her.

Sol's an honest man, she recited, a good and honest man. He loves you. He's given you a new life. Everything you wanted. He deserves your love and loyalty.

"Miss Romeyn?" said Harlan Kasebier, the clerk, beckoning her toward his postal altar. She had known him since he was three and had dimpled knees. "Well," he said, his official face breaking into a smile, "I heard something real nice about you."

Jottie trailed out of the post office. Dispirited by her own failings and blinded by the glare of the sun on the macadam, she didn't notice the Lloyd boys sitting on the stairs until she nearly fell over them.

"Miss Romeyn!" squawked Jun. "Y'all right?" He leapt to his feet and held out his hand to steady her. "I'm sure sorry! Gee!"

Jottie smiled into his sweaty, sorry face. "It's all right, Jun. I'm fine. I seem to be banging into everyone I meet today." Her eyes moved over the three brothers. They were arrayed in their Boy Scout finery, and she could see that their shirts were turning their necks blue.

"Jun," said Dex meaningfully. He looked hard at Jottie.

Jun swung around and tried again. "You *sure* you're all right?" he asked. "I ask because we can help if you're not. All right, I mean."

Jottie's heart lifted. To the Lloyd boys, at least, she had intrinsic value. Obligingly, she slumped. "Well, I do feel kind of dizzy, Jun. It's awful close, you know?" He nodded vigorously. "I'd feel a lot better if you boys would help me across the street." She tried to look pitiful.

"I'll do it!" yelped Frank, leaping to his feet.

"You get out!" cried Dex. "It was me she tripped over."

"Oh," said Jottie hastily. "I'd feel better if it was all of you." She swayed.

Jun grinned at her. "Thanks," he said in an undertone, as he stiffened into a military posture. "Get on over to her side, Dex! Whatsamatter with you?" he barked. "Frank, get her elbow!"

With Dex and Frank supporting an arm apiece, and Jun grandly striding ahead to stop traffic, Jottie tottered into the crosswalk.

A car slammed against the curb, and Sol slung himself out into the street with his face askew. "Jottie!" he called, rushing to her side. "What happened?"

Jottie saw the Lloyds exchange glances, expecting betrayal. She was glad to have the opportunity to redeem herself. "Oh, Sol, I was feeling real flimsy from the heat, and these nice boys said they'd help me across the street. Aren't they good boys?"

"Yeah." Sol nodded cursorily at Frank. "Thanks, fellas. I'll take her from here." Without even knowing he did so, he nudged Dex out of the way and slid his hand under Jottie's arm. "Come on, let's get you in the car, honey, and I'll take you right home."

Jottie cast a helpless look at Jun. "Thanks!" she called to him. He nodded bitterly.

"Don'tcha want a glass of water, even?" yelled Dex.

Sol glanced at him and then turned away without answering as he opened the car door for her. "There you go," he said, as she settled herself on the seat.

She turned to wave at the Lloyds. "Thanks, boys!" It was the best she could do. "Sorry!" she called.

Sol took his place behind the steering wheel and turned to inspect her soberly. "You feel dizzy? You look a little pale."

Jottie doubted it. "I'm fine, Sol. It was a—" The impossibility of explaining it overcame her and she fell silent. Even if she could explain it, he wouldn't think it was funny. "It was nothing."

Sol nodded sympathetically. "It's damn hot. Let's get you home where you can put your feet up. I stopped there a few minutes ago to find out where you were." A pause. "I wanted to tell you my news, honey. I wanted you to be the first to know."

She knew then, but she turned to him expectantly. He took her hand. "Shank's out," he said. "And guess who's in?"

"Oh, Sol, that's wonderful," she said, squeezing his hand. "You deserve it, you truly do. You'll be a wonderful president." He would be, she knew.

He let out a long, amazed breath. "Honey," he said in a low voice, "I have everything I ever wanted."

❖

August 29, 1938

Dear Layla,

My God, you've pulled it off! When Gray told me that you were refusing to attend your mother's party *in order to finish your manuscript,* I thought perhaps the Second Coming was at hand—and in Macedonia, West Virginia, of all places! (You didn't miss much, by the way. Both Lance and Alene looked as though they'd prefer the rack. Your mother was in her element.) Then I figured you'd come down with boils or lice or some other rural affliction and didn't dare show your face. I'm sure you'll understand when I tell you my first thoughts were for my own safety; you know your father well enough to know that he'd happily shoot me before he'd allow one hair on your head to be mussed.

But you were actually *working,* by God! Ursula sent me the copy, not to edit, but to crow over. She's delighted, and I can see why. It's informative, interesting, and well written, an excellent example of what we've been trying to pull out of these small sponsored projects. Ursula may not effuse—against her policy, I believe—but in her letter to me, she said, "The manuscript is much better than I would have believed possible from an untried young woman. She is obviously someone we can, and should, use for other projects." In other words, watch out. Ursula's told me of some problems she's been having with the Field Assistant in Martinsburg—Iliff or Liffle or something. It seems he's incapable of producing copy, and she's had to compose his material for the State Guide herself, which is not only against project rules but quite an annoyance to her. However, now she's seen what you can do, she's had the bright idea of hiring you to take over, not on the State Guide, which is nearly done, but for a couple of other projects she has in the hopper. Ursula's a go-getter, and I'd advise you to consider the offer. You've made a real success of this business, Layla, and I extend you my heartiest congratulations, along with a few apologies for ever having doubted you.

Fondly,
Ben

P.S. I wish you could have seen Gray at the party, torn between the desire to brag about your industry and the shame of admitting that you're on relief. He solved the dilemma in his usual way—a couple of bottles of Champagne and he couldn't say anything.

51

"Just let me try it." Mae ran her fingers through Emmett's hair.

"Leave me alone," he grumbled, peering at the frayed electric cord on the lamp beside him.

"But you'd look so handsome. Wouldn't he?" She appealed to Minerva.

"You'd look like Tyrone Power," Minerva said. "Don't you want to look like Tyrone Power?"

"No." He picked up the lamp and looked at the bottom.

Layla drifted through the hallway. "Don't *you* think Emmett would look handsome with his hair combed straight back?" called Mae.

Layla returned to the doorway and stood there, looking slightly dazed.

"You don't have to answer that question," said Emmett, embarrassed.

Layla hesitated. "My mother used to straighten my hair when I was a child," she said softly. "I thought it was a violation of the Fourth Amendment." Her eyes sought Emmett's. "Unreasonable seizure."

Emmett's face lit up. "That's right! You're exactly right!" He turned to his sister. "Hear that, Mae? Touch me with that comb and I'll call the attorney general."

Layla gave him a small smile and disappeared.

Mae's eyes followed her. "I could just kill that Felix," she said after a moment.

Minerva nodded. "Me too."

"What's so wonderful about him, anyway?" demanded Mae. "Nothing."

"Nothing," agreed Minerva. "Nice teeth is all, and that's not much to write home about. Plenty of people have nice teeth."

Simultaneously, they turned to glare at Emmett. "To hell with all of them," said Minerva.

Emmett's eyes widened and fled to his lamp.

*

It was hot everywhere and it was hottest upstairs, but I didn't care. I liked to visit Father's room. Every day, I checked on it, not to see if he was there—I knew better than that—but to make sure no one had touched anything or messed it up. I closed the door behind me and looked around. It looked nice, nice and tidy. There was a stretch of wall between his dresser and his desk, and I liked to sit there. I didn't disturb anything; I just sat on the floor with my back to the wall and thought about nothing. It was my own place. Probably not even Father had ever sat right there. When he left, there'd been a penny on the floor, under his dresser. It had made me feel good, seeing it there—just something he'd dropped and would pick up some-day. But one week when Jottie cleaned, she found it and put it on his desk. I don't know what upset me more, that it wasn't where he'd left it or that his desk was changed.

One afternoon, just the most stifling afternoon you can imagine, I came to his room to sit for a while. I attended to the door, closing it without making a noise, and then I turned. Something was different. I couldn't quite tell what it was, be-cause most things were the same, but after a moment I got it. The window was open more than it had been. One of his pic-tures had been moved. The penny was gone.

Father had been there. I quick went to his closet, to his dresser, to his table drawers, and searched for things missing—had he come for clothes, money, what? There was a pair of shoes gone—his other black ones—but besides that, every-thing was there. I stopped in the middle of the rug, breathing hard, and then I got a wild hope that he was somewhere in the house. I raced out of his room and down the hall, opening doors. I checked our room first and then I went into Miss

Beck's room without knocking, but she wasn't there anyway, and neither was he. I banged into Jottie's room—I didn't need to be sly about that—and saw at once why he'd come. On Jottie's faded pink bedspread, there was a package wrapped in white cloth gone yellow with age. It just sat there, where he'd set it. He had given it to her.

I hadn't smiled in so long, my face nearly cracked into pieces when I did. I clattered down the stairs as fast as I could without falling and slammed into Jottie in the kitchen. "Come upstairs," I croaked. I hadn't said anything at all in a couple days, and Jottie was so excited to hear me speak that she didn't understand what I'd said for a few minutes. But when she did, she came right along.

In her room, I gestured to the yellowed cloth. "It's from Father."

She frowned at me. "What? Felix is here?"

I shook my head. "No. He was. Open it."

She gave me a worried look and lifted the package up to pull away the cloth. Vause Hamilton's coat came sliding out into her hands. She did just what I'd done, down in Tare Russell's basement: She held it up casually, wondering what it was. And then she realized—or, really, recognized—what she was holding. I saw it come over her face, how she knew that it was his, how she'd seen him wearing it, how it was what he'd been wearing the last time she'd ever seen him. She brought the cloth to her face and breathed it in, and then her eyes closed and she smiled, so happy and beautiful. I sat down on the bed and watched her. I hadn't seen her that happy in a while.

After some time passed, she smoothed the coat flat on the bed, brushing it a little with her hand, not because it needed brushing but because she wanted to take care of it. She glanced at me and then reached to the inside pocket. There was the little square photograph of her. She gazed at it for a moment, then shook her head like she couldn't believe it and put the photograph away and went back to brushing the coat with her hand. Then she looked at me again and reached into a side pocket. She found the buffalo nickel and then went to the next pocket and pulled out the scrap of paper with Father's writing on it. She read it and her lips folded into a line. "Too late, Felix."

She caught me watching her and sighed. "Now he's willing to let me see it. Now. But it's too late. You can't just wipe away eighteen years. You understand that, don't you, Willa?" She looked at me and nodded to make me agree.

I shook my head. I'd hoped that the sight of the coat would melt her heart, and I was pretty sure Father had hoped the same thing. I even opened my mouth to say so, but the thought of trying to gather all those words made me so tired I closed it again.

She waited until she was sure I wasn't going to reply. Then she said, real gentle, "Honey, he'll never change. He'll never— tell you the truth about anything or act like other men, and he'll never, ever change."

I frowned at her, trying to understand what she meant. Finally, I cleared my throat and whispered, "I don't want him to change."

She pressed her lips together and shook her head. Like she didn't even know she was doing it, her hand reached out to stroke the coat, and she was gone, imagining poor dead Vause, how he had been inside it and how, probably, she hadn't paid a moment's mind to the coat he wore and yet now that was all there was of him left to her. Gentle and slow, as if she wanted to make it last a long time, she folded the coat along its creases, smoothing it and touching it as she went. When she was done, she tilted her head, looking at it. "Was it like this? In Tare's basement?" she asked me. "Folded so neat?"

I nodded.

"And wrapped in this cloth?"

I nodded again.

"Oh Lord," she sighed. She rubbed one finger down the cloth. "It would've been easier just to go to the penitentiary."

I didn't know what she was talking about. I watched her slip the coat back into its white package. She cleared out the whole bottom drawer of her dresser and put the cloth bundle inside. She gave it a last stroke, and then she closed the drawer and rose. She paused, then went to the window, and my spirits rose because she was looking for Father. But then she made a little noise, a little disgusted noise, and she marched real quick out the door. I heard her heels thumping on the stairs.

That night Jottie seemed almost lighthearted. She and the others played pinochle, the way she liked to play it, with the curtains drawn tight so that the police chief couldn't see that they were gambling if he walked by. I didn't play, of course. I sat on the sofa, not reading my book and wondering where Father was. Two times that night, Jottie went upstairs. She pretended she needed a hankie and then she pretended she couldn't find her pen, but I knew better. She was looking at Vause Hamilton's coat.

✳

"Jottie?"

"Yes?"

There was a short, embarrassed shuffle on the other end. "This is—well, it's Hank Nole."

"Hank!" She straightened, shoring herself up against all the reasons he might be calling. "How are you?"

"Fine, thanks." There was another slight ripple, which Jottie now recognized as the sound of the police chief stroking his walrus mustache. "Ahm, can I talk to Felix?"

"Sorry, Hank, he's not here," she said. And then, firmly, "He doesn't live here anymore."

He sighed. "Yeah, I know. What I really mean is, do you know where he is?"

"No." Oh God, what had he done? "Why?" Not that she cared.

"Well, Jottie, ahm, guess he's been drinking pretty steady past couple weeks, and he got up to disturbing the peace last night."

"Disturbing the peace?" It didn't sound like Felix. He generally took pains to maintain the illusion of peace. "Did you arrest him, Hank? Is that why you're calling me? Because I'm not—"

"No! No, I don't have him. But I'm going to have to arrest him if I find him. So if he, ahm, turns up, let him know that, will you?"

"Hank, if I let him know, you won't even see his dust. Whose side are you on?"

"Jottie," said Hank reproachfully. "Felix has always been real good about keeping his business outside my jurisdiction. I'm returning the favor. I don't want to see his dust."

———◆———

52

Seated at the kitchen table, Layla glanced up from her letter. "Parker Davies tenders you his respects."

Jottie shifted her cigarette from one side of her mouth to the other without touching it. "He tenders them? He actually used 'tender'?"

"Yes."

"Huh," said Jottie. "Ain't he nice?"

"He'd like to come by and discuss the manuscript tomorrow afternoon."

Jottie raised her eyebrows. "Old Parker reads pretty fast, doesn't he?"

Layla nodded.

"He wants to come here?"

Layla looked down at the letter again. "Yes. At three. He doesn't exactly sound thrilled."

Jottie smiled around her cigarette. "Let's make sure Minerva and Mae are here, then."

"All right," said Layla apathetically, setting the paper down.

Parker Davies was dressed for a bank. In his gray suit and hat, he looked like a chip off a bank that had gone for a walk. He stood on the sidewalk in front of the house and eyed the porch mistrustfully.

Layla got up and opened the screen door. "Mr. Davies, please do come in and sit down."

"Miss Beck." He smiled with his mouth closed and came heavily up the stairs. "Seems to get hotter every day, doesn't it—" He broke off as his eyes adjusted to the shade of the porch and he saw Jottie, Minerva, and Mae arrayed before him in light summer dresses.

"Parker," said Jottie, rising to shake his hand.

"Jottie. Mae. Minerva." He inclined his head to each. "An unexpected. Pleasure."

"Likewise," murmured Mae. Jottie nodded seriously. Minerva grinned at him.

He looked away. "Miss Beck. Shall we—proceed?" He tapped a folder that he held under his arm.

"Oh, yes," she said. "Please have a seat."

He glanced at Minerva. "It's a business matter. No need to bother these"—he gestured to the Romeyns—"ladies with our discussion."

"Oh, Parker, I've been looking forward to it all day," said Minerva.

"I just love businesslike discussions," said Mae.

"And, do you know, we've come to feel a real personal interest in *The History of Macedonia*," said Jottie. "Would you like some ice-tea?"

He cleared his throat. "Ice-tea. Thank you. Ice-tea would be very pleasant." He let himself down stiffly into a wicker chair and balanced his folder on his knee. "Miss Beck, I will not beat around the bush—"

Mae held up a finger. "Wait just one moment, Parker, while I get the tea. I couldn't stand it if I missed what you're going to say." She rose. "Back in two shakes!"

Jottie and Minerva looked at each other and clamped their mouths shut. Layla gazed at the porch screen.

After a moment's silence, Jottie asked, "Isn't the part about Mrs. Lacey's backyard good? I never knew they burned amputated limbs. Could have knocked me over with a feather."

"Limbs?" he said, his lips pursing around the word. "I did not care for it, Jottie. I'm surprised you did."

"You're squeamish?" asked Minerva. "Is that why you never became a doctor?" She wrinkled her nose sympathetically. "I remember way back when, you wanted to be a doctor."

"Not that there's anything wrong with being a lawyer," said Mae, reappearing with the tray.

After the tea was handed around, followed by a plate of cookies that Parker Davies did not touch, he turned, with a genteel puff of impatience, to Layla. "As I said, Miss Beck, I will not beat around the bush. There are passages of this manuscript which must be expunged; there are fabrications and outright lies, all of which must be removed. I cannot think"—he looked at her severely—"why you saw fit to invent such ridiculous falsehoods when the true history of Macedonia is a model American tale!"

Layla straightened in her chair. "To which passages do you refer, Mr. Davies?"

"The General!" he exploded. "You—you—presume to—you call him insane! The General was in no way at all—could never be said to be—*insane*! And here, here"—he ruffled pages hurriedly—"you say he maimed his only son! He didn't maim anyone!" He leaned toward her, breathing heavily.

"You mean except Indians?" said Mae.

He glanced at her and then back at Layla. "Where did you get these ridiculous ideas, Miss Beck?"

Layla sat up even straighter. "I stand by my history, Mr. Davies," she said, flushing. "According to my sources, there is ample evidence that the General was unhinged. In fact, it is the most generous interpretation of his behavior, and, as for your objection to the word 'maim,' I don't know what else you'd call it when a man cuts off his own son's toes."

"What?" he rumbled. "What toes?"

"Yes, indeed," said Jottie smoothly. "The General cut off his son's toes. With his sword. To keep him from running off with a girl. Stabbed him right through the boot. He limped for the rest of his life." She took a sip of tea. "Mrs. Lacey told me all about it."

"Mrs. Lacey!" he cried. "What does she know?"

"I expect," said Layla, "that, having lived here for eighty-seven years, she knows even more Macedonian history than you."

Parker Davies clenched his jaw. "I have marked places in this manuscript that require revision," he said. "The material about the General—nonsense! Reverend Goodacre! Reverend Goodacre established the first Baptist church in Macedonia! If he happened to incur the—the—attentions of a madwoman—and that is exactly what I believe to have happened—there is no cause for you to air old rumors and gossip! I think that I made it perfectly clear, Miss Beck, in my first letter to you, that the subject of *The History of Macedonia* was not merely the history of the town but an account of its first citizens." He patted the manuscript. "I do not say that you have not included fair descriptions of our best families. You have, and I am pleased, quite pleased, with those passages. But the book"—he glared at her—"the book is tainted by lurid tales and sordid allegations!"

"Well, they stopped being lies, at least," said Mae.

"The roundhouse! The firemen didn't blow it up!"

"They surely did," Jottie snapped.

He glowered at her. "Jottie, my argument is with Miss Beck."

"Your argument's with all of us," Jottie said. "We think it's a fine book. An interesting book that people will want to read."

"*I* don't want to read it," growled Parker. "It's sordid!"

"A lot of people think it's excellent," said Jottie.

"Who? What *people*?" he sneered.

"Layla, what's that uncle of yours?" said Jottie, turning to Layla. "I never can remember his title—"

"Her uncle? I don't see how her uncle is germane in the least!" Parker interrupted.

"Her uncle is the supervisor of the Writers' Project in Washington," said Mae. "Jottie keeps forgetting what his title is. Honey"—she turned to Layla—"weren't you telling us about how he had dinner at the White House recently? Or was that your daddy? Her daddy's a senator," she explained helpfully to Parker.

"It was Ben," Layla said. "My uncle."

"And her uncle—the supervisor—thought the book was wonderful," said Jottie, producing a piece of paper from beneath her cushion. "Let's see, what did he say? He said, 'Ursula sent me the copy'—Ursula's the state director, Parker, the lady who's running the State Guide—'Ursula sent me the copy, not to edit, but to crow over. She's delighted, and I can see why. It's informative, interesting, and well written, an excellent example of what we've been trying to pull out of these small sponsored projects. In her letter to me, she said, "The manuscript is much better than I would have believed possible from an untried young woman. She is obviously someone we can, and should, use for other projects." '" Jottie looked up at Parker. "They're going to use it for an example."

"An example," he repeated. He slid his jaw forward and back, thumbing the papers in his lap.

"And she wants Layla to write more," added Mae. "Lots more, all about the area around here. Isn't that right, Layla?"

Layla smiled. "That's what Ben says."

"Because she thinks *The History of Macedonia* is so good," said Jottie.

Parker's eyes moved from face to face. "Huh," he said. "But—" he broke off.

"I thought she did real well with the General's knee pants," said Minerva softly. Parker jumped as though he'd been stuck with a pin. "She even described that stain he got from George Washington's gravy." She smiled into his eyes. "Anyone would think it was true."

"Minerva!" he groaned.

"Parker. You think I forgot a single thing you ever said to me? I never did." She slouched gracefully against the back of her chair and smiled at him. "Not one word."

Two pink spots appeared on his cheeks. There was a silence that stretched out into minutes, during which Parker Davies kept his eyes on the manuscript in his lap. "Puh," he said finally. He looked at Layla. "I insist that you check your facts, Miss Beck. Thoroughly. You will see the places I've noted with a question mark. Please see to them particularly. I am not persuaded that you have looked closely at the statue of Charity. And your description of the operation of the looms at American Everlasting is incorrect; the proper term is 'take-up mechanism,' I believe, though of course Mr. McKubin will be the authority—" He stopped speaking as Layla held out her hand.

"I'll check them," she said.

"There's no need to include that—that story about Ridell Fox," he said to Jottie. "Mr. Fox will be most displeased."

"Nonsense," said Jottie. "We showed it to Belle Fox and she

was thrilled. Said it was about time someone got it all down in black and white."

In silence, Parker meticulously stacked the papers and tapped them on his knees before passing them to Layla.

"I'll check these facts," said Layla crisply. "And with that proviso, am I correct in assuming that the manuscript is now approved by its sponsor?"

Parker glanced sourly at Minerva. "Yes."

"I'll need a letter to that effect. If you like, it can be printed in the front of the book," Layla said. "They'll do that if you want."

"The town council will write you a letter," he said. "There will be no need to include it in the book. Which will, I presume, be ready in good time for the festivities?" He looked at her sternly.

"I have every reason to believe it will," said Layla. "Though the printing is out of my hands, of course."

"September twenty-fourth," he reminded her.

"Will there be a parade?" asked Mae.

"I think not," he said. "A picnic has been decided upon."

"Oh, goody," said Mae. "I love a picnic. Don't you just love a picnic, Parker?"

As his steps resounded down the front walk, Willa's head became visible next to the porch. She'd heard it all, thought Jottie, from under the house. Her smooth brown hair shone in the sun as she followed Parker's progress down the street, and then she peered up into the screen.

"Come on in," said Jottie. "Come have some tea."

"There's cookies, too," said Minerva.

Slowly, Willa made her way around the rhododendron bushes and up the stairs. Her face was the color of cream except for the purple smudges under her eyes, but she glanced around at all of them—even Layla—before she sat down. At least she was that interested, thought Jottie, scooting over to make room for her niece. Silently, Willa accepted a cookie and a glass of tea and set them on the table in front of her.

"You're a dark horse, Minerva," said Jottie. "You truly are."

"Do you really remember every single word he ever said to you?" asked Layla.

"'Course not," Minerva said. "I was asleep most of the time."

They were still laughing when Emmett drove up in his truck. They watched as he parked and approached the house, unconscious of his audience. He opened the screen door and caught sight of the five of them, all in a row, all smiling at him, and froze. "Do you-all have any idea how frightening you are?" he asked.

They laughed harder than ever.

53

"Emmett!" It was Sol's voice. "Hold up!"

Emmett paused, one hand on the door of the New Grocery, his eyes sweeping over Prince Street. He frowned, puzzled—

"Over here," Sol said breathlessly, banging open the door of Statler's Ice Cream. In his hand was a very large heart-shaped pink satin box emblazoned with the motto Sweets to the Sweet. "Glad I caught you." He shifted the box to whack Emmett on the arm. "Listen, I have to meet with George and the strike committee, so I can't come over—you know, to see Jottie tonight. Will you give her this?" He nudged the box into Emmett's stomach.

Emmett looked at it and quickly back at Sol. "Why, sure! I'll take it right over!"

"Thanks, pal. I owe you. It's just a little something for Jottie," he said, nodding with pleasure and pride. "Got to stay on her good side."

"Right," said Emmett, nodding back with gusto. "Right you are! Candy! I'll tell her you're tied up tonight."

"Good, okay." Sol glanced at his watch. "I'd better get going. Thanks. Tell her"—his smile was wide and guileless—"sweets to the sweet."

"You bet!" said Emmett, and watched as Sol hurried away, past the barbershop, café, hardware store. Then, glancing with distaste at the box in his hands, he entered the New Grocery.

Back on Prince Street, he juggled a coffee can with the box of candy. They couldn't be combined. Scowling, he stuffed the candy under one arm and held the can casually in the same hand. It was stupid. He put the can in one hand and the box in the other. Damn Sol and damn his candy. Walking fast, he turned up Council Street and found himself swiftly overtaking Layla's back. He'd recognize that back anywhere.

There was nothing for it. "Hello," he said too loud.

She spun around, startled first and then, he saw, pleased. "Oh, hello there!" Her eyes fell on the pink satin box and veered away. "Have you been shopping?" she asked, and then gave a flustered laugh. "Obviously."

"This"—he jabbed the box in the air—"is not mine. It's from Sol. To Jottie."

"Oh," she said. She stole another look at it. "My."

He grimaced. "Yeah." He matched his steps to hers, and they walked in silence for a bit. "I don't think Sol understands Jottie very well," he said.

She glanced at him. "I was thinking the same thing. Though," she said slowly, "I couldn't say why, exactly. I mean, it's just candy. Candy's nice."

"It's the box," said Emmett, eyeing it. "I think there's something the matter with the box."

She began to laugh.

"What?" He stopped, his brow furrowed. "What's funny?"

"What you said." Layla smiled. "I think you're right." She looked up at him, her eyes sparkling. "Can you imagine Jottie's face?"

He laughed and shook his head. Then he sobered. "I thought they'd make each other happy," he said worriedly.

Her smile faded. After a moment, she said, "Do you remember him?"

A sidelong glance. "Vause?"

She nodded.

"Yes."

"Was he so—so—what was he like?" she asked.

"Well, I was nine years younger than Vause, so what I remember is kind of piecemeal, you know?" He hesitated, thinking himself backward. "Everyone shouting because Vause had won something—a race or a football game or something.

Him lighting the bonfire on Halloween. That kind of thing. Mostly I remember having the feeling that wherever he was, he and Felix, and Jottie, too, that was the most exciting place to be. That's where everyone was laughing and happy and, you know, lively." He paused mid-step on the sidewalk. "I can see that smile of his now—he had one of those devil smiles, you know?" He glanced at Layla and she nodded. "I was only eight when they left. For the Great War. And then Vause didn't come back until—what?—1919. He had a cane when he got back, and everyone was worried about him. But not me." He grinned. "I hated him."

"You hated him?" cried Layla. "Nobody hates Vause Hamilton!"

"Yeah, well, I did. He stole Jottie."

"Ohh."

"Yep. She was mine; she raised me, more than my mother ever did. She was like a mother, only fun. She took me everywhere, she played with me, she saved my hide when I needed it. She made us a secret code and wrote me notes in it. She told me things, too, about what she thought and what she studied." He smiled. "Though she never mentioned anything about Vause. Not a word about him. I only found out after he got back. I guess everyone could see it then, but not me. I didn't know a thing until they started using me as a decoy."

"A decoy?"

"You know, Let's you and me go to the river for a swim, Emmett, and we'll take a picnic, too. Won't that be fun? And of course I fell for it every time, so off we'd go to False River, *putt putt,* have our picnic, and then—surprise!—who would show up but Vause Hamilton! I guess Daddy and Mr. Hamilton were trying to stop the whole thing, which is why they had to meet out of town. But was I mad! Sometimes Vause would try to make it up to me—he'd throw a ball with me—but I couldn't stand it. I couldn't stand him. I'd go off in the trees and sulk." He shook his head ruefully. "I can't say I put much of a damper on the two of them, though. Jesus, they were in another world." He hesitated and then said slowly, "One time, I came sneaking back; I guess I had some idea I was going to throw a rock at him. But even then, when I was a stupid kid, I was . . . I don't know what's the word—jarred, maybe?—by the sight of them. They were just holding hands and talking, but—well, I'm glad I had the sense to go away and leave them alone."

Layla nodded dreamily. "It must have been something special, what they had."

"Nah." He looked fixedly ahead at some distant point. "That's just what being in love is like."

Her face flamed.

※

Sol took his cigarette out of his mouth. "If I were you," he called to Bird, "I'd find a branch that was thicker than a pencil."

"Pooh." From the throes of the maple, Bird waved her hand dismissively. "I'm a bird, ain't I?" She tested her weight on a slender bough.

"You're a birdbrain, I can tell you that," he laughed.

Jottie looked at him sideways. "Twenty years ago, you would have been climbing up there after her, trying to save her life."

His eyes flicked toward her and back to Bird. "I've learned a thing or two since then."

She nodded. He had.

"Sol?" called Bird.

"What?"

"I'm stuck."

"Told you."

"Come get me."

Sol laughed and nudged Jottie, didn't-I-say-so? "Here I come," he said, stubbing out his cigarette.

Jottie watched him trudge sturdily over the grass toward the maple tree. In the future, she would see this again and again; this would be a common scene. Now he held up his arms, his white shirtsleeves slipping backward, his kind face upturned as he coaxed Bird down. She was going to drop on him, Jottie knew. He wouldn't be expecting it, but he would catch her. Might hurt his back a little, but he wouldn't mind. He'd look at Bird, cradled there in his arms, and he'd forevermore take her into his heart, because that was the kind of heart he had.

Jottie turned around to peer into the mesh of the screened porch, where Willa perched like a raven, a ruin, stringy with exhaustion, her ferocious, unswerving heart indifferent to its own injuries, enduring in wreckage that anyone else would flee. For as long as Jottie watched her, she didn't move.

When Jottie finally turned away, she saw that it had happened just as she expected. There was Sol, with Bird in his arms, dappled, smiling, delighted.

What's it worth if it's so easy, she asked herself.

It's not worth a nickel.

It was getting to be the end of summer. You could feel it happening. Not that it wasn't hot; it was—sweltering, even, in the afternoons. But it wasn't crushing anymore, and there was a winey tang in the morning before the heat came on. From where she stood on the front-hall rug, Jottie looked through two layers of screen out to the tree-lined street, panning for the sheen of gold among the leaves. None yet; only the exhausted green of late summer. School would start soon, and Emmett would stop coming. He'd been there every day since Felix left, his steady presence masking the other's absence. They would miss him. Beyond the porch, trees rustled in some slight gust, and Jottie opened the coat closet in the front hall. Soon they'd resume their duties, the coats. Before she could stop herself, she hoped that Felix had enough money to buy a coat, wherever he was. She closed the closet door and leaned against it for good measure. Her eyes fell on the hall table. "Letter here for you!" she called. Silence. "It's from Charleston," she called again.

"I'm coming," said Layla, stepping into the hall. Jottie looked at her approvingly. The disheveled phase was over. Soon, very soon, she'll be all right, Jottie thought as Layla slit the envelope.

"Well?" prodded Jottie. "What's she say?"

"She likes it," said Layla, reading.

"Of course she does!" Jottie said. She couldn't help feeling proud.

Layla let out a whoosh of air. "She wants me to do another one."

"Well, that's no surprise," Jottie said. "Didn't your uncle say she would?"

"About *apples*." Layla grimaced. "She wants me to write a book about apple farming in the Eastern Panhandle." She handed Jottie the letter. "Sounds deadly, doesn't it?"

"Huh," said Jottie, reading. "They're more interesting than you think, apples."

Layla eyed Jottie closely. "Are they?"

"Sure," said Jottie. She began to sing, "Autumn's jewel, fruit on the bough, a treasure far greater than gold—"

Layla raised her eyebrows.

"Don't you know that song?" Jottie asked, nonplussed. "I thought everyone knew that song." She smiled at Layla. "What?"

"Let's do it together!" Layla said. "You and me! You could show me the wonderful world of the apple. We'd have fun."

"Pooh." Jottie flapped her hand. "I can't write a book."

"Pooh yourself," retorted Layla. "You can too. You wrote half the last one."

"I did not," said Jottie. "And, besides, it's a WPA job. You got to be on relief."

"If I can be on relief, you can, too."

"No, I can't. I've got those farms, remember? Even though they don't make a dime nowadays."

Layla's eyes narrowed. "Listen, Jottie, do you want to do it? This apple book?"

"You live here as long as I have, you end up knowing a lot about apples." Jottie read the letter again. "I know a lot more than *she* does, that's obvious."

Layla peered over the edge of the paper. "You're a better writer than she is, too."

"Well." Jottie had to agree.

"Listen." Layla's voice grew strong. "If you can't get on relief, that's all right. We'll share it between us, and they don't have to know a thing about it down in Charleston." She nodded encouragingly. "We'll write it together and I'll give you half the money, and they'll never be the wiser."

"But that seems like tricking Mrs. Chambers," said Jottie, wavering.

"Oh, *her.* She wouldn't care if a goat wrote it, as long as it came in on time."

"It's not like I couldn't use the money," said Jottie reflectively. "It'll save us from the poorhouse, anyway."

"I doubt Mr. McKubin would let his fiancée go to the poorhouse," Layla said, smiling.

Jottie looked furtive. "I guess not."

"You're still—going to get married, aren't you?"

"'Course I am," Jottie said. "Yes, indeed." She nodded for emphasis.

Layla hesitated. "If we did it, this book, is it all right about—me?"

"What about you?"

"If I stay?" Layla asked, gazing at a point slightly to the right of Jottie.

"Oh, honey." Jottie touched Layla's shoulder. "Of course. But I thought your daddy said you could go home now."

Layla nodded. "I don't want to go home." Her eyes remained on the point to Jottie's right. "I want to stay here."

Jottie glanced at her worn front room. "I don't know why. I bet your house is real nice."

"It's you-all," muttered Layla.

"Us-all?"

"I want to stay with you-all," Layla said. "When Parker came the other day, all of you helped. Minerva and Mae and you—you sat there and fought for me, even—even after what happened. Even though I made such a mess."

Jottie reached to brush back Layla's curls. "Honey—"

But Layla wasn't finished. "You treat me like I'm one of you, even though I've caused so much trouble and made such a fool out of myself. You don't hate me. Except for Willa, no one hates me."

"She'll get over it," said Jottie. She'd said it before.

"At home, they hate me," Layla continued.

Jottie smiled tenderly. "I don't see how that could be true."

"Well, I'm a black sheep, anyway."

"Then they must be awful particular," said Jottie. "There's one good thing about Felix," she added. "He made the rest of us look like angels. Listen, you can stay here as long as you want. I don't know why you'd want to be, but you're practically family."

Layla caught up Jottie's hand and squeezed. "That's what I want."

54

"Jottie!" yelled Emmett, thundering up the front stairs. "You need any butter?"

"What?" she squawked from the cellar.

"What?" he called, moving into the kitchen. "I *said*—oh." He caught sight of Layla and broke off.

"She's in the cellar," said Layla, pointing to it unnecessarily.

"I'm here," said Jottie, rising into the kitchen with her hands full of tomatoes. "What are you yelling about?"

"I'm going to big farm," said Emmett, his voice sliding awkwardly from loud to quiet. "Wren called. The DeLaval broke, so I'm taking the other Reliance from mountain farm."

"Honest to God, I don't know what Wren does to those separators."

"What does it separate?" asked Layla. "A separator?"

They both looked at her as if she had grown horns. "The wheat from the chaff," said Emmett.

"Oh."

"She doesn't know you're joking," said Jottie, shaking her head. "These city slickers."

"They'd starve to death if it weren't for us," said Emmett.

"I was just asking a question," protested Layla. "Don't I get credit for being interested?"

Emmett shook his head. "No. If you want credit, you got to come to the farm and touch a cow."

"All right. But isn't that how you get scarlet fever?"

"Oh, for God's sake!" he exploded.

"I'm joking!" she interrupted, rising from her chair.

His eyes moved over her summer dress and her high heels. "You really coming?"

"Yes. If"—she hesitated—"that's all right?"

He nodded, flushing a little. "Yes. Of course." He looked at Jottie. "Can I borrow a towel?"

"I'm sorry to put you to the trouble," said Layla after a few minutes.

"What?" said Emmett, glancing from the road to her.

"The towel," said Layla. She plucked at the towel she was sitting on, embarrassed.

He smiled. "You're less trouble than Bird. She won't ride inside. Because of the smell, she says. I have to tie a rocking chair in the back, so she can sit on it like a queen."

Layla laughed. "You're an indulgent uncle."

"I guess." He looked toward her. "It does smell pretty bad, doesn't it?"

She nodded.

"One of the hoses leaks," he said. "I just roll the windows down, but I guess it kind of knocks you out if you're not used to it."

"It's, um, bracing," said Layla.

"That's a nice way to say it."

They fell silent then, passing through a spate of dark trees and emerging on a flat road lined by fences and marked at long intervals by gates and mailboxes. Layla stared out the window at the undulating green dotted with cows and rocks. The engine whined over an incline and dropped the Model T into a valley where a wide, deceptively smooth river seemed to repose on one side of the road.

"False River?" asked Layla.

"Mm-hm," said Emmett. "Yes."

There was another silence. She looked sideways at Emmett's quiet profile. What did he think? What did he think of her? He had every reason to despise her. She despised herself, and he was not the kind of man who wanted a woman to be a fool. Surely he thought her ridiculous and weak. Not to mention loose. A tramp. How could he think otherwise? Except, she thought, the way he looks at me sometimes, with those unreadable black eyes, like he's waiting for something. No. Probably my imagination. Probably he's waiting for me to go away. She stole another glance at him. He can't think any worse of me than he does already. She licked her lips. "You—" she began.

"You—" he said at the same moment. They stopped. "Go ahead," he said.

"I was," she said laboriously, "going to say that I feel—well, that you must think I'm an awful fool. After what happened."

"A fool?" he said, frowning. "No. I don't think that."

"I meant tramp," she said harshly. "That's what I meant."

Emmett slowed the truck and pulled over to the narrow edge of the road. After a second, he flicked the key; the engine coughed and fell silent. "Smells better now, huh?" he said.

Layla stared ahead.

"As far back as I can remember," he said carefully, "girls have fallen for Felix. Practically every girl he ever looked at, she'd be crazy about him inside of five minutes. If that long. I thought it was normal until I was, you know, interested in girls myself. One time, when I was fifteen, he took me along with him and some of his friends to—well, I guess you'd call it a roadhouse. Strictly illegal. He was going to show me the ropes, he said. Meet some girls." His eyes widened, remembering. "They were arguing over him, who'd get him. He thought it was funny. No one paid me any mind, except when Felix told them to, and then they'd come over and dance with me to get in good with him." He glanced at Layla. "I guess they were tramps. But what I'm trying to say is that I've seen a lot of girls that Felix . . . well"—he swallowed—"who liked Felix, and I never heard one of them say no to him, not about anything. But you did. You said no. He gave you hell for it, too, but you didn't give in. You stood up to him."

Layla ducked her head in a little nod. I did do that, she thought, with a tinge of pride. I did.

"That was something else, Layla. I was—surprised isn't strong enough. Amazed is what I was. You're tougher than I am. About eight years ago, I decided it would be better in the long run, for Jottie and the girls especially, if I tried not to notice the things Felix was doing." He lifted his eyebrows. "It's been a lot of not noticing, but—I didn't want to hate him. I didn't want to wish him dead." He glanced sideways. "I wanted to kill him when he was saying those things to you."

"I'm glad you didn't," Layla muttered.

"Why? You still love him?" he asked bitterly.

"No. No, I think he's dangerous," she said, lifting her eyes to his. "He might've hurt you."

Emmett's smile was like light itself. "Yeah, I think he probably would have."

She frowned. "That thing he does. The way he moves without making any noise. Why would he *do* that?"

"No idea," Emmett said, watching her.

Her shoulders hunched. "It gives me the willies."

"Me too," he agreed.

"This is Miss Beck," said Emmett, untying a rope in the back of the truck. "She doesn't know what a cow is."

"That right?" said Wren blankly. He stared at Layla.

Emmett snickered. "Those ones are cows." He nodded to the fence behind her.

"And those over there are sheep," said Layla, pointing to the pigpen.

"That's right," said Emmett.

Wren looked shocked, but he said nothing.

"Okay, you pull," Emmett directed him, climbing into the bed of the truck. He looked at Layla. "Why don't you go commune with nature? This is going to take a few minutes."

She nodded and wandered toward the cows. Several lifted their heads at her approach; most didn't. Their unconcern was comforting. Carefully, Layla turned and backed herself onto the top rail of the fence, hooking her high heels over the rail below. She smoothed her skirt and watched Emmett heave a metal barrel into Wren's arms. "Don't drop it," she heard him say. Wren shuffled into the darkness of the barn, and Emmett pushed a contraption of wheels and levers toward the tailgate and then eased it onto the ground. "Wren! Just set it down and get out here," he called, sounding irritated.

"Okay." Together, the two men lifted the machine up, Emmett stooping a little to match Wren's height, and moved slowly into the shadow of the barn.

On the fence, Layla listened to the wind, to the jaws of the cows, to the sizzle of flies, to the quiet snorts of the pigs, to the isolated squeals of metal inside the barn, to a few far-off, weary birds.

Emmett came out, wiping his face on his sleeve. She watched him reach into the truck and gather the rope into a neat coil. Then he turned, squinting a little in the sun, to find her.

He stopped a few feet away from the fence. His hair was damp with sweat, she saw, and his dark eyes were doubtful.

"Well?" she said at last, stretching out her hands. "Are you going to leave me here?"

He moved forward to lift her down, and she heard the intake of his breath as his hands closed around her waist.

Oh, she thought. Oh. Not my imagination, after all.

⸺⬦⸺

September 7, 1938

Dear Father,

Thank you for your pithy communique of the 2nd. Was that permission or a summons? I couldn't tell. Pleased as I am to know that the drawbridge is down, the oil removed from the boil, and the arrows returned to their quivers, I'm afraid I can't comply with your request (invitation?), because I've taken another job on the project, which requires me to stay here in Macedonia through the fall, at least. This time, I'm to write about apples of the Eastern Panhandle, a subject in which I have been deeply interested for—oh, about three days. Really, though, I do wish you could observe my newfound apple-expertise; I'm sure you would be terrifically impressed. The merest glance now suffices for me to distinguish Grimes Golden from Golden Delicious, and just yesterday I had an invigorating half-hour conversation about apple scab and twig-cutter weevil with a man who has promised to escort me to see a particularly fine example of sawfly infestation this weekend.

You should be proud of me, Father, for I have learned the lesson you set out to teach me this summer: I am no longer afraid of work. I've come to believe that there's very little difference between submitting to the requirements of a job and submitting to the requirements of being your daughter. Both provide a salary. Both require devoted attention. The one distinction is that the former allows me the freedom to choose my own husband, which I cannot help but consider an advantage, especially when I think of Nelson.

My education has been broader, perhaps, than you intended. In addition to my new dedication to labor, I've also widened my social perspective, and I now include teachers, farmers, union agitators, and people who have never been to a country club among my friends, which is a great improvement, in my opinion. I've learned other lessons, too. I've learned that history is the autobiography of the historian, that ignoring the past is the act of a fool, and that loyalty does not mean falling into line, but stepping out of it for the people you love.

I tell you these things, not bitterly or from a desire to punish you (maybe just a bit from a desire to punish you), but because I know that you of all people treasure liberty—haven't you sworn to defend it three times?—and that you will understand and even respect my new ideas. I gaze into the future and predict howls of dismay, thundering excoriations, outraged diatribes against my choices, but I know you, Father. I know you, and in your secret heart, you'll admire me for getting what I want. And in your even more secret heart, you'll say to yourself, That's my child.

Love always,
Layla

Sol paused in the hectic lobby of Sprague's Palladium. "Dr. Averill! Good to see you, sir. And Mrs. Averill." There was a flurry of pleased surprise, a dispensing of benignant smiles.

"May I introduce my fiancée, Miss Romeyn? Jottie, Mrs. Averill and Dr. Averill."

Wider benignant smiles, exclamations of polite joy. "Your fiancée! Sol!" Dr. Averill proffered the obligatory nudge. "You sly dog! Here I thought you were a confirmed bachelor!"

Mrs. Averill leaned forward, her eyes sparkling. "Why, Sol! I had no idea! How long has this been going on?"

Sol threw a proud look at Jottie. "Well, Mrs. Averill, we were childhood sweethearts, Jottie and me, but we just recently were, um, reunited."

Childhood sweethearts? Jottie struggled against the launch of an incredulous stare at Sol. Childhood sweethearts? *That's* what you're telling yourself? When you know the only one I ever loved was Vause? Helpless outrage choked her. How dare you throw him away like that? How can you? But she knew the answer; she'd heard it weeks before: *Vause would be out of the way, and Sol'd get what he never had in his whole life—the chance to edge out Vause Hamilton with a girl.*

"Isn't that lovely! Childhood sweethearts reunited!" Mrs. Averill turned in sentimental ecstasy to Jottie. "You never stopped caring for him? *So* sweet."

Jottie smiled coyly and twined her arm through Sol's. "I certainly remembered him fondly," she said. "But it was only after I was widowed that, well, my thoughts *turned* to him." She sent an adoring glance up into Sol's startled face.

Hours later, after Sol had retreated, unenlightened, from her house, Jottie took off her shoes and stockings and went to stand in the dark, cool grass. A few final, hardy fireflies cycled around her, pursuing their impenetrable rites, oblivious to their approaching doom. Not, after all, an honest man, she concluded. But it's himself he lies to. She watched a firefly gleam and lapse and tried to endure her growing certainty that if Sol had been in Felix's place, he would, after a time, have come to believe that what he had told her was the truth.

✳

Anybody else besides Jottie would have been mad. Bird was. She said it wasn't fair she had to go to school and I didn't and Jottie should make me. "You ain't sick," she said.

I lay still on the bed and didn't say anything.

Bird bent over and searched my face. I watched her blue eyes. "Maybe you are sick, though," she said. She touched her finger against my cheek. "Willa?"

It was a struggle, but I spoke. "I'm tired, is all." I sounded like the inside of a pipe.

She put another finger against my cheek.

"I'll be back at that damn school before you know it," I said.

Bird giggled. "You swore." She didn't say she was going to tell.

My eyes shut against my will, and I shook my head to jostle myself awake. Bad enough to dream once a day. If I had to go through it twice, I didn't know what I'd do.

Jottie took me to Dr. Ecks, just to make sure, she said. He looked down my throat and banged my knee and thumped my back and listened to my heart. He even peered with a little funnel into my ears, which I enjoyed. Then he looked at me for a long time, tapping his gold pen against the table. "Willa, go on and get dressed and sit out there in the waiting room," he said. "I'm going to talk to Jottie a minute."

I didn't care very much what he had to say, but it was a reflex by now, just like my leg jumping when he smacked it with his rubber mallet. I got dressed and stood outside his office door and listened. It was pathetic the way grown-ups believed their word was law.

"She sleeping?" he asked.

"No," said Jottie. "She goes to bed, but she doesn't sleep much."

"I could give her something," he said, "but it'll make her pretty woozy."

"She's already pretty woozy," Jottie said.

He tapped his pen some more. "All right. Let's leave her alone," he said. "Let her be."

"She won't go to school," Jottie said.

"That's all right," he said. "Let her stay home." I loved Dr. Ecks. "It'll give the other children a chance to catch up."

"Won't do them any good," said Jottie proudly. She was wrong, of course. I could never do a thing about angles, not in my whole life, because of that time.

"She'll be all right," he said.

In some little part of myself, I was relieved to hear that. I was beginning to think I maybe was dying. I had never heard of anyone dying of tiredness, but that didn't mean it didn't happen. Leprosy was the only disease I really knew about.

So Jottie and I spent the first two weeks of school driving around, looking at apples. She and Miss Beck were writing a book for the Apple Growers Association of the Eastern Panhandle, all about apples. Jottie said she was doing fieldwork—I think she just liked to say the word—so almost every day we drove to this orchard or that, looking at Golden Delicious or Grimes Golden or Winesap, and along the way Jottie would tell me about the farms we passed and all the things that had happened there. Floods, mostly. She talked and we both ate apples. Sometimes, when the drive was long, I'd fall asleep, but that was all right because I never dreamed in the car. I felt safe in the car, which was funny, considering what a terrible driver Jottie was. I liked to wake up, slumped against the car door, and realize that we had covered miles without my knowing it. I didn't want to know everything anymore; I didn't want to know anything. Once, I woke, more or less in a heap on the floor of the car, and I saw through my tangled eyelashes that Jottie was crying. I watched her wipe her tears with one hand while she gripped the steering wheel with the other and then switch when her hand got wet. I watched her, and I thought about how, just a month or so back, I would have driven myself distracted wanting to know why she was crying. But now I didn't want to know. I didn't ask. I just felt sorry. Sorry and tired.

Miss Beck stayed on. She didn't do fieldwork with Jottie and me, and I was glad. Instead, it was Emmett who took her around to look at apple farms, even though he didn't have anything to do with it. They went on the weekends, because he was teaching school the rest of the time. *The History of Macedonia* was done. Five copies arrived in a box, and Jottie baked a cake to celebrate. Emmett came to supper that night, still wearing his schoolteacher suit and tie, and afterward, on the porch, Jottie and Minerva and Mae took turns reading pieces of it aloud with dramatic emphasis, while Emmett and Miss Beck applauded like crazy. Bird tucked a book under her arm and sashayed down the street to impress Jun Lloyd with it, which it didn't. Mr. McKubin stopped in for a moment and said it looked real official, but he couldn't stay, because something was happening at the mill. He was the president of it now and he was busy. Harriet came by; Richie was down at the mill, too, she said. She talked on and on, and I watched the sky grow dark, even though supper was barely over. Marjorie Lanz came in and sat down with a thump, and Mrs. Fox, too.

I went inside. Father's room was still hot, but not like it had been a few weeks before. I slid down the wall and stretched my legs out in front of me. I checked the place where the penny had been, out of habit, and then I closed my eyes. I wasn't so comfortable I was in danger of falling asleep. I let myself drift away. I had plenty of time. Nothing was going to change.

55

⟡

Layla peered over the rim of *Apple Cultivation Practices,* trying to track the source of her nervy awareness. Suspiciously, she scanned the humid expanse that stretched from the heavy trees behind her to the dark mud at the river's edge. Nothing. Her eyes moved from the blue sky down to the lumpy, shaded grass where she sat.

"It's the cicadas," murmured Emmett. He was stretched out on the blanket beside her, his eyes closed, a battered copy of *Our Constitution* face down on his chest.

It was the cicadas. They were silent. In the whole world, she could only hear a soft, occasional swirl of wind and the light lapping of the water. The summer's sound, the frantic orchestra that had sawed behind every scene—it was over. She relaxed against the gray bark at her back. In the quiet, she watched Emmett take even breaths, the minute ripples of his dark eyelashes telling her that he was awake. She wondered at his stillness. His hands were perfectly still. His mouth, too. How could he be so still?

She leaned away from her tree trunk, fascinated by his repose. Carefully, she shifted closer to him, the better to see the straight line of his forehead; the shadows over his deep eyes; his firm, even mouth.

She reached out and brushed her fingers across his lips. As his eyes flew open, she smiled and bent over him.

Some time later, she broke away.

"Mm-mm," he murmured, "no. Don't do that."

She leaned on one hand, watching him.

"No," he said again. "Come back here."

"Would you *ever* have kissed me?" she asked.

Smiling, he reached up to explore her curls. "No."

She pulled his hand around to her mouth. "Why? Scared of me?"

He frowned. "Of course I am," he said. "I've been trying not to care about you ever since the day I met you."

"Oh," she said, deflated.

He watched her for a moment. "I didn't succeed," he said, and reached for her.

The sun was low and pink in the sky when they drove back to Academy Street. Emmett stole another glance to his right.

"What?" she said, catching him.

"I'm marveling."

She blushed.

"Was it a dream?" he asked. "Maybe I was really asleep all afternoon. Seems like it might be a dream."

"You were awake," she said. "We were both awake." She touched the back of his hand.

He glanced sideways again. "You're so beautiful. Every time I look at you, you're just as beautiful as I remembered. It's not fair." He laughed. "I might drive off the road, you're so beautiful."

"You're going to feel bad if you kill me," she said, smiling.

"I won't," he promised. "I won't kill you. I'm going to keep you safe with me." He sent her another sideways look. "Did you know that? Did I mention that before?"

"Which?"

"That I want to be with you forever. Did I say that already? Because I've been thinking it for a long time. Don't know if I said it."

She shook her head.

"Well, hell!" He slapped his forehead. "Must have slipped my mind. You know, in the press of events. I'd better pull over." He drew the truck to a stop. "You got to pull over if you're going to propose," he confided, shutting the engine.

"Propose?" Layla exclaimed. "You're going to propose?"

"Watch," he said, turning glowing eyes to hers. "Watch this."

He took her hands in his. "Will you marry me? Please?" He bent to kiss her fingers. "Please."

"But Emmett—"

"Do I need to get on my knees?" he interrupted. "I'll be glad to."

"No, sweetheart—"

He recoiled, his eyes wide. "Oh shit."

"Oh shit?" she repeated, baffled.

"Are you going to turn me down?" He stared at her. "Is that what you're about to do?"

"Emmett, please, will you let me get a word in?"

He winced, pressing his hand over his heart. "I was so happy. I'm a jackass, I was so happy—"

"Emmett!" Layla cried. "I'm not saying no!"

He looked up, still wincing. "You're not?"

"No. Honestly." She rolled her eyes. "I'll marry you, for heaven's sake. I just want to know you before I do."

"You'll marry me?" he demanded. "Say it again."

"I'll marry you," she repeated, "once I know you."

"You know me plenty," he said. After a second, he added, "What do you want to know?"

"Everything," she said. "I want to know everything."

"Everything?"

"Everything that ever happened to you. And what you thought about it."

"That'll take forever!" he roared. "We'll both be dead before we're done."

"Then you'd better get started," she said. "What's your first memory?"

"Oh, for God's sake. Jottie trying to stuff me into a doll buggy."

Layla laughed. "That's good. That's exactly the kind of thing I want to know."

"Why?" he groaned. "Why do you want to know that?"

"Because it made you," she said. "And I love you."

"Jesus Christ," he muttered. He reached across the seat to grip her hand.

56

People drove in from miles away for the sesquicentennial of Macedonia; I'm not sure why. It was a beautiful day, and I suppose that had something to do with it. The sky was bright blue, and for all the air was warm, you could feel fall on the other side of it. I liked fall. I guess everyone else did, too, because the crowd was tremendous. By ten-thirty in the morning, all the ladies were having conniption fits about not enough food, even though they were charging a quarter a plate. There were hundreds of people in Flick Park, surging around, eating on benches and rocks and the fenders of their cars. I saw Sonny Deal eating in a tree. He waved and pretended to throw a cookie at me, but he didn't really. It was nice to know there were no hard feelings.

"Listen"—Jottie sounded tense—"if we get separated, and I don't see how we won't, I'll just see you at home, all right? Do you hear me?" She peered into my face, and I nodded.

"I hear you," said Bird, but she was already straining to get away. I think she saw Berdetta Ritts in the distance. "Can I have some money?"

Jottie unexpectedly pressed a quarter into each of our hands. "That's supposed to be for lunch," she said. "But do as you will." Bird lunged off in pursuit of Berdetta. "You want to stick with me, Willa?" Jottie shouted as the Rotary band began to play. I nodded and held tight to her hand. Carleton Lewis had got his drum out of hock, and the noise was enough to wake the dead.

Jottie and I wandered over to watch the ladies at the long tables. Mrs. Fox and Mrs. Dews and the others looked like windmills, their arms pumping up and down to slap potato salad and fried chicken and pie on hundreds of plates. "Think I'll eat when I get home," Jottie said in my ear. I agreed. That pie looked a little careworn. Some of the country people had brought their own box lunches—probably they didn't have a quarter to spend on food—and they looked content, munching on bread and apples with babies laid over laps and men squatting on the ground.

"Lord, what a crush!" said Mrs. Tapscott, grabbing hold of Jottie's arm. "I'm about ready to faint dead away. Listen, Jottie, will you tell that girl I'm just wild about her book? I never would've thought an outsider could do it, but she did a real nice job. Real nice."

"I'll tell her, Inez," said Jottie. "She'll be pleased."

"I'm going to send it to my cousin Cincy down in Romney." Mrs. Tapscott giggled. "He never would believe Jackson stayed in Mother's house. That book will just shut him right up."

Jottie laughed, and Mrs. Tapscott blew away with the crowd. "Bye, honey!" she called to me as she went.

Jottie looked down at me sideways. "Guess we should have charged to get in that book, huh?" I nodded. "Let's see if we can get us some ice cream," she suggested. "Armine Statler said he was going to set up a booth somewhere." She was under the impression that I didn't know she was trying to feed me up. "That is the Lord's own racket," she muttered, heading away from the Rotary band.

"Jottie." It was Mr. McKubin. He put his hand on her arm. "How's this suit?"

He stood back a little ways so she could see.

"You're a vision," said Jottie. She poked my shoulder. "Isn't he?" I nodded, even though he didn't look any different than usual. "They won't hear a word you say," she added. "They'll be so struck by your suit."

Mr. McKubin had to make a speech and he didn't want to. He'd practiced saying it on our porch the night before, and he'd made a lot of faces while he was doing it. The speech was called "Labor and Honor," and it was about how working made you better, and the more you worked, the better you got. The strike was over. Mr. McKubin had decided that the workers could get up a union if they wanted to, and he threw them a big party to celebrate the fact. All the strikers came and ate cake, and everyone was happy until the TWOC sent in a man who said they should be getting more money. Mr. McKubin said there wasn't any more money to get. He also said the whole damn thing was Emmett's fault when you got right down to it and he couldn't believe he was marrying into a hotbed of Communism. Then Emmett said he didn't know which was better for the sock business, dying on your feet or living on your knees, and everyone laughed.

But Mr. McKubin wasn't laughing now. He said, "I'd better go on up there." He looked real glum. "Wish me luck."

Jottie patted him on the arm. "You don't need luck, Sol. You'll do better than you think."

That made him happy, I could tell. He was smiling as he turned to go.

"Come on, honey, let's find Armine," said Jottie. We started toward Prince Street, but a lady in a green hat blocked our way.

"Jottie," she said, kind of haughty.

"Anna May," said Jottie.

"I haven't seen Felix in a while." She didn't look at Jottie's face when she said it. She looked at the top of her head.

"No. He's on an—an extended business trip," said Jottie. She closed her mouth tight, looking a little haughty herself.

"Ah," said the lady. "Well." She turned and walked away without another word.

"Honest to God," muttered Jottie.

I looked up at her and raised my eyebrows.

"Puh!" she said indignantly. "If you can't be bothered to talk, you can't expect to find everything out!"

I decided I didn't care.

The crowd was getting thicker. Jottie ran into Harriet, and then Mrs. Sue came along, and pretty soon the knot of ladies was big enough to stop traffic. They didn't notice, though. They were busy talking. I could see Geraldine far away, across Flick Park, stomping toward some blackberry canes that grew by the side of the creek. She looked important and busy, with her brothers and sisters scuttling after her. It seemed like a long time ago that we had played together.

I yawned. Jottie and her friends were talking about the price of hats. Jun Lloyd loped by. I wondered if he'd ever buried Neddie that day.

The knot of ladies unfurled itself into a straggling line of attention. Mayor Silver was about to give his sesquicentennial speech, and there were lots of preliminary squawks and blasts as Carl Inskeep adjusted the microphone on the stand. Someone's magnified laugh washed over the park, followed by a wave of laughter from the crowd. Mayor Silver climbed the stairs to the bandstand and smiled—he looked a little nervous. "Thank you," he said, which reminded everyone that they should clap, so they did. "Thank you, thank you," he cried.

I jerked on Jottie's sleeve. "I'm going home," I said.

She was so pleased to hear me say something that she nodded enthusiastically, as if she couldn't wait to see me leave. "All right, honey. I'll be along in a while. I think I saw Emmett with Layla, so there's no one at the house. You don't mind, do you?"

I shook my head and left. I didn't want to hear Mr. Silver say thank you again. I didn't want to hear him say anything.

That microphone had a terrible echo, but once I turned up Council Street, all the sounds fell away. Everyone was at Flick Park, and the rest of Macedonia was deserted, which suited me fine. I liked it peaceful.

I turned from Council to Kanawha Street.

"My God, you walk fast," someone said behind me. "Nobody's going to believe you're sick when you walk that fast."

My heart almost choked me and I stopped dead. I didn't dare look around.

"Unless you have Saint Vitus Dance."

"What's that?" I asked very quietly.

"Saint Vitus Dance? It's a disease. A dread disease that causes excessive movement of the limbs. I think it's going to be a tough sell, though. You don't look sick."

I spun around then, and there he was, smiling at me.

"You look fine." He opened his arms and I crashed into them. "Hey," he said, rocking me back and forth. "Hey, Willa."

"I missed you," I choked out. "Something awful."

Father nodded, holding tight to me. "I missed you, too, honey. Especially when I heard you were sick."

"I'm just tired," I said, but my face was pressed up against his shirt, so he couldn't understand me.

He held me a little away. "What?"

"I'm—I was just tired. That's all."

He was looking all over my face. "Tired? Jottie let you stay home from school for that?"

I nodded. He looked pretty tired himself. His eyes were bloodshot.

He shook his head disapprovingly. "I had to fall down and practically knock my brains out before they'd let me stay home from school. Had to be almost dead. Jottie's a patsy."

"Will you come home?" I begged. "Please?"

"You know I can't," he said. "I seem to recall you were present at the hanging." He tried to smile, but it didn't turn out.

"Please." I couldn't stop begging him. "Please, just for a little. No one'll know. They're all down at Flick Park, all of them. And I won't tell."

One eyebrow shot up, and I remembered that he didn't have any reason to trust me.

"I'm sorry!" I burst out, hiding my face in his shirt again for shame. "I'm sorry for telling—I couldn't stand for Jottie to cry like that."

"I know," he said, stroking my hair. "Don't fuss. It's better she knows."

"I didn't mean to tell. If I'd had another minute, I would have thought of something else," I mourned. "I should have figured out a way."

He put his hand under my chin and lifted my face to look at his eyes. "I never figured out a way, and I worked on it a lot longer than you." He patted my cheek. "You did fine."

It was forgiveness, but it sounded like good-bye, too. I clapped my hand over my mouth to keep from sobbing.

His shoulders sagged a little. "Don't, sweetheart. Don't take it so hard."

A wail escaped from under my hand. He was going to leave again.

"Oh God," he breathed. "Tell you what." He took my hand

away from my mouth and wrapped it in his. "Let's go sit on the roof. Just for a little bit. Just this last time."

I clung tight to his hand. "Really?" I hiccuped. "I've never been on the roof."

He was appalled. "What? You've never been on the roof?"

"Jottie said she'd skin us alive."

He made a disgusted sound. "This is what comes of letting other people raise your children."

"Jottie's not other people."

"Well, obviously she is. Don't sit on the roof! She spent half her childhood on that roof. Roof's the best part of the house." We walked together along Academy Street, swinging our hands between us, and I tried not to think that it would end. When we got to the house, he moved right past the front path to the cellar door and pulled it open. "Come on," he called to me.

"Why don't you go in the front door?" I asked, even though I was already following him.

"You said there was no one home, but you don't really know," he explained. "You can't be too careful."

Inside the cellar, he fished himself an apple from the bin and then skimmed up the stairs and through the kitchen so fast I was hard put to catch up with him. "Wait," I panted. "Wait for me."

"I'm trying to stay on the right side of the law," he said over his shoulder. "For once. Hurry up."

"I'm hurrying," I gasped. I caught up with him at the door to his room. "It's all right in there," I said, breathing hard. "Nothing's changed."

He nodded and moved across the room to the window, opening it wide. "Out you go," he said, gesturing for me to go first.

"After you," I said. I was a little nervous. Dex Lloyd had broken his arm, and that was only falling out of a tree.

Father laughed softly, the way I loved. "What nice manners you've got, honey." He swung his legs over the sill and then helped me out, taking my hand so I wouldn't be scared. There was an almost-flat part outside his window—it was the roof of the porch, really—and we sat down there, facing east so we could look along Academy Street. Some of the trees had yellow leaves already. He took off his coat and sighed in a contented way. "Ah, thank God. Home," he said, stretching out and wadding his coat up under his head for a pillow. Then he glanced over at me. "You don't have a coat."

I shook my head.

He stood. "Just a minute." The way he walked, he might have been on a sidewalk. He slipped through the window again and came back out with his own bedspread. He folded it into a neat pad and put it down for me. "There," he said.

"Thanks."

"Think nothing of it."

I lay back and he did, too, and for a long time we didn't say anything. Then I propped myself up to see if he was asleep, because if he was, I'd keep watch to make sure he didn't roll off the roof. His eyes were closed, so I studied him. He looked kind of raggedy, not so spruce as he usually was. He had a stain on his pants. I wondered did he wash his own clothes. It hurt my heart to picture that. Without opening his eyes, he spoke. "Why'd you do it, Willa?"

"What?" I asked, even though I was pretty sure what he meant.

"You know." He waved his fingers. "Tare's basement. Looking in those cases." His eyes opened and he stared at the sky. "Why?"

"I wanted"—I chased after the right words—"I wanted to know about you. I thought that if I knew what you were doing and where you were, I'd be part of you. Like we'd be working together, even if you didn't know it." I gulped a little. "When I went down to Mr. Russell's basement, I thought I was going to find whiskey."

"Jesus," he breathed.

"I'm a bootlegger, too," I confessed. I wanted him to know everything. "But I buy my whiskey from Mr. Houdyshell."

He hitched around to look at me. "What the hell are you talking about?"

I explained about Mrs. Bucklew and Mrs. John and the basket and the Four Roses whiskey. While he was listening, he put his hands up to his face to shade it.

"So we're both outlaws," I finished.

Father lifted his hand away, and I saw that he was laughing. At me. He shook his head in wonder and said, "Who would have thought it? You, of all people. I would have put my money on Bird."

I drew myself up. "I am a natural-born sneak. I did it all summer long, and I didn't get caught."

His smile disappeared. "And you think it's fun?"

That gave me pause. "No," I said slowly. "I'm just good at it."

He nodded, and his face was grim. "Yeah, I know. I'm good at it, too. It's a goddamn curse, how good I am at it."

"Same here," I said, thinking of my dream. If I'd gone to Minerva's like I was supposed to, I would never have had to dream that awful dream. It was a curse.

"You should probably stop, then," he said.

"I have," I said with dignity. "I don't want to know anything anymore."

"You're something fierce, Willa," he said with a little smile.

"That's because I'm like you," I said. "I get it from you."

"No," he said quick. "Don't wish for that." He propped himself up on his elbows and looked out into the trees. "How's Jottie?" he asked quietly.

"I think she misses you," I said.

"I doubt it." He let his breath out through his teeth. "She has Sol, the Honest Injun."

"He's honest," I agreed. But I was thinking about Mr. McKubin sitting on our porch and how Jottie was when he was there. "I don't think she's going to marry him, though." I listened to myself say the words and thought, She won't.

He swiveled his head to look at me. "Says who?"

"Says me," I said slowly, fitting my ideas together. "He likes everybody, Mr. McKubin does, and he's nice, I guess, but that's not what Jottie cares about, just being nice. Any old body can be nice." I frowned. "And then, when he's around, she's quiet. Not the way she really is. It's like she doesn't want to talk, because he won't understand what she means." Father's eyes narrowed. "The happiest I saw her since—you know—was when she got that coat." I smiled to think of it. "She was like me: She didn't know what it was at first, and then she knew. She remembered it. And she closed her eyes and was so *happy*. She was happier with Vause Hamilton's coat than she is with Mr. McKubin."

"Well, yeah," Father said, like it was perfectly reasonable that she would love a dead man's coat more than the person she was supposed to marry. "It's Vause."

"And it's Jottie, too," I started to say, when suddenly he sat up straight, looking down Academy Street.

There she was. She was walking, alone, past the Caseys' house. I could see her perfectly, her locket shining against the front of her dress, her tan hat on her dark hair, her worn purse hooked over her wrist. Plenty of people would have thought she looked just like anybody, but she wasn't, and all the ones who say that's the truth about most people don't understand what she was.

Father smiled, watching her.

She passed the Lloyds' house. "Stand up," I said. "She'll see us then."

"Nah," he said, his eyes following her. "I'd better go."

"No!" I cried, but he rose, moving quickly toward the window. Leaving. "No!" I didn't even think about falling off. I stood up, grabbed his hand, and pulled him around, and for the first time in my life, I was faster than he was. "Jottie!" I called.

She looked from side to side before she looked up. "Willa! What in God's name do you think—" She stopped. She didn't say anything, just looked and breathed in and out.

Father didn't say anything, either.

"Come on up," I said finally.

"Hey, Jottie," Father croaked. He cleared his throat. "Hey."

She frowned. "I told you not to come here, Felix."

"Oh, Jottie, *please,*" I begged. "Please come up. For just a minute."

She didn't say anything. After a moment, she went inside.

Father sat down—dropped, practically—and we waited. For a while I was worried that she wasn't going to come. But then we heard her at the window. I turned around to watch. Jottie could walk the roof just like Father could—you'd think she did it every day of her life, that's how graceful and calm she was.

I made room for her on my bedspread and she sat beside me. She and Father didn't talk and they didn't look at each other, either. They just sat in silence for ages.

"How was the sesquicentennial?" I inquired politely.

"Boring," said Jottie. "You're talking, I notice."

I made a face at her and tried another subject. "Did you have some ice cream?"

"No."

This from Jottie, who was always telling us that polite conversation was the ball bearing of civilization. I began to get scared. What if they didn't speak at all? Father would leave, and she'd never let him come back. Anxiously, I peered out into the leafy emptiness for a topic.

Finally Jottie said, "Hank's got a warrant out on you."

Father looked at her quickly and nodded, but he didn't speak.

All of a sudden, she shuddered all over, the way a horse does when it's got something on it. "No," she said, and got to her feet. "I'm sorry, Willa. No. It's too late." Father turned his head away.

She made to go, but I quick grabbed her skirt in my hand. She'd rip it if she kept walking. "Jottie. Stop. I can explain." I couldn't wait for them.

She stopped. "You can explain what?"

"What happened." I closed my eyes so I could tell her how I saw it in my head. "He didn't expect it," I began. "He didn't think it would happen the way it did, with the flames burning up the walls so quick." I looked at Father. He was still facing away, but he was listening. "He never thought that they'd get hurt or that one of them might die. He'd never thought that could happen, but then, all of a sudden, it was happening, and he didn't know what to do." Jottie lowered herself down, listening. "And later, when he found out Vause was dead, he felt so sick he thought he might die himself, because in just that one little minute, he'd lost everything." I was still holding her skirt, and I yanked on it. "*Everything.* And he'd done it to himself. It was all his own fault. Just like me. I ruined everything. I wrecked Father's life and my own, too, and, Jottie"—I had her now; she was watching me—"if I could have thought of it quick enough, I would have lied, too. I would have said anything to keep you from sending Father away."

"Oh, sweetheart," she said, squeezing my hand. "It's not the same. Not at all—"

"I feel like it is," I said. "I feel sick every time I think of it. I feel so sick I wish I could disappear."

"Me too." Father turned to look at me. "How'd you figure all that out?"

"I thought about it until I could picture it."

"Yeah, well, you got it right." He shook his head, so tiredly I could hardly bear it. "And like you said, when I think of it now, I wish I could disappear. Or maybe smash my head in so I don't have to remember it anymore." He swung around to look at Jottie, with his red eyes, but she ducked away so she wouldn't have to look back. He pulled in a breath. "The last time I saw him alive, the last minute, was when we came through Parnell's door and saw the whole corridor was on fire. I couldn't believe how big it had gotten." He ran his hand over his face. "It had been almost nothing before. Just a half hour before, it had been nothing. I yelled that we should go through Arlie's office; it was burning, but we could still get out if we ran fast. Vause didn't answer; he was turning around and around, trying to find a way out, but he looked over, and I could see what he was thinking. He was thinking, I've wasted my life on you, Felix. It was right there on his face, like he'd finally figured it out, like I'd been playing him for a sucker his whole life." Father stopped for a second, remembering. "He looked at me like I was something he wouldn't touch. I tried to pull him, come on, come on, let's go this way, but, you know, he was stronger than me—he hit my hand away and ran, back toward the stairs, because he didn't believe me anymore. He didn't believe I would have done anything to get him out." He hunched his shoulders. "I would have done anything, Jottie."

She didn't lift her head.

"There was so much smoke," he went on, "I couldn't see, and it was so loud I couldn't hear. I was shouting and I couldn't hear it. I ran back the way he'd gone, but I couldn't see him—I couldn't see anything. Then I thought maybe he'd made it down the stairs, so I ran down; they were just about to collapse, and I crashed into the door. That's how I found it. Okay, I thought, he's outside, he's safe, so I went outside and then"— he gave a little groan—"there were people everywhere. I ran, I looked for Vause, all up and down the streets. We hadn't made a plan to meet up, because I thought we'd be together, so I just ran up and down and up and down, looking for him, until I had to hide, you know, at Tare's." Father rubbed his hands against his knees, back and forth. "I had a few hours where I still thought he'd gotten out, for sure he'd gotten out, and maybe the pair of you were leaving town without me. That's what I hoped for, I swear I did." He looked up, wanting to see if she believed him.

Jottie still wouldn't look at him. She shook her head.

"I swear that's what I hoped for, Jottie," Father begged.

But she shook her head again, and her face was like stone. She hated him for what he'd done, and there was nothing I could say, nothing I could do, to change it. I wasn't sure what God would think about Father, but I prayed anyway, with my hands smashed between my legs.

"It was when I climbed in your window the next morning and saw that you'd cut your hair off, that's how I knew he was dead. And I wished to God I was, too. I felt so sick, I wanted to die. It'd happened so fast, Jottie, it was only an hour, maybe an hour and a half, and right up until the last two or three minutes I thought it would be all right, we'd be fine. And then it was too late and I couldn't stop anything; I couldn't undo it and I couldn't change it." He pressed his hands onto his eyes, hard. "I killed *Vause*."

She nodded, her lips folded tight.

"I knew you'd believe me," he said, taking his hands away. "I knew that if I told you the right way, you'd believe that Vause had done it alone. And then you'd stay with me. You wouldn't leave me, and you wouldn't hate me like Vause did, and I wouldn't have lost every single damn thing I cared about." He swallowed, and it looked like it hurt. "I wasn't—wasn't able to do anything else, Jottie."

He stopped talking and waited. But Jottie didn't say anything. She stared out into the leaves, not moving, not hardly breathing. I didn't know what she was deciding; I didn't know anything except I would probably be alone forever at the end of it.

"Jottie?" I said, as gentle as I could. She turned her eyes to me. "Jottie, we all three of us wish we could go back in time. We'd give anything to go back and change it. But we can't, Jottie. We can't."

"How can you forgive him?" she burst out. "How? After what he did?"

I guess she meant Miss Beck and casting me aside and lying. "You're right, Jottie, but what good is it? Rightness is nothing. You can't live on it. You might as well eat ashes." I glanced at Father, his bloodshot eyes and the stain on his pants. I loved him so. Once more, I tried to explain. "This is all we can do; it's all we're allowed. We can't go back. The only thing time leaves for us to decide"—I picked up Father's hand and held it tight—"is whether or not we're going to hate each other."

Father gave me a grateful squeeze.

Jottie watched the pair of us for a moment. "Willa, honey," she said sadly, "wouldn't it be better to give him up?"

I almost smiled. "Like you said, too late for that."

She almost smiled back. "Listen to you," she said, shaking her head. "Throwing it right in my teeth." Her eyes slid over Father, calculating what she could bear. After a moment, she said, "No, you can't live on ashes."

He swung around, hardly breathing.

She heaved a sigh so deep it must have started at her ankles. "Poor Felix," she murmured. "Poor old Felix."

She reached out and took my hand, the one that wasn't holding Father's. They didn't touch, they didn't say another word, but we made a chain, the three of us, and that was fine. That was fine for a start.

In the quiet, I lay back and looked at the sky. It was a circle, what I could see, a circle of blue over our house. Just on the edges there were a few green leaves, ruffling a little, and some spots of gold that shimmered and waved until my eyes crossed and then closed and I went to sleep.

When I woke up, Jottie was still beside me, but Father was gone. I didn't mind. He'd be back.

Epilogue

Jottie broke it off with Sol not long after that. He got married within the month, to a Maryland lady no one knew, but it didn't last, and by the next summer he was back on our porch again, somehow managing to appear only when Father was away. Bird reckoned he spied on us from inside the sewer pipe, but however it was, he knew when he could climb the stairs and take a wicker chair. He must have spent a thousand nights that way, listening to Jottie and the rest of us and then walking back to his house alone. Even then I wondered how it could be enough for him, but I guess it was more than he had expected for himself, except during those few weeks when he thought he had won his war with my father.

Father came and went the way he always had. I never knew exactly what he was doing, and of course it was no use to ask him. I think he did sell chemicals, sometimes, but I don't know. Late in 1940, he came home from a trip with his leg badly broken. He said he'd been thrown from the top of a railroad car by an enraged animal trainer. Jottie said she didn't know anyone who was *more* likely to be thrown from the top of a railroad car than Father, but she also said that didn't mean she believed him. She fussed over him with pillows and breakfast trays, and he laughed and let her, and I was as content as I would ever be in my life, because I knew where he was.

Father was never quite as fast after that. His leg hurt him, and he was getting old, too. He still disappeared, sometimes for weeks, but he didn't come back with as much money, and I think what he got was hard-won. I remember one night—in

1943—he came home during a terrific storm. The electricity was out, and he mumbled something about how we should count our blessings and went upstairs to bed. We didn't know what he meant until the next morning, when Jottie came into the kitchen looking like she was about to faint. She wouldn't even let me see him for two days. I guess he'd been beaten up pretty bad.

Jottie picked up the slack. She continued working for the Writers' Project—without their knowing it—until it folded. Some of the books were pretty silly. She wrote a book about water sports on the Potomac that nearly killed her. But writing grew on her, and after she was done with project guides and histories, she took up writing mysteries, most of them about a dead librarian who went poking her ghostly nose into other folks' business. She sent herself into stitches writing those books, and she got four of them published, too. She said she was just trying to earn an honest crust, but I know she liked writing, and she liked being an authoress. I never in my life heard her laugh so hard as the day the Beacon Light Ladies' Study Club invited her to come speak on the subject of "Modern Literature and Good Taste." She went, though, and she bought a big black hat to impress them in.

The war began just as the Writers' Project breathed its last, and then, of course, the farms prospered. Jottie had a lot to do to manage them after Emmett enlisted, but she set her hand to it, and before long Wren Spurling got the shakes every time he saw her coming. Once the war was over, and you could get gasoline again, Jottie and Father traveled. She said she'd had a circumscribed youth and it was time she saw the world. Father drove. They went to New York and California and other places. I always hoped they were running whiskey into dry states, because Jottie would have relished that, but I never knew for sure.

Those were good years for them both. Jottie lodged all of us on this earth, but no one more than my father, and he recognized it and was grateful. As for her, I believe she knew all along that hatred was a poor bone to chew; she had been trying to hate Vause Hamilton for years, and she saw, after it was over, that it would have dried her to dust if she'd succeeded. It was the same with Father. The truth of other people is a cease-less business. You try to fix your ideas about them, and you choke on the clot you've made.

Besides, Jottie and Father had loved the same person, and each knew where the other went for dreams. In the years that followed the sesquicentennial, Father and Jottie came to talk about Vause Hamilton like he'd just left the room. Between them, he was a little alive, always, but they knew better than to weaken that faint heartbeat by speaking of him before others. He was theirs in private, and when I heard of him, it was only because I sat so quiet they'd forgotten I was there.

In 1940, Minerva surprised everyone—including herself, I expect—by producing a daughter, my cousin Elizabeth. Not to be outdone, Mae had a son, whom she insisted on naming Omar. Waldon almost put his foot down about that, but not quite.

Layla and Emmett got married on New Year's Day of 1939, after she had finished grilling him on everything he had done in his entire life, Emmett said. He pretended to be exasperated about that, but he wasn't. They held the wedding in our parlor, fresh-dusted for the occasion, with Jottie as the bridesmaid.

Somewhere along the line, I forgave Layla. I'm not sure when. On the day she got married, I watched her walk down our hall to the parlor, hanging on to the arm of the senator's fancy suit, and I didn't forgive her a thing. I thought about her lifting up her face to Father's to be kissed, right there where she was walking. She thought about it, too, I could tell. She looked at me as she turned toward the parlor, and her face went pale. I was glad.

A few years later, it had all melted away. Why? I can't tell you. Right after the war, Bird and I went to see Emmett one day. He'd gotten shot up in the Kasserine Pass, and he'd just had the second operation on his shoulder. He couldn't drive or do anything, and Layla asked us please to come out and enter-tain him. So we drove up to White Creek, Bird and me, in Jot-tie's new car. Over the course of our drive, we summoned up what we thought were some real amusing anecdotes, but when we saw Emmett there on his porch, looking like he'd been run over, they fled our mind and we just sat and stared at him. He'd always been so tall and strong, so generally big, and there he was, white as a sheet and shrunken up with pain. We didn't know what to do. Layla saw our faces and came out and sat down. She started talking real nicely, asking us questions about school and our dates and Jottie and whether Father was away on business. At first we answered stiffly, casting glances at Emmett, but as she went on, we relaxed and started to talk. We told stories and made fun of people, like usual, and Emmett smiled, even if he didn't talk much. But I watched. I saw him shift his good arm over the side of his chair so that one of his fingers touched Layla's skin, and I saw her look at him. As we walked back along their drive to our car, I said to Bird, "I don't hate her anymore." I was kind of surprised to come to it.

"Yeah." She nodded. "Seems like her days as a harbinger are over."

Acknowledgments

Over the long course of writing *The Truth According to Us,* I found myself requiring expertise about—or at least a nodding acquaintance with—a wide array of 1930s phenomena: products, machinery, diversions, occurrences, and individuals. The quest for authenticity is a task both endlessly receding and endlessly fascinating, and though I was time and again obliged to curtail my ravening curiosity in order to get on with the job, research was one of the few unalloyed pleasures of my creative process. There is no thrill like the thrill of finding the name of the manufacturer of the top brand of cream separator in 1938. A full accounting of my sources would run about fifty pages, but I'd like to acknowledge here some of the larger debts.

Like nearly every author who has written about the Federal Writers' Project, I relied upon *The Dream and the Deal,* Jerre Mangione's lively history of that improbable program. William F. McDonald's more sober *Federal Relief Administration and the Arts* was also valuable. For specifics about West Virginia, Jerry Bruce Thomas's *An Appalachian New Deal: West Virginia in the Great Depression* supplied me with helpful information about the state's resistance to Roosevelt and the New Deal. Likewise, Dr. Thomas's article "The Nearly Perfect State," about the political controversies surrounding the Federal Writers' Project's state guide to West Virginia, offered extremely useful background.

The History of Macedonia is, of course, an imaginary publication, but it was modeled on a 1937 history book entitled *Historic Romney,* produced by the Federal Writers' Project for the town council of Romney, West Virginia. I have also used *West Virginia: A Guide to the Mountain State,* the Project's state guide, as both a model and a source of information. Berkeley County, in the eastern panhandle of West Virginia, is home to a magnificent, professional-grade historical society. I was lucky enough to visit their archive early in the course of my work, and several of their publications have been key resources, particularly *A Martinsburg Picture Book,* which was both a good visual reference and a spur to the imagination.

In investigating the Works Progress Administration and the Federal Writers' Project, all roads lead to the Library of Congress, which has by far the world's largest collection of original documents and papers from those programs. While most researchers in this archive are interested in materials relating to the big-name authors who worked on the Project, I was looking for administrative correspondence, regulations, and instruction manuals, which are harder to find. I am therefore grateful to my sister, Sally Barrows, for doing the sleuthing— and ordering the photocopies!—that made these materials available to me.

Virtually all other research took place at the University Library at the University of California in Berkeley, for the proximity of which I give thanks daily. Histories of labor relations in the southern textile industry in the 1930s, the 1938 Sears catalog, advertisements for finishing schools in West Virginia in 1920, World War I songbooks, 1938 restaurant menus, specifications of safes manufactured in the United States in 1919, *LIFE* magazines, Federal Writers' Project publications of unimaginable unimportance—these are just some of the treasures I needed and found in the University Library.

Obviously, *The Truth* was not built on facts alone. Or, indeed, at all. Fiction was by far the more fractious element of the compound, and I owe enormous thanks to my editors at Random House for their contributions to the making of this novel. Susan Kamil, the first and most faithful advocate of my work, endured some terrible early drafts and labored long and hard to help me excavate the story I was trying to tell. Kara Cesare was invaluable in guiding the craft in the latter part of its journey, and I am deeply grateful for the attention, appreciation, and kindness she brought to the project. Dana Isaacson's positive response came at an opportune moment and was greatly appreciated.

Throughout this long and convoluted process, my agent, Liza Dawson, has manifested true Macedonian ferocity and devotion, and I am profoundly and permanently grateful to her. I do not believe that this book would exist had it not been for her efforts.

Closer to home, I'd like to express my thanks to my mother, Cynthia Barrows, chief teller of family stories, chief authority in all matters West Virginian, and tireless answerer of annoying questions about regional speech. Thanks also to my father, John Barrows, for his historical contributions and for allowing me to test him on certain points. A few people read the manuscript in various states of undress; I am indebted to Alicia Malet Klein, who read it *twice,* and to Margo Hackett, who loved what I loved and consequently made me feel like I wasn't insane. Thanks, too, to Lisa McGuinness and Tom Klein for their good opinions.

Even closer to home—inside it, in fact—is my best reader, Jeffrey Goldstein. He has read every word of every version of this book and has nonetheless managed to remain interested in the book's characters, integrity, and fate. From the very beginning to the very end, he has always understood what I was aiming for, and he has always liked what he was reading. When everyone else, including me, wanted to throw the manuscript off a cliff, he believed in it. Grateful is too chilly a word, but he, as usual, will know what I mean.